LISA WINGATE

Tending Roses

NAL
ACCENT

FICTION FOR THE WAY WE LIVE

NAL Accent
Published by New American Library, a division of
Penguin Group (USA) Inc., 375 Hudson Street,
New York, New York 10014, USA
Penguin Group (Canada), 90 Eglinton Avenue East, Suite 700, Toronto,
Ontario M4P 2Y3, Canada (a division of Pearson Penguin Canada Inc.)
Penguin Books Ltd., 80 Strand, London WC2R 0RL, England
Penguin Ireland, 25 St. Stephen's Green, Dublin 2,
Ireland (a division of Penguin Books Ltd.)
Penguin Group (Australia), 250 Camberwell Road, Camberwell, Victoria 3124,
Australia (a division of Pearson Australia Group Pty. Ltd.)
Penguin Books India Pvt. Ltd., 11 Community Centre, Panchsheel Park,
New Delhi - 110 017, India
Penguin Group (NZ), 67 Apollo Drive, Mairangi Bay,
Auckland 1311, New Zealand (a division of Pearson New Zealand Ltd.)
Penguin Books (South Africa) (Pty.) Ltd., 24 Sturdee Avenue,
Rosebank, Johannesburg 2196, South Africa

Penguin Books Ltd., Registered Offices:
80 Strand, London WC2R 0RL, England

Published by NAL Accent, an imprint of New American Library, a division of
Penguin Group (USA) Inc. Previously published in an NAL Accent trade paper-
back edition.

First NAL Accent Mass Market Printing, February 2003
10 9 8 7 6 5

Novels by Lisa Wingate

The Blue Sky Series
A Month of Summer
The Summer Kitchen
Beyond Summer
Dandelion Summer

The Tending Roses Series
Tending Roses
Good Hope Road
The Language of Sycamores
Drenched in Light
A Thousand Voices

The Texas Hill Country Trilogy
Texas Cooking
Lone Star Café
Over the Moon at the Big Lizard Diner

To my grandmothers,
for tilling the soil in which we grew
and for watering our roots
with stories of all the old things

Acknowledgments

When you sit caged in some lonely corner slowly tapping out the pages of a novel, one of the things you dream about is who you will acknowledge when the book is finally published—sort of the way actors dream of their Oscar speech. So here is my Oscar speech. I will try not to leave out anyone.

My heartfelt thanks go out to all of the friends who suffered through editing and reediting countless versions of the manuscript. You are the saving grace of a lousy typist. Thank you also, Amanda Carter, for your incredible proofreading, for your valuable input, and for the little jokes written in the margin. Yes, my spelling is laughable, but you're the best.

Thank you, Mom, for suffering through each and every rewrite of this book, and all my others through the years. Thank you, Sam, for always having so much faith that I could do this and for making the children peanut butter and jelly sandwiches all of those times dinner was nowhere in sight. You are just what every writer needs: a supportive, patient spouse with a good eye for plot lines.

Gratitude beyond measure goes to my wonderful agent, Lisa Hagan, for showing this project such devotion, for always being positive and determined, and for giving me affirmations when I needed them. You are exactly what every writer dreams of in an agent and a friend.

Thank you to everyone at NAL, but especially to my incredible editor, Ellen Edwards, for knowing exactly what *Tending Roses* needed. You have an amazing sense of things, and you have been a dream to work with. Without you, the book would still be missing something.

Last, my thanks go to my grandmother, who, at eighty-five years old, came for a visit after my first son was born and sat with me in the long evening shadows, telling the stories that were the genesis of this book. Thank you, Grandma, for showing me how to rock a colicky baby, how to plant iris bulbs, and how to prune roses. Thank you for helping me to see the value of where I was and for telling me about the times when the roses grew wild. . . .

Chapter 1

INDIAN wisdom says our lives are rivers. We are born somewhere small and quiet and we move toward a place we cannot see, but only imagine. Along our journey, people and events flow into us, and we are created of everywhere and everyone we have passed. Each event, each person, changes us in some way. Even in times of drought we are still moving and growing, but it is during seasons of rain that we expand the most—when water flows from all directions, sweeping at terrifying speed, chasing against rocks, spilling over boundaries. These are painful times, but they enable us to carry burdens we could never have thought possible.

This I learned from my grandmother, when my life was rushing with torrential speed and hers was slowly ebbing into the sea. I think it was God's plan that we came together at this time. To carry each other's burden. To remind ourselves of what we had been and would someday become.

Floods are painful, but they are necessary. They keep us clear and strong. They move our lives onto new paths.

A winter rain was falling the day we drove the pot-holed gravel drive to the Missouri farmhouse my great-grandparents had built on a bluff above Mulberry Creek. As straight as one of the grand porch pillars, and as much a part of the house, Grandma watched as we wound through the rivers of muddy water flowing down the hill. She frowned and wrung her hands as the car tires spun, throwing gravel against the ancient trees along the drive. No doubt she was worried that we would damage her prized silver maples.

A sick feeling started in my throat and fell to my stomach like a swallowed ice cube. I looked at Ben in the driver's seat and the baby asleep in the car seat behind us. This would probably be the longest December and the worst Christmas of our lives.

It would only be a matter of time before Grandma figured out why we had come and war broke out. Even now, she was looking at us with mild suspicion, no doubt calculating why we were arriving three weeks early for Christmas. She wouldn't be fooled for long into thinking this was just a casual visit. That was the wishful thinking of a bunch of relatives hoping to postpone the problem of Grandma Rose until they were off work for the Christmas holiday.

In a perfect world, all of them would have been rushing to Grandma's side, whether it was convenient or not. In a perfect world, I wouldn't have been looking at my grandmother with a sense of dread, and I wouldn't have been looking at my baby and wondering if the trip was too much for him and if it was wise to take him so far from his doctors. In a perfect world, babies are born healthy, and medical bills don't snowball into the tens of thousands of dollars, and grandmothers don't almost burn down their houses, and family members don't go years without speaking to one another, and Christmas is a time to look forward to. . . .

But those of us who aren't perfect do the best we can. With me on maternity leave and Ben able to do most of his work in structural design anywhere there was a computer and a phone line, we were the logical choice to stay at the farm the next few weeks and make sure Grandma Rose didn't burn down the rest of the house before the family could figure out what to do about her.

But I never imagined how I would *feel* when we turned the corner to the house. I never thought the sight of my grandmother, ramrod straight on the porch, would turn me into that six-year-old girl who hated to enter that house. It wasn't *Grandma* I hated. It was the house: the constant fuss about scuffing the floors, and scraping the walls, and tracking mud on the rugs—as if the house were more important than the children in it.

From the porch, Grandma flailed her arms and yelled something we couldn't understand.

"She's"—Ben squinted through the rain—"telling me how to park."

"If it weren't raining, she'd be climbing into the driver's seat." I was joking, of course—mostly. I wondered if Ben had any inkling of how difficult she could be. He hadn't been around her much in the ten years we'd been married. He'd never seen her standing at the door inspecting people's shoes for mud like a drill sergeant, or putting coasters under people's drinks, or listening to the plumbing to make sure no one was flushing too much toilet paper. He didn't know that food was forbidden in the living room and that you were not allowed to step from the bath until every ounce of water was drained from the tub and toweled from your body. And that the towels then had to be folded in triplicate and hung on the bar immediately so they would not mildew. . . .

He didn't have a clue what I was thinking. He grinned as he put the car in park, stretched his neck, and combed his fingers through the dark curls of his hair.

"We made it. I'm ready for a rest. Then I need to get the computer plugged in and see if there's any more word on that Randolph stores job."

The undercurrent of worry about money was unmistakable. Since Joshua's birth, it was the unspoken nuance of every conversation we had. It was all Ben thought about. He didn't have time to consider how we were going to get along with our new landlady. Besides, he always got along with everybody. It was one of the things I loved and hated about him.

Sun broke through the clouds as we covered Joshua and hurried to the porch. Grandma waited for us at the steps and pushed open the screen, holding around her shoulders a psychedelic afghan I had made in art class. The picture of her standing there in my awful crocheted creation with her hair flying in the wind made me smile.

Coming closer, I noticed how much she had aged, how her cheeks, once plump and naturally blushed, were now hollow and pale. Her shoulders, once straight, now bent forward as she moved. I realized how long it had been since I had come to the farm, and I felt an intense pang of guilt. Six years. Gone in the blink of an eye. The last time I came was for my mother's funeral.

Grandma squinted as we drew nearer, as if she were looking at strangers. "Katie? Is that you?" She craned forward and took on a look of recognition. "Oh, yes, I'd know those Vongortler brown eyes anywhere. You're just as pretty as ever . . . but you've let your hair grow long."

The last part sounded like a complaint, and I wasn't sure what to say. I found myself self-consciously smoothing the wisps of shoulder-length dark hair into my hair clip. I wondered how she had expected me to look.

Grandma didn't wait for my reply. "My word! I've been worried sick." She looked as if she'd been walking the floors since before dawn. "I expected you this morning, and here it is two o'clock, and with this rain going on, I just thought the road was icy and you had slipped into the ditch."

"Grandma, I told you we wouldn't be here until afternoon." I would have blamed her forgetfulness on the stroke, except that for as long as I could remember she'd been purposely forgetting things she didn't want to hear. I took comfort in the fact that in this respect she hadn't changed. "Besides, it's fifty-five degrees. There is no ice."

She gave me a blank smile that told me she wasn't digesting a word. "I thought for sure you'd be here for lunch. Katie, you look like you could use a little farm cooking. You're far too thin, just as you always were. Now, I've got biscuits, some green beans, green-pea salad, and a good roast, but it's cold now. Oh, look at the baby!" Joshua was still sound asleep in his carrier. "I'll put it in the oven and warm it up."

I hoped she meant the roast.

Ben shot me a grin and crossed his eyes as she went through the side door into the kitchen. His crooked grin made me laugh, and I coughed to cover it up as Grandma looked suspiciously over her shoulder.

When she turned away, Ben pointed to the huge stain around the doorframe and his eyes widened.

I stopped, taken aback by the extent of the smoke damage. The sheriff hadn't been exaggerating when he called Aunt Jeane in St. Louis to warn her that Grandma's mental slips were getting dangerous—more dangerous than her occasionally puttering to town in the old car she refused to part with, even though the doctor had told her she shouldn't drive anymore and she had promised Aunt Jeane she wouldn't. She had also promised Aunt Jeane she would use a timer to make sure the iron and the coffeepot weren't left on, but in truth, what she had tried to pass off as "the iron getting too hot" had been a potentially serious fire. The iron must have been left unattended for hours.

If I had been in denial before, I was now fully awakened to the fact that something had to be done about Grandma Rose.

Still talking, she walked past the soot, as if oblivious to it, ignoring the evidence that she'd almost burned down the utility room a few days before. "Well, come on in. It's cold out there," she snapped. "Now, I'll take care of the baby and you two can just eat and rest. You can wait a while to bring in your things. Just make yourselves at home in here. I had that neighbor boy help me move some of my things to the little house out back. I'll stay out there so as to ease the strain on that septic line here in the basement. All of us in the house might just be too much waste going down."

She set the stoneware plates in the oven and lit the gas with a long match. "Now, I never leave this pilot running on the oven. It's no problem to light it each time, and it saves on gas." Closing the oven door, she paused to clean the fog from her eyeglasses, then let them hang from the chain around her neck and walked back to the table. "There now, you two just get what you need. I'll look after the baby. He'll surely be waking up."

Joshua obliged with a squall the moment we turned our backs on Grandma and the baby carrier.

And so began our trip down the rapids.

It's strange how it's always easier to tolerate other people's grandparents than your own. Ben, who had been so concerned about getting to work on his computer, didn't even raise a protest when Grandma solicited him to drive her to town for her daily grocery run and visit to the church office. Grandma wrote the church news for the local paper, and it was very important, according to her, that she stop by so as not to miss a thing. Normally, a neighbor man took her, but she had canceled him today because we were coming. And by the way, she didn't want us to think there was anything going on between her and Oliver Mason, despite what we might hear in town. He was too old for her, had a bad leg, talked too much, and smoked cigars. She had been on her own for thirty years and had no need for an old man eating her food or messing up her house, and besides, cigar smoke would stain the ceilings, which she had paid a great deal of money to have painted. . . .

Just in case we were wondering. Which we weren't until she brought it up.

Leaning close to me, Ben fanned an eyebrow and grinned as he grabbed Joshua. Grandma insisted the baby should accompany them to town, even though I argued against it and Ben would have preferred to leave him home. It was Grandma's firm opinion that I would be more successful in getting unpacked if Joshua went with them. Of course, the truth was she wanted to take her only great-grandchild to town and show him off to all her friends.

It's hard for a mother to argue with logic like that, and as was often the case, Ben took Grandma's insistence in stride.

He laughed about her pointed denial of a romantic relationship with Oliver Mason. "Hear that?" he told Joshua. "We're going to town with a hot babe. Hope old Oliver doesn't decide to knock me in the head with his cane."

The picture made me laugh even as they piled into Grandma's old Buick and disappeared down the driveway. Watching them go, I engaged in a quick moment of mother-panic about whether Ben knew how to properly buckle Joshua's baby carrier into the car seat. I suddenly realized that, in Joshua's four months on earth, this was the first time he had gone somewhere without me. We'd been at the farm for only a few hours, and Grandma Rose had already kidnapped my husband and my infant son.

I shook my head, chuckling at myself as I started unloading our suitcases and tried to figure out the rocket science of setting up Joshua's portable baby equipment.

The house was completely still after they left except for the faint hum of the furnace. I wandered down the dogtrot, looking up the wide oak stairway where pictures of my aunts and uncles on birthdays, graduations, and wedding days had always hung. After the fire, someone had taken the pictures off the wall. The outlines of the frames were yellowed into the paint, so even though they were gone, they were still there, like ghosts.

Standing on the first step, I touched the shadows, wondering where the pictures were, and if Grandma had even noticed they were gone. But I knew she must have. Nothing out of order in the house escaped her notice.

Every inch of the place whispered of the relentless pursuit of perfection that was Grandma Rose. The house was Grandma, and Grandma was the house, married since she had come as a bachelor farmer's bride sixty years before. I wondered how we were going to convince her to give it up, and if she could, and what would happen if she wouldn't. I wondered what she was going to say when the family confronted her, and whether I should try to prepare her ahead of time. I wondered what would happen when all of us saw one another for the first time since my mother's death. Six years of drifting apart puts you at opposite ends of the ocean, and it takes something cataclysmic to push you into the same port.

Looking at the ghosts on the wall, I had the vague sense of an oncoming storm.

The uneasy feeling stayed with me through the rest of the afternoon, though I wasn't sure why. The rain had stopped and the day turned bright and unusually warm for December. Joshua returned from town in a fine humor, and Ben was more relaxed than I had seen him in months. Only Grandma seemed to be in a foul state. Ben chuckled as he quietly told me that Oliver Mason had shown up in town and, much to Grandma's disgust, tagged along on their rounds of the grocery store and the church—as Ben put it, like an old stray dog trailing a T-bone steak. Ben said he figured poor Oliver had nothing better to do.

It was so good to see Ben loosened up, I decided not to tell him that another enormous hospital bill was in our stack of forwarded mail. They just kept arriving. Maybe that was where my uneasy feeling came from. Even here at the farm, in the middle of nowhere, there was no escape from the hospital bills and the house payments, car payments, credit cards—all just a little behind, getting worse. Ben was right. I shouldn't have taken this last month of unpaid family leave to be with Joshua. We couldn't afford it. . . .

Grandma came by and patted me on the arm, and I jumped like a nervous cat.

She stopped and looked at me for a moment, frowning as if she were seeing right through me. "Well, Katie, you look worn-out," she said finally. "Why don't you put on a sweater and come sit on the porch with me? It's seldom we get such nice weather this time of year."

"All right," I muttered, glad for the distraction.

"Benjamin, you can come sit out with us, too," she said to Ben, who was headed up the stairs with his arms full of computer equipment and cables.

"No, thanks," he said without turning around. "Probably too late to talk to anyone in Chicago, anyway, but I'd better get this thing plugged in and give it a try. I need to download some plans so I can get a bid in on a job tomorrow. It's a design for four big new Randolph stores like the one in Springfield. Can't miss the chance at a contract like that."

He gave Grandma one of his most charming smiles, but beneath that was the undercurrent—the one that said if he didn't get the contract to do the structural design for the new Randolph stores, disaster was imminent.

Grandma watched him go with a narrow-eyed look, moving her lips as if she were chewing on a thought, or as if she were reading the undercurrent, too. She had that look of being just about to sink her teeth into a new worry, and Grandpa had always said that she could jump on a worry like a bulldog on a fresh bone.

Hoping to distract her with a change of scenery, I grabbed my jacket and Josh's carrier and headed for the porch. "We'd better hurry up before the sun starts to go down and it gets cold." The last thing she needed to be doing was worrying about us.

She followed me onto the porch, and we sat on the swing, enjoying the warmth of the Indian summer afternoon. For a moment, neither of us said anything. Grandma's eyelids drifted downward and her head sagged, as if she were falling asleep. I had never seen her let herself drift off like that before. It was one of the habits she had always disdained in other old people. Watching her filled me with a sense of sadness and regret for having stayed away so long from the farm, and from her. I couldn't explain it now. After my mother's funeral, I just went back to Chicago, buried myself in my work at the Harrison Foundation, kept busy, kept moving up the ladder, kept raising more money for worthy environmental causes, and kept my mother's unexpected death out of my mind.

Suddenly, six years were gone and Grandma had burned down the utility room. It shouldn't have taken that to bring me back.

Grandma's head jerked up as Ben came through on his way back to the car for more equipment. She glanced at me with an addled look, and I pretended I hadn't noticed her falling asleep. I stared at a pair of deer moving in a field of winter wheat in the valley below.

She cleared her throat, patting her cheeks as Ben carried a computer monitor into the house. "My goodness, that boy is a hard worker." It almost sounded like a complaint. "But I thought the two of you were coming here for a vacation."

My mind was on the deer. "We can't afford a vacation," I heard myself say, and I instantly realized my mistake. Glancing at Grandma, I saw that narrow, calculating look, and I realized she was trying to dissect our situation. "I mean, Ben has to take his contracts when they come. Randolph stores is a big chain. If he can get the structural design contract, it'll pay really well."

Grandma gave me a very earnest look. "Now, you know, if there is a problem about money, you can come to me. I don't have much, but my children are welcome to all that I have."

I just nodded, smiling at her because I knew better. Grandma loved to play the martyr about helping other people. The truth was that she managed her nest egg of farm-rental income and railroad stock with an iron grip. Ben and I would never have dreamed of accepting any of it, and if we did, everyone in the family would forever hear about how she'd gone without groceries for a month and sold her favorite knitting needles at auction, but was happy to do it because her children were welcome to all that she had. The truth was, she had refused to sell or deed over even an acre of the farm to anyone in the family, even after my grandfather died. The truth was, she hung on to what was hers, and she didn't share, and she wasn't going to give any of it up without a fight.

"We're all right on money, Gram," I assured her, hoping to nip any rumors she might start about us arriving destitute.

Her lips moved again, as if she had a piece of gristle between her teeth. "Well, I only ask because I saw all those bills and notices coming in your mail . . ."

I turned to her, openmouthed, flame rising into my cheeks. I wondered if she had been steaming open our envelopes. She didn't look at me, but out at the deer, her chin tilted stubbornly, her arms crossed over her chest, fingers drumming impatiently.

I took a deep breath and swallowed what I was going to say. Instead, I calmly falsified the truth. "It's just a little hard right now with Ben new at consulting and me on unpaid leave with Joshua. There were some hospital bills that the insurance didn't cover. It'll be better next month when I get started back at work."

Grandma huffed an irritated breath. "It isn't right that mothers these days have to give over their children so quickly to go back to work. In my day we women waited at least until the children were school-aged—if we worked at all."

Her out-of-date philosophy only tightened the knot of maternal guilt inside me. I felt the perverse need to defend myself and my whole generation. "Well, Grandma, things aren't that way anymore. These days it takes two incomes to have a nice place to live, and cars, and money for retirement funds, college funds, and a meal out or a vacation once in a while."

Grandma huffed, sticking her chin out like a wooden

Indian. "In my day, we didn't *expect* vacations." She was clearly determined to pick a fight.

Looking at her, I was reminded of the other reason why I didn't come back to the farm anymore. For most of my life, all I could remember was her picking fights. She had a talent for stirring up unpleasantness, she was an expert on every subject, and she felt the need to control everyone. Which was probably why my father was that way, too. I switched to the defensive to keep from being eaten alive.

"Well, these days that's what people want, and—" I snapped my mouth shut and forced myself to take a breath. *One . . . two . . . three . . . four . . . five. . . .* I didn't finish until I'd counted all the way to ten and calmed myself down. "It's not that I'm dying to send Josh to day care, Grandma, but there's a lot to consider. I've worked hard to get where I am with the Harrison Foundation. It's an important job. We fund a lot of critical environmental research, and I'm the one who raises the money that funds the projects."

She turned her face away, impatient with my explanation. "I don't know that I believe all the malarkey about hairspray killing the fish in the world anyway."

I smiled and rubbed my forehead, unsure of whether to laugh or get a headache. "I don't think we've ever funded a research project on hairspray killing fish, but my point is that I can't put off going back to work forever. Ben's income isn't steady yet. Next year we want to sell our town house and buy a bigger house with a yard for Josh." The list went on, up to and including paying off the hospital bills, of which Grandma didn't even begin to know the extent. "If someone can tell me how to do all that without working, I'd like to hear about it."

I looked at the deer, and my mind continued whirling with the problems that would face us when we returned home—day care, work, hospital bills, payments on cars, payments on the boat, payments on the house . . . My stomach started to churn, and I felt my pulse going up as it did every time I considered how we were going to keep so many plates spinning at once.

"So these are the things young people want these days?" I heard her ask, but her voice seemed far away, coming from somewhere beyond the din in my head.

"Um-hum," I muttered.

I could feel Grandma watching me, and when I turned to her she met my gaze with an extremely lucid look—as if, just for a moment, all of her mind was in the present. "Maybe you should start wanting less."

The whirlwind inside me stopped. I sat there looking into her eyes, the soft, clear blue of a robin's egg, and whispered, "Maybe so."

We sat for a long time in the quiet of the waning afternoon, watching the deer come into the wheat field on the river-bottom land below. Finally, the sun fell below the edge of the blue, tree-clad hills, and the feeling of winter came into the air.

Josh woke up, and I took him out of his carrier, snuggling him inside my jacket.

Grandma patted my hand and smiled. The hints of her former ire were gone, and I wondered if she even remembered our conversation. "Don't you two look sweet?" She sighed, rocking forward and rising slowly to her feet. "There's nothing more precious than a mother with a baby in her arms." After shuffling to the screen door, she started down the steps. "I have a few things to do out in my little house. I'll be back in a while."

I stood up and caught the door before it slammed. "Grandma, you don't have to stay out there. There's plenty of room in the main house for all of us."

She paused on the steps and craned her neck as if I were speaking gibberish. "No, no. This is better. I don't want to put too much strain on that sewer pipe in the basement. The little house has its own septic. I'll just stay out there until everyone goes back home again. Then I'll have to get back in the big house and wax the floors after everyone . . ." She turned and started down the stone path, still muttering about how the gathering crowd of family would put us all in danger of ruined floors and a sewer-system meltdown.

I let the door close and watched her go, thinking that there wouldn't be any *after Christmas*. She didn't seem to have an inkling that Aunt Jeane was looking into nursing homes in St. Louis and my father couldn't wait to sell the farm.

The whirlwind started in my head again.

I went inside to see if Ben had locked down the Randolph contract. He was sitting in front of his computer in the second-story bedroom that had once been Aunt Jeane's. Seeing him surrounded by the white French-style furniture and the pink ruffled curtains and bedspread made me laugh.

"Nice digs," I said. Even the flowered wallpaper went back as far as my memory could reach.

Ben glanced sideways at me and grimaced. "I feel like Thumbelina." He tapped the keyboard impatiently, waiting for a file to download. "But this is the only phone jack in the whole place. All the rest of the phones are hard-wired in. Not that it matters much, because I can't get the stupid phone lines to cooperate. I keep getting bumped off the server. If this thing doesn't straighten up, I'll have to—"

"Good-bye," the computer said, sounding gleeful.

Ben slammed his hand against the desk and closed his eyes. "Oh, shoot!" He stood up, scattering architectural blueprints onto the floor. "Shoot! Shoot! Shoot! I've been trying to get that file for an hour."

Josh whimpered on my chest, and I bounced him around to keep him quiet. "Well, maybe it'll be better in the morning," I suggested. "It's always hard to get on this time of the evening."

Ben went back to the computer as if he hadn't heard me. I hated it when he did that, and he knew it. He wasn't in the mood to be social, and he was hoping Josh and I would leave. When we didn't, he finally sighed and said, "I think it's something with the phone exchange out here."

"Oh." It occurred to me that, if he couldn't get his computer to log on to the Net, there was no way we would be able to stay for the next three weeks. "Well, we can call the phone company in the morning. Come downstairs and have a sandwich with us. Josh is ready to have a bottle, play a little, and go to bed." I turned Josh around, hoping he would lure Ben in. As usual, it didn't work.

Ben shook his head, looking grim and determined. "I'd better stay here and try this file again. I wanted to look John's specs over tonight so I can talk to him about the Randolph job tomorrow. He was already out of the office this afternoon."

As usual, it was hard to argue with his logic. "All right," I said. And, as usual, we said good-bye to the back of his head and left him to his work. "Don't stay up here all night," I called back, but I knew he probably would.

He was still there grumbling and trying to get his computer to cooperate an hour later when I went upstairs to bathe Josh. After the bath, I stood in the doorway with Josh while Ben told the computer exactly how he felt about it. No love lost, that was for sure.

Ben combed his fingers through his hair irritably and swiveled in his seat to look at me. "This thing is a piece of junk."

I shook my head. "Sounds like you'd better give it up for a while."

He grumbled something about not letting it beat him and turned around to face the dragon again. I left. I could tell Joshua was about to descend into his usual evening crying hour, and Ben had enough aggravation already.

By the time I reached the bottom of the stairs, Josh had worked himself into a full-scale colicky fit, as he always did in the evenings. Nothing, but nothing, ever distracted him from it. Gritting my teeth, I walked him up and down the dogtrot, mentally reviewing the advice of pediatricians, baby magazines, and the child psychologist on the evening news. *Colic is harmless. . . . Don't let yourself get aggravated. . . . It's just an underdeveloped nervous system reacting to too much stimuli. . . . Some babies need a crying hour to relieve their frustrations. . . . Colic is harmless. . . .*

Joshua's cries echoed through the house like the blast of a trumpet, and my head felt as if it were swelling with every wail. Then Grandma appeared suddenly around the corner from the living room, startling both of us.

She smiled and reached for Josh. I, quite gladly, relinquished him. During crying hour, I would have given him to almost anybody.

Grandma Vongortler, it appeared, had the magic. She held him close under her chin, whispered something in his ear, and apparently a bargain was struck. He took his pacifier, and the two of them went to the living room to rock in her recliner. I went to the kitchen to put away the dishes, and suddenly all was right with the world.

Silence, at last.

Later, I found them asleep in the chair. They looked so right together, Joshua's head tucked beneath the stubborn line of Grandma's chin, her glasses hanging askew on her nose, his tiny fingers gripping and releasing the pale blue fabric of her dress, his lips pursed as if waiting for an invisible kiss.

I stood in the doorway watching them, afraid that if I entered the room I would break the spell. Finally, I turned and left them there, curled up together.

Chapter 2

BEN and I finally went to sleep in our first-floor bedroom sometime close to midnight. Joshua was settled upstairs in a room that had once been my father's, and, after sleeping for several hours in the living room chair, Grandma finally padded off to the little house, complaining of insomnia.

In the dark hours of the morning, I heard the low shuffle-creak, shuffle-creak of her walking the floors, then rustling in the kitchen, then progressing slowly up the stairs. A small squawk came over the baby monitor sometime later, followed by the dim sound of Grandma rescuing Josh from the crib and settling into the rocker nearby.

With the true devotion of a mother who hadn't had a good night's sleep in three months, I rolled over and closed my eyes again.

The sun was streaming through the tall east windows when I awoke. Ben was gone from his side of the bed, his suitcases opened and clothes strewn around so that I could tell he'd already dressed. I couldn't believe I'd slept right through his usual morning racket, and I couldn't believe the mess he'd left behind. The bedroom looked as if a hurricane had just blown through.

His attempt at damage control was on the bedside table in the form of a note:

Kate,
Sorry about the mess. Gone to town to see about the phone lines. Grandma and Joshua up together early. Joshua ate, pooped, back to sleep now. Grandma same as Joshua. See you this evening. Have everything put up by time I get home.

Ben

His attempt at sounding like an autocratic husband made me laugh, even as I fished through his jumbled clothes for mine, then proceeded to tidy up because I knew Grandma would have a fit about the condition of the bedroom. Ben still had a lot to learn about vacationing at Grandma Vongortler's.

The smell of brewing coffee tickled my senses just as I was hanging the last few shirts in the closet. After closing the suitcases, I stuffed them under the bed, pronounced the room reasonably in order, then headed to the kitchen to fix myself some breakfast.

Something wet sloshed into my shoe as I rounded the corner into the kitchen. Looking down, I stared in disbelief at the huge dark stain on the toe of my shoe, then at the puddle of brown liquid that ended at my feet, ran upstream across the kitchen floor, and originated at the coffeemaker, which was happily spewing coffee onto the counter. The coffeepot sat nearby filled with water. At the sink, the faucet was running, and bubbly dishwater was gurgling from the full side of the sink into the empty one and disappearing down the drain.

"Grandma?" I muttered, staring at the coffeemaker cord dangling in the puddle and marveling that no one had been electrocuted. "Grandma?" I called louder. No answer. No sign of Grandma.

Confused, I tiptoed around the coffee puddle and turned off the coffeemaker and the sink faucet, then grabbed a bunch of kitchen towels and threw them on top of the burgeoning oil slick in the center of the room.

A movement caught my eye outside the window, and I saw Grandma in her old brown overcoat, calmly hanging towels on the line beside the little house, completely unaware that the kitchen was being flooded. I suddenly had a very clear picture of how she had left the iron turned on next to a stack of clothes and set the utility room on fire a week before.

Carrying the wet towels to the washing machine, I surveyed the damage to the utility room. Not as bad as I had thought. Just smoke damage and a hole in the wall where the old ironing-board cabinet had been. It was fortunate that Oliver Mason had been there when the fire started, or it could have spread to the rest of the house.

I glanced out the window at Grandma as I walked back to the coffeemaker. I didn't suppose it would do any good to tell her she'd just flooded the kitchen. It would only make her nervous and upset to know that she was doing things she couldn't explain. Besides, she would probably deny it anyway. She still vehemently denied responsibility for the fire in the utility room. Grandma's version of the facts was completely different from everyone else's. And, as usual, she was sticking to her story.

Instead of going out to talk to her, I took advantage of the few minutes of privacy to call the hospital in order to make payment arrangements for the new bill. Lately, it seemed as if I talked to the hospital billing department at least once a day. For the most part, they had been pretty understanding about the delay. Unfortunately, the woman on the phone today didn't care that my son had endured emergency heart surgery shortly after birth, or that I'd had to take an extra month of unpaid leave to care for him, or that we were still grappling with the insurance company over deductibles and coverage limits, or that there were no guarantees Joshua wouldn't need further heart surgery. All she cared about was whether we could send two hundred fifty dollars by the middle of December. Merry Christmas.

By the time I got off the phone, my hands were shaking and my nerves were stretched like fiddle strings. Upstairs, Josh had started to cry in his crib. After sticking the bill back in the envelope, I buried it under the stack of mail and went to rescue my son.

The phone rang as I was coming downstairs again, and I answered, bouncing Joshua on my shoulder to quiet him.

"Hello?" I said, wondering if the bill collector from the hospital was calling back to give me more bad news.

"Hi . . . Kate, is that you?"

"Liz?" There is nothing like hearing your best friend's voice on the other end of the phone when you're in a moment of crisis.

"Yes, is something wrong? I hear the baby crying."

"No, he's all right. He just woke up and he doesn't think I got to the crib fast enough."

I was only half joking, but Liz laughed on the other end of the line. Not having any children of her own, she thought all the trials of motherhood were pretty funny.

"I just called to see how the trip went and how your grandmother's doing."

"What . . . I . . . Just a second, Liz. The baby just spit up on my shoulder. Oh, yuck."

"Sounds like you have your hands full." Liz laughed again as I wiped away the mess, then repositioned Joshua so that he could look out the window. Finally, he quieted down and I could hear myself think.

"So, how was the trip and how is your grandmother?" Liz repeated.

"The trip was fine," I said. "Josh slept most of the way in the car, so it was a nice drive. No snowstorms, so we made good time. My grandmother seems to be doing pretty well, but wow, is the utility room a mess. There's smoke damage all around the window and the outside doorframe and a big burned-out hole where the ironing board used to be. She acts like it's not there."

"Hmmm. That doesn't seem good," Liz said, sounding as if she were analyzing one of her legal cases for the Harrison Foundation. "Well, have you tried confronting her about it?"

"No," I admitted. "It's been so long since I've seen her, I hated to come in here and get her upset. I think I'll try to keep things calm until the rest of the family gets here for Christmas."

"Oh, well. I don't blame you. Sounds like kind of a mess."

"It'll work out all right." I couldn't imagine how, but I didn't feel like talking about it anymore. "Anyway, how's the town house?" Liz was between apartments, so she had agreed to house-sit for us while we were away.

"The house is great. I was lounging on your balcony just this morning, watching people play golf and feeling pretty suburban."

That made me laugh. Liz had lived in an apartment downtown for the seven years I had known her. "So, you like it, then? I told you you would. It's nice to be out where there's a tree or two to look at. You know, the town house next to us is for sale."

"You're not sneakily trying to suggest that I become your next-door neighbor?" she quipped.

"We could commute together," I said, thinking of how nice it would be to have company on the ride into the city. "Play golf on the weekends . . ."

"Neither of us plays golf, and besides, every weekend

we're in the city for some kind of fund-raiser or something."

"Well, we could golf between fund-raisers." A twinge of nervous adrenaline shot through me at the thought of the office. "So . . . I hate to ask, but what's going on with the audit?"

Shortly after I had left for maternity leave, my boss found out that the foundation was going to be audited, which was no big deal until some important paperwork wasn't where it was supposed to be, and word leaked out to a few influential people in Chicago. Sloppy accounting practices are a terrible black eye for an organization that depends on government grants and the endowments of noteworthy people.

Liz let out a long sigh, and I knew the news was not good. "It hit the papers this morning. We're already getting calls, but we don't know what the fallout will be."

"Oh, no," I muttered, my mind reeling. "That's bad."

"I know. I wasn't going to tell you with everything else you've got going on."

"Ohhhh, I wish I were there. I wish I could get Larry Shaffer by the neck and strangle him. He knew he was leaving for that other job, and he just blew off keeping the foundation paperwork in order." My hand tightened around the phone cord. "You know this means people will pull funding, and it'll cut down the usual December revenue."

"I know. We're already making calls to try to do damage control. Don't worry about it. Dianne's doing her best to fill your shoes while you're gone."

"I know, but . . ." I wasn't sure I liked the idea of my assistant filling my shoes.

"Just relax and take care of your family stuff. Now I'm sorry I even told you."

"No. Don't be. I can make some calls from here and

try to spin things with some of my bigger givers." Joshua wiggled on my shoulder and started to cry again.

"Sounds like somebody's hungry," Liz said. "I'll let you go. Don't worry about things at work and tell Ben not to worry about the town house. Tell him I'm busy sampling all his favorite wines and driving this cute little golf cart up and down the street. Tell him on Saturday I might go sail his boat around Lake Michigan."

"I think it might be a little cold." I laughed. "But feel free to use all of Ben's toys. Someone should. We pay for all that stuff and then he never has time to use it anyway." Which was so true, it was embarrassing. Ben had a bad habit of taking up expensive hobbies. "You should have seen the place before we got rid of his antique motorcycle collection to pay off a couple of hospital bills. You know, boys and their toys."

"Yes, I know. That's why I'm not married."

Joshua let out a loud squall and kicked his feet, fed up with the supper delay.

"Oops!" Liz said. "I'm really letting you go this time. Tell Ben I said hi."

"O.K. Thanks for calling, Liz. It was great talking to you."

" 'Bye, girl. Have a good Christmas. Miss ya'."

"You, too. 'Bye."

I hung up the phone, feeling homesick and nervous about the events at work and the fact that I couldn't be there.

But Joshua had a more immediate problem, so I grabbed a bottle from the refrigerator and walked into the hall. Through the window, I could see Grandma sitting on the porch, enjoying the warm weather, so I wrapped a jacket around Josh and went outside to sit with her while he had his bottle.

Sinking into the quilted cushions of Grandma's swing, I took in a deep breath of the warm air. It smelled of green winter wheat and freshly tilled earth, drying puddles of water and decaying leaves. Just a hint of winter. Compared to Chicago, Missouri felt like a heat wave and not like December at all.

It was quiet. I wasn't used to such a deep silence—no cars, no voices, no commuter trains, no doors slamming, no cell phones ringing, no pagers beeping, no horns honking. At this time of the year, not even any insects buzzing. Just silence as the sun crept through the screen and settled over us, soothing my nerves like warm bathwater. I let out a long sigh, trying to forget my troubles. Grandma turned to me with her brows knitted, and I was afraid she could tell something was wrong. "Oh, I can just imagine what all this activity has done to the floors." She gave me a look of deep grief.

I was relieved that she wasn't questioning me again about our stack of bills. I was afraid this time I might spill. I needed to talk to somebody, but good sense told me Grandma was not the one.

I listened absently, running financial calculations in my head and deciding which of my clients I should call to do damage control, while Grandma proceeded to tell me a long story about paying a traveling salesman three hundred dollars to refinish the wood floors—not with just ordinary finish, mind you, which would have cost one hundred dollars, but with the best finish available, which was warrantied to last ten years, and, of course, people thought she was crazy to pay so much, but if you do things right the first time, it is always worthwhile. And she always took care of the floors just the way . . .

It was impossible to tell whether she was talking about two months or twenty years ago. I wasn't sure she knew either, but the payment made had something to do with saving up milk and butter money, and there hadn't been cows on the farm in ten years, so I assumed it had been that long. Strange how she could remember every detail of an event so long past, but couldn't remember people's names, or conversations from a day ago, or whether the iron and the coffeemaker were left on.

Ben drove up in the middle of her story, and she fell silent as he came through the screen door. The look on his face made my heart sink like a lead weight.

"What's wrong?" I wasn't sure I wanted to know.

He glanced at us as if he couldn't decide what to say, then shook his head and walked past. "I lost the Randolph contract. I couldn't get the computer logged on this morning." The kitchen door slammed behind him.

Grandma jerked at the sound and Joshua spat out his bottle and started to cry. I buried him under my chin and closed my eyes as the disasters came crashing down on me.

Grandma stroked my hair the way I was stroking Joshua's. "Be patient, Katie. Everything doesn't have to work itself out today."

I knew I should get up and leave before I made her any more upset. "I'm just disappointed, Grandma." I tried to sound calm, but the words trembled. "Without that contract, things will be"—*impossible, hopeless, a financial disaster*—"tight." Josh wailed louder, so I got up to walk him.

Grandma rocked back in her chair and looked at the long afternoon shadows on the lawn. "The Lord gives us what we need, but we have to do our part."

I gritted my teeth. Lately, it felt as if we'd been doing our part and God hadn't been doing His.

Joshua's crying quieted to a whimper. "I'm sorry, Grandma. I'm probably just overreacting. I'd better go in and talk to Ben."

Joshua erupted into a full-scale colicky fit when I went into the house, and Ben gave me an irritated look as he poured himself a glass of soda. "Feed him or something. I'm not in the mood for this right now."

"And you think I am?" I tried to give Josh his pacifier, which only made him angrier and louder. "What's wrong with the Randolph contract?"

"Nothing. They hired somebody else this morning while I was down at the phone company finding out this is some kind of private exchange and there's no local server. If I can't get plans in, I can't—" He slammed his glass on the table and foam leapt out the top. "I can't talk with him doing that!"

The noise made Joshua wail louder. "Oh, good job." I wanted to pitch both of them out the window. Joshua's holler echoed through the house like a siren, and my head swelled with every blast. Grabbing his stroller from the utility room, I headed for the door to keep from going out of my mind.

I caught my breath a few minutes later as I pushed Josh's stroller along the lane that ran past the barn to the pasture gate. He quieted somewhere along the way and lay looking up with wide eyes at the spindly clouds floating overhead. Gazing down at him, I turned the stroller around and started back to the house. I wondered if all new parents started family life in such a mess, or if Joshua had been cheated by the luck of the draw—born with a heart that wasn't right, into a family that was floundering.

As we pushed up the hill to the farmhouse, he twisted his head to look at me and gurgled a smile, as if to tell me he wasn't worried at all. I smiled back and wondered how I could be so in love with something so tiny. He seemed so fragile a vessel to hold all my devotion.

Grandma was asleep on the swing when we came back to the porch. Our car wasn't in the driveway, so I knew Ben had gone back to town, probably to hash things out with the phone company, which was probably for the best. Both of us needed some cooling-off time. I wasn't ready to talk things out with Ben yet, and I figured he probably wasn't ready to talk to me either. He wasn't much for talking over problems anyway. He didn't feel it helped anything.

I parked Joshua next to Grandma's swing and watched as he drifted off. Next to Grandma on the swing, a book lay open, and I picked it up as I sat down in the rocking chair beside her. Absently, I turned it over in my hands and looked at the cover. Someone had made it by hand, laminating pressed wildflowers against pretty peach-colored parchment for the cover and binding it in the center with a sky-blue ribbon. The pages inside were blank except for the first few, which I guessed Grandma had just been writing in, because a pen was lying on the arm of her chair. It wasn't my business to read it, but I looked at the first few words, anyway.

Yellow Bonnets, it was titled.

I read on, though I knew I shouldn't.

When my mind and body were filled with youth, time barely passed around me. Years, seasons, even days crept by with the sloth of an inchworm. . . .

I paused and looked at Grandma, knowing I should put down her book. But I turned my eyes to the words anyway. It was hard to imagine her so young. I didn't know much about her childhood. She never talked about it—almost as if she hadn't existed before she married my grandfather.

. . . . and I waited, anxious for them to pass. Summer days were the longest of all, but in many ways the best. The pastures around our old white house bloomed thick with yellow bonnets like a carpet over the bright green grass. And when there was no work to be done in our tilled fields, we children galloped through the yel-

*low bonnets, snorting and tossing our tawny manes like
fine horses.*

In my mind's eye, I can still see our small, bare feet,
brown from the summer sun, parting the windswept
flowers, scattering grains of pollen to the breeze. We
were ever without shoes in the warm months, as our old
ones were worn through or outgrown by winter's end.

When summer was at its height, the children's fair
would come to town, filling the field beside the church
with autos, buggies, and bright gypsy wagons. On Saturday, my father would take five dimes from the coffee
tin in Mother's kitchen and give one to each of us children. Laughing, we clasped our money in our palms
and ran along the dusty road to town.

When we reached the fair, we dashed wide-eyed into
the fray. My brothers and sisters spent their money
quickly, on candied apples or chances to win popguns
and china dolls. I stood back, instead, and thought of
how I would get the most for my pennies, for I knew
they were precious. Always, I went first to the carousel,
where I could ride for half of my dime. When they
opened the gate, I rushed forward, looking at one fine
horse and the next, white, black, and silver-gray—some
wild-eyed with teeth bared, some meek and sweet with
heads neatly bowed. With their jeweled harnesses
trimmed in gold and silver, they were the finest things I
had ever seen, ever touched. In my mind, I can see them
yet. When I rode, I threw back my head and closed my
eyes, feeling music, feeling wooden muscles gather and
stretch beneath my legs. It was magic, and those moments have never left me.

All too soon, the horses spun to a halt, and the music
quieted. I touched each satiny mane as I walked back
to the gate. Then I bought a cotton candy with my other
nickel, and sat on the hill above the fair, trying to make
it last as long as I could. Below, I saw other children
still at play. Some rode the carousel four or five times,

spending more pennies than I and my brothers and sisters had between us. And I would think: Oh, how wonderful to have so much money to be able to ride the carousel four or five times! Sometimes I prayed that I would find a nickel on the ground as I walked home so that I might ride the carousel again, but I never did. Those nights, I often went to bed angry with God.

The next day as I held my father's hand on the road to worship, I often repented my anger. Guilt was ever my shadow as I walked past the field, empty now, except for blowing bits of streamers, torn tickets, and trodden grass. In worship, I confessed my sin of greed to God, then left with my family to pass the empty field again, and again think of the carousel horses.

The sun was ever high and hot when we reached our home. No work was to be done on the Lord's day, so we children pulled loose from our parents' hands and ran to the pond, galloping wildly through the yellow bonnets. Those fields, the feel of the grass, the scent of pollen in the air are ever with me when summer days grow hot. And now, looking through the tunnel of these many years, I can see what in my youth I could not— that time is a limited and precious gift. I wish I had not spent my hours worrying over another nickel for the carousel, but instead running barefoot through the fields of yellow bonnets.

Closing my tear-filled eyes, I hugged the book to my chest and pictured those tawny-haired children running barefoot through fields of yellow. I knew why Grandma had chosen today to write down that story. And whether she intended to leave it for me to read or not, I knew it was for me—to tell me something she couldn't frame into words when we sat together talking. She wanted me to see what things were precious, to know, as she knew, after eighty-nine years of life.

I watched her and Joshua as the afternoon grew soft

and silent. They looked so peaceful, asleep in the bright winter sunlight, and I felt peaceful also—as if every muscle in my body were dissolving into the cool breeze and the soft sunlight. I looked at the last line of Grandma's story again, and then I set the book on the seat just as I had found it. Later, I would tell her I had read it and how much it meant to me.

> *I wish I had not spent my hours worrying over another nickel for the carousel, but instead running barefoot through the fields of yellow bonnets.*

There were yellow bonnets in my life—things I had set aside in my rush to establish my career and buy all of the things we thought we needed. In ten years of marriage, Ben and I had probably spent less than one year in the same room, and even less time actually talking. We were a far cry from the college lovers we had started out as. It seemed hard to imagine those days now, as if they had happened between two people I didn't know. It was hard to picture us strolling through the city hand in hand, or curling up to watch old movies all day, or calling five times a day just to say, "I love you," or hear the sound of the other's voice. Now we couldn't carry on a conversation without someone getting paged, or called, or e-mailed.

Grown-up life has a way of doing that to you—taking up a little more and a little more of your time until you're never together, and when you are together, you're exhausted. I guess I'd thought having a baby would change all that, but it hadn't changed anything. Ben was still busy, I was still busy, and life was rushing by like a speeding train. Jump on board or get left behind. . . .

Chapter 3

BEN didn't come back until late in the evening, and when he did, he said he had driven all the way to Springfield to pick up some software for a local Internet provider, in hopes of correcting his problem with the computer. He went directly upstairs to install it and stayed there until late that night.

I didn't bother arguing with him, or trying to coax him into eating supper or coming to bed. I left him alone, then finally went to bed. I could tell he wasn't in the mood to talk. He wanted to be alone, which was how he always wanted to be when things went wrong at work.

By morning, he was in a better mood. He slept late, so I ate breakfast with Grandma, then put Josh in his stroller for her, because she wanted to push him to the mailbox and back while I made some phone calls. By the time I was done, they had finished their walk and were resting on the porch, Joshua nodding off in his stroller, Grandma's head bobbing forward and a Wal-Mart ad slowly falling from her hands.

Stepping quietly onto the porch, I slipped the ad and the rest of the mail gently from her fingers and set the pile on the table beside her.

Ben was standing at the corner of the porch when I turned around. He gave me a hangdog look as he leaned against the wall, and I could tell he was ready to kiss and make up.

"Want to go for a walk?" he whispered.

I nodded, glancing at Grandma and Josh, both sound asleep in the gentle winter sunlight, just as they had been the day before. I remembered her story about the yellow bonnets and wondered where the book was now. "Not too far, in case Josh wakes up."

Ben chuckled. "You mean Grandma might not hear him if he wakes up?"

"Not likely." It felt good to laugh together. "Her hearing aid's on the table." I opened my mouth to tell him about the story she'd written, then stopped. It felt as if I'd be betraying something secret between Grandma and me.

Strolling silently across the lawn, we reached a wrought-iron bench next to one of Grandma's rose trellises. Winter-bare vines hung thick around the trellis, testifying to the heavy stand of roses that grew there in the summer months. For as long as I could remember, Grandma's yard had been filled with roses.

We sat on the bench, neither of us knowing quite what to say.

Finally, Ben leaned forward and braced his elbows on his knees, his blue eyes gazing at the green winter wheat in the valley below. "I'm sorry, Kate. Yesterday was a frustrating day. I didn't mean to take it out on you. I still can't get the computer logged on. There is too much interference on the lines out here. I can't get a viable connection to the server."

I swallowed a lump of disappointment. "I didn't know there were still places where you couldn't get Internet service."

Ben rolled his eyes. "Well, we've stumbled onto one,

unfortunately, and there's no cellular service out here, either. Anyway, I called James. He needs some detailing design work done on the steel for that building he's putting up in New York."

I grimaced. I couldn't help it. "Is he going to pay you what you're worth this time?" Jobs for Ben's old friend James always ended up paying about half the normal rate.

Ben gave me a narrow sideways look. "He's a friend, Kate."

"He's a friend with a half-million-dollar house, two boats, and a Mercedes. He can afford to pay you what you're worth." The retort was a knee-jerk response, out of my mouth before I stopped to think. I could see Ben start to stiffen, and I could feel us winding into a fight again. "I'm sorry," I said quickly. "That's just my opinion. Another hospital bill came yesterday, and things are a mess at work because of that audit, so I'm not in the best mood."

Ben let out a long sigh, looking at the ground, digging his fingers into his dark hair. "Another hospital bill? How bad?"

"Ninety-five hundred," I answered. "The insurance already denied the claim, but I'm going to file a complaint. Again."

Ben just nodded, then reached over and laid his hand on my knee. I put my hand over his and we sat together in silence, listening to the faint lowing of cattle in the wheat field. I felt the tension ebbing from my muscles, the warmth of Ben's body next to mine, and the comfort that came from knowing I wasn't alone. It felt good to be there with him, quiet together.

Looking at the sea of waving winter wheat below, I thought again of Grandma's story. I pictured the field blanketed with yellow bonnets, waving slightly in the gentle summer breeze, parting as tiny feet passed by. I pictured the children running, laughing, carefree ... and that sense of peace came over me again. Even though I didn't think God was listening, I closed my eyes and prayed. ...

The dinner bell rang at the house, startling me from my thoughts. I glanced at my watch and realized it was practically lunchtime.

Ben stood up, seeming in a better mood. "Either Joshua's learned how to pull the string, or Grandma's got lunch ready."

I stood up and followed him to the porch. Grandma was in the kitchen fixing a plate of sandwiches. "I hope roast beef is all right," she said, seeming more cheerful than usual. I wondered if she was trying to smooth the wrinkle between Ben and me. "I've got some good cucumber rings and the leftover green-pea salad." The sweet tone in her voice told me she was up to something.

The three of us sat down with Josh's stroller parked by the table, and Grandma said grace—quickly, as if she were in a hurry to move on to other things. Ben and I started eating, and she sat eyeing us as if waiting for one of us to bring up our problems.

When no one did, she offered what, I think, was supposed to be a solution. "They will be cleaning out the produce bins at Shorty's Grocery today. Katie, I thought you and I would go this afternoon and salvage what we can use. It's a terrible waste, those things they throw away. One or two bad spots and they will pitch something out. I go every week and take oranges, apples, lettuce, and potatoes—all without it costing a cent. Some weeks, I even get enough to do some canning."

I stared at her, not quite digesting what was being said.

Ben cracked a halfhearted smile. "At least we won't starve."

Grandma gave him an earnest look and raised a finger to make a point. "That was always the good of living on a farm. When other folks had nothing, we always ate, even if it was only potatoes and buck-flour pancakes." I felt like a naughty child as she shook that craggy finger in our direction. "And I'll tell you something else. We children knew not to complain or we would leave the table hungry. My father would say the Lord served up the meals and it wasn't our business to complain about the menu."

Grandma had the most uncanny talent for putting things in perspective. When you gave thought to how it would feel to be unable to buy *food* for your children, a few medical bills and a tightening of purse strings seemed minor problems. Neither Ben nor I complained anymore.

Grandma clapped her hands together, looking triumphant. "Oh, and Benjamin, I've called Brother Baker down at the church about your problem with the phones. There are several empty offices in the fellowship building, and he says you are welcome to attach your computer to the phone lines there. He says you shouldn't have any problem on that exchange there in town. His son uses that intra-net all the time to do his college work."

Ben and I sat staring at her with our chins hanging somewhere near the floor.

Ben recovered first and numbly said, "Thanks, Grandma. That sounds perfect."

Grandma smiled, chirping, "Very good," with a self-satisfied glint in her eye. "Sorry to say none of those offices are done in pink paint and ruffles, but I suppose you can make do."

"I guess I'll have to." Ben chuckled, grinning sideways at me. He picked up his plate and put it on the counter, looking as though he had the wind in his sails again. "Thanks again, Grandma Rose. You're a lifesaver. Guess I'll go load up the computer and head to town."

Grandma flushed as if the praise were more than she could bear. "Good-bye, Benjamin. Brother Baker will be at the church. He'll show you to the offices." Her gaze followed Ben as he hurried from the room and trotted up the stairs, and I saw the faintest hint of a smile on her lips.

She wiped it away as soon as she caught me watching. "Well, I suppose we should get going. They always change the produce on Saturday after lunch; then it goes to the trash bin at three. I think they'll be putting out bags of potatoes today. I saw them getting rotten earlier in the week."

"Grandma, potatoes only cost a dollar fifty-nine a bag. Why don't we just buy some?" I was thinking of the insurance claims I needed to write out and the files I had brought along from the office, the phone calls I needed to make and about a dozen other things I could be doing—none of which included picking through rotten vegetables.

Grandma jerked back, looking at me with a white-rimmed blaze in her eye. She raised that craggy finger and shushed me. "And that would be a dollar fifty-nine we wouldn't have in our pocketbooks tomorrow. That is the problem with you young people today. Everything is just a dollar here and five dollars there, and ten dollars that time, and then you don't have any money when you need it and you have to borrow from the banker. My father used to say: 'The man who buys what he does not need will often need what he cannot buy.'"

"O.K., Grandma, don't get so upset." She was turning red in the face. I knew better than to get her started on the subject of debt. That was a hellfire-and-brimstone sermon, and it could go on for hours.

So I packed Joshua's diaper bag, and we climbed into the Buick, me in the front to chauffeur and Grandma keeping Joshua company in the backseat. Away we went to dig through rotten potatoes.

Grandma was in a foul mood about debt on the way there, and it didn't take long before I was in a foul mood too. Grandma could have that effect on people when she wanted to. When she was finished preaching about debt, she started handing out unsolicited parenting tips.

"Time we took that pacifier away from this baby, Katie." Josh, strapped beside her in his car seat, was peacefully unaware of the tempest brewing in the old Buick, and he cooed happily as Grandma tried to extract his sucker.

"Grandma, leave it be." Too late. The pacifier flashed across the corner of my peripheral vision, gripped in Grandma's hand. Josh whimpered, trying to decide if he really felt like crying.

"He'll become spoiled on it."

"He's only four months old," I reminded her, glancing over my shoulder and wishing I could reach the pacifier, now on the seat beside Grandma.

Josh waved a hand in the air as if to cheer me on, then started babbling at his own fingers.

"It'll ruin his mouth." Grandma looked out the side window and moved her lips like a cow chewing a cud.

Gripping the steering wheel tighter, I faced forward again, reminding myself of the doctor's advice that she avoid stress. Too bad that didn't stop her from dishing it out to other people. "It helps him sleep," I said.

"The child doesn't sleep because his little stomach isn't satisfied. A tablespoon of rice cereal will take care of that."

I resisted the urge to stop the car and make her hitch the rest of the way to town. Instead, I stared ahead, determined not to let her get to me. "He's too young for cereal. Giving solid foods too young causes earaches."

I should have known better than to reason with her.

She spat out a puff of air as if she had a bad taste in her mouth. "Oh, nonsense. I never heard of such."

"It's been proven."

"Fiddle. I gave cereal to every one of my children and you grandchildren, and not a one of you got earaches."

Confronted with eighty years of child-rearing experience, I was helpless so I settled for, "He doesn't need cereal."

"We'll purchase some at the store." In the rearview mirror, I saw her cross her arms tighter and draw her chin back, pressing her lips into a stern line.

"We're *not* getting any baby cereal."

"*I'll* buy it." As if I were too cheap to buy my son what he so desperately needed.

"No, you won't." Beads of sweat squeezed from the skin under my collar and dripped down my back. No matter what, I wasn't going to let her bait me onto her hook. . . .

"I can buy what I want." Snatching her purse from the floorboard, she clutched it in her lap. "I have my money. I'll take care of little Jackie." Jackie was her son, my father.

The next thing I knew, I was half facing Grandma and making the most ridiculous statements. "Joshua! It's Joshua! And you come near that baby with cereal, it'll be the last time! No cereal, no cookies to chew on, no drops of brandy for colic! No . . ." The word ended in a gasp as something in the road caught my eye and I slammed on the brakes.

Grandma rocked forward, catching one hand on the seat back and the other on the baby carrier as we slid to a stop.

Heart rapping in my throat, I looked at her and Joshua, then glanced ahead at the road. Doe-eyed in our path were a big dog and a dark-haired girl crouched above an overturned bike. The car had stopped not more than ten feet short of them. We were all frozen, looking at each other agape with horror.

My mind ran over the preceding moments with lightning speed. Where had she come from? How could we have come so close to hitting her? How long were my eyes off the road? What would have happened if I'd seen her a moment later?

The clatter of something against the pavement shook me into action. Hitting the hazard lights, I put the car in park and got out just in time to catch a can of pork and beans as it rolled toward the side of the road. On my way to the overturned bike, I gathered what could be salvaged of the groceries that had spilled from the basket.

"Are you all right?" I asked, stopping a few feet away when the dog started to growl.

The girl nodded as she stood up and righted the bike, reaching across the dog to regain her groceries, her chin tucked and her face hidden. "Rowdy, hush," she told the dog. Her voice sounded so young, it shocked me, and I realized that though she was tall, she was probably only about nine or ten years old. Too young to be biking down the highway three miles from town all alone.

"I'm sorry. I just didn't see you," I apologized, wanting to touch her to make sure she was all in one piece.

Stepping back as if she'd read my thoughts, she crossed her arms nervously over her stomach. "I shouldn't've been in the road."

Bracing my palms on my knees, I bent over and tried to make contact with the face hidden beneath a mass of too-long bangs and tangled hair. "It was my fault. I'll be glad to replace your groceries or just give you the money."

I caught a glimpse of wide dark eyes as she looked around at the spilled milk, squashed chips, and broken jelly jar.

"I'm really sorry," I tried again as I started picking up

the remaining groceries. "Can I give you a ride home and explain it to your mom?"

"No, ma'am." She ran three steps and hopped on the bike before I could react. The dog followed quickly after her, and they disappeared around a bend in the road as I retrieved the last of the crumpled groceries and stood there with no one to give them to. Finally, I just carried the ripped bag back to the car and set it in the trunk, leaking jelly and all.

"Well, let's get on to town." Grandma was clearly put out by the delay as I climbed into the driver's seat. "The vegetables will be in the trash before we get there, and now we have spoiled groceries leaking all over my trunk." I glanced after the girl, and Grandma leaned forward to follow my line of vision, adding matter-of-factly, "That little Jordan girl. It will be a miracle if something terrible doesn't happen to her before she's grown."

"What was she doing on the road?" I asked, ignoring the ire in her tone.

Grandma tipped her chin up and righted herself in her seat like a judge at a hanging trial. "Well, probably going after cigarettes for her granny. She's a big fat woman and too lazy to get out of the house. Has emphysema so bad she can't walk to the mailbox, but it doesn't stop her from buying cigarettes." She pointed a finger into the air and then at me. "And I'll tell you what else. They take welfare. Spend it on cigarettes and potato chips. Just white trash—that's all. That little girl's been sent home from school for lice probably a half-dozen times."

The thought made my skin crawl. "Where is her mother?"

Grandma huffed out a long sigh as if even telling the story were a waste of time. "Ran away to St. Louis and got herself pregnant by some Mexican or Indian or maybe even a Negro man. No one knows, and she didn't either. Then she died on drugs and left that baby for her gran to raise. They're just no better than white trash. Hurry up, Katie. I have to get to the grocery."

"Where does she live?" I asked, keeping the car at a moderate speed. One near miss was enough.

Grandma craned forward to glance at the speedometer, huffed, then gave me a blank look in the rearview mirror. "Where does who live?"

"That little girl on the bike."

"Oh," she muttered absently, her mind obviously drifting. "Down Mulberry Road in an awful little hovel that ought to be condemned. Larry Leddy rents it to them, and he ought to be ashamed. Needs to be torn down. You can see it across the river bottom from our place. Katie, land sakes, slow down. Do you know you went forty-five around that curve? No need to rush us into an accident."

And so it went the rest of the way to town. *Speed up, Katie. Slow down. Land sakes. Curve ahead. Joshua needs cereal, but no pacifier.* And an occasional, *The Jordans are white trash. Welfare ought to haul them away. Land sakes, what's wrong with the world?*

Chapter 4

FEW things smell worse than rotten vegetables. When we began our salvage operation in the back room of the grocery store, my mood matched the stench—completely foul. I set Josh's carrier as far away from the smell as I could and reluctantly started sorting through some apples with one finger.

But as we went along, I started to see the humor in Grandma and me digging through bins of spoiled fruit and bags of rotten potatoes like a couple of vagrants. No one at work would ever believe this was how I had spent my vacation.

When Grandma found something good, she would cry out as if she'd discovered a gold nugget: "Ah-hah! Here is a perfectly good orange. Not a mark on it. Can you believe anyone would throw such a thing in the trash?" or "Um-hum, um-hum, look at how many good potatoes are left in these bags. I thought so. We can store these in the cellar and have them all winter. Terrible how much people will waste these days. In my day . . ."

Meanwhile, I sorted through bags of apples, trying not to laugh and not to breathe at the same time. When we were done, we had netted about a half-dozen oranges, slightly bruised; two bushels of apples, rotten only in places; some yellow stalks of celery; four cucumbers, shriveled on one end; and enough potatoes to feed an army.

Grandma was giddy. We would not starve over the long winter ahead, or go into debt to buy potatoes. She went into the store to thank Shorty, the grocer, while I loaded down the trunk of the old Buick, then picked up Josh and drove around front to wait for her. She was still inside talking, so Josh and I sneaked over to the hardware store to buy a can of paint and a brush for the utility room. I tucked it in the trunk under the baskets, then sat with Josh on the bench by the curb, enjoying another unseasonably warm day.

Taking a deep breath of the clean Ozark air, I gazed at the town, sleepy at midafternoon on a Saturday. It looked like a picture postcard, an ancient native-stone town nestled amid oak trees on the banks of the Gasconade River. Hindsville probably hadn't changed much since its founding over a hundred years before. The storefronts, brownstone with neatly painted porches and trim, were built around a picturesque central square with stone walkways and a gazebo where folks still came on Saturday nights to pick guitars, fiddle, and sing.

I had vague memories of going there a few times as a child—twirling in a floral-print dress on the grass in front of the bandstand. The memory made me feel warm and grounded. There is something special about a place that smells and sounds and feels like your childhood. Hindsville was the place where I bought ice cream cones at the drugstore and sat on the curb to eat them. The place where Mom and I bought new school shoes from the dry goods store at the end of every summer visit. It was the center of nearly every tradition I remembered about my family—the only place where the four of us were together with no one in a hurry to go somewhere.

I'd never realized I missed it. Throughout my adult years, I'd never felt a need to return. Too slow. Too boring. No skyscrapers. No shopping mall.

My last memory of Hindsville was of coming for my mother's funeral at the family cemetery next to the farm. Ben and I had stayed only three days. Three quiet, solemn days in which all of us looked for someone to blame for Mom's car accident. Three days in which we fell apart instead of coming together . . .

So why did I now feel an overwhelming sadness that I would probably never return to Hindsville? This Christmas would be the end of it. The end of the farm. The end of that nagging guilt that Grandma was here alone and no one ever visited her. After Christmas, Grandma would be settled in a nursing home near Aunt Jeane . . .

My mind couldn't frame the picture.

The chimes rang three o'clock on the Baptist church next door, and I stopped to listen, looking at the glittering stained-glass image of a dove landing in God's hands. Brother Baker stood on the front steps and waved at me, then walked across the alley to Shorty's. I stood up, hoping Grandma would come out before Brother Baker got around to loading on the Christian guilt about Ben and me not being churchgoers.

"Well, your husband is all settled in with his computer," he announced as he stepped onto the walk.

"That's wonderful," I said, thinking how much Brother Baker seemed to have aged. My mind conjured a fleeting image of him in a much younger state, red hair instead of gray, dunking me in the baptismal pool behind the pulpit. "We sure appreciate this. Grandma's farm doesn't seem to be Internet-friendly."

Brother Baker chuckled, then gave me a round-cheeked smile that made the essence of my childhood stronger. "Well, you know, we haven't quite joined the modern era around here."

I laughed with him. "That's not all bad." Strangely, I meant it. "We're enjoying the quiet."

Brother Baker nodded as if he understood. "It has its benefits." He reached down and rubbed Josh's fuzzy head, then sidestepped to open the door to the grocery store as Grandma hobbled out carrying a half-dozen loaves of bread and two boxes of doughnuts.

She tipped her chin up, looking triumphant. "The bread man was going to throw these away." She peered over the stack and realized it was Brother Baker holding the door open, not me. "Well, hello, Brother Baker. How is young Benjamin getting along?"

"Just fine, Mrs. Vongortler." Brother Baker stood at attention like a foot soldier addressing a cavalry captain. "He's all settled in one of those offices off the fellowship hall."

Grandma nodded approval. "Well, very good. I guess that's a problem solved, then." She squared her shoulders so that she could look at Brother Baker more directly. "Now, if any of the church elders have a question about him using the facility, you have them call me."

"I'm sure things will be fine," Brother Baker said, then told us good-bye and scooted into the grocery store, clearly relieved to be escaping the conversation with Grandma unscathed. "You ladies have a good day now."

Grandma nodded after him, then proceeded to the car, and the three of us headed back to the farm with our loot.

By the time we arrived and carried the baskets to the kitchen, Grandma and Josh were both exhausted. Grandma padded off to the little house to rest, and I put

Josh in his crib, then retrieved the paint from the car and started on the utility room.

An hour and a half later, the room was greatly improved, and I had touched up around the outside doorframe and ceiling too. It looked pretty good, except for the burn damage on the wall where the ironing board had been. Since I know nothing about replastering walls, there wasn't much I could do about that, so I set the new stand-alone ironing board in front of the hole and went outside to clean the paintbrush and put the paint away. I heard Grandma coming in the front door as I went out the back, so I hurried to get out of sight. The less Grandma was reminded of the fire damage, the better.

When I came onto the porch again, she was in the front yard near the rose trellis, carefully pruning the winter-browned vines with the tenderness of a loving parent. A pair of squirrels, accustomed to her throwing out corn, dashed back and forth around her feet, looking for food. Every so often, she paused and reached into her pocket, tossing out a handful of seed to keep them busy.

Her hand reaching into the printed blue polyester brought a memory to me with startling clarity. I could see her in that very apron on some long-ago summer day, tossing bits of corn to the guinea hens that years ago roamed the farmyard. In my ears, I heard the sputter of the old red tractor and the rattle of the wagon puttering down the lane. I could see my grandfather motion to me, then stop the tractor and wait by the gate. I remembered running across the lawn with my hand in Grandma's and laughing when she swung me into the wagon for a ride. As we left, I saw her squeeze Grandpa's hand and give him a peck on the cheek.

Then the memory dashed away like one of Grandma's squirrels.

I found myself standing with one hand pressed against the screen. The memory was one I never knew I had, from a summer visit when I was only three or four years old. It was the only recollection I had of my grandparents together—surprising in its tenderness, considering that no one in the family ever talked about how they were toward each other. I guess I'd never thought that they might have been in love, and never considered how truly sad it would be to go on for almost thirty years after the one you loved was gone. I wondered if that was the source of the melancholy that had been with Grandma ever since I had known her. I remembered her as solemn and rigid, fussy about things and critical of people, often difficult to be around. I just assumed she had always been that way. I could not remember a time when she would have burst into laughter and run across the lawn with me on her arm.

Leaving her there with her roses and her squirrels, I went inside to fix myself a cup of tea and air out the utility room. The kitchen was quiet and peaceful, no overflowing dishwater or lakes of coffee on the floor—just long rays of late-afternoon sunlight streaming through the tall west window, and the dishes still there from lunch, waiting to be washed, and several baskets of slightly unappealing fruits and vegetables waiting to be stored, or canned, or whatever Grandma had in mind. Choosing to ignore the mess a little longer, I poured the tea, then turned to sit at the table. There, as if it had appeared while my back was turned, was Grandma's book. It reminded me that I'd never confessed snooping the day before, or told her how much the yellow bonnet story meant to me. I wasn't sure why I hadn't mentioned it—perhaps because I was embarrassed about snooping, or maybe afraid she'd be angry. One thing I had learned on my childhood visits to the farm was not to touch her things.

Still, if the book were private, she wouldn't leave it lying around. . . .

I subdued my conscience in a flash and opened the book with curiosity and a sense of anticipation, hoping to read the story about the yellow bonnets again.

But the pages of the story had been removed from the book as if they had never existed. *Milk*, *bread*, and *oleo* had replaced the words that had shown me children running through yellow fields.

"A shopping list," I muttered, feeling strangely let down and even more guilty. My theory that Grandma had written the story for me to read was a wash. If it were for me, she wouldn't have taken it out of the book and put it away.

The next page was blank except for dots of ink that had bled through from the page after. Turning the page, I found writing that quivered like Grandma's hands.

"Time For Tending Roses," I whispered and thought of the beautiful rose garden that bloomed on the lawn in summertime. It had been there for as long as I could remember, carefully manicured, every bloom perfect— just as perfect and neat as everything else in Grandma's household.

I read the title again, then dove into the story with a strange hunger for the words.

When I was a young woman, I seldom owned anything of which to be proud. When I was old enough to work in a shop in St. Louis and live on my own, most of my wage was sent home to provide for my younger brothers and sisters, for my parents had not even their health by this time. When I was married, I came to my husband's farm with all that I owned packed in a single crate. Everything I saw, or tasted, or touched around me belonged to my husband. I felt like the air in that big house, needed and used, but not seen.

God sent an answer to me in worship that spring, when an old woman told me she wanted the gardens cleaned around her house, and if I would do the work, I might have flower bulbs and starts of roses as my pay. My husband pretended to think the idea rather foolish, as I was needed on the farm, but he was patient with me as I worked through the early spring, cleaning gardens and moving starts to a newly tilled bed by our farm-house. He was older than I, and I think he understood that I needed something of my own.

Those roses were the finest things I had been given in my life, and I tended them carefully all spring. As the days lengthened, the roses grew well and blossomed in the summer heat, as did I. Coming in and out of the house, I would look at them—something that belonged to me, growing in soil that belonged to him.

Even passing folk admired my roses, for my work made the blooms large and full. Once, a poor hired lady came with a bouquet of roses and wildflowers clasped in her hands. She told me that her children had sneaked into my garden and picked them for her, and that they would be punished. I bade her not to scold the children, for I was proud to give them this gift. She smiled, and thanked me, and told me that, with so many children, she had no time for tending roses.

I did not understand her words until my own children were born. When the first was a babe, I took her outside and let her play in an empty wash barrel so I could have time for tending my roses. I was often cross with her cries while I was at my work. As she grew, and as my second child was born, I understood what the hired lady had told me—that motherhood leaves no time for selfish pleasures. Only time for tending others.

My roses grew wild and died as I busied myself with feeding and diapering, nursery rhymes and sickbeds. I missed those bright blooms that had been mine and felt it unfair that I must leave my hard work there to die. But

I did not think of it overmuch. My mind and heart were occupied with the sorrows and joys of motherhood.

The day came, it seemed in no time, when my children were grown and gone, and I again found time to tend the roses. I could labor over them from dawn until dusk with no children to feed, no husband needing meals, and few passersby on the old road. My flowers have come thick and full and beautiful again. From time to time, I see neighbor children come to pick them when I am silent in my house. I close my eyes and listen to their laughter, and think that the best times of my life, the times that passed by me the most quickly, were the times when the roses grew wild.

The sense of sadness in those last words was overwhelming. For a moment, I glimpsed my own future, considered a day when I would sit alone in a quiet house trying to fill my time, at the end of things rather than at the beginning. The beginning of a journey is always uncertain, but with uncertainty comes hope. Never had I appreciated the value of that. Through all of my adult life, I had wanted to know exactly where I was going and what path to take to get there. I had never considered the beauty of where I was. Sitting there in Grandma's kitchen, holding her book, I thought of her as a young woman not able to see that something wonderful was passing. Not appreciating the noise until she was surrounded by silence.

For the first time in my life, I was very glad just to be where I was.

Joshua stirred upstairs, and I left the kitchen, setting Grandma's book on the table, just as I had found it. When I reached the upstairs bedroom, Joshua was lying in the crib, stretching his hands into the air and watching faded plastic horses dance on an old crib toy Grandma had hung above the bed. Gazing at him from the doorway, I wondered if my grandmother had once stood in that very spot watching my father in that old wooden crib, and if my mother had once stood there watching me.

The feeling of missing my mother was suddenly overwhelming. The six years since her death seemed to have passed in the blink of an eye. Here at the farm my grief felt fresh. This was the place where I remembered her most, where she was never busy with patient consultations and college courses. This was where I *loved* her most, where we picked blackberries and baked cobblers and roasted hotdogs on the stone grill out back, where we really spent time together. I wondered if she had felt that way about it too, or if she even found time to think.

Josh grew restless, and I picked him up and sat in the rocking chair by the window, feeling the weight of him on my chest and gazing at the waning day—thinking of Grandma's story about the roses and about the fact that time is so invisible, you never see it passing.

I was drifting somewhere among the crimson-rimmed clouds when Joshua grew impatient and made it clear he was ready for a bottle. Leaving my thoughts behind, I went downstairs to feed him and fix supper. The book was gone from the table, and Grandma was sitting there drinking a cup of coffee, looking slightly chilled. She reached for Josh and fed him while I worked on creating a casserole from leftover breakfast sausage and some of our salvaged vegetables. The kitchen was heavy with the odor of paint from the utility room, but Grandma didn't mention it.

Ben walked in the door just as I was putting the plates on the table. Hanging his coat on the hook, he looked over his shoulder with a frown. "Why does it smell like paint in here?"

I gave him a warning glance as I finished setting the

table and started serving the food. "Must be the casserole."

He knitted his brows in confusion, but just nodded, afraid to say anything else. "O.K." And he sat down, wisely keeping silent until he could survey the lay of the land.

We sat there quietly for a while, at peace until Grandma heard a sound somewhere in the house and decided to start up about the plumbing. "That septic drain is going to back up in the cellar, I can tell by the way it sounds." She paused in the middle of a bite of casserole, listening. "Oh, if it backs up, it will be expensive to fix. It is too much paper, that's all. Too much paper down it with so many people in the house. We will all have to be more careful, and no . . ." A semi roared by on the county road, and she paused in midsentence, then seemed to lose her train of thought. "Oh, those awful trucks. The way they come racing through. That little Jordan girl might be on the road."

"Grandma," I scolded. "Stop worrying."

She gave no indication that she'd heard me, but turned to Ben instead and reported, "We nearly ran right over the little Jordan girl today."

"Grandma!" I squealed.

Ben gave me a quizzical look.

Rubbing the growing ache in my head, I rolled my eyes. "It was nothing," I said to Ben. And to Grandma, "Eat your casserole."

Ben smirked at me, trying not to laugh, then bent over his plate shaking his head. Grandma huffed and ate some casserole, then decided to fill Ben in on the day's successful salvage operation. That cheered her up, and by the time we finished eating, she had a gleam in her eye and a plan for how the three of us could get the potatoes stored in the cellar and the apples peeled, boiled, and made into apple butter and preserves. To my com-

plete amazement, Ben complied, and we spent a couple
of hours storing up food for the next century. After he
had carried the potatoes to the cellar, he even helped to
mash and strain the apples. The extra helpfulness and
the overly cheerful tone of his voice told me that he was
up to something, but I didn't dare ask about it in front of
Grandma. Whatever it was, he knew I wasn't going to like
it, and he was trying to butter me up.

He brought it up after Grandma went to the little
house and Joshua was put to bed. He took a deep breath
and dropped the bomb as we were cleaning the last of
the canning supplies. "Kate, I have to go out of town for
a couple of days."

It took me a minute to register what he was saying;
then a pang of disquiet went through me. "What?"

"I can't help it," he went on quickly. "James needs me
at a job site to solve some detail problems. They've got
some steel that's not fitting like it should and it's holding up the job they're on. It'll only take a couple of days,
a week at the most."

"A week?" My disquiet erupted into full-scale panic.
"What if Grandma sets the house on fire again? What if
Joshua gets sick and needs to go to the doctor? You
know any kind of infection could put strain on his heart,
and ..."

Ben reached out and grabbed my shoulders. "Josh is
fine. Grandma will be fine. It's only a couple of days. We
need the money."

"You already agreed to go, didn't you?" I looked at
him, and suddenly I knew there was no point in fighting.
He'd already decided.

He nodded, looking guilty about it. "James really
needs someone who can get this figured out in a hurry
and get the job on-line. His detailer wants them to re-
make all the parts, but I looked at the design on-line, and
I have an idea. I told James I think I can save him a lot

of money and man-hours." Beneath the surface guilt there was that look of excitement and job lust that he always got when presented with a challenge. Once again, he was Superman, out to save the world from poorly designed buildings and metal parts that didn't fit.

I knew there was no point in arguing anymore. He was going. Sighing, I pressed the palm of my hand against my forehead, wondering if the rest of our lives would be Ben coming in on one flight and leaving on another. I had a flash to the two of us in some former life planning all the traveling we would do together. "When do you fly out?"

"First thing in the morning, and it's a two-hour drive to the airport, so I'll be gone early."

"Promise you'll be back before any of the family gets here. You know James's jobs always run overtime." Being left alone with Grandma was bad enough. I couldn't face the idea of being there without Ben when the family arrived for Christmas.

"I'll be back." He sat at the table, and I sat with him as he went on, frowning. "Stop worrying about them coming. It'll be the same as always—they'll fly in, make a little small talk about jobs, houses, cars . . . whatever, and then they'll fly out. Aunt Jeane will take care of all the details, like she always does, and that will be the end of it."

I sighed, afraid he was right, afraid he wasn't, and wondering why I cared. Things with my family had been hopeless for so many years now, I thought I'd learned to accept it. We weren't at war, but we weren't at peace, and mostly we just stayed away from each other.

It seemed to matter more now that we had Josh and now that Grandma was one step away from a nursing home. "I was just hoping things would be . . . different," I admitted, even though I didn't know what I was hoping for.

Ben scoffed, reaching over and rubbing my shoulder. "Don't get your hopes up, Kate. Your dad's too wrapped up in himself to care about anyone else, and I'll be surprised if Karen even shows up at all. Neither one of them gets along with Grandma, and you know they both hate this farm. They've never made any secret of that."

"I know." Something sharp twisted inside me. "I guess, once in a while, I just wish things were better."

"But they're not." He sighed, probably because we'd had the conversation before and he was tired of going over the subject of my family. His family was so unemotional, it made mine seem like a certifiable disaster. "Stop torturing yourself, Kate. Just forget about it."

"You're probably right." But I knew he wasn't. No matter how much you want to cut your family out of your heart, you can't. The bond is born when you are born, like an organ in your body. There is no surgery to remove it. When it is diseased, you live with a dull ache telling you that something inside you is not right.

I rubbed my eyes as they started to burn. Then I stood up and walked to the window to look out at the little house. "I'm afraid Grandma is going to go off the deep end when they tell her they want to take her to a nursing home and get rid of the farm."

I heard Ben get up. "Let's cross that bridge when we come to it. Maybe it won't be as bad as you think. Maybe Grandma will like the idea of being in St. Louis close to your Aunt Jeane."

I sighed, shook my head, and turned from the window.

Chapter 5

THE clatter of pans awakened me sometime in the early morning. Opening one sleepy eye, I watched a squirrel trying to raid the bird feeder outside my window. The noise in the kitchen stopped, and I wondered if Grandma had seen the marauding squirrel and gone outside to chase him away. On one hand, she practically hand-fed the squirrels; on the other, she hated it when they got into her bird feeders. Like everything in her world, she felt they should know their place.

Rolling over slowly, I reached for Ben, but realized that he was already gone. I dimly remembered him kissing me good-bye and leaving while it was still dark outside. The reality of him being away filled me with a profound sense of loneliness. I closed my eyes, knowing I was being childish, and trying not to think about it.

A voice inside my head admonished me for being so emotional. *It's just postpartum hormones, Kate. Don't be such a baby. Get your head together. He'll be back in a few days. No point going off the deep . . .*

A strange, putrid smell assaulted my senses suddenly, cutting short my thoughts.

"Eeewww," I muttered, my empty stomach rolling

over as I stood up and slipped my feet into my house shoes. Whatever Grandma was cooking, it smelled like rotten eggs. She . . .

The jingle from a public-service commercial twittered through my mind: *If you sniff that rotten-egg smell, turn off the gas, open the windows really fast . . .*

My heart leapt into my throat. *The propane!* My mind cleared, and I rushed toward the kitchen. The smell there was stifling, but the room was undisturbed except for a smattering of mixing bowls and an open flour sack beside the stove.

Over the hum of the refrigerator, I heard a faint hiss coming from the oven. Covering my face with a towel, I rushed forward and turned off the dial, then threw open the window and screen door, gagging. My legs trembled like wet spaghetti as I rushed from room to room in the house, opening windows and doors.

Sitting on the stairs as the smell faded away, I held my head in my hands, thinking about what might have happened if I hadn't awakened when I did. Josh was still sound asleep in his bed . . . helpless . . . What was Grandma thinking, turning on the oven and not lighting the pilot? And then to walk away while propane spewed into the kitchen . . .

A desperate anger welled up inside me, and I grabbed my coat, then stormed out the door, slamming it behind me. "Grandma!" I hollered, heading for the little house. "Grandma, come out here!"

She poked her head out the door, her blue eyes wide over two circles of fresh pink blusher on her cheeks. "Katie, what's wrong?"

I stopped at the bottom of the steps, gripping and ungripping my fists. "The house is full of propane gas! You left the oven on and the pilot wasn't lit."

Confused, she stepped out, darting a glance toward the house, then back to me. "I haven't *used* the oven this morning. I was going to make a coffee cake, but there wasn't time. I have to be ready for church."

"Grandma, you *did* use the oven," I insisted, my temper boiling hot into my throat. "You got out the flour. You got out your mixing bowls, and you turned on the oven, but you didn't light the pilot." I waved a hand toward the house. "The kitchen was full of gas. I could smell it all the way to my room!"

Looking dazed, she shook her head. "That pilot on the oven must be broken. . . ."

Mouth hanging open, I stared at her in complete shock. "Grandma, you won't ever leave the pilot lit! You light it every time with a match—don't you remember? You said it wasted gas!"

The mist cleared from her eyes like fog evaporating from a mirror. Fingers trembling, she brought them to the sides of her face. "Oh, Katie, I'm sorry. Oh, I'm sorry. I'll pay for the propane."

The hairs rose on the back of my neck, and my mouth sped ahead of my self-control. "I'm not worried about the propane. I'm worried about getting blown up in my sleep!" I looked away from her, not wanting to see her expression of horror and dismay. I was too angry, too scared to care how she felt. "From now on we're leaving the pilot lit. It's made to stay on all the time. It doesn't use that much propane. Don't turn it off again."

"I'm sorry," she said a second time. "Oh, Katie, I can't believe I . . . I don't remember . . ." The word disappeared into a sob.

"Don't cry," I muttered, my anger suddenly spent. "It's all right now. I opened the windows and cleared out the gas." Too exhausted and frustrated to comfort her, I turned away. "I'm going to go take a shower."

The smell was gone from the house when I returned, and by the time I'd showered and dressed, it was gone from me. I felt bad about being hard on Grandma, so I went looking for her to smooth things over.

I found her on the porch, rocking in the glider and drinking a cup of coffee. If she was upset with me, she didn't show it. She smiled as I came through the door. "I must say, I don't know when I remember such a stretch of mild weather in December." She paused to take a deep breath of the sun-warmed winter air, looking toward the driveway. "And where is Benjamin gone to this morning?" She didn't mention the propane incident, so I didn't either.

"He had to go out of town for a couple of days on a job. He flew out this morning."

"My, that boy is a hard worker."

"I guess he is," I muttered, but I failed to completely conceal my irritation that once again he was not at home when a crisis arose.

Grandma was acute about those things, and as usual, she honed in, looking for a worry to pounce upon. "Is something wrong?"

Shaking my head, I pretended to rub my eyes because they were tired. The truth was, I felt lonely and lost, and I wondered if I could survive two more weeks with Grandma. I had the overwhelming urge to run home to my house and my job, and forget all about smoke damage, coffee-stained floors, defective sewer pipes, and spewing propane. I wanted Grandma Rose to be completely sane again and the crisis to be over. "No. Everything's fine."

"I see," she said, and I was afraid that, as usual, she was seeing more about me than I wanted her to. Looking me in the eye, she took a deep breath, and for a moment, I thought she was going to offer some grandmotherly advice. Then the expression on her face went blank, and she patted the seat beside herself, saying, "Well, sit down for a while. This is just the kind of morning when the roses smell heavenly." She pointed to the trellis in the yard, but of course the vines were winter-bare. "I planted some Peace roses and some Mr. Lincolns at the cemetery last spring."

A quick stab of panic went through me at the mention of the cemetery, and I wondered if she was going to press me about visiting my mother's grave. She always went there on Sundays after church. I wasn't ready to go and didn't know when I would be. I hadn't gone there since we'd laid my mother in the ground.

I sat beside Grandma on the glider, and we rocked slowly back and forth in silence. Pulling my knees to my chest, I rested my chin on them and watched a cottontail hop lazily around the lawn, looking for something to eat.

After a moment, Grandma laughed under her breath and shook her head, watching the bunny.

I glanced sideways, wondering why she was laughing when only a moment before she had been stirring up turmoil.

"It's terrible to get old." She was smiling as she said it, though. "I was thinking I would roust old Trooper for not keeping the rabbits from the yard." Another chuckle burst from her lips, and she slapped her hand to her chest. "That dog's been dead for twenty years!"

Throwing her head back, she laughed until tears squeezed from her eyes. I couldn't help laughing with her, and we kept at it for a long time, rocking and laughing, then finally catching our breaths. Our noise frightened the cottontail from the yard, and we laughed harder, both thinking that now there was no need for the dog.

Grandma's face was red when she stopped, and tears had traced lines around her eyes. She wiped them with the handkerchief from her pocket, then fanned her cheeks. "Oh, I'll be a mess for church. People will think I've been drinking."

"That'll give them something to talk about," I teased, taking the handkerchief from her hand and helping her dab away the tearstains. I had a fleeting thought of how beautiful she must have been as a young woman and how much time had changed her. Her eyes were still the blue of a summer sky. "There, now no one will know your secret."

She smiled, and for just a moment we sat gazing into each other's eyes like lovers.

She turned away, looking suddenly somber. "Your grandfather had the most beautiful deep brown eyes. Just like yours." A long sigh, and then, "He always called me Rose."

I wasn't sure if she was talking to me or not, so I kept silent. Her tone was wistful, and she turned her face away so that I could not see her expression. I wondered if she had thought, just for an instant while we were looking into each other's eyes, that she was with him.

"It wasn't even my name," she went on. "One day after we married, he just started to call me Rose. He said he never liked Bernice for a name, and he thought I ought to be Rose. And that was that."

"I never knew," I said quietly. I'd always thought Rose was her middle name, and that was why we called her Grandma Rose.

"It was just a pet name, I guess." The words ended in a wistful exhaled breath. "I'd better get my things for church." Without looking at me, she stood up and shuffled toward the side door off the porch.

I watched her go. I didn't know what to say when she became melancholy and reminiscent. I was never sure whether she was talking to me or just remembering out loud, and whether she wanted me to answer. Maybe it was enough that I was there to listen. After so many years of being alone, perhaps she was glad someone would hear what she was saying.

I went inside as the neighbors pulled into the drive to take Grandma to church. In spite of my conviction that it was my prerogative not to go, I found myself embarrassed to be seen sitting on the porch sipping coffee in my old jeans on Sunday morning.

Joshua was cooing in his bed, so I got him up and fed him, then answered a phone call from Aunt Jeane. We talked about how Grandma was doing and how our visit was going. I told her about the vegetable salvage operation and the cottontail in the yard, and she laughed until she gasped for breath and sputtered like an old car. I didn't tell her about Grandma leaving the propane on. It seemed as if I would be betraying Grandma if I told—as if I would be putting her one step closer to the nursing home.

"I'm glad she's not driving you too crazy," she said with a note of sympathy. "So you and Ben are doing all right with her, then?"

I answered yes, because I knew that was what Aunt Jeane wanted to hear.

"Well, that's great." She sounded genuinely surprised. "I don't know what we'd do without you, Kate. I found a wonderful facility only a few miles from here called Oakhaven Village. It has lots of activities for those who are able, and indigent care if they need it as time goes on. I talked it over with your dad and he wants me to come get Grandma next weekend and bring her up now so you and Ben won't have to stay off work through Christmas."

A note of panic went though me. I was not sure why, because Aunt Jeane was offering to let me off the hook. "It's not a problem for us to stay," I said quickly, wondering why my father didn't want us anyplace where we might be forced to see one another. "Grandma is all excited about a family Christmas, and if you try to come get her now, you're going to have to drag her out of here kicking and screaming." I wondered if they had the power to do that. "Ben and I are fine here through the holiday. I don't go back to work until January sixth." I couldn't help adding, "Tell Dad to mind his own business unless he has a better idea."

"Now, Kate, don't get your feelings hurt." Aunt Jeane went into her usual peacemaking mode. "Your Dad just hated to see you two mess up your work schedules and you have to take extra leave to stay there."

"I'm sure he did."

"You know, in his mind there isn't much worse than having to spend three weeks on the farm. He's just trying to spare you and Ben some trouble."

"Um-hum. I guess I should go. Joshua's crying." Which wasn't true, but I didn't want to get into a conversation about Dad or Karen. Aunt Jeane had been trying to smooth us back together ever since Mom's death—ever since that awful night after the funeral when cruel things were said and my sister accused my father of being responsible for my mother's death.

Aunt Jeane was unwilling to quit on a sour note. "I can't wait to see that baby. Tell Grandma I'm still planning to come that week before Christmas. We have teacher in-service for one day after the kids get out, and then Robert and I will drive down. But if you have any problems or you need me before then, I'll take some time off and come. Let me know if you need me."

"We will." What I wanted to tell her was to get in the car and come *now*, but she'd ask what was the matter, and I wouldn't know what to tell her. *Nothing. Everything. Grandma almost blew us up this morning.* "We'll be fine," I said instead, then good-bye, and I hung up the phone. I knew if I said anything more, they'd only be more determined to haul Grandma off right away. If they were with her now, if they could see the look in her eye, they would know that the family coming home this

Christmas was important to her. She was building a chest of hopes for all of us, and I knew we were going to let her down. I didn't know how to stop it from happening.

The house seemed too quiet and too empty. I called the office and checked my voice mail to see if anyone had tried to call me, but there were no messages. Even that was a disappointment. In the past, there would never have been a day when no calls came in, when no one called with an idea of somewhere new to solicit donations, or an invitation to speak at a public event, or an invitation to some high-profile party where the foundation might find friends with deep pockets. Now it seemed as if all those contacts had simply melted away, as if everyone had forgotten me, and ten years of hard work had evaporated like smoke. It felt as if I had dropped off the edge of the known world.

Finally I gave up torturing myself and put Joshua in the belly sling to take him for a walk down the old river path. The trail looked as clear and well-traveled as it had when Karen and I were kids, which seemed strange since there was no one there to walk it anymore. I wondered if the children across the river on Mulberry Road used it. Grandma complained that they raided her blackberry patch regularly in the summer.

Skirting the overgrown blackberry patch, I stepped onto the path and started walking back in time. In my mind, I heard the laughter of little girls and the patter of hurried footsteps on the path. I heard my mother calling after us, telling us not to jump into the water until she got there.

The riverbank opened before me, and I saw my mother there, picking daisies from the grass at the edge of the rocky shore and weaving them into a chain. I saw myself running through the shallows, long dark hair streaming behind me, and Karen sitting in the ripples watching the water wash over her sun-browned legs. I saw my mother putting daisy chains around our necks and smiling, then just sitting on the bank and watching us with a wistful look in her eye. I wondered what she was thinking.

I remembered stopping my play and asking my mother about the glittering bits of sun on the water. I wanted to know where the sunlit patches came from and where they would go. Strange, now I couldn't remember her reply—just the question and the sensation of wondering. And the sense of confidence that she would have all the answers.

Standing at the edge of the water, I saw the vision fade—green leaves turn to dead branches, wildflowers to brown grass, summer to winter, a dream into reality.

I realized again how precious those times at the farm were, and how much I missed them when we went home to Boston, where I grew up. Boston was all about busy schedules and baby-sitters, and days when I came home upset about something at school and there was no one to tell. All I wanted on those days was for my mother to be there when the school bus dropped me off. But, of course, she wasn't. She was an M.D. when few women aspired to such a height, and that consumed her time like a ravenous dragon. There wasn't much left except the two weeks a year we went to the farm, and there she tried to make up for all the rest. Dad just brought his work with him and continued on with business as usual.

I wondered if they considered their lives successful. Certainly, we had all the trappings—expensive cars and homes, good schools, nice clothes. But is life a success when it doesn't include time for after-school talks, and curling up to read books on winter nights, and weaving daisy chains in the summer? Is it a success when you have all the big things but none of the small ones? Is it as it should be when everybody grows up and moves to opposite coasts and doesn't care if they ever see each other?

I thought of Grandma's story about the roses—something grand that seemed important at the time, when in reality all the important things were passing by unnoticed. I could hear the last words in my mind,

. . . the best times of my life, the times that passed by me the most quickly, were the times when the roses grew wild.

I didn't want my life to be like that. I didn't want Joshua's childhood to pass by while I was working sixty hours a week. I didn't want him to look at me one day and see a stranger, someone he only met two weeks a year on vacation. I wanted to give him a family that spent time together and really knew one another.

But I didn't know how to get from where we were to where I wanted to be. As things stood, I had to keep my job, but there were things we could give up—the vacations, the country-club golf membership, the boat, the house plans.

Maybe you should start wanting less. . . .

Maybe Grandma Rose was right.

Staring into the water, I thought about what our lives would be like if I changed to part-time work or didn't work at all. So many of the things we enjoyed and wanted would no longer be a possibility. Still, I knew the bigger house with the white-fenced yard could be postponed, but Joshua could not. He was only a baby for now. We would open our eyes one day and he would be gone, and we would be sitting alone in a house somewhere, missing him.

What would it matter then how big the house was?

Tiny fingers opened and closed against my chest, and I looked into Joshua's wide eyes, blue as the morning sky and filled with contentment. In that moment, it didn't matter where we were or what was around us. There was only he and I in the world, and I was filled with a devotion so consuming, its intensity was painful. Never had I felt that for another person—not for my parents, not even for Ben. Nothing in my former life had shown that within me I had such a deep and profound ability to love.

The clatter of a rock in the water shattered the moment, and I looked up to see the Jordan girl hopping from rock to rock across the shallows like a wood sprite. She stopped midstride when I looked at her, watching the way deer will just before they bolt for cover.

"Hello there," I said.

She didn't answer, but lowered her other foot to the rock on which she was perched. Peering at Joshua from beneath too-long bangs, she finally said, "I didn't know you have a baby. I heard him laughin'."

I pulled him out of the carrier and held him up so she could see. "This is Joshua." Holding his wrist, I waved his tiny hand at her. "Say hi, Josh."

A yellow blur darted from the bushes at the sound of my voice and splashed across the river, stationing itself between the girl and me. The dog didn't growl at me as it had the day before, but stood watching with the hair raised on its back. Fleetingly, I contemplated how I would defend myself and Joshua if it decided to attack. "He won't bite, will he?"

Jumping the rest of the way to the bank, she hollered, "Rowdy, go on," and kicked halfheartedly at the dog, who dodged the attack without taking offense. Flopping down on the bank, he went to work routing fleas, but kept watching me out of one eye.

The girl and I stood there for a minute like two shy toddlers, both just watching Joshua watch us.

"You stayin' up at the Vongortler house?" she asked finally, a hint of pretty dark eyes peeping suspiciously from beneath long raven lashes.

I sat on a boulder and propped Joshua in my lap. "Um-hum. We're here for a few weeks until Christmas."

"I heard she was sick with a stroke like my granny." Leaning down, she tickled Joshua's palm until his tiny hand closed around her sun-browned finger. Her lips held a solemn line, but there was a sparkle of delight in her eye as Josh gurgled and gave her a baby smile.

"Well, she had a stroke several months ago, but she's better now," I said, thinking about the little house on the other side of the river and what Grandma had said about the girl's grandmother. "Is your grandma sick?"

She stiffened noticeably, breaking the link between herself and Josh. "No, ma'am."

"It's Kate," I offered. "Kate Bowman." I could tell I was treading on fragile ice, so I didn't ask anything more about her situation at home. "What's your name?"

She seemed surprised by the question, and for the first time looked me straight in the eye. I was struck by what a pretty girl she was underneath all the tangled hair and dirt. She had a hint of a Native American look about her, with wide almond-shaped eyes and full copper lips, the lower one pursing out in a permanent pout.

"It's Dell," she told me with an air of importance. "Dell Jordan."

Smiling at her grown-up demeanor, I stuck out a hand for our formal introduction. "Very nice to meet you, Dell Jordan. I guess we're going to be neighbors for a few weeks."

She shook my hand in a hurry, then pulled back and wrapped her arms nervously around her stomach. "Yes, ma'am," she said, but she didn't seem very excited about the idea.

"You should come over some time and play with Joshua," I suggested, though I wasn't sure why I felt the need to get to know her better. She seemed to need a friend. Perhaps Josh and I seemed the same way to her.

The invitation made her uncomfortable, and she glanced over her shoulder toward home. "I gotta go."

Pushing off the rock, I stood up. "Me too." But I was wishing we could sit there a while longer—just a little while so I could win her trust. "Well, I guess we'll be seeing each other around. I'm sorry we almost ran you over on the road to town the other day. That's not a very safe road for bike riding, no shoulders and all those blind curves. If you need a ride to town while we're here, have your grandmother call me. I'd be happy to take you."

Her narrow-eyed look told me I was pushing too hard. "Granny wants me to ride my bike." She ended the conversation abruptly, turning and bounding across the rocks to the other bank. The dog hurried after her, sliding into her legs when she stopped suddenly and turned back to me. "I come here almost every day. Maybe I'll see ya'."

"O.K.," was all I had time to say before she grabbed a hanging tree root, climbed up the steep bank like Tarzan, and disappeared into the underbrush.

I stood there a while longer, enjoying the sound of the water and the tranquil quiet of the day. Finally, I left them behind and headed back to the house to see if Grandma was back.

As I walked, I started thinking again about the possibility of my working less. In my mind, I listed the things Ben and I could give up and how much each would cut our monthly expenses. I calculated whether I could work part-time and still be able to make the payments on Joshua's medical bills and other necessities. I thought about how I might tell my boss, and I imagined what he might say. He was not an easy man to get along with and not very family oriented, so I pictured him questioning my decision and asking how I was going to do my current job when I was only there part-time. Public relations and fund-raising for a major organization are all-consuming endeavors, not part-time occupations. The job required me to attend a lot of high-profile functions, public events, and political gatherings. There was no way I could work part-time and still maintain my position as head of public relations. I could give up the title and work behind the scenes, but that would be a hard pill to swallow. Being highly visible in an organization as well known as the Harrison Foundation had definite perks—lots of free invitations to events and free tickets from wealthy benefactors, lots of ego gratification, and the satisfaction of championing worthy environmental causes. The job was truly one of those once-in-a-lifetime opportunities, almost a calling for someone like me, with a college degree in environmental science and a love for the natural world. I hated to think about what might happen to my pet projects and ongoing research grants if I left the foundation.

I wondered if I could really give it all up. I wondered if we could really survive on less income or if I was just dreaming.

Joshua grabbed my shirt, then smiled as if to tell me that all things are possible. . . .

But as I sat in the kitchen after supper that evening, the bills and checkbook spread around me, the possibilities didn't look so good. The things we could give up didn't add up to enough savings, unless I went on the blind assumption that Ben's business was going to grow significantly in the near future. That was hard to say, since he was new at consulting and we had no idea what the future would bring.

Looking at the figures, I felt hopelessly trapped in my own life. But the more I thought about the reality of going back to my job full-time, the more I became determined to find another way, at least for a while. For the next year, there would still be questions about Joshua's heart, and I knew I couldn't pay someone to love him and watch over him the way I would. Deep in my mind, I feared that something would happen and I wouldn't be there.

Grandma saw the papers and calculator and was curious about what I was doing. Then she grew irritated with me for having everything spread out on the table, especially when it got in her way during supper. After we were finished, she informed me that her ankles told her a cold front was coming, and she was going to the little house to soak her feet and work on her article for the Monday printing of the local paper. No edition ever went to press without the Baptist Buzz by Bernice Vongortler.

I worked on the bills and the figures until my eyes started to cross and my brain hurt; then I stacked everything up and put it away, still wondering if I should talk to Ben about it. By the time I finally got in touch with him, it had all started to seem like a ridiculous fantasy. I chickened out and didn't say anything important. Nothing about Joshua and my job, nothing about Grandma leaving the propane on, nothing about Ben and me possibly selling the boat and giving up the plans for a bigger house. Mostly, I talked about nothing. Ben didn't even seem to notice. On the other end of the line, I could hear him muttering calculations and rustling papers, working as he pretended to listen to what I was saying. I knew there wasn't much point in talking. His mind was on the job and not on me.

The noise of a car backfiring on the farm highway caught my attention, and I listened as it passed by, the engine sputtering as if it wouldn't make it up the hill.

The sound tugged a memory from somewhere deep in my mind. "Ben, do you remember that old yellow car we had in college?" I wasn't sure why I asked the question. "What kind of car was that?"

"What, hon?" More papers rustling, then a momentary pause. "I didn't hear what you said. What about Grandma's car?"

"No. Not Grandma's car. I was talking about that old

yellow car we had in college. What kind of car was that?"

"The yellow one?" A note of curiosity entered his voice, and silence came from the other end of the line. For the first time, I felt as if he was really hearing me.

"Yes. The yellow one. A car just went by that sounded just like it. It made me think of the old yellow car."

Ben chuckled—a deep, warm sound that made me feel as if he were right beside me. "Wow. I haven't thought about that thing in years. It was a Firebird. Remember, James used to call it 'Big Bird'? "

"Well, James had a Beemer from his dad, so he could afford to make fun," I pointed out, remembering how Ben's friend had everything in college while Ben and I were practically destitute. Ben's parents didn't have any money to help him with college, and mine weren't inclined to pay for a degree in something as impractical as environmental science. They wanted me to attend medical school. Aside from that, they didn't want to pay any expenses for me while Ben and I were living together, so we just went our own way, worked part-time jobs, and scrounged the best we could. At the time, it seemed like a terrible struggle, having no money. Strange that now I was looking back on those years fondly.

Ben's laugh broke into my thoughts. "Yeah, but we had more fun in that old yellow car than James did in his slick Beemer. That car had personality."

"Is that what you call it when you can see the road passing through the holes in the floorboard?"

We laughed together and both ended in a wistful sigh. Ben chuckled again. "Remember on our honeymoon when Big Bird broke down at the Canadian border and we pitched our tent in the park there by the road?" Another wistful exhaled breath. "That was one great night."

I scoffed, shaking my head. "Ben, what are you talking about—great? We woke up in the morning smack in the middle of a Harley biker rally. Big guys in black leather and tattoos everywhere. We were scared to death."

"Yeah, but before the bikers showed up, that was *some* night."

I remembered, and blushed red from head to toe. "O.K. You're right. It was."

"Um-hum." A low, passionate sound. "Besides, the bikers weren't so bad. They fixed Big Bird for us."

"Oh, you're right. I forgot about that!" I laughed, the scene coming back with comical clarity—two petrified college kids standing on the side of the highway while a half-dozen leather-clad Samaritans debated what was wrong with Big Bird. In the end, they sent us on our way with a greasy handshake and a slightly used Harley bandanna holding together the battery cables.

"That really was a great trip," Ben said wistfully. "We should do that again someday."

"We should," I agreed. "Without the bikers." But I knew we never would. We wouldn't find the time, and we wouldn't find the money, and it just wouldn't end up happening. Still, it felt so good to talk about it, to laugh and remember. I wanted to keep him on the phone all night, as I had that first year after college, when he had started traveling with his job, and he would call and we would talk and talk and talk.

"We could plan . . ." Ben paused, and I heard noises in the background, then someone talking. When he came back on the line, his voice was different. "Kate, James is here to look over some things. I've got to go."

"All right," I said.

We said good-bye and the moment was over. After I hung up the phone, I went to bed, thinking about Ben and me in the old yellow car, driving the highway to Canada without a care in the world.

I fell asleep to the sound of the old family clock ticking on the mantel in the living room. Grandma must have sneaked around and wound it again. Now it would chime all night, every hour and half hour, echoing through the house. But the ticking faded, and I drifted into someplace dark and quiet, peaceful . . .

"Katie . . . Katie . . ." The sound of a voice floated through the dark stillness in my mind. "Katie . . . Wake up!"

My body lurched to consciousness, and I struggled to sit up, blinking into the darkness as my heart pounded like a hammer in my throat.

Dazed, I looked at Ben's side of the bed and remembered he was gone. I glanced at the clock. Twelve-forty. I must have dreamed that someone was calling me.

"Katie, wake up." The call came again from the hallway, demanding and urgent.

"Grandma?" I jumped up and rushed across the room, my mind spinning a web of terrifying reasons why she might be knocking at my bedroom door in the middle of the night. Throwing open the door, I stood blinking, blinded by the hallway lights. "Grandma, what's wrong?"

She motioned nervously across the hall to the open bathroom door. "There were three rolls of toilet paper under the sink last week. Have you moved them? I have looked and looked, but they are nowhere to be found."

"Toilet paper?" I stammered, my vision clearing so that I could see the nervous twitch of her lips as she waited for my answer. "I don't know. I guess we used it up."

"That couldn't be," she insisted, looking desperate. "We could not possibly have used so much in a few days."

Rubbing my forehead, I tried to comprehend the conversation and why we were having it in the hallway at midnight. "I'm sure we did. We can buy some more toilet paper tomorrow."

"Almost a whole package in less than one week," she stammered, looking horrified. "It's too much down the septic. That pipe will back up in the basement."

Taking a deep breath, I fought to control my overtired temper. "Grandma, please," I pleaded. "Just go back to bed. The plumbing is fine. Do you know what time it is? It's *after midnight.*"

"Benjamin should go down and check the pipes. We'll have to call a plumber before the basement floods."

"The basement is fine. I was down there this afternoon getting potatoes, remember? It's fine. Go to bed."

"But Benjamin could . . ."

"He isn't here!" I snapped, hitting the end of my rope with a twang. "He's out of town."

Grandma backed up a step, then stood looking around my shoulder at the empty bed. "Oh," she muttered. "Oh . . . I . . . I must have forgotten. Well, perhaps I should leave him a note to check the pipe when he gets back."

"All right," I sighed, having no idea what good leaving a note would do when Ben wasn't coming home for a few days. "Do you need me to help you get back to the little house?"

Shaking her head, she shuffled toward the kitchen. "No. I'll be fine. I don't want to keep you from your rest. I'm going to go soak my feet. My ankles are stiff. Must be a cold front . . ."

Growling in my throat, I closed the door and went back to bed, staying awake just long enough to hear the porch door slam.

Chapter 6

GRANDMA'S ankles were correct in their prediction. The weather turned cold the day after Ben left. Three days later, it was still rainy and unpleasant outside, and Grandma and I were starting to get cabin fever. I was actually glad when she volunteered us to help set up the inter-church Christmas village in Town Square Park. The Senior Baptist Ladies were in high spirits, because for the first time in several years they had been awarded responsibility for decorating the Santa House—the crème de la crème of the Christmas Village display. Plans included a dozen freshly cut Christmas trees, decoration of the gazebo, and the election of Mrs. Santa Claus.

When we arrived at the church on the crisp December afternoon, the ladies were already sorting through boxes of supplies and discussing decorating ideas. They paused for a moment to pass Josh around, and then three of them hustled him off to the nursery, ignoring my protests that I could carry him in the belly sling while I worked. Grandma patted my shoulder and told me not to worry, that the ladies had been taking care of babies longer than I had been alive. Still, I felt a little strange with Josh gone.

Surveying the room, I noticed with some relief that I

was not the only under-sixty person who had been drafted into temporary membership in the Senior Ladies. There were a couple of women around my age, a few younger than I, two teenage boys, and one captive husband, who was doing all the heavy lifting. Everyone seemed excited and cheerful, even the husband, who was being henpecked nearly to death by his wife, his mother, and his mother-in-law.

When the Senior Ladies started singing Christmas carols together, I knew without a doubt that Christmas fever had come to Hindsville. By the time we began setting up Christmas trees in the square, Grandma was afflicted with it and was angling to play Mrs. Santa Claus in the pageant.

"But I wouldn't want anyone to think Oliver Mason and I are a couple. You know they have chosen that old coot as Santa Claus?" she was saying. "People could get the wrong idea."

I hid behind a Douglas fir, trying not to giggle. This was, after all, the serious matter of Grandma's reputation. "I'm sure they won't. But if you're worried about it, don't play Mrs. Santa Claus."

Wringing her hands, she let out a long, soulful sigh. "Oh, but I wouldn't want the *children* to be disappointed." As if no one else in town could possibly play Mrs. Claus.

"That's something to think about." I bit my lip to keep from laughing and pretended to be busy fluffing out the tree. "I guess you'll just have to do it."

Raising her chin steadfastly, she gave one swift nod. "I suppose I shall."

And so she left me there and wandered off to begin campaigning in earnest. I continued working on the Santa House with Wanda Cox, a sixtyish neighbor of Grandma's who was tall and slender and wore a beauty-shop hairdo that reminded me of the 1960s. With us were her daughter, Sandy, who was the fourth-grade teacher in town, and three other elderly ladies whom I didn't know. With all of us working, the task went quickly, which was good, because evening was coming and it was getting cold. To keep warm, we talked as we worked, about kids mostly, because that was the one thing we all had in common.

"I worried about everything when Bailey was born, but with Justin, I just let things go. It's a lot more fun," Sandy was saying. She was pretty, a few years younger than I, with short blond hair, and a friendly personality that made you feel like you'd known her forever. I figured that made her good at teaching.

One of the ladies hanging garlands laughed. "It's easier with the second one, isn't it? By the time you've had four, you're satisfied just to keep them all fed, diapered, and bathed. Mine were eighteen months to twenty-two months apart. It seemed like I never would get through washing diapers. Every day, another load of diapers. We had that old wringer washer, and I'd stand there and churn that thing, and churn that thing, then wring the diapers, and hang the diapers, and in the meanwhile, the children would be tearing up the house, or running in the mud hole, and here I'd go again."

Wanda giggled along with her. "My mother used to put the babies in those long dresses, and when she had work to do in the kitchen, she'd pick up the table leg and set it down on the end of the baby's dress. That way she'd know right where we were. Of course, she married at seventeen and had seven, so she had to do something."

"Seven," I breathed. "Wow." I was thinking of how I felt half out of my mind raising one, and was trying to picture how it would be to have seven, still be in your twenties, and be living in the dark ages before wrinkle-free clothes and disposable diapers. It made my life seem like cheesecake.

The conversation went on like that for quite some time. We covered cooking, husbands, childbirth, weddings, college coursework then and now, and a touch of politics. And all the while we covered the Santa House with garlands and lights. With so many hands, it hardly seemed like work. Everyone was laughing and talking, discussing, humming Christmas songs. In spite of the cold turning fingers and toes numb, it was the best day I could remember.

We ate a potluck supper in the fellowship hall of the church, which had once been the chapel. Built of native brownstone with ancient stained-glass windows in hand-hewn frames, old candelabra chandeliers, and beaded board paneling, it was a perfect setting for a Christmas dinner. Townspeople added to our number, and the supper soon looked like a major happening in Hindsville.

It was a picture-postcard event—long tables decorated with red tablecloths and garlands, and filled with food in dishes of a hundred different shapes and colors. The room was alive with a wonderful sense of community, people laughing and talking, discussing the events in one another's daily lives. I was struck by how well they knew each other and how fortunate they were to have that sense of belonging. Watching the old people pass Josh around, I wished Ben were there to share the evening. He would have enjoyed the food and the conversation, and he definitely would have enjoyed watching Grandma campaign for the position of Mrs. Santa Claus.

She was working the room like a professional, shaking hands, kissing babies, calling in favors, even doing a little blackmail. She hardly paused long enough to eat supper. She finished up the evening by sitting with old Oliver, so everyone could see how they looked together. Watching the two of them made me laugh.

Oliver looked like a smitten fifteen-year-old boy, and
Grandma looked as if she were trying to swallow a dose
of castor oil. When he laid a hand on her arm, she gave
him a look that could have fried an egg. He didn't seem
to care. He just smiled and chewed on the end of his
unlit cigar.

By the time the evening was over, Grandma had the
election in the bag. No one was surprised when she won
the position of Mrs. Santa Claus by an overwhelming
margin. Grandma pretended to be honored and aston-
ished, and laying her hand on her chest in a gesture of
false humility, she walked forward to accept her costume. Then she promptly sat beside me, leaving old
Oliver to fall asleep in the corner.

Grandma spread the Mrs. Claus costume on the table
and began to discuss how embellishments could be
made. When we got home later that evening, she started
her work.

Over the next two days, I received sewing lessons and
was endlessly tortured over the appearance of the costume, and whether Grandma should sit next to Oliver in
the Santa House or on a chair beside it so she could
hand out candy canes, or perhaps old-fashioned pep-
permint sticks would be better, and perhaps the line of
children should file by her before they went in to see
Santa Claus, because . . .

Meanwhile, I was growing more immune to
Grandma's rambling and complaining speeches. Even
though Ben's three-day trip turned into a week plus
three days, the time seemed to pass quickly. He was due
home the day after the pageant, with a nice paycheck—
enough to catch up on most of the bills, at least for another month. I still hadn't talked to him about my
occasional fantasies of a life change, but the desire for
something different in our lives was becoming real in
my mind.

The day of the Christmas pageant dawned sunny and pleasant for December. Grandma fretted over last-minute preparations all day, until finally it was time to get ready for the pageant. I dressed Joshua in a red snowsuit, took pictures of him in the arms of the most perfect ever Mrs. Santa Claus, and away we went. We arrived at the secret Santa rendezvous location behind the post office with no time to spare, and Grandma was hoisted onto the firetruck by three volunteer firemen. She rode next to Santa Claus and even managed to hold hands with the old coot. Oliver's red cheeks were a perfect addition to his costume, and there was no rouge involved.

At the Santa House, Grandma sat outside the door, handing candy canes to hopeful kids and admonishing them to be good. I recognized Dell Jordan in the line and was relieved when Grandma didn't refuse her a candy cane, mention anything about welfare, or tell her that her Christmas wishes probably wouldn't be fulfilled. She didn't treat the girl with any special kindness, but she wasn't cruel either, which I knew from experience she could be. Apparently, the Christmas spirit had improved her disposition.

When the Santa line was finished and the trees were lit, everyone stood around the gazebo enjoying the lights and trays of cookies and gallons of hot spiced apple cider provided by groups of church ladies. Grandma sat near the gazebo with Joshua in her lap, amid a crowd of admirers, and I sat on a bench near the edge of the park with Sandy and her husband, Troy. Their daughter, Bailey, was playing on the ground in front of us, so bulky in her snowsuit that she could barely walk. We were laughing and talking about kids and whatnot.

"Now, our little one is a rascal." Sandy giggled. "Bailey was so sweet and so easy, but this new one is a whole

other thing. We left him home with his gramp tonight."
She glanced over her shoulder at a group of boys who
were sitting on the sidewalk behind us with their plates.
"Y'all quit throwing your food," Sandy admonished
them. "If you don't want it, put it in the trash."

The rowdy crew quieted and hunched over their
plates, giggling and talking in whispers.

Sandy rolled her eyes and shook her head. "Boys! I
deal with that sort of thing all day long in fourth grade."

I glanced up just in time to see Dell Jordan walk by
looking at the Christmas trees, her dark eyes alive with
wonder, reflecting the twinkling lights. She dropped her
gaze to the boys on the sidewalk and started to walk
away.

"Smelly Delly," one of them chanted, pitching a half-
eaten cookie in her direction. The rest of them joined in
instantly. "Smelly Delly, Smelly Delly, Smelly Delly,
Smelly Delly . . ."

Sandy glanced at Dell as she hurried away; then she
shook a stern finger at the boys. "Y'all leave Dell alone.
That's mean."

Mean? I thought. Mean? It went beyond mean. It was
unspeakably cruel. Setting my plate aside, I stood up,
but Dell was already gone, rushing behind the gazebo
like a deer bolting into the woods. I turned on the boys,
suddenly angry. "You boys should be ashamed of yourselves. She didn't do anything to you."

The oldest one, who was probably about Dell's age,
rolled his eyes as if I were stupid. "Well, she does smell.
It ain't a lie. She's got gross old clothes."

I wanted to wring his neck in spite of his age. "She's
just a little girl." Then I realized who I was talking to,
and I sat down again. Dell was just a little girl, and they
were little boys, and children could be cruel.

Sandy's husband turned around and addressed the
boys. "You boys throw your plates in the trash and go

play. And don't say those things again or I'll tell your mamas." They sluggishly obeyed, and when they were gone, he said, "Some of these kids around here just have so much more than others."

"I guess so." I nodded as if I understood, but I didn't. I'd lived in upper-middle-class suburbs all my life. A house and two cars for everyone. Two parents usually. Games and toys, nice yards, and nice clothes for school. Poverty and ignorance were characters we saw on TV, or sometimes passed on the highway while traveling to some vacation hideaway. They were not our neighbors. They did not have faces with soft brown eyes and down-turned mouths that never smiled. . . .

Troy stood suddenly. The abruptness of his movement broke my train of thought. Looking up, I saw Grandma coming our way, her face stern, her pale blue eyes flashing with anger, her Mrs. Santa hat gone, and her wig askew. Shuffling across the grass in a hurry, she had two boys by the shirt collars. Two other boys followed meekly in her wake. She parked the boys on the sidewalk behind us, her hands retaining a shuddering grip on their collars, as if she intended to hang them right there.

"At the very least, you boys should clean up the food you have wasted." Her voice was loud and authoritative, her face dangerously red. She glared at the youngsters, who, in turn, stared at their shoes. "And when you are in church tomorrow, ask the Lord to show you a better way to act. There are some children who do not have enough to eat, and you are throwing good food into the street." She pitched the two of them forward with impressive strength, then grabbed the other two and forcibly added them to the pile. The four landed in a sprawl in the dry grass beside the curb.

Troy and Sandy stared at her, openmouthed.

"Grandma!" I exclaimed, looking around to see if anyone was watching. I could just imagine what the boys' parents would think if they saw her pitching their children into the dirt.

She blinked at me, seeming surprised by the sound of my voice, then teetered backward unsteadily. Troy rushed to her side, grabbing her upper arms to steady her. With short, careful steps, he helped her to the bench.

"Sit down, Mrs. Vongortler," he soothed, his face lined with concern. "It's all right."

"It isn't," she insisted, but the red had drained from her face, and the fervor faded from her voice. "Those boys should be ashamed and so should their parents." Tears welled up in her eyes, and she blinked as they spilled onto her cheeks. The gnarled line of her mouth quivered with withheld emotion.

My heart dropped into my stomach, and I sat beside her, feeling completely helpless.

Sandy leaned close and whispered in my ear, "Do you want me to go get Dr. Schmidt?"

I shook my head, not knowing what to say. I had no idea if her behavior was typical or not. I only knew I'd never seen anything like it in the past. My helplessness reminded me of how ill prepared I was to be her care-taker.

"Grandma." I leaned close, feeling better when she looked at me with tearful recognition. "Are you all right? Do you need Dr. Schmidt?"

"No." Her voice was small, as if it were coming from somewhere far away.

"Do you want me to take you home?"

"No."

"Would you like cider or some water?"

"Cider." She wiped her eyes and ran her hands self-consciously over her wig, straightening it, then looking up to see if anyone else had noticed us. "I would like to sit with the others before they wonder about me."

"All right." I helped her up and dabbed the moisture from her cheeks with a napkin, relieved to see her acting like herself again. I was also relieved that no one else had noticed the incident. Grandma looked embarrassed enough with just the three of us watching. I was embarrassed for her and wished Sandy and Troy weren't there. I could tell they were wondering, just as I was, what had set Grandma off and why she'd taken the boys in hand. I wondered if she was angry over what they'd done to Dell Jordan, or because they'd wasted the food. Probably the food. She'd already made her feelings about the little Jordan girl quite clear.

As we joined the others for the last of the evening's Christmas carols, I looked around for Dell, but she was nowhere to be found. I wanted to make sure she was all right and to let her know the boys had been reprimanded, but she was gone, so I tried to put it out of my mind. Grandma's outburst kept replaying in my thoughts. I couldn't even begin to guess at her motives. I never would have imagined she was capable of manhandling someone else's children.

The truth was, we really didn't know each other at all.

By the time we headed home, Grandma seemed to be in high spirits again. She had apparently forgotten all about the incident with the boys and was now focused on preparations for our family Christmas, which was, for me, about as unpleasant a subject as the awful event in the park.

"We should hurry home," she said. "We have so many things to do before Christmas. Now, I don't want one of those store-bought trees this year. We'll go on Christmas Eve and cut a cedar from the north field, and . . ."

The rest of the way home, she talked about the family coming for Christmas, and who would stay in what room, what sheets and quilts we would use, how we would fit everyone at the table, and where she had

stored the Christmas decorations in case I wanted to
pull them out when we got home.

Guilt rushed over me, making me unable to discuss
the plans with her. Christmas was only a week away, and
I had not called my father to ask when he would arrive,
or if he was coming at all. It was childish of me, I knew,
but I was waiting for him to call me. Fortunately, Aunt
Jeane was making arrangements with Karen and her
husband, so that was out of my hands. As far as I knew,
they were to arrive on December 23rd and leave four
days later. It would be the longest visit to Hindsville of
Karen's adult life, and I wondered what sort of emotional blackmail Aunt Jeane had used to convince her to
come. Aunt Jeane wouldn't say.

I wondered if Karen was as nervous about the visit as
I was. I supposed not. Karen was always confident of
her position, seldom rattled by anything.

I called my father that night after Grandma had gone
to the little house and Joshua was put to bed. In my
mind, I rehearsed what I would say if he answered.
Hello, I'd say matter-of-factly. I'd make some inquiry
about his health or his work. Tell him how much it mattered to Grandma that he come for Christmas. Make
sure he knew it didn't really matter to *me.*

Of course, the truth was that it did matter. I thought
about Joshua, and the fact that he was nearly four
months old and no one in my family, except Grandma,
had even seen him.

I was relieved when Dad's answering machine
picked up. I quickly left a message. "Hello, it's Kate.
Grandma has been wondering when you're coming for
Christmas. She says she hasn't seen you since she was
in the hospital in June. She's really looking forward to
this Christmas. Please let us know as soon as you can."
I hung up the phone hurriedly, afraid he would answer.
Then I sat at the kitchen table, catching my breath,

feeling as if I had been running from something in a nightmare.

The sound of the television in the living room caught my attention, and I walked through the dogtrot, wondering if Grandma had decided to come back into the house. I hoped she hadn't heard me on the phone. I didn't want her to know I was having to beg my father to come.

When I entered the living room, it was empty. Shaking my head, I turned off the TV and stood looking around the room for a minute, having the irrational feeling that there were ghosts in the house. The mantel clock chimed, and I jumped, surprised by the noise.

I thought I hid the winding key where Grandma wouldn't find it. . . .

Something white caught my eye near the clock, something fluttering just slightly in the draft from the register. Grandma's book. Glancing around the room again, I walked to the mantel and picked it up, looking at the words in the dim light from the floor lamp. The story about the roses was gone, replaced by something new.

Fragile Things, the story was titled. In the back of my mind, I thought of Joshua.

I remember a time when I was too young to know the worry of money or work. I knew only the little things in the world around me—the grasshoppers and the flowers, the sound of dragonflies, the silk of milkweed pods, the taste of honeysuckle. I knew nothing of larger things.

I was too young to understand the need that forced us to load the old box wagon with all that we owned— mother's quilts and linens and dishes, the birchwood cradle she used to rock my baby brother, the blue-rimmed china that came from the old country with my grandmother, the mantel clock that had been handed

down to my father. We were like that clock, proud and
solid—something that shouldn't have been moved, but
was. My soul was like the china, fragile and white.

I touched the china with reverence as we folded it
among old linens in the trunk. Mother stood above me,
her hands poised in the air as I touched the fine golden
flowers painted like windsong along the blue edge. She
hovered there silently, nervously, watching me, warning
me, waiting to catch the fragile things should they fall.

When the wagon was packed, I sat near the china
trunk, my legs swinging off the rough tailgate, bare and
brown, no stockings or shoes. I did not watch our small
farmhouse disappear behind us. Instead, I watched my
shadow slide over the ground with the silence of a ser-
pent, the grace of velvet. I did not wonder where we
were going or why. I knew our journey would end
someplace wonderful.

I saw it ahead later in the day—a settlement of fine
whitewashed buildings and a tall stone church with
beautiful colored glass windows. I imagined it a castle
as we stopped in front, and I imagined myself a princess
in the tower. From the churchyard, I heard the shouts
and laughter of children, and I watched them with interest as they played. Never had I seen so many young
people, and I wanted to jump from the wagon and run
to join in their games.

I was angry when my mother kept me beside her in
the wagon as father climbed down. I watched him stop
for a moment before he went forward to the men gathered nearby. I saw his hat clenched tightly in his hands,
his strong shoulders rounded like an ox yoke, his dark
head bowed as if in prayer. I saw my mother hold her
hands just an inch above her lap, as if she were waiting.
I did not know why these things made me feel heavy
and small. My mind had no words to frame it.

I turned, instead, to watch the children play with tiny
arks and carved animals, miniature people and dolls. I

imagined myself among them in a starched print dress, blue like our china, with tiny golden flowers. I thought of the fun we would soon have together, and I knew our journey had, indeed, ended someplace wonderful.

The wagon swayed suddenly, and I heard my father clamber to his seat. Shouts and laughter followed him into the street. I started to laugh also, but the voices made me silent.

"We don't want beggars here!" they called. "Move on, white trash, no charity here!"

A rock flew close to me and struck the wagon like brimstone. My mother cried out, clutching me and the baby as stones drove the mule to bolt. I huddled there, my heart fluttering like a tiny bird as the wagon bounced and swayed. Behind me, I saw the china trunk slide to the back of the wagon, then slowly topple over the edge. I cried out as it fell to the street, splintering against the ground and spewing bits of china like water drops. My father did not draw up the mule, but instead allowed him to run until the town was far behind us.

Burying my face against my mother's breast, I cried in anger and fear and sadness. She wrapped me in her arms and promised that things would be all right. But I knew things would be different. I knew I would be different. I understood the truth that had hidden beyond the smallness of my world—that I was not good and perfect, that others would live in wonderful places while I would not, that others were greater and I was less.

I knew my father was right in not going back for the china. It was no longer perfect, no longer whole. It was now fragmented and sharp and, as with all things fragile, could not be made whole again.

In that moment, I understood so much about Grandma Rose that I had not before. I understood why she was so worried about someone spoiling the things that belonged to her, why she obsessed so over her house and her savings. I understood why she couldn't stand the sight of Dell Jordan. Dell reminded her of a past she was trying to forget, a girl she used to be. The incident with the boys in town had brought it all back to her, and she lashed out at the people who had long ago broken her own spirit.

After reading her words, I understood how much the safety of that big white house and the security of her land and her belongings meant, and how deeply she feared losing them. I understood why she had never been willing to let even a piece of it go.

Somewhere inside, she was the little girl in the back of a wagon, trying to hold on to something that was heavy, and fragile, and slipping away.

Chapter 7

THAT night I dreamed of flying. In my dream, I leapt from the bluffs above the river and soared high over the farm. Below, the maple trees were bright with fresh spring leaves, and the fields were filled with yellow bonnet flowers. Dell Jordan was running through them, her feet bare, a long yellow dress flowing around her like sunshine. Two brown-haired girls ran with her, their hands clasped together. Laughing, they fell onto the carpet of yellow bonnets and lay gazing skyward with long dark hair tangled in the grass. The smiles were mine and my sister's, our faces young and bright with innocence.

A child appeared from the flowers, her hair in tawny curls, her feet and legs bare and brown. Her eyes were blue like the summer sky, my grandmother's eyes. Smiling silently, she coaxed us to our feet, and we joined hands, darting through the flowers like untamed horses. Then we ran to the bluffs above the river and disappeared into the sky.

My limbs were leaden as I drifted between sleep and consciousness, as if my spirit had been away and had suddenly come back to the shell of my body. I lay listening for the sounds of summer outside, thinking about waking my sister and going out to play in the fields. The rattle of dishes clinking in the kitchen brought to my mind an image of Mom and Grandma cooking breakfast for all of us. For just an instant I hung suspended in the mists of my dream, forgetting who and what I was.

A baby's cry came from somewhere far away, and the dream rushed away like a genie disappearing into a bottle. Reality struck me with a suddenness that stole my breath, and I sat up, realizing Joshua was crying.

I walked upstairs, feeling like an impostor in my own body.

Joshua was wiggling in his bed with his eyes still closed, so I slipped the pacifier into his mouth, watched him settle into sleep again, and tiptoed to the window. Outside, the first long rays of a winter dawn rose into the sky like outstretched fingers. The hillsides and farmyard remained shrouded in dusky gray, and a pair of deer had come to graze just outside the yard fence. They started suddenly, raising their heads and flicking their tails, then darting into the murky darkness beyond the glow of the yard light.

Grandma appeared in front of the little house and walked slowly along the path toward the main house, her gray wool coat wrapped over her pajamas. Leaving the window, I went downstairs and found her in the kitchen.

"Katie!" She jumped and slapped a hand over her heart when she saw me. "What are you doing up?"

"Josh was crying," I whispered, as if there were someone else in the house to hear. "Are you O.K.?"

She smiled, starting to fix the coffee. "Oh, yes. Fine. I just couldn't get back to sleep. Don't let me keep you up. You go back to bed."

"All right," I said, turning to leave.

"I had the most wonderful dream." Her voice was almost a whisper, her face turned away. I wasn't sure if she was talking to me or not, but I stopped to listen. "It was all about spring and yellow bonnet flowers. I was young again." The last words faded into a sigh, and she stood looking out the window. Silent.

Watching her, I thought of the tawny-haired girl in my dream—the girl who had my grandmother's summer-sky eyes. I wanted to ask if her dream had been like mine—if our souls had truly become young again and galloped together through the fields of yellow bonnets. Words came to my mind, but not to my lips, and finally I turned away and left her there staring out the window.

Still thinking about her, I slipped into bed and fell into a dreamless sleep. When I woke, the sun was bright and the morning mist had already evaporated from the bedroom windows, telling me I had slept late. I lay trying to decide if I had been awake at dawn and seen Grandma, or if it was merely part of my dream. I wondered if she would remember and could tell me.

I didn't hear anyone in the house, so I dressed, then headed for the coffeepot. No one was in the kitchen.

The phone rang just as I was finishing breakfast. It was a woman from the insurance company calling to tell me they were refusing another claim, but if I wanted to, I could certainly send it in for re-review. But this item was definitely in excess of coverage limits.

"This charge was preapproved," I protested, thinking of all the years Ben and I had paid for insurance and never used it. Now that we needed it, it wasn't paying. "I already talked to Cynthia Bell about this last week. She assured me this would go through."

"Ma'am, I don't have authorization to . . ." And so we went through the usual drill. I knew it so well that I didn't even have to listen anymore. When it was over, I hung up the phone with a slam, feeling as if I wanted to rip it out of the wall.

It rang again, just as I turned to walk away. I hovered

for a minute, considered not answering it, then finally picked it up.

Ben was on the other end, and I was so glad to hear his voice, I instantly felt better. Then I realized that, if he was calling, he wasn't coming home that afternoon.

He made small talk for a minute, then got around to the point. "So, I thought I'd stay an extra day here. Bill and Carl are in town, and James has tickets to the Knicks game tonight. I can get a flight home tomorrow."

I rubbed the bridge of my nose, trying to smooth away the rising screams of protest in my head, but they came out anyway. "Well, you know what, Ben? This is the third time you've called to tell me you weren't coming home yet. Frankly, I'm a little sick of it."

"Come on, Kate, it's just one more day." He sounded self-righteous and offended. "What's wrong with you?"

A list ran though my mind, but I simplified it down to, "I could just use a little help here. In case you've forgotten, Aunt Jeane is coming day after tomorrow. The house isn't clean, there's grocery shopping to do, and I still have files I need to go through for work. They called me again today needing those grant applications. The insurance company called with another rejected claim that I'll have to protest. That means more paperwork. We have no Christmas shopping done, and there's a four-month-old baby upstairs who has to be fed, burped, diapered, fed, burped, diapered, unless he's sleeping, and then there're laundry, dishes, dirty bottles to wash, and food to fix. Josh could use a little more attention, and every time I turn around, you're either gone or you have your face in a computer." The truth, too long bottled up, spewed forth like venom.

"What, so now I'm a bad father?" His voice was angry and indignant. "You know, someone has to make a living here. I can't do that if I'm sitting home baby-sitting.

I thought we both agreed the most important thing right now is get the stupid hospital bills paid off."

Tears crowded into my eyes. It seemed as if we were thinking in two different universes. "No, the most important thing right now is our son. It seems as if you should want to see him more than you want to go to a Knicks game with your friends."

Ben scoffed as if I were being idiotic. "Let's not make a federal case out of this. It's just one day. I've already changed my flight and I'll be back in town tomorrow around noon. I've got to go by the office at the church for a while. Then I'll be home."

"Before midnight, I hope," I said, wondering how we were ever going to see eye to eye on raising our son. To me it was everything; to him it ranked behind a Knicks game and stopping at the office.

Josh was growing up without Ben even seeing it. I wondered if it seemed wrong to Ben that he didn't know how to quiet Josh when he cried or what to feed him when he was hungry. Ben's own father had always been away from home struggling to build a business, and I wanted more than that for Joshua. I thought Ben did too. He had been every bit the proud, expectant father before Josh was born. But when Josh finally came home from the hospital, tiny and frail, needing special monitoring and extra medical care, Ben backed away, and I let him. I was afraid to let anyone help with Josh's care, even Ben. Now I was wondering if things were ever going to change.

Ben finally broke the silence on the line. "I don't know what you're on my case about. The check from this job is going to make the payments for this month. We needed the money."

"I know that," I said quietly, trying to keep the tremor from my voice. I didn't want him to tell me I was getting overly emotional. My frustration with the

realities of our life came spilling out. "I've been thinking maybe we should cut down our expenses. Get rid of
some"—*boats, memberships, house plans, car
payments*—"things. I was thinking of only going back to
work part-time. I could probably stay with the foundation part-time and still keep my insurance. I could do a
lot of work from home—set up an office in the den,
maybe."

Silence again, and then, "I don't see how that's possible financially." Another pause, during which he covered up the phone receiver and talked to someone else.
When he finally came back, I could tell he was ready to
end the conversation. "Everybody's waiting for me in
the lobby. I need to go. Stop letting Grandma get you all
emotional, all right?"

I exhaled my disappointment and said good-bye because I could tell there was no reason to keep talking.
He was probably right, and besides, I should have
waited until he was home to bring it up. But time was
running out. In a couple of weeks, I was supposed to be
back at work.

The screen door slammed outside, and I dried my
eyes, then sat at the table with my cup of coffee.

Grandma gave me a suspicious look as she came in
the door, nose tipped upward as if she had scented trouble. She looked pale and chilled, and there was dirt on
her hands.

"Grandma, you shouldn't be working in the yard
today," I said as she washed her hands at the sink. "It's
too cold, and you know Dr. Schmidt said light exercise
only. Your blood pressure is still too high."

She batted a hand behind her back, shooing me away
like a nagging insect. "Yes, yes. I was only cleaning the
leaves out of the flower bed."

"And you shouldn't be doing that," I insisted. She'd
been sneaking into the yard for days and doing things

she wasn't supposed to. She was determined that every-thing would be perfect for the family's arrival. "Leave it for Ben and me to do."

Pouring a cup of coffee, she tipped her chin up stub-bornly and walked to the table to sit down. We sat silent for a while, and then she asked, "Was that Ben on the phone?"

I glanced up from my coffee cup, wondering how she could have heard the phone ringing from outside. "Yes."

She nodded thoughtfully. "Did you have a tiff? I heard yelling."

I stared at the swirling liquid in my coffee cup, getting the mortifying image of her listening at the door while Ben and I argued over life's realities. "No."

Grandma made a tsk-tsk sound, and from the corner of my eye I saw her shaking her head as if she knew better.

I put the best light on it I could. "It was nothing major. He wanted to stay another day and go to a Knicks game with his friends and I wanted him to come home." Then the truth spilled out. "I just get aggravated because he doesn't make any effort to help with Josh. Everything else is more important."

Grandma made the tsk-tsk sound again, shaking her head at me. "Give him some time. Men are selfish crea-tures. Sometimes it takes a little while for them to adjust to the demands of fatherhood."

A dozen snide replies ran through my mind. I didn't like her making excuses for him. I had to adjust to the demands of motherhood the moment Joshua was born. Why should Ben be allowed six months to step up to the plate?

"I just don't feel like talking about this," I said fi-nally. No sense hollering at Grandma. It wasn't *her* I was mad at.

"Oh, I could tell you stories about your grandfather,"

she went on. "He had been living here alone for twenty years when I married him. Now, there was a man who was hard to break in. And stubborn! Oh, he was stubborn!" She glanced from the corner of her eye to see if I was listening. "Of course, back then, we womenfolk just went on and did the best we could because we didn't know any other way."

For a moment I thought I was going to get the lecture about how spoiled young people are, but she fell silent, as if she had lost her train of thought. Her hand slipped from my arm and she folded it in her lap, staring out the window. Finally, she said, "I don't suppose women do that anymore. I think that is some of what is wrong with families these days. Raising children is an occupation of self-sacrifice, but these days young people don't want to give anything up."

I felt the need to defend myself. "I don't want Josh to grow up feeling like he's a sideline occupation. I was thinking that we could cut back our expenses, give up some luxuries, and both have more time with him. But the truth is, when I go through all the figures, it doesn't seem possible. Even if we give up the boat and the idea of a bigger house and get less expensive cars, I'm not sure we can make it."

Grandma laid her hands on the edge of the table and looked at me for a long time, her eyes clear and sharp. "It sounds like you have a good idea, but you are lacking in faith."

"It isn't that simple," I said, and my vision for the future dimmed until I could barely see the picture. "Even if it were, I don't think Ben is willing."

"Oh." She nodded, as if she had suddenly gained a profound understanding of things. "Well, you won't make progress by fighting with him on the phone, that much I can tell you. It takes time to turn a heart, and it cannot be done with hard words. I lived nearly forty years with your grandfather, and that was the most important thing I learned."

I rolled my eyes, feeling like a teenager getting my first dating advice. "I wasn't trying to pick a fight. He's just so . . . self-centered sometimes. He only listens to about half of what I say, and I'm just . . . sick of it. It's just frustrating."

She smacked her lips, nodding again. "A man has his own way of thinking. Sometimes it is hard for us womenfolk to understand." She smiled, patting my hand. "Give things a little time. Be patient, Katie. Everything doesn't have to work itself out today."

"I'll try."

"Good girl." She stood up abruptly and shuffled to the coat hook, wrapping her coat around her shoulders. "I have some things to do in my little house."

"All right," I said, wondering at the infinite changes in her moods. She seldom seemed able to maintain a conversation.

She wrapped her scarf loosely over her silver hair, tucking the corners into her collar, then opened the door. "You know, there is a big house here with no payment due on it," she said, stepping into the winter chill. "I don't mind staying in the little one." And then she walked out the door, leaving me stunned in her wake.

I sat there for a minute waiting for her to come back and recant what she had said, because I knew she couldn't possibly mean what I thought she meant. The idea of Grandma giving up her house was almost as outrageous as the idea of us moving into it permanently.

But she didn't come back, and finally, I just shook my head, put my coffee cup away, and then went upstairs to get Josh and take him out for a walk.

The day was brisk, but it felt good to be outside in the fresh air and sunshine. I walked past the field of long winter wheat and watched the cattle moving lazily about, their backs turned to the wind. I pictured my father and grandfather working there, turning up the black earth, planting seed, harvesting, and planting again. I wondered what they had been like together, if they had understood each other, or if they had battled as we were battling now.

I thought about my conversation with Ben again, and that sense of frustration twisted inside me like a rubberband, winding tighter and tighter, until I couldn't stand to think about it anymore. *Be patient,* Grandma had said. But time was running out. Christmas was almost here, and then it would be over, and we would be back to our old lives, so busy that there wasn't time to think about changing things. . . .

A cold wind blew across the field, tugging at our coats, chasing away my thoughts. Turning away from the wind, I pulled Joshua's hood tighter around his red cheeks and walked back to the house.

The kitchen was dark and quiet. Grandma was nowhere to be found, which was odd at lunchtime, but I figured she had exhausted herself working in the yard and had fallen asleep in the little house. As I hung my coat on the hook, something familiar caught my eye beside the row of old blue and white porcelain canisters. Grandma's book.

I didn't waste time considering whether or not it was right for me to read it. I went to it like an old friend.

Breaking.

I thought about what she had told me earlier and wondered if the story would be about my grandfather.

As a young woman I had a deep and abiding love for all living things. Farm life was joyous for me, as there were so many animals to care for. I was fond of each of them, especially the young ones, and in particular the horses, perhaps because I had so loved the carousel.

When we married, my husband purchased two draft mares and said that we might raise a pair of foals each year to sell. Money was scarce in those Depression years, and the purchase of the mares was a terrible risk. I knew he was pressed by the need to support a wife and the children that would come.

My heart was filled with guilt for the burdens I had brought by coming to our marriage penniless. I sought to do penance by giving special care to the mares and fretting over their stalls and feeding. On the early spring nights, I rose from my bed to watch for signs of foaling and sat with the mares when the time came to bring the young ones into the world. My hands were the first to touch the foals as they struggled, still damp, into life.

Summer found me slipping away from my farm labors, passing time in the company of the horses. In my stolen moments I watched my little Kip and Dutch run through the tall grass or sleep among the Queen Anne's lace. I was as proud of those foals as if they were my children, and they loved me as much as their own mothers. I coaxed them to it with bits of sugar and melon rinds. My husband thought me foolish and said I would spoil them, but I knew better. I was determined that they would learn to find comfort, not fear, in the touch of a human hand.

Winter came, then spring and new foals. Kip and Dutch were yearlings and ready for harness breaking. I shall never forget how it was begun. I watched, banished to the house, as they were bound with ropes and strapped into the belly harness. Wild with terror, they rose, running and bawling, falling and crashing into the fences. Sweat and foam covered them as my husband mastered them with the pull of the ropes and the slash of the black snake whip. Wildly, they struggled, until they had no more strength to fight.

I hid myself away in the house, but I could not escape the thunder of his voice and the crack of the black snake. My heart was filled with anger. It is there still— a tiny blackened place only I know, like a bruise deep within an apple.

I did not speak of it to him. He never knew what was in my mind. I did not know what was in his. I do not believe that he intended to cause me pain, but that he knew no other way of breaking horses. His thoughts were ruled by the work that needed to be done, while mine were ruled by the feelings of my heart. In the end, the result was the same. The horses were trained and sold, and our lives went on. Each year, our union endured the breaking of the horses. He became as gentle as his work would allow, and I as hardened as my heart could manage. What we cannot change, we must endure without bitterness.

Sometimes we must try to view the actions of those around us with forgiveness. We must realize that they are going on the only road they can see. Sometimes we cannot raise our chins and see eye to eye, so we must bow our heads and have faith in one another.

Looking through the window, I watched the little house. I wondered if Grandma was thinking about me, or maybe just sleeping away the noon hour in her chair.

Turning to the book, I read the last line again. *Sometimes we cannot raise our chins and see eye to eye, so we must bow our heads and have faith in one another.*

It was a good lesson—one I had tried to master before, but it was like a big fish on a thin line. I couldn't quite get it into my grasp. Maybe I was making life too hard by trying to get Ben to see things my way. Maybe I needed to be a little more accepting of him and have faith that he was getting through the best way he knew how. Josh's premature birth, the ongoing medical problems, and all the hospital bills weren't easy to deal with.

Maybe I just needed to be patient and have faith that we would somehow find our way.

What we cannot change, we must endure without bitterness. . . .

The screen door slammed on the little house outside, and I jolted from my chair, setting the book on the counter where I had found it and glancing out the window. Grandma was crossing the yard with a gardening apron strapped over her coat and a pair of rose trimmers in her hand.

She seemed not to notice as I descended the steps and stood next to her while she pruned the branches from a rosebush. I wondered if she was afraid I'd tell her she should be in the house resting.

"It's kind of cold out here," I said finally.

"I just thought I'd give this bush a quick trimming." She ignored my observation. "Normally, it is best to trim them back in February, but I'm doing this while I can this year. Always trim the small stems away and keep the old wood so the bush will sprout there next year. Like this. That way the new blooms will be larger."

"All right." I wondered why she was talking to me as if she didn't expect to be able to prune the roses herself. "Are you feeling O.K.?"

She stopped midclip and frowned at me. "Do I look bad?"

Her consternation made me laugh. "No, but I thought you were resting this afternoon."

"Oh . . . no." She glanced at the driveway as if she were expecting someone. "I want to finish this before Jeannie arrives day after tomorrow. You go on with your paperwork in there. Sort things through before Ben comes home. I was thinking we would go to town tomorrow for groceries and whatnot. What time is Benjamin coming in?"

"About noon tomorrow. Why?" That sweet, agreeable

tone bothered me. Grandma only talked that way when she was scheming something.

"No particular reason." Still far too congenial for Grandma Rose. "If you and Ben wanted to stay in town and have a supper out together, I could have Oliver bring me home after we finish the grocery shopping."

"No. I can bring you home. Ben heads right for his computer when he comes in from a job. I'll be lucky if I see him before midnight."

Grandma stopped clipping and frowned at me over her shoulder. "Then perhaps you should go see him at the church office."

She was probably right, but I was still smarting over the Knicks game, and I wasn't about to go making nice with Ben just yet. "No. I'll just wait," I said. Then a wicked thought came into my head, and I added, "But if you want to make plans with Oliver, don't let me get in your way."

Grandma looked as if she might faint. The blood drained from her face, and she craned her head away from me, eyes widened and nostrils flared. "Certainly not!" she exploded with a volume that probably cleared the nearby woods of wild game. "That old coot! Why, do you know that just the other day he was going around town with a *hole* in the *seat* of his *pants*? It was obscene. His daughter needs to take better care of him. It's terrible to let someone go around in such a senile condition, and—"

"All right, Grandma," I said, trying to stop her before she sent her blood pressure skyrocketing. "We'll go to town and come back together."

"Well, I guess so!" And she went back to pruning the roses with a righteous vigor, this time grumbling about Oliver and not about Ben and me. Which was just what I'd wanted. For once, I had beaten Grandma Vongortler at her own game.

But by the next day she was again trying to put me in

checkmate. I knew she was up to something, because she was in that unusually good mood again. Not a cross word to say, not one bit of her usual ire, even when I fed her bran cereal for breakfast, which she normally said tasted like it belonged in a horse trough.

"You should write that on our list for the store," she said as I threw away the empty box. "Dr. Schmidt says I should have more fiber."

I blinked at her, wondering who she was and what she had done with Grandma Vongortler. "All right. Are you about ready to go?" Josh was dressed. I was dressed. The diaper bag was packed, but she kept putting me off.

She chewed the last of her bran cereal thoughtfully. "I have to fix my hair and get my article together for the paper. We should get those sheets changed, also. Just in case Aunt Jeane comes early."

"She won't be here until lunchtime tomorrow." I was getting a little tired of Grandma yanking my chain, and I had a feeling she was putting me off so that we would run into Ben in town. "I'm going to start some laundry. You let me know when you're ready." So I gave up and went on with getting the house ready for Aunt Jeane's arrival. I tried not to think about the fact that a few days after Aunt Jeane came, the rest of the family would follow. It was just too hard to consider the Christmas gathering, and what might be said and not said, and what might be decided about Grandma, and how she might take it. I felt like a traitor about to give my general over to the enemy.

It didn't help that as we sat down to lunch, Grandma was still in a congenial mood. She complimented my housecleaning and told me how glad she was to have Josh and me there and how very much she had enjoyed the house not being empty over the past weeks. It just wasn't like her at all, and I wondered what she was conjuring up in that evil mind of hers.

"It's been a nice visit," I said, guilt sloshing around in my stomach like seawater, because this wasn't a visit at all. This was a covert mission to supervise Grandma Vongortler, and I was the family's spy. Her being so nice to me only made me feel worse about it.

There was a knock at the front door, and I jumped up like a trapped cat looking for an escape, then hurried into the breezeway. When I answered the door, little Dell Jordan was standing on the porch in a faded pair of blue jeans that were too short and a windbreaker that wasn't heavy enough for the cold day. She was looking down at her tennis shoes.

For a moment, I couldn't think of anything to say. Finally, I choked out, "Hi. Well . . . what can I do for you today?"

She shrugged, as if she wasn't sure, muttering, "My granny said I could come carry in Mrs. Vongortler's groceries for a dollar." She kicked a toe into the tangle of leaves that had wandered onto the porch, then pushed her hands into her pockets, watching the leaves crinkle under her shoe. "Granny said Mrs. Vongortler sent a note with the postman."

"Well . . . I . . . umm . . ." I stammered. "I don't . . . Grandma didn't . . . Can you wait here a minute?" And I went to the kitchen to see what was going on. If Grandma had something mean to say, I didn't want Dell to hear it.

Grandma was depositing her plate in the sink when I stepped in. "Now I'll just be a minute." She headed for the little house, as if she hadn't heard the knock at the door. "I'll meet you at the car."

"Grandma," I protested, confused. "Dell Jordan's at the door. She says she's going to carry in your groceries for a dollar. Do you know anything about this?"

Grandma stopped halfway out the door, crossed her arms, and gave me that wooden-Indian look. "Yes. But I thought we would be back from the grocery store by now. I told her grandmother we could use help bringing things in and also hauling the leaves out of the yard, and that I would pay her." She smacked her lips and huffed. "Well, we need to get to town now. I guess she will just have to ride along with us. Tell her I'll give her five dollars for helping me this afternoon."

With a smack of the screen door, she was gone. It took me a minute to reel my chin off the floor and go to the front door to talk to Dell.

"We were just on our way to town to get the groceries," I said. "If it's all right with your grandma, you can ride along with us. Grandma . . . er . . . Mrs. Vongortler said she would pay you five dollars, if that's all right."

I caught a glimpse of wide brown eyes as she nodded vigorously, then tucked her chin again. Stepping tentatively in the doorway, she followed me like a shadow as I put Josh in his carrier and headed for the car.

Grandma Rose's sunny mood was apparent when we got to the Buick. She had opened all four doors and was waiting for us in the passenger seat, wearing something other than her usual scowl.

"Don't forget your seat belt back there," she said as Dell slid uncertainly into the back next to Joshua's car seat. "Katie drives too fast."

Dell glanced at me with one brow raised and one lowered.

"She's in a good mood," I whispered as I leaned over to buckle in Josh.

Grandma strained to turn her good ear to us. "What?"

"Nothing, Gram." I winked at Dell and she giggled behind her hand.

Grandma started working her scheme before we were out of the driveway. "I have quite a bit to do at the

church. You could go over to the church office and see
Ben for a while. It's twelve-thirty. He'll surely be there."

Her plan was becoming clearer, like an image material-
izing on a computer screen. "I think I'll just go to Shorty's
and get started on the groceries," I said. "We've got a
really long list." It was about like trying to outsmart a
computer. Amazing how acute Grandma Rose could be
when she was plotting something. She wanted me to make
up with Ben, and she was determined to have her way.

"Well, you can't do that until I am finished at the
church," she retorted, clearly irritated that I wasn't coop-
erating. "There are things we need that aren't on the list.
And if I'm not there, that butcher at Shorty's won't give
us the best cuts of meat. Dell can help me with my things
at the church, and then she and I can start at the grocery
store while you visit with Ben. No *sense* putting *that* off."

Dell's eyes looked like baseballs in the rearview mirror, but she didn't say a word. She was clearly just as
confused as I was, probably more so because she was
young and not accustomed to Grandma's puppet work.

"That's silly," I protested. "You do your work and
we'll just go to Shorty's and get started on the things
that are on the list. If Ben wants to talk to me, he can
come home." I knew I was cutting off my nose to spite
my face. Ben and I needed to talk, but I didn't want to
get into another fight, and I wasn't ready to be contrite,
and I wasn't doing a very good job of taking to heart the
advice from Grandma's book.

An irritated sigh puffed from Grandma's lips, and she
looked out the window. I knew I hadn't heard the last of
the argument. She was just falling back to muster a new
plan of attack.

The car fell into an eerie silence. I felt like a prisoner
standing before a firing squad, waiting for the crack of a
rifle.

"Katie, where does this road go?"

"What?" For once, her thoughts had lapsed at the right time. We had tacked in another direction.

"Where does this road go?" She sounded as if she really couldn't remember, and I felt a note of panic. Maybe the fight had pushed her blood pressure up and caused a stroke. The doctor had warned us that a small stroke could cause a sudden memory lapse.

"It goes to Hindsville, Grandma." I tried to sound calm, but I wasn't. She had lived on this road for sixty-some years. If she really didn't recognize it, something was terribly wrong.

She chewed her lip as if thinking about that, then asked, "Did we drive this road yesterday?"

I wanted to stop the car and shake her back to reality, but instead, I calmly answered, "Yes."

"Where did it go?"

"To Hindsville." My heart hammered so hard in my ears, I could barely hear her. *Three more miles to town, then straight to Dr. Schmidt's. Please, God, let us make it there without having an emergency.*

"Will we drive it tomorrow?"

"Probably." *Two more curves, then across the bridge to Dr. Schmidt's. Please let him be in the office.*

"Where will it go?"

"To Hindsville."

She didn't look at me, but stared straight ahead at the road instead. "If we got on this road trying to go somewhere else, how would that be?"

Dell laughed in the backseat and piped up with an answer. "That would be pretty stupid."

Slowing the car, I took a long look at Grandma. In one startling, maddening, murderous moment, I realized she wasn't out of her mind at all. She was reeling me in like a guppy.

Looking over her shoulder, she pretended to be talking to Dell. "Yes, it would. The same road always leads to the same place. If we get on it expecting to go somewhere different, we'll be disappointed, won't we? As you said, it isn't very *smart.*"

Not a word was said the rest of the way to town. I didn't have a reply. I didn't want to reply. I didn't want to ever speak to Grandma Vongortler again.

But her point was made. If Ben and I kept doing the same things, we were always going to end up in the same place. Do the same things, get the same results. Simple, stupid.

Chapter 8

BEN'S car was in the church parking lot when we got to town. Grandma looked at it and tipped her chin up triumphantly. As soon as I brought the Buick to a halt in front of the church, she was shooing me out.

"Now, Dell and I will be just fine. I have to finish my newspaper article and organize some things in the choir room. It's a mess in there with all of the things coming in for our Christmas drive. She can help me clean it up, and then we'll get started on the grocery shopping."

Standing on the curb, I gave them a questioning look. A couple of weeks ago, Grandma didn't care if we ran Dell over on the highway. Now she was trying to help Dell earn extra money. If I hadn't read Grandma's book, I would never have understood.

Grandma huffed an irritated breath and fanned a hand at me. "Go on and talk to Ben. We will be just fine together, won't we, young lady?"

Dell gave Grandma a look of respect, then ducked her head and nodded. "Yes, ma'am."

I left them there and carried Josh around the back of the church to the fellowship building. Walking down the hall, I saw Ben in the office at the end, at work on his computer just as I had predicted. That old sense of resentiment stirred inside me again, and I started to turn around and leave.

Ben saw me coming and pushed away from the desk, rubbing his eyes. "I don't have time for a fight, Kate," he said flatly. "I have to get this report finished."

"I don't want to fight." *Get on a different road, end up in a different place.* "I thought maybe I could help you get your work done, and—"

"Kate, I didn't . . ." he interrupted defensively. Then he paused and looked at me, snapping his mouth shut. "I'm sorry. What did you say?"

You can't turn a heart with hard words. "I said, I thought I could help you get your work done. You look tired."

He nodded, combing a hand through the tangle of dark hair on his forehead. "Um-hum. But everything is about done. I stayed up last night and finished the report. It's over there if you want to proof it for me. And that ought to pretty well wrap it up."

It was my turn to be surprised. "You mean you're finished with the project?" Looking at him, exhausted and unshaven, I realized he probably hadn't slept since we talked on the phone the day before.

"Pretty much." He stood up, rolling his head back and yawning, his blue eyes partly closed. There was a hint of a wicked gleam there. "I thought you told me to finish up and get my butt home for Christmas."

I smiled, glancing at Josh as he yawned and stretched his arms, looking like his father. A tender sense of family love warmed inside me. "I did . . . but I didn't think you were listening."

Ben leaned forward, kissed me on the forehead, and then kissed Josh, grinning slyly. "I was listening."

He sat down at the computer and went back to work. I took Josh to the nursery down the hall and laid him in one of the cribs, then went back and helped Ben finish his paperwork. Within an hour and a half, we had packaged the blueprints, specs, and reports for mailing, and Ben was ready to go home and fall into bed. I had the romantic notion of going with him, but then realized I had Grandma and Dell and the Buick to drive back, so I kissed him good-bye, picked up Josh from the nursery, and went to look for Grandma and Dell.

I found them on a bench in the church lobby. Everything looked surprisingly peaceful. Grandma's chin was tilted up in a self-satisfied way, and Dell was wearing a rare but adorable smile.

"You two look like you had a good time," I said, stopping in front of them. I couldn't imagine why both of them looked so pleased.

Grandma didn't volunteer any information, but Dell was quick to point to some brown paper sacks at her feet. "We did. Look what I got."

Squatting down, I looked in the first sack. It was full of notebooks, pencils, pens, coloring books, and some costume jewelry. Confounded, I opened the other sacks and saw adorable little-girl clothes, some new and some looking as if they had been worn a few times. As hard as it was to believe, I could only assume that Grandma had taken Dell . . . shopping? It was like Elmer Fudd buying gifts for Bugs Bunny.

"What's all this?" I asked.

Grandma just shrugged and glanced away, but her lips were trembling with a withheld grin. "The Baptist Ladies Mission in Springfield sent far too much for our Christmas drive this year. I thought Dell might take some of the things home with her and get them out of our way."

I knew this was all far from accidental. I suddenly understood why Grandma had stalled me all morning. She was waiting for Dell to show up, not so Dell could carry groceries or help her at the church. She had planned to take Dell shopping in the donated goods.

My throat prickled as if I had swallowed a cocklebur, and I just sat there unable to say anything, thinking of what a wonderful thing Grandma had done. Beneath that mask of curmudgeon, there was a heart that cared whether Dell Jordan had decent clothes to wear and supplies for school.

We didn't talk much as we climbed into the car and started toward home. In the rearview mirror, I could see Dell resting her head against the backseat with the grocery sacks clutched in her lap. She looked excited and happy, as a child should look at Christmas. Grandma looked like a girl at Christmas herself. Her pale blue eyes glittered with emotion, and she was struggling to maintain her trademark frown.

When we arrived at home, Grandma fixed tea and cookies, and we sat in the dogtrot for an impromptu fashion show. Dell carried her bags upstairs, changed in one of the bedrooms, then paraded down the stairs in one outfit after another. Grandma had washed Dell's face and tied her hair in a ribbon, and she looked like a real little girl. The rag doll with the frown was gone. It was impossible not to smile with her. Even Joshua joined in the excitement, giggling and cooing as Dell paraded in her new clothes.

When the fashion show was finished, Dell sat on the bottom step in a daisy-print dress she was reluctant to take off.

I picked up the teacups and leftover cookies as she dangled a string of plastic beads over Joshua's carrier while he flailed his hands in the air, babbling happily.

"Now, don't let him get hold of those," Grandma scolded. "He'll put them in his mouth and choke."

Dell pulled back as if she'd been accused, and sat with the beads and her hands in her lap.

I frowned at Grandma's harshness. "She's all right. He's enjoying looking at the beads, and he can't reach them." I wondered why Grandma felt the need to throw cold water on such a perfectly wonderful day.

Dell ducked her head, and the room fell silent. Disappointed, I finished picking up the tea things and walked to the kitchen. Sometimes Grandma's timing could be so bad. She always picked the most vulnerable moments to pull out her Mr. Hyde personality.

The silence in the hall continued until I heard Joshua fuss. I moved close to the door, but he stopped grumbling and started jabbering, and I could tell someone had picked him up. Stepping into the hall, I saw Dell sitting on the rug at the bottom of the stairs with her legs folded and Joshua balanced in her lap. Grandma was poised behind her with hands suspended in the air, as if afraid Dell would suddenly drop him. Dell didn't seem to notice. She was too enthralled with Joshua's baby talk.

I stood by the doorway watching them, and a sense of amazement filled me. It was as if the spirit of a real child had come to inhabit the body of the somber little rag doll. Her face was flushed and bright, her raven eyes alive with laughter and tenderness. There was the little girl I had wondered about, but never seen—the one who could smile and giggle, make silly sounds and funny faces.

Grandma spoke, and that girl disappeared like a mirage.

"Now, you must be sure to keep hold of him. He can wriggle out of your hands in a hurry." The harsh tone was gone from her voice. "He surely seems to enjoy sitting there with you."

I guess Dell was pleased. It was hard to tell. She ducked her head, but didn't offer to give Josh back. I had the distinct impression that she would have been just as happy for Grandma to leave and the baby to stay.

"I know how to give him a bottle if he's hungry," she

offered. "And change his diaper. I used to have a little brother."

"You did?" Grandma sounded surprised.

I wondered what "used to" meant.

"Um-hum," Dell said, but she didn't offer any more information. She brushed a few strands of grass off the rug as if it were of great concern.

"What was his name?" Grandma pressed, sounding curious and slightly suspicious.

"Angelo." Dell played patty-cake with Josh's feet, seeming uninterested in the conversation. "He didn't look like me. He looked kinda like Joshua. He didn't have a ugly no-good daddy."

A sickening lump rose in my throat and descended to my stomach like bile. She had said the words as if they were the most natural thing in the world, just a fact of life, something simple and of no consequence, barely worthy of conversation.

Grandma was silent for a long time. She dropped her hands to her sides and her shoulders sagged. Finally, she said, "Where is your brother now?"

"Mama took him and give him to his daddy," Dell answered nonchalantly. "She was afraid he'd fall in the river and get drowned. Granny says she didn't hear no more about him after Mama died. I had a dream about him one night. I think he lives in a big house."

. . . *that others were greater and I was less. That others would live in wonderful places while we would not.*

Grandma's words drummed in my mind. I wondered what she was thinking and what she would say.

They sat silent for a while, Dell seemingly engrossed in playing with Josh and Grandma with her chin tilted back, looking toward the ceiling, dabbing her eyes with her hankie.

Dell looked up finally, watching Grandma with an intense expression. "Do you think I have a ugly no-good daddy?"

Grandma cleared her throat and looked at Dell. When she spoke, her voice was trembling. "I think that's not a very nice thing to say," she said quietly. "You are a child of God and a beautiful gift to this world."

Dell sighed and tilted her head to one side, frowning, obviously not satisfied with the answer. She watched Grandma Rose, her dark brows slightly lowered, the question still in her face. "God don't know me. We didn't ever go to church."

My eyes filled with tears as Grandma reached out, her aged hands trembling, and combed back the dark strands of Dell's hair. Dell didn't move away, and she met Grandma's gaze. "God knows you, child. He is mindful of every bird in the air, and every fish in the sea, and every flower that blooms in the field. They are beautiful to Him, just as you are." She cupped Dell's chin in her hand lovingly, leaning forward so that their faces were close. "You must remember that when people are unkind to you and try to make you feel as if you are less than they are. Your Father in heaven made every strand of hair on your head and every ounce of flesh on your bones. You are perfect, and beautiful, and just the way you are intended to be."

The phone rang, and I jumped, then rushed into the kitchen to answer it. My voice shuddered as I said hello.

"Kate?" I recognized the voice of Dianne, my assistant at work.

"Hi, Dianne." Clearing the lump from my throat, I tried to sound a little more businesslike.

"Is everything all right? You sound upset."

"No. I'm fine. I've just got something in my throat." The last thing I needed was for Dianne to think I was falling apart emotionally. She was good at her job, but also young and ambitious. She had a way of taking over things if I didn't keep clear lines between her job and mine. Of course, with me being away so long, the lines were quickly disappearing. "Did you need something?"

"Yes." She sounded as if she were in a hurry and frustrated. "Paul wants a copy of the original packet on the MTBE oxygenates contamination study, and I can't find it. He says it's important, and he needs it yesterday."

"Is there a problem?" Alarm bells rang in my head. When my boss wanted something that quickly, it usually spelled trouble, and the study of gas additives in the drinking water supply was one of my favorite projects.

"I don't know. I think he's just in a grouchy mood because you're not here."

I chuckled. "He's that way when I *am* there. That's just Paul. It's your day. Just give him the packet and try to stay out of his way. Tomorrow it'll be someone else's day."

"All right." She sighed, sounding demoralized. "Where is it?"

"In the basement files under the project code number. That's why you couldn't find it. I already sent it off to the morgue, because there shouldn't have been a need for it anymore."

"O.K. Thanks."

"No problem. Don't let him get to you."

"I won't." She sounded a little better. "Everything all right down there?" she asked, but I could tell she was in a hurry to get off the phone and didn't really want to talk.

"Fine, thanks."

"Oh . . . um . . . good," she muttered, sounding distracted. "Well, have a good Christmas and I'll try not to call you again."

"Call me if you need me. It's not a problem."

We said good-bye and I hung up. I stood for a moment looking into the hallway at Dell and Grandma, now sitting silently together. Chicago and the trouble at work flew from my mind and I thought again about what Dell had said, and about Grandma Rose's book and how little had changed in her long life. Poverty and ignorance still existed, and cruelty was the house they lived in. It still wasn't fair that some children had many nickels for the carousel while others had few. It was still true that some were greater while others were less.

For a long time, I stood watching them as Dell played with Joshua, and Joshua laughed, and Grandma sat watching the two of them with her hands in her lap, very still, as if she had slipped so far away that she was oblivious to the movement and noise of the children.

Finally, I walked into the hallway and broke the spell. Dell looked at me as if she were afraid I would be upset with her for picking up the baby. She carefully put him back in his carrier, then stood up.

"Lay your dress on the bed in the upstairs bedroom," Grandma told her. "I'll mend that button on the back and press it for you so that it will be ready for church."

Dell nodded at Grandma, then turned to me with a look alive with wonder. "Mrs. Vongortler says I can go to Christmas church with her on Sunday." Then she turned around in a flash and dashed up the stairs in a cloud of billowing green daisy-print.

"Are you sure she *wants* to go to church?" I asked.

"All children want to know the Lord," Grandma replied flatly, busying herself with picking lint off her dress. "It is perfectly natural that she would want to learn. Just because her family are heathens does not mean she must be."

I watched her for a minute, trying to gauge her answer, but she was looking away from me toward the stairs.

"All right," I said. "As long as it's her choice and it's all right with her grandmother. I don't want Dell to think she has to go."

Grandma gave me a long, steady look. "I don't make *you* go. The Lord only wants those who come freely."

I didn't have a reply for that, so I changed the subject. "It was really nice of you to get those things for Dell. The kids in town were teasing her about her clothes."

Grandma shrugged as if she didn't have great interest in the matter. "She shouldn't have a problem now. Those things are all washed and ironed, and if she needs them cleaned or mended, she can bring them to me and I will get them fixed for her."

"That's nice of you," but it didn't sound like Grandma at all.

"Lord knows, her Granny can't be counted upon to keep her things cleaned. Too busy smoking cigarettes and watching television." That sounded like Grandma.

"Anyway, you did a really nice thing," I repeated for the third time. I didn't know why I wanted to force her to accept the compliment. Maybe just to prove she wasn't the old Scrooge she pretended to be.

She didn't reply, just sat staring out the window. I was about to go help Dell get her belongings together when Grandma Rose spoke.

"It occurred to me that I should do more for other people. I never once considered that there were people just down the road who cannot afford proper clothing, or care for their children. Dell tells me they won't even have a Christmas dinner because her Granny can't afford such." She sighed, shaking her head, looking into the past. "I've been a pretty horrid woman most of my life. I mostly concerned myself with having life my own way and with gaining the things I never had as a youngster. I have been bitter with the world and ungrateful too often. In the meanwhile, I have raised two children who never come around and two grandchildren who moved to the far corners of the earth and send me cards at Christmas instead of coming here. It isn't a right way to end up in life. Time gets by so fast. It seems like I was Dell's age just yesterday, and I thought I'd never be old." She paused, seeming to lose her train of thought, then let out a long sigh. "I should have done more good."

I wasn't sure what to say, so I stood up, laid a hand on her shoulder and kissed her cheek. "You've done a lot for me," I said quietly. There was so much more to say than I could put into words.

She patted my hand, then slipped hers into the pocket of her apron and sat staring at the waning day outside the window. I left her there and went to say good-bye to Dell, who stood at the door with her packages.

"Could you tell Grandma thank you before you leave?" I asked. "I think she's feeling a little sad."

"O.K." Dell set her sacks by the door and trotted across the room to Grandma's chair.

Glancing back as I went into the kitchen, I saw her lean down to give Grandma a hug. I knew then that they understood each other better than I'd realized.

After Dell left, Grandma was melancholy. The phone rang, and she hurried to answer it, then shook her head and hung up. "Just a wrong number." Her eyes glittered as she turned away from me. "I thought it might be Jackie."

"I'm sure he'll call soon." I didn't know what else to say. The truth was, my father hadn't called and I was beginning to wonder if he was going to. "He's probably just out of town."

"I suppose." She put on her coat and walked outside. Looking out the window, I saw her in the twilight, sitting on the porch of the little house, her pale blue eyes watching the driveway intently. Taking the hankie from her apron pocket, she raised it slowly to her face, dried her tears with a trembling hand, then clutched the hankie in her lap and continued to watch the driveway.

Stroking my fingers absently over the phone receiver, I wondered why she kept watching when she knew no one was coming. Yet, she had done just that for as long as I could remember. Every summer vacation memory was framed by the image of her standing on the porch steps forlornly watching us drive away. We had always assumed the performance was for our benefit and that it ended as soon as we rounded the driveway. I could see now that we had had no inkling of what she was really feeling.

I picked up the phone and dialed my father's number. Either he hadn't received my first message, or he just didn't care. If I had to drag him personally, if I had to grovel, beg, or threaten, I was going to get him to the farm for Christmas.

My heart was in my throat as the call connected. I wasn't sure I'd be able to talk if he answered. Relief melted through me when, once again, his machine picked up.

I swallowed hard, waiting for the tone, then rushed through the message. "Dad, this is Kate again. We were wondering when you were coming ... umm ... Grandma really has her heart set on everyone being here. It's ... umm ... really important to all of us. Let me know when you'll get here. 'Bye ... Dad."

I love you. Hard to know. Even harder to say, so I just hung up the phone. Another missed connection between my father and me.

I warmed up the tea and called for Grandma to come in.

"You look cold," I said, pouring two cups of tea as she came through the door.

"I'm not cold." She shook her head at the tea, waving off my concern as she sat down. "I'm eighty-nine years old. I might not be here three months from now. Nobody seems to understand that."

Setting my tea aside, I rubbed the growing ache between my eyebrows. I knew that martyred tone like I knew the back of my hand. It grated on my spine like a fingernail scratching on a blackboard. "Oh, Grandma, everything's fine."

"You never know," she insisted gravely. "I had a pain just this morning. I don't know what it could be. I should probably see Dr. Schmidt."

Funny, you were practically dancing a jig at the church this morning. "It's five o'clock. Dr. Schmidt is closed for the day. I'll take you in the morning if you still feel you need to go."

She gave my suggestion a quiet *humph*, stood up, and shuffled toward the door to put on her coat. "I'm going to walk up and get the mail. Maybe there will be a letter."

I didn't bother to remind her we had picked up the mail hours ago and there was no letter from my father. I just let her go. I figured the walk would clear her head, and she would come back in a better mood. Meanwhile, I started warming up some leftovers for supper. I was hoping Ben would wake up and we would have some time to talk.

I wanted to tell him about everything that had happened while he was gone—about the propane and the midnight toilet paper inventory, about the Christmas festival and Grandma giving Dell clothes from the donated goods at church. I wanted to explain the changes in the way I was thinking about our lives.

But I wasn't sure what I wanted him to say. I didn't know if I wanted him to understand, or to give me a reality check and talk me out of my Vongortler-induced insanity.

Grandma appeared at the kitchen doorway as I was putting the last of the leftovers on the table. Her face was brighter, and she was carrying a potted plant with stems of delicate purple flowers.

"Look what Mrs. Owens brought by," she said. "She thought we would enjoy them for our table."

"They're pretty," I replied. "I thought you went to get the mail."

Stopping midstride, she looked at me as if my head had suddenly popped off my body and rolled across the floor. "Katie, the mail comes in the *morning.*"

"You're right." Bested again. What else could I say? "Everything's ready. I guess Ben's still sleeping. We might as well eat."

She set the plant in the middle of the table. "Doesn't that look nice?"

"It does," I agreed, glad she was over her unhappy spell. "I wonder what it's called."

Touching the leaves, Grandma studied them as if the answer might be written there. "I'm not sure. I don't believe I've seen one before, but Mrs. Owens raises all sorts of plants in her greenhouse. The flowers look a little like lilacs. I'll have to ask her what they are called. Maybe it can be planted outdoors in the spring."

"Sounds like a good idea." *But in the spring no one will be here . . .*

We ate supper in silence, me feeding Josh and Grandma studying the flowers.

When we had finished, she pushed her plate aside and fingered the flowers thoughtfully. "These would be nice to plant in the cemetery," she said, not looking at me.

"That would be good." I didn't want to think about the cemetery. I still hadn't been to my mother's grave. After the farm was sold, I probably wouldn't be back . . .

Grandma, of course, had an agenda. "Aunt Jeane will want to take a visit there."

"Yes. I'm sure she will." Standing up, I started clearing the dishes, hoping to put an end to the conversation.

"Your mother would have wanted you to come." I

could feel her watching my back as I rinsed dishes at the sink. "She loved you girls very much."

Tears clouded my eyes, and a plate slipped from my fingers, clattering against the counter. Bracing my hands on the sides of the sink, I tried to gather myself before turning around to tell her I did not want to talk about the cemetery or my mother.

Tears rushed from my eyes and spilled over my cheeks. I was overwhelmed with grief for my mother and guilt about selling the farm. It isn't easy to sell the land for which your ancestors have given their hearts and their bodies. I supposed Dad and Aunt Jeane would retain ownership of the burial plot, but probably nothing else. . . .

The last hours of my charade with Grandma were about to end. In the morning, Aunt Jeane would come and she would talk to Grandma about Oakhaven Village. And I hadn't even warned Grandma. I'd let the weeks go by without saying anything. At the very least, I should do what I could to cushion the blow.

Wiping my eyes impatiently, I turned around, but the flowers and Grandma were gone, as if she knew I was about to say something she didn't want to hear.

The thought was still with me later that evening as I curled up on the sofa to watch the news. The house was ready for Aunt Jeane and Uncle Robert to arrive in the morning, but I was not. Aunt Jeane's arrival would be followed by Karen's a few days later, and finally by Dad's, assuming he decided to come. They would come with their agendas and their time constraints and their scars, and we would all start opening wounds. The farm would be dissected; the peace would vanish; Grandma Rose would be gone. My time home with Joshua would be over, and I would be back at work trying to dig up files to pacify my boss's senseless bad moods. Joshua would spend his days with a baby-sitter. Ben would be away on some job. Life would be filled with all the familiar noise—like static turned so loud you couldn't think.

I wasn't ready. Closing my eyes, I tried to make it go away.

. . . The best times of my life, the times that passed by me the most quickly, were the times when the roses grew wild.

There was so much that the rest of them didn't know, that they didn't understand.

. . . time is a limited and precious gift. I wish I had not spent my hours worrying over another nickel for the carousel, but instead running through the fields of yellow bonnets.

I wished I didn't understand. Things would have been easier. . . .

My mind drifted into the past, to a summer vacation filled with picnic lunches and daisy chains. I could see my mother's fingers braiding necklaces and crowns, balancing them on our heads. I could see her young and laughing, her feet bare and her brown hair tumbling in curls around her shoulders. Her laughter was like music.

I could see her singing above my bed as I lay in my room. The scent of fresh grass clung to the daisy chain around her neck. Beside me, Karen's breaths were long and slow. Mother's hand smoothed my hair, and I closed my eyes, floating . . .

The blaring sign-off of the evening news awakened me, and I sat up, wondering if the scene in my mind was a memory or just something from my imagination. The sensation of my mother was so close and so real that I could almost smell her Chanel perfume, just faintly in the air. It made me feel warm and grounded, as if I had found an island amid a sea of mental conflicts.

Switching off the television, I walked through the house turning off the lights until only the one in the kitchen was left. I didn't want to think about anything. I just wanted to go to bed and forget that Christmas was only a few days away.

As I turned out the light in the kitchen, I noticed that Grandma's flowering plant had reappeared on the table. Beside it, the wildflower book waited for me. Running my fingers reverently over the pressed flowers on the cover, I looked around for Grandma. As usual, she was not to be found, and it was as if the book had appeared by itself.

Lifting the cover, I settled in a chair and read the first words.

Blooming, it said, the word written in a steadier hand than Grandma's usual. The title made me stop to look at the flowers—tiny, bell-shaped blooms hanging in clusters like dresses waiting for fairies to slip into them and dance.

I turned my eyes back to the words, whispering as I read, as if the flowers could hear.

As a child, I could not understand the unfair nature of my world. As I grew, injustice seemed to grow with me. My father was called to war, and we children were left cold and hungry. In his absence, a baby boy was stillborn in our home, and my mother's heart was broken. Ever after, she was fearful and sad, and taken with spells that made her unable to care for my young brothers and sister. My time, and what money I could earn, were taken from me to care for the younger ones. I was proud of my ability to help, yet bitter about my sacrifices. I was angry with my mother for not seeing that I, too, was still a child. I felt as if I were invisible to her. When my father returned, I felt as if I had disappeared from her eyes altogether.

At the school fair the year my father came home, I ran in the girls' footrace and won the prize of fifty

*cents. It was the greatest accomplishment I could re-
member in my life, and more money than I had ever
been given for myself. Passing by the store, I was
tempted by the things I could buy, but my desire to
show my prize to my mother was greater. When I
reached our farm, I bounded into the house like a
spring lamb, anxious to show my prize and gain her
admiration. Yet when I told her of my triumph, she had
no joy for me. She took the coin from my hand and put
it in the jar, saying winter was coming and the young
ones would need shoes and coats. I do not know why
she was so hard with me, but even so many years later
the memory is like a stone in my heart.*

*I fled the house that day in anger and hid beneath
the lilacs by the garden wall. My father came to me
there, and together we sat surrounded by the heady
scent. Cradled in his arms, I cried out my anger at my
mother and my sadness with my life. I wanted him to
change our lot, to change my mother's heart, and to
make her well again. I wanted him to give me a life in
which I could have hope and joy.*

*There was great torment in his face as he rested his
head against the garden wall and stared at the branches
stretching skyward above us, crowned with fragrant
blooms.*

*"This lilac tree is too beautiful for this old garden,"
he said sadly. "It should be growing in front of a fine
home where people would water and prune it, and cut
the flowers to put on a long dinner table."*

*I did not speak. I only looked at the strong branches
above us and watched the flowers sway in the breeze
like purple lace. I imagined how they would look on a
fine dinner table. I felt my father take my small hand in
both of his and kiss my fingers, then hold them near his
heart. Looking at him, I saw tears in his eyes.*

*"But God planted this tree here," he whispered. "It
would do no good for it to wither because this soil is*

too hard and this place too common. God gave it the
ability to be fine and full and beautiful, but not the abil-
ity to go somewhere else." Laying my hand in my lap,
he dried the tears from my face. "We are like this lilac
tree. We cannot change where God has put us. If we are
to bloom at all, we must bloom where we have been
planted."

Closing the book, I set it beneath the flowers, then just sat there with my head in my hands. Finally, I wrapped my coat around my shoulders and walked onto the porch, looking at the farm below, bright in the glow of the rising winter moon.

This was the soil into which we had been planted. We had made it bitter, filled it with anger and resentment so that nothing could grow here. But it wasn't the farm we were destroying—it was ourselves. We were rooted here like Grandma's lilac bush, tied to this place, this family, one past. The soil was not going to change. If we were to bloom, we would have to change.

Yet, I didn't know how to begin. The anger and the resentment were as natural to me as breathing. Without them, I didn't know who I would be.

The door opened behind me, and I glanced over my shoulder as Ben came onto the porch with a blanket around his shoulders. A sense of comfort floated through me at not being alone anymore.

"It's getting cold," he said, slipping behind me and wrapping his arms and the blanket around me. The warmth felt good against the winter chill.

Leaning against the solidity of his chest, I closed my eyes. "Christmas will be here before we know it." And all the questions that needed to be answered. I couldn't keep them inside me any longer. "Ben, Grandma is never going to agree to go to some nursing home with Aunt Jeane."

He rested his chin on the top of my head. "Calm down, Kate. No one has even talked to her about it yet."

"She's been talking to me about it ever since we got here," I told him. "Not in so many words, but she's been letting me know how she feels—what is important to her. She won't leave. She shouldn't have to. It isn't right."

He sighed, his breath tickling the stray strands of hair on my cheek. "It's never right when people get old and can't take care of themselves. Hard decisions have to be made."

"But not yet," I pleaded, searching desperately for some solution. "We could stay a while longer. I can take up to six months' unpaid family leave. By then maybe she'll be feeling better, or Aunt Jeane will be off school for the summer, and she could stay a while. And by then Joshua will be through his six-month checkup, and we'll know more about his heart, and . . ."

"Slow down a minute." Ben's voice was calm, slightly patronizing, as if I were engaging in hysterics. "The last thing I heard, you and Grandma were one step short of a fistfight and you couldn't wait to get Christmas over with and get back home. I go away for a little while, and you've done a complete U-turn. You want to explain to me where all this is coming from?"

"I can't explain it." I watched the rising moon, large and amber on the horizon, creeping up as if it were too heavy for the sky. "I know it's not logical, Ben. I do. But it's the way I feel. I think it's wrong to drag Grandma away from the farm when everything she loves is here. I don't think she'll survive it. And I don't feel right about leaving Joshua while he's still so little and he hasn't even made it through his six-month checkup with the heart specialist. I just want to wait a little longer."

"Well, Kate," he began, and I could tell by the tone of his voice that he was going to give me a reality check.

"You don't know if the family is going to agree to this. Your dad and Aunt Jeane pretty well have their minds made up about the nursing home. Even if they go for your idea, I don't see how we can get by financially for three or four more months. We're about to go under now."

I rushed on, feeling suddenly desperate to make him see. "We could make it work, Ben. We could sell the boat and get rid of the golf membership, cut off most of the utilities at our house while we're gone, or maybe Liz would stay there and rent it from us. If we had to, we could take a loan against the retirement fund. One thing about being here, we don't spend any money on eating out and entertainment."

Ben gave a quiet, rueful laugh. "Because there's nothing to do here."

I laughed, too, relieved he wasn't rejecting the idea completely. "Well, you know, the best times in our life together were when we didn't have the money for all this . . . stuff. Remember when we first came to Chicago, and we lived in that old apartment building? We used to sit up on the roof with the couple from across the hall and play records and dance?" I sighed, wondering how we had come so far up in income and so far down in the things that really mattered. "Those were good times, Ben. We weren't always in such a rush. It would be nice to take a break and just have some"—I couldn't think of a word for it, so I finished with—"time."

He was quiet for a minute; then he took a deep breath and said, "Do you realize you're talking about trying to scrape by on half of what we're used to?"

"I know." I tried not to sound as shaky as I felt. "But we'd be getting rid of the payments on some stuff."

"Mostly *my* stuff," he reminded me, but he didn't sound angry about it. I wondered if he was taking the discussion as seriously as I was. He almost seemed to be joking now.

"Who knows?" I said, not willing for the discussion to end so frivolously. "We might learn to like the simple life. At least think about it."

"I will," he said quietly, and we fell silent. I gazed overhead at the Milky Way, never visible in the neon-bright city sky. Here on the farm, it was as clear and white as the dust of crushed pearls. The sky was filled, every inch, with stars and constellations that once guided sailors as they traveled to new worlds. I wished it were that simple for Ben and me—just read a map and suddenly we would know where we were meant to end up and how to get there. But growing up is never that easy, no matter what age you are.

I wondered if Ben was thinking about it also. I wondered if he was considering what our life might be like, what things we could change, what our options were. I wondered if he was realizing that there was something better out there, if we could only find our way through the maze of everyday problems. . . .

The touch of his lips on the back of my neck told me otherwise. As usual, we were thinking in two completely different directions. The featherlight sensation of his fingers running over my thighs brought me into his.

His voice was throaty and passionate in my ear. "How'd you like to make love to a poor boy?" It was an old line he hadn't used on me in years—the same one he'd used the day he came home from physics class and asked me to marry him—right then. *How'd you like to marry a poor boy?* My mind rushed back in time. . . .

I felt my body quicken in response. "I don't know. Is he good-looking?"

"Very," he whispered against my shoulder, his fingers loosening the buttons on my shirt. "And smart."

"Is he tall?" The words trembled from me in a gasp as

the chill of the night air and the warmth of his hands touched my skin.

"Really tall."

I turned slowly in his arms and slid my hands into the silky darkness of his hair. "What's his name?"

His blue eyes twinkled brightly in the amber moonlight, and I remembered all the things I loved so much about him. "Zorro."

"Mmmmm, *mi querido*," I whispered, the only words of Spanish I knew: *my beloved.* "Take me away, Zorro."

Just as he had on the day we got married at a little chapel down the block from our college apartment, Zorro swept me into his arms and carried me to our bedroom. Only this time Zorro paused just beyond the bedroom door. Instead of kicking it shut, he closed it quietly, so as not to wake the baby.

Chapter 9

AUNT Jeane and Uncle Robert didn't arrive until almost noon the next day. Grandma had been pacing the floor for hours, describing all sorts of scenarios as to what might have happened to them on the road. When they finally drove in, both of us were overjoyed.

Aunt Jeane was the closest thing our family had to a rock. She was solid and steady—the same for as many years as I could remember. She'd never been able to have children, but had been a devoted fifth-grade teacher for thirty years. She had been a perfect aunt to my sister and me, sending us special presents on our birthdays, sewing Halloween costumes and ballet dresses. She lived about a half-day's drive from the farm, but always made the trip to see us when we were in Hindsville.

After we exchanged the initial greetings, Uncle Robert wandered off to the living room to read the paper while Grandma, Aunt Jeane, and I sat at the kitchen table over coffee. Aunt Jeane put Joshua on her lap and cooed at him until he started to laugh.

We talked for a while about the unusually mild weather, and the details of Aunt Jeane's trip up, and how pretty the Christmas decorations looked in the park in Hindsville.

"We need to get to work around here. This place could use a little Christmas spirit," Aunt Jeane remarked, lowering a critical brow and looking around the house. "We should buy a tree and put it up. Mother, where are all the old Christmas decorations?"

Grandma pursed her lips and wrinkled her nose as if she had caught a whiff of something unpleasant. "The Christmas decorations are in that old trunk in the third-floor attic. But I don't want any store-bought tree, and it's too soon for a Christmas tree, anyway. We'll cut a cedar from the pasture on Christmas Eve, like we used to. A Christmas tree shouldn't come from town—it should come from the land."

Aunt Jeane nodded patiently. "All right, Mother. But how about if we get the other decorations out, so the house will look nice when everyone else gets here? It's been years since this place has been decorated for Christmas. It would be good to see all those old things again."

Grandma nodded. "Yes, now that I think about it, it would. Maybe some neighbors will see the lights and stop in. Back in my day, that's what folks did. Every night of the week before Christmas, folks kept a pot of cider or hot cocoa on the stove, and neighbors would just stop in and visit and bring Christmas cookies or loaves of bread. Then we would wrap up something for them to take home. Some nights we would go around and visit other folks' houses—maybe five or six in a night—and we would come home with good things to eat, or sometimes a little present for us children. We would ride the babies on our sled if there was snow ..." She sighed, looking out the window, seeming to drift into the past. "It doesn't seem right that there isn't any ..."

Aunt Jeane and I sat waiting for her to finish the thought; then we just looked at each other and shrugged.

"Well, how is teaching this year?" I asked finally. Aunt Jeane always had some funny story to tell about her fifth graders.

This time, she only looked down at her hands and shook her head. "One of my kids was removed from her parents by social services. I'll tell you, it's awful the kinds of families some of these children come from these days."

Grandma huffed, obviously put out at being left out of the conversation. She never liked having to share Aunt Jeane's attention. "Things are no different than they ever were. Only back in my day, there was no welfare agency to take care of people's problems for them, and we didn't air all our dirty laundry on television." She raised her lecture finger into the air. "When I was in the fourth grade, I had to miss most of the school year taking care of my mother." She lowered her finger as if she had forgotten why she was telling the story. "That was a hard time. Father was away fighting in the war, and mother lost a baby boy. She sat rocking hour after hour, crying for that baby and saying her heart was broken. It seemed like the world was coming to an end all around us. Oh, it was a bad time."

"Mother!" Aunt Jeane scolded in a tone so sharp it made me jump. "You're drifting off again. We all know that story, and there isn't any reason to tell it again now. It just makes everybody sad."

Grandma looked at Aunt Jeane for a moment, then lifted her chin, stood up, and walked toward the door. "I need to finish my article," she said, but I had a feeling she was hurt by Aunt Jeane's rebuke.

Aunt Jeane shook her head at Grandma, then sighed. "I'm sorry, Kate. I didn't mean to start up with her." She turned to me with an expression of monumental sadness. "I swear, she is getting more addled every time I see her. Half of the time she can't even carry on a conversation anymore. She gets halfway through a sentence and forgets what she was saying."

It bothered me to hear her complaining about Grandma. "She's just a little excited because you're here," I said, hoping to make her see that Grandma wasn't ready for Oakhaven Village just yet. "She's doing a lot better lately." *She hasn't flooded, burned down, or blown up anything in over a week.*

Aunt Jeane clearly wasn't ready for me to come to Grandma's defense. "I guess I'm just expecting too much. It's natural to be more impatient with your parents than with other people." She laughed. "Of course, after all those psychology classes, you'd think I would know better."

We laughed, and I considered telling her about Grandma's book, but I quickly changed my mind. I found myself hoping Grandma wouldn't tell her either. I wanted it to remain our secret.

"So, staying here hasn't been too hard on you and Ben?" Aunt Jeane asked.

"No. It's been a good chance to slow down and think about what's important." At least for me, it had been. "Ben was gone working most of the time. I'm hoping this break over Christmas will give him and Josh some time together."

Aunt Jeane narrowed her eyes like a hawk zeroing in on a target. "Where is Ben, this noon? I thought he would be here." The way she said it made her sound just like Grandma.

I pretended to be busy adding sugar to my coffee. The truth was, I was embarrassed and disappointed that Ben wasn't home to greet the guests. After last night, I'd hoped things were going to improve, but one call from a client at 7 A.M., and he was up and gone to the office first thing despite the facts that there was company coming, there were a million things to do, and Grandma was in a nervous snit. We had made love until late in the night and talked about old times, and I thought that meant we were reconnecting. I thought he would spend the morning with Josh, but Ben had barely seen Josh since he'd come home. I guess that fact hadn't even occurred to Ben.

"He's at his office," I said finally. "I was hoping he'd be back by now. He must have gotten tied up with something."

Aunt Jeane clearly smelled a rat. "You two having a fight, or something?"

"No." Which was true. "He got a call from one of his clients this morning, and off he went."

"And?" Aunt Jeane probed. I wondered why she was pushing so hard and if Grandma had told her about the problems between Ben and me.

Aunt Jeane laid a hand on my arm, and the next thing I knew, I was spilling the whole story. "I guess I'm just disappointed that it didn't occur to him to stay home and help get things ready here, or to spend a little time with Josh. You know, he hasn't even seen Josh in over two weeks, and it didn't occur to him to stay around this morning and put the client on the back burner for the day." I sighed, wondering if Aunt Jeane would think I was being petty and self-centered. "I understand that he's a perfectionist about his work. I do. I love my job, too, but it's not my top priority anymore. Just once in a while, I'd like us to come first with Ben. It seems he and Josh barely know each other. Josh hardly even notices when Ben comes into the room. That just isn't right, and it isn't fair to Josh."

Aunt Jeane quickly put on her psychologist's cap. "Well, Kate, lots of men don't feel that child care is their responsibility. For years, society has been telling them they're good fathers if they make a good living and show up on Sundays for dinner. I see it all the time with kids at school. A lot of dads think they're doing their jobs because they make lots of money. Moms, too, for that matter. In the meantime, their kids are lonely and needy. They don't have anyone to go to, and they end up disrespectful and mad at the world. I'll tell you, things have changed in the thirty-six years I've been teaching."

"I don't doubt that." I could tell I was in a hornet's nest, so I started trying to back out. When Aunt Jeane got stirred up about something, she didn't quit easily.

She raised a finger into the air, looking frighteningly similar to Grandma. "I'll tell you, it isn't bad schools that are to blame for the problems kids have today—it's insufficient families and lazy parenting. People don't put their children ahead of themselves. You are right to think hard about your priorities, Kate. Do what you can to bring Ben around." Pausing, she looked at her finger, then slapped her hand over her mouth and started to laugh. "Listen to me. I sound just like Mother."

I burst into giggles because that was exactly what I had been thinking. "I guess it runs in the family." I motioned to Joshua, who was pointing his finger, trying to examine the buttons on Aunt Jeane's shirt.

We laughed some more, and Joshua squealed and waved his arms. Aunt Jeane bounced him, smiling and chattering. I was struck again by what a shame it was that she'd never been able to have children. She would have been a wonderful mother and grandmother.

"Speaking of family," she said finally, "have you heard anything from your father?"

I shook my head, feeling guilty, though I didn't know why. "I called and left messages twice, but I don't know if he's coming."

"If you called, he'll come. He's just staying away because he thinks you don't want to see him."

"Why would he think that?"

She dropped her chin as if she couldn't believe I was

asking. "Kate, you haven't so much as called the man in years. You didn't send him a birth announcement for the baby, or any pictures. You didn't call when Josh was born or during all that time he was in the hospital. Your father had to find out about Joshua's progress second-hand. What was he supposed to think?"

I stared at a warped board on the kitchen floor, feeling as if we were speaking two different languages. "What?" I muttered, trying to find reality. "Did he tell you all that?"

"He's really hurting over it." She skirted my question, but looked at me directly. "And you're hurting over it, and your sister is hurting over it, and Grandma is hurting over it. So am I. We've let ourselves fall apart these last few years. This family needs to put itself back together before any of us can be right again."

"I don't think it's possible to put us back together," I confessed. "I can't believe you even got Karen to come, but you can be sure she isn't coming here to kiss and make up." Karen blamed Dad for the fact that Mom was emotional and driving too fast when the car accident happened. A few Christmas cards had been the extent of my sister's contact with the family since then.

"She and James are putting in for time off so they can be here." Aunt Jeane's voice was steady—as if she were laying out a map of things to come. "That is a start. Have a little faith, Kate. Open your mind a little. You may be surprised."

Cold dread gripped my stomach, churning it like a boiling pot. "I wish I could." To hash things out with Dad and Karen was to go back to the event that began our separation.

Aunt Jeane stroked my hair just as Grandma sometimes did. "Kate, it's time. Six years have gone by. Have you even been to visit your mother's grave since you've been here?"

"No."

"Then it's time."

"I know." I thought about what Grandma had said. *It seemed like the whole world was coming to an end around us.* Why did I feel that way? Why did it seem as if gathering the family here would bring about something terrible?

I tried to push the answer into a dark corner of my mind and lock it away. But I knew. Gathering the family would bring back my mother's death.

And that was when the world had ended for all of us.

Aunt Jeane put her hand over mine as if she understood. "I know it's hard, but it's time we let go of all this grief. We can go to the cemetery now, while Grandma is busy in the little house." She looked hard at me. "Just you and me, all right?"

I nodded, and we quietly gathered our coats, slipped Joshua into his carrier, and left without telling anyone.

Looking at Joshua lifted my spirits as we made the trip to the family cemetery, which was on the back side of the farm on a hillside overlooking Mulberry Creek. For a hundred and thirty years, members of my father's family had been buried there. Legend said the site had been selected by his Cherokee ancestors because all four horizons were visible. Shaded by ancient oak trees and circled by a weathered iron fence, the cemetery had the feeling of sacred ground.

Aunt Jeane entered first, clearing overgrown honeysuckle vines away from the gate, then stepping inside. She went to the grave of my grandfather and lovingly brushed the leaves away from his side of the stone. She left covered the side that waited for my grandmother, as if to promise we would not need it soon.

Standing outside the fence with Joshua in my arms, I gazed at the hillside, remembering it filled with cars and people with dark umbrellas. So long ago, but yesterday in my heart. The grief was fresh and untouched.

Drinking in the cool afternoon air, I remembered further back—to a time when this was no more than an interesting place to play and a spot where we occasionally came with Grandma to put flowers on Grandpa's grave. I remembered a day when Karen and I read the ancient headstones, contemplating the fact that children were buried here, some only babies. The idea made us sad, and we went somewhere else to play. If you are lucky, you know a time in your life when graveyards are that easy to forget.

Rustling leaves announced my entrance into the graveyard. Aunt Jeane glanced at me, then went back to cleaning Grandpa's gravestone with a rag. I knew she wanted to let me make peace with my mother's death in private.

I walked forward and stood a few feet from my mother's grave, staring at the headstone and thinking of all the pain attached to it. Resentments rose like sludge dredged from the bottom of a riverbed. They mixed with sorrow and left a strange taste in my mouth. I was angry that she had died and left us in tatters, that with her went the last thread that stitched our family together. I was sad that she was gone, that there would never be another chance for us to talk, that she would never hold Joshua, or read him a bedtime story, or weave a chain of daisies for him. I was sorry that I had wasted so many chances to call her on the phone and just talk. I was bitter because we had let our lives go by in such a hurry that we never got to know each other.

I never again wanted to make that mistake in my life. Closing my eyes, I hugged Joshua to my chest and prayed that I would be there to care for him as he grew up, to cheer him on at Little League games and graduations, to kiss his cheek when he married, and to someday be a grandmother to his children. . . .

I was glad when the creak of the gate told me Aunt Jeane was ready to leave. Turning away from the stones, I walked to the car and climbed into the passenger seat, feeling numb.

She knew what I was thinking and didn't press me about my feelings. Instead, she concentrated on the living. "Your mother would have wanted us to do what we can to patch this family back together."

I sighed. "I know." *But I'm not sure it's possible.* "How long do you think everyone will stay?"

"A few days probably. Your dad might want to stay longer now that he's retired. He'll probably want to stick around and get to know this baby."

I scoffed bitterly at that, wondering if we were talking about the same person. He'd never been interested in getting to know his *own* children.

"Katie, you need to consider what is best for your son." Aunt Jeane's retort brought me up short. "It isn't right to keep him from his grandfather because *you* are angry. Yes, you will make an empty space in your father where Joshua should be, but you will also carve a hole in Joshua where his grandfather should be. As he grows up, he will feel that he was not good enough to warrant his grandfather's attention. *Your son* deserves to know the love of his family."

I nodded, feeling ashamed. Aunt Jeane had Grandma's way of putting you in your place.

Looking out the window, I felt the essence of my mother around me, like a spirit. Silently, I promised I would do everything possible to heal the family and to keep the farm. I knew that was what she would have wanted. The farm was the one place in the world where my mother really seemed to be at peace.

I took a deep breath and told Aunt Jeane what I was thinking. "Since we're talking about family, I want to say something about Grandma."

Aunt Jeane gave me a strange sideways look as we pulled into the driveway of the farm. "All right."

The car crept closer to the house, and I could see Grandma standing on the porch watching us curiously. I hurried with what I had to say. "I think you and Dad are wrong in wanting to move Grandma Rose to a nursing home. She doesn't want to leave the farm."

Aunt Jeane's mouth straightened into a stubborn line that reminded me of Grandma's. "Kate, don't let her play on your emotions. I know she doesn't want to leave, but the fact is she can't live here alone anymore. She's a danger to herself, and she can't even drive anymore. If anything happens, she'll be trapped here alone. This move is for her own good."

I straightened my shoulders, trying not to feel like one of Aunt Jeane's fifth graders. "I'm not letting her play on my emotions. I'm not stupid, Aunt Jeane. I know she's trying to manipulate me, but I also understand some things I didn't before I came here. This farm is her heartbeat. She won't leave willingly. If you force her away from here, you'll be killing her."

Aunt Jeane turned to me, looking surprised and wounded. "I'm not trying to hurt her, Kate, but there isn't any other way."

"Ben and I can stay a few months longer," I rushed on, though I knew I shouldn't offer without talking to Ben again. "I'm not ready to go back to work yet anyway. We've figured out some ways we can cut our expenses for a while."

Aunt Jeane stared at me, openmouthed, clearly shocked by my offer. "And after that?"

"I don't know," I admitted. Glancing out the window, I saw Grandma advancing on the car and I knew we had to end the conversation.

"It isn't fair to you and Ben to . . ." Aunt Jeane

stopped in midsentence, jumping in her seat as Grandma opened the car door and stuck her head in.

"You should have told me you were going for a drive," she complained. "I might have come along."

Aunt Jeane just shrugged and climbed out of the car. "You were busy on your article. Besides, we only went to the cemetery. I'll take you back this evening if you want to go."

Grandma stepped away from the door, nodding at me with a profound expression, as if she knew how much the trip meant. "No. I was out there last Sunday. I can wait a while longer." As I walked around the car, she laid a hand tenderly on my shoulder and whispered, "Good for you, Katie. Next spring we can plant Mrs. Owens's flowers there. It is good soil."

Aunt Jeane looked at us, narrowing one eye suspiciously and tapping the knuckle of her index finger to her lips. She shook her head as we walked to the house. I had a feeling she thought Grandma had bewitched me and that I was in need of an exorcism.

When we stepped onto the porch, Grandma motioned us toward the front door. "Now, don't go in through the kitchen. The floor is wet in there and the front bedroom. I just finished mopping."

Aunt Jeane glanced at me and frowned with disapproval, then stood back with her arms crossed over her chest as we walked into the dogtrot. I could tell this was a test, and Aunt Jeane was waiting to see how I would handle it.

"Grandma," I said, "you know you're not supposed to be mopping. Dr. Schmidt said light exercise only."

Grandma slipped her hands into her apron pockets and pulled out a dustrag, shaking her head. "Well, the work *has* to be done." She sighed. "And with you so busy, and Ben gone all hours . . ."

I could tell she was in her highest state of martyrdom,

no doubt putting on a performance for Aunt Jeane, so I stopped her before she could go on. "But *you're* not supposed to do it."

Wringing the dustrag between her fingers, she pretended to feel guilty. "Well, after dust-mopping the rest of the house, I usually do wet-mop the kitchen."

"You mopped the whole house!" I gasped.

"It *had* to be done. That coffee boiler went haywire again and made a mess all over the kitchen." She sighed in a voice that sounded as if it were drifting from her deathbed. "That mess gets on there, and it gets ground around by everyone's feet. The finish will become scratched, and we'll be paying to refinish the floors."

Clearly, I was supposed to be grateful that she had sacrificed herself to save the floors. Instead, I was ready to choke her, whether Aunt Jeane was watching or not. Once again she had flooded the kitchen, and she didn't want to admit responsibility. "No digging up flower beds, and no mopping! *I* will do it. If your blood pressure goes any higher, Dr. Schmidt is going to put you in the hospital!"

Grandma gave absolutely no indication that she'd heard me. Instead, she wandered a few steps away and began nonchalantly dusting the knickknacks on a table. Her face was tilted stubbornly aside, as if I were no longer there.

"Grandma." I heard the word come from my mouth as if I were addressing a child, but I was too angry to care. "I *know* you can hear me."

She didn't say a word, but batted a hand beside her face as if I were an insect droning in her ear.

My temper went up three notches, and I gritted my teeth to keep from losing it completely. Things had already gone too far, and it wasn't doing my blood pressure or Grandma's any good. It wasn't helpful that Aunt Jeane was seeing the two of us at our worst. Taking a deep breath, I lowered my voice. "Let *me* do the floors from now on. Your face is all red. You need to go sit down and rest."

She stood for a moment, then turned and shuffled away, muttering, probably not to me, about finishing her Sunday school lessons.

Shifting Josh onto my hip, I called after her as a peace offering, "Do you need me to drive you to town later so you can turn in your article?"

For just an instant, she stopped, and it looked as if a treaty might be signed. With a *humph* that was audible across the room, she continued on, calling back to me, "*Oliver* will come for me."

Watching her disappear into the back room, I knew I had no future in diplomacy. I had succeeded in getting her away from the mopping, but I was now lower on her list than old Oliver Mason. And I had, most certainly, not impressed Aunt Jeane.

Aunt Jeane just sighed and shook her head. "My point exactly, Kate." She uncrossed her arms and watched Grandma go. "She is just impossible these days. She's lost her mind. Why in the world would you want to subject yourself to that?"

Looking at the doorway where Grandma had disappeared, I shook my head, wondering if I was out of my mind, too. "I don't know," I said, because I couldn't possibly explain the way my feelings had changed since I came to the farm. "I just know it's the right thing to do." I couldn't find the words for everything that had happened over the past weeks, and I didn't want to. "After I feed Joshua, I'm going to town to see what's keeping Ben," I told her. But the truth was, I just wanted to get out of the house and clear my head. I was starting to feel as if I was crazy and everyone else in the family was sane.

I needed a reality check, so I called Liz at work. It was

good to hear the receptionist answer. For just an instant, I had the sensation of being back home in Chicago.

"Hi, Andrea," I said. "This is Kate. Is Liz in the office today?"

"Well, hi, Kate!" Unfailingly enthusiastic and perpetually cheerful, Andrea could talk faster than any person I had ever met. It was a running joke around the office. "We haven't heard from you in a while. How's everything going out there in the boonies? How's your grandmother? Is she feeling better? John Ducamp called earlier today and wanted to talk to you. He wouldn't let me put him through to Dianne. He said he wanted to talk to *you*. I sent you an e-mail. Did you get it? I hope he's not going to withdraw his support. You know, that audit thing came out in the paper, and it's made a mess of things around here, but I don't know if that's what Ducamp called about. He said he'd be out of town for a few days, but you could call him next week."

Andrea paused for a breath, and I quickly cut in. "I'll call his office and leave a message that I'm trying to get in touch with him. In the meantime, tell Dianne not to worry about it. I know Mr. Ducamp pretty well. I'm sure I can reassure him that nobody's mismanaging from his endowment. Great, this is just what we need at the end of the year." My head started spinning with office business, and I almost forgot why I had called. "So . . . is Liz in the office today?"

"Oh . . . ummm . . . no, she's downtown. She's down working on the stuff for the audit. I can page her for you."

"No. Don't bother." I suddenly felt like an idiot for calling in the middle of a workday to talk about my grandmother. The past weeks had turned my brain to Jell-O. I always hated it when people interrupted my workday with personal business, and now I was the one interrupting. "I can talk to her later." But I probably wouldn't. The fact was that she couldn't possibly understand, anyway. She didn't know Grandma, and she didn't know the farm, and she hadn't read Grandma's book. Liz was in another world—one where things were mostly black and white. In my family, there was nothing but gray area. All the normal guidelines were a blur.

"... all went down yesterday and looked at the Christmas trees, and watched everybody skate on State Street ..." I realized that Andrea was still talking. "The trees are positively gorgeous this year and all the decorations are amazing, better than last year. They must have about a million lights down there on the buildings and in the trees. Too bad you're not here. Yesterday, the Vienna Boys' Choir was in town performing, and they were just wonderful. We listened to the concert while we ate lunch, and we were saying that you would have liked it."

"Sounds like I would have," I said, picturing all that she was describing and suddenly feeling as if I were back home, where things were safe and uncomplicated. "So, did Mr. Halsted send everyone free tickets to *The Nutcracker* again this year?"

Andrea laughed, and the sound strengthened my memories of home. I could remember that giggle echoing through the office at least a dozen times each day. Everyone said it carried like a bugle. "Yes, he did. We went last Friday, and it was too fun. Dianne, Liz, Kristen, and I shopped at Bloomingdale's last week for dresses, but you know Liz was the only one who could afford a dress there, so the rest of us just scrounged. I wore last year's. I figured nobody would know the difference. Besides, I was pretty happy to know it still fit. Anyway, the ballet was great, and Halsted had the whole section again. Paul even went this year."

"Wow," I muttered, trying to picture my boss, a died-in-the-wool analytical type, at the ballet. "I'm sorry I missed that. It would be good to see him loosen up a little bit."

Andrea giggled again, then whispered into the receiver, "He claimed he didn't enjoy it, but he was swaying with the music all the way through. I think he's a frustrated ballerina."

That made me laugh out loud. "Now I'm really sorry I missed it." A strong twinge of homesickness pinched me unexpectedly. I felt like a kid left out of the playground games.

"Well, we thought about you. I took some pictures. I'll send you some . . . Oh, well, I guess no point in that. By the time they get there, you'll be back from vacation."

I didn't reply, just sat silent, wondering where we would be when Christmas was over, and thinking that my time at the farm seemed more like a life event than a vacation. It was as if I'd been gone from Chicago for months. . . .

"Oops, the other line's ringing." Andrea's voice cut short the silence. "It was good talking to you, Kate. I'll let Liz know you called."

"Good. Thanks."

"We sure miss you around here."

"I miss you guys too. It was good talking to you, Andrea."

Good didn't describe it. It was an experience in altered reality, a temporary teleportation back to Chicago. " 'Bye."

I hung up the phone, keeping my eyes closed for just a minute, pretending I was on the other end of the phone shopping at Bloomingdale's and watching the skaters on State Street. I had a strange sense of missing all the things that a few moments ago I had thought didn't matter.

I felt a little like a wishbone in a tug-of-war. Stay or go, town house or farmhouse, executive or stay-at-home mom, glitzy downtown Christmas or Christmas pageant in Hindsville, ballet or dancing on the front porch with Ben and Josh. Go home and let Aunt Jeane move Grandma to St. Louis, or stay and try to help Grandma keep the farm. Forget what I learned about her over the past weeks, forget I read her book, forget about the fragile things and the yellow bonnets and the times when the roses grow wild . . .

Or listen and try to change.

Sometimes life moves so fast, the road splits in an instant, and you only have a heartbeat to decide which way to turn.

Right or left . . . fast or slow . . .

My head started spinning again, so I gathered up Joshua, told Aunt Jeane good-bye, and headed for town to find Ben—just to talk, I wasn't sure about what. I wanted somebody to tell me I wasn't going crazy. That staying with Grandma for months wasn't an insane plan that would ruin us all. It seemed strange, because I'd been so sure a day ago. One dressing-down from Aunt Jeane, one argument with Grandma, and one phone call to Chicago and I was doubting it all. Maybe I wasn't as sure as I thought.

When I walked past the little house, Grandma was sitting on the porch, huddled over a meal of Dinty Moore straight from the can. Undoubtedly, the cold stew was intended to make me feel guilty for driving her from the big house—and it worked.

"We're headed to town to see what's keeping Ben." I stopped on the path and held Josh up like a peace pipe. "These are the little booties you made for him. Aren't they cute?"

"Y-yes." A feeble voice and one squinty eye rose from the can of Dinty Moore. "Don't let me trouble you. You go on about your business. I'll be fine." She huddled over her lunch and looked at me no more, her aged hands barely able to raise the spoon to her lips.

Swinging Josh onto my hip, I vacillated in place a minute, then decided to try one more time. "Are you sure you don't want to go with us?"

Setting the can on the table next to her, she looked forlornly down the driveway, and I knew I was playing right into her hands. "No." She gave a terrible sigh. "I'll ride with Oliver."

"We'll see you later then," I muttered, giving up. I wasn't sure what she wanted me to say, anyway. I certainly wasn't going to apologize for trying to make her follow her doctor's orders.

I just walked away and left her there, sitting round-shouldered in the rocking chair, gazing down the driveway looking sad and lost. She was still there, in exactly that position the last time I checked over my shoulder as we drove away.

I wondered if the expression wasn't completely contrived.

Driving the winding road to town, I thought of how it must feel to be unable to do the things you'd done all your life, how frustrating it would be to have to ask for help when you were accustomed to doing for yourself—as if you were a child again, only as a child you know you'll grow out of your problems. For Grandma, the problems would only grow larger, the list of forbidden activities longer, the need for help greater. She was like a prisoner in a cell with the door slowly being boarded shut.

Rage against the dying of the light.

Now I understood those words. Grandma was angry with the passage of time more than she was with us—frustrated with her own body, and the fog in her thoughts, and her doctors telling her what to do, and her children trying to take away what was familiar.

I thought about her as I wound down the hill into Hindsville. I thought about how many times she must have descended that hill over the years, in the old Buick, in Grandpa's old farm trucks, in a horse-drawn wagon before that. I thought about how familiar and comforting that view must be to her—the same town, the same gazebo, nearly ninety years of memories. Her feelings for Hindsville and the farm had to be so much stronger than mine for Chicago. Hindsville was the backdrop for her entire life. Chicago was little more than a ten-year career for me, some friends, and a sterile west-side town house that still didn't have pictures on the walls or furniture in the dining room.

The two places didn't compare. If I felt homesick for Chicago, how would Grandma feel when she was taken away from Hindsville—from the house with pictures on all the walls and furniture older than any of us?

My reasons for wanting to stay started coming back to me as I pulled into the church parking lot and took Joshua, sound asleep, from his car seat. I started feeling grounded again, rooted in family history and the familiarity of the place.

I touched the church cornerstone with my great-grandfather's name carved in, as I passed. This place not only held Grandma's history—it held mine. . . .

From somewhere inside, I heard Ben's laugh and Joshua stirred on my shoulder, then sighed and fell asleep again. Opening the door quietly, I saw Ben sitting on one of the benches in the lobby, talking to Brother Baker. I stood in the entry and watched them for a moment, surprised to see them laughing and conversing about basketball like a couple of old friends.

The sound of the door shutting caught their attention, and Brother Baker stood up, looking guiltily at his watch. "Well, I should have started on my home visits a half hour ago. How are you this afternoon, Kate? Oh, boy, look at that sleeping baby. I'll tell you, we sure have enjoyed having your husband around here. This church is too quiet most of the time."

I nodded, thinking that it would be nice to have Ben at home instead of hanging around town. "I could send Grandma by a little more often to liven things up."

Brother Baker laughed, then blushed red. "No, ma'am, that's all right. A little Grandma Vongortler each day is about all this old building can handle."

The three of us laughed.

"I'll tell her you said that," I joked.

Brother Baker turned another shade of red and shook his head. "I guess I'd better get going on my rounds before she shows up and puts me on the path of the righteous."

We told him good-bye, and he headed out the door, in an unusual hurry, I think, because he expected that Grandma Rose was right behind me.

Ben rolled his head from side to side, yawning. "Where's Grandma?"

"At home." I sat beside him on the bench, thinking that I should explain to him about the fight and why Grandma wasn't riding to town with me today. I knew she would be telling her side of the story to whoever would listen as soon as she got to town. "I made her mad and she wouldn't come to town with me."

Ben looked as if he'd just bitten into a sour persimmon. "What happened?"

The accusatory tone of the question put me on the defensive. "I caught her mopping the floors, and I told her to quit." I threw up my hands in frustration. "We got into a fight right in front of Aunt Jeane. If Grandma doesn't stop acting like that, they'll be shipping her off to the nursing home on the next boat. I'm telling you, she could outstubborn a mule!"

Ben thought that was funny. "You two should be a good match."

"Ben Bowman, you'd better wipe off that smile. This is *not* funny."

He cleared his throat and made a pathetic attempt to rid himself of the annoying grin. "Sorry. You're right. It's not." Reaching behind himself, he pulled a folded-up newspaper from his back pocket and dropped it across my knees. "But you might want to read your grandma's newspaper column before you lock her in the dungeon for being a crotchety old lady."

Confused, I picked up the four-page *Hindsville Register* with one hand while balancing Josh with the other. The paper was neatly folded to the Baptist Buzz, by Bernice Vongortler.

This year, the Lord has indeed blessed us with the most bountiful harvest I can recall. Looking out upon the wheat fields and the hay meadows, I am often reminded of how much things have changed in my sixty-odd years as a farm wife. I am brought in mind of progress when I see fields planted in the blink of an eye and harvested with the touch of a button. Steel arms and hydraulics have replaced the strong arms of men, and one man can do the work that once required neighbors to come together. Where once we needed one another, now we need no one.

I think of my first threshing season as a farm wife, of men in plaid shirts and soiled overalls cutting the wheat, of women in flowered cotton dresses and starched white aprons laying billowing red-checked tablecloths over yard tables, and I wonder if this modern way is better. Perhaps the Lord did not wish our harvest to be easy. Perhaps hard work was a gift to gather us together.

This brings me in mind of something that was recently brought to my attention. While many of us are sitting down to bountiful tables this Christmas day, there will be families and shut-ins in our midst who will not have even the most basic Christmas meal. I remember the young boy on the mount who gave his meager basket of bread and fish and found that it could feed thousands. I have been wondering if perhaps the Lord did not create this challenge so that friends and neighbors might come together to share from our own harvests so we might feed the souls and the bellies of the hungry in our community this Christmas day.

In this hope, the Senior Baptist Ladies' Group will be organizing a workday at the Church Annex building on Wednesday, December twenty-third, beginning after the lunch hour. All who would like to gather are welcome and should bring canned corn, cranberries, and dishes of dressing. Shorty's Grocery has graciously agreed to donate twelve turkeys in the hope that many Christmas meals can be cooked, packaged, and delivered by those of us who have been given the ability to do so.

As we gather on Wednesday, I know we old folks will be blessed with memories of threshings, barn-raisings, hayings-in, and holidays past. I believe it is good for us to share these experiences with the young people who drive today's tractors through the fields, reaping harvests in solitude, so they might understand what we once knew—that the volume of crops brought in is not the only measure of a harvest.

I sat staring at the paper for a while, then swallowed hard and cleared the tremors from my throat. "Now I *really* feel bad for picking on her."

Ben patted my knee sympathetically, chuckling under his breath. "You should. She's a saint and you're an ogre."

"She could turn a saint *into* an ogre," I joked, handing him the paper. "I don't think I'll ever figure her out. I guess I should smooth things over with her when she gets into town."

Ben gave me an evil sideways grin. "Aw, let old Oliver chase her around for a while. It'll put her in the mood to make up. Just get it all settled before the twenty-third so we can get in on some of that turkey dinner."

"Ben, you're awful," I said, and shook my head at him, wondering if perhaps he understood Grandma Rose better than I did.

Chapter 10

WHEN I found out why Ben had stayed so long in town, I felt doubly like an ogre for complaining about him to Aunt Jeane. Ben had spent most of the morning helping Brother Baker clean out a storage shed behind the church and, in the process, had ferreted out several boxes of Christmas decorations, which Brother Baker said he was welcome to borrow. He sparkled like a child with a new toy when he showed them to me and described his plans to decorate the farm for the upcoming holiday. Apparently, Aunt Jeane wasn't the only one who had noticed that the farm was lacking in Christmas cheer.

I caught a dose of Ben's high spirits as he struggled to carry an enormous box into the house. "Ben, what in the world . . . ?"

"Surplus from Christmas pageants past." He gleefully lowered the box to the kitchen floor. "Can you believe all this stuff was just sitting in the storage shed at church? Look. We've got lights." He held up a tangled mass. "Garland, life-size gingerbread men." Diving into the box again, he came up holding a felt tunic, and he fanned an eyebrow at me. "And an elf suit in case you want to dress up later."

The image made me laugh and blush. I looked over my shoulder to make sure we were alone in the kitchen.

"Dad's lost his mind," I whispered to Josh, setting his carrier on the floor so he could investigate a strand of glittering tinsel. "Grandma said there was a trunk of old Christmas decorations in the attic. Maybe we can get the house decorated and put Grandma in a better mood when she gets home from town."

Ben chuckled. "That would take some serious Christmas magic. She looked like she was about ready to slug old Oliver when they came out of the grocery store." He gave me an evil, sideways wink. "I think maybe he was getting a little fresh."

Aunt Jeane chuckled at Ben's joke as she entered the kitchen. "That poor man. She's always picking on him." She took Joshua and made goo-goo eyes at him.

"I wouldn't worry too much about old Oliver," Ben said. "He looks happiest when he's bothering Grandma V. I think it's a love-hate relationship both ways." Ben set aside the tangled lights and rubbed his hands together in anticipation. "So, let's go get the trunk out of the attic and see what's in the old Vongortler Christmas stash."

"You guys go on," Aunt Jeane said, holding Josh above her head like an airplane. "Josh and I will go sit in the living room with Uncle Robert for a while."

So Ben and I left Josh in the capable hands of his auntie and proceeded to the third-story attic, up a short flight of stairs at the end of the upper-story hall. I opened the door cautiously, peering inside as the overhead light blinked, crackled, and finally came to life.

The room looked as though a tornado had blown through, depositing empty wooden crates, old toys with wheels missing, a couple of bald baby dolls, chairs with broken parts, trunks with old clothes and quilts spilling out, lamps with torn shades, a dress dummy lying on its side like a headless Rip Van Winkle, and an old-fashioned shopping cart tilted on three wheels. A layer of fine dust covered everything, giving it the appearance of a faded still-life painting.

Ben looked curiously around the room. "What's all this?"

"Grandma's treasures," I said, moving aside a couple of hideous framed paintings of Spanish knights and unearthing the trunk marked CHRISTMAS. I remembered the old red steamer trunk from my childhood. "She never goes to the county dump without scavenging something. Karen and I used to think she was a little nuts."

Ben skewed a brow as if he agreed. "But all this stuff is . . . broken. It's junk."

"Not to Grandma." I dragged the trunk out of the corner. "Karen called it junk once, and both of us got a thirty-minute lecture on wastefulness and how people shouldn't throw away useful things just because they need a little extra care." The last statement made me think of Grandma's situation, and I felt a painful twinge inside me.

Ben met my gaze for just a moment, and I wondered if he was thinking the same thing.

He cleared his throat and grabbed the other handle of the trunk. "Well, let's get this thing downstairs and see what's inside." Closing the door as we left the attic, he took one more look at the mess and shook his head. "Hope the trunk's not full of bald angels and three-legged reindeer."

I chuckled as we lugged the trunk downstairs. "No telling what's in here," I said, suddenly fascinated by the possibilities. "I'll bet no one has opened this thing since the last Christmas we came to the farm. I think I was about twelve. There used to be some real family heirlooms in the Christmas trunk."

Ben and I set the trunk at the bottom of the stairs and

spent the next hour poring through the old Christmas decorations. The trunk was a time capsule of my family's history—ancient carved wooden ornaments initialed by my grandfather, a dangling Roy Rogers and Trigger that must have been ordered off a cereal box or soap flakes, an official Red Rider BB gun ornament that had probably been my father's, a tiny cloth angel with Aunt Jeane's initials stitched on the back, a glittered hickory nut made by my mother, a skinny Santa Claus my parents sent to Grandma from a trip to Germany, several homely macaroni angels crafted by Karen and me in Girl Scouts, and a handmade manger scene that Grandma once told me her father had made for her. All of us were there in that old trunk, frozen in time.

Ben and I strung artificial pine garlands in the dogtrot and along the stair banister, then hung the ornaments carefully on the garlands, where they could be removed and later put on the tree. As Aunt Jeane and Uncle Robert prepared supper in the kitchen, Ben and I stood in our bedroom doorway and surveyed our handiwork.

"These bring back a lot of memories," I whispered, looking at the ornaments again. I was sad and happy and tired all at once. "Christmas was always my favorite time of the year when I was little."

"It is for most kids." Ben flipped the light switch, and we stood in the twinkling blue glow of Christmas lights. "New bikes, new skateboards . . . new laptop computer with a ten-gig drive, high-res screen, and turbo processor . . ." He paused hopefully.

I chuckled at his joke, knowing there would be no new laptop computer under our tree this year. Then I went on reminiscing. "You know, for me the best thing about Christmas was that we were going to have a few days when no one was rushing off to be somewhere, and there were no baby-sitters coming to stay with us. Mom loved Christmas. She always made Dad take time off, and we'd decorate the tree and drive downtown to look at the lights. She got so excited looking at the decorations. I think she liked it as much as Karen and I did."

Ben slipped his arms around me from behind and rested his chin on my head. "That's the first time you've mentioned your mom in years," he said quietly.

I realized suddenly that he was right. "I guess I just sort of pushed her out of my mind. Maybe I've been pretending she's gone away to one of her symposiums, and she's coming back."

He held me closer, his arms like a warm blanket around me. "She isn't coming back, Kate."

"I know." It was hard to face that my mother and I had spent so little time together, even harder to face that my father was still alive, and I didn't even have the desire to see him. I wondered if I had ever felt love for him, or he for me. He was little more than a wax statue in my memory—a figurine present at birthdays, holiday dinners, graduations, and not much else. He had spent his life studying cells under a microscope, yet he was blind to the events going on around him. He was a paradox I could not understand.

His mistakes were mistakes I did not want to repeat.

"Ben, I don't want our family to end up like this," I said quietly. Stepping away from him, I walked into our room and sat on the edge of the bed.

He followed me and leaned against the dresser, looking confused. "Where is that coming from? I thought we were hanging Christmas decorations and having a good time."

"That's just it." I wished I could find the words to explain the sense of lost opportunity that gripped me. "Twenty years from now, I don't want Josh to be hanging Christmas decorations somewhere with his mind full of bitter memories and disappointments. I want him to remember good times—to remember us together as a family, to know how to build a family of his own some-day." I sighed, looking at Ben, who was looking at me with an expression as blank as the summer sky. "You don't build family memories by being at work all the time. We deserve more than the back of your head in front of a computer screen."

He rolled his eyes as if it were a tired subject. "It's a little hard to sit around bouncing a baby on my knee when I've got a business to build and bills to pay."

"I understand that." I felt surprisingly calm, yet determined, as if I knew I was on the right path this time. "But the fact is, there will always be more work that can be done, more contracts you can get, one more little detailing job for James. There are tons of things I could and probably should be doing for work right now. But at some point, you have to put it aside and get busy with the things that really matter."

Ben threw up his hands, looking helpless. "All right, I admit it. I'm just not very good with little babies. My dad never changed any diapers or washed any bottles. It didn't scar us for life. I think you're worrying too much."

I took a deep breath. Ben's family got along on the surface, but the truth was more complicated. "You've been complaining about your dad for as long as I can remember. He was never there. You never played football together. He didn't have time to help you fix your bike, your car, your curveball. He never attended your baseball games, your football games, the school play. All he did was struggle fifteen hours a day to build a business, and everyone in your family seemed to think that was acceptable. But you always felt the absence, remember? Don't you remember telling me that years ago? Don't you remember us talking about how life shouldn't be that way?" I raised my hands, pleading to be heard. "Why would you want to repeat that pattern?"

He tipped his chin up confidently, looking out the window as Oliver Mason's car drove up in the twilight. "It's not going to be like that with Josh and me."

I sighed, watching Grandma come up the walk. "At what point do you intend to step into Josh's life and make him your buddy? And what if, by the time you're ready for him, he has already given up on you?"

Ben just turned and stared at me, blinking, as if maybe what I'd said had finally gotten through to him.

The supper call came from the kitchen, and our conversation ended. Ben was unusually quiet during dinner and through the rest of the evening. He went to sleep that night without a word, turned toward his side of the bed, not seeming angry, just silent. I wondered what he was thinking.

I lay on my side of the bed, staring out the window at the heavy full moon, thinking about Ben and me—where we had come from and where we were now. Ten years ago, we had arrived in Chicago with nothing but a little secondhand furniture and a stack of college loans to pay. At the time, the most important thing was to get the best-paying jobs we could and bury ourselves in the business of getting ahead. All we wanted at that point in our lives was to pay off the college loans. When we had the loans paid off, all we wanted was a new car. When we had the new car, all we wanted was a house, then a bigger house, then a boat, a country-club membership, a baby, a family . . .

Maybe you should start wanting less. . . .

Maybe we kept wanting more because all the possessions in our lives were taking us further away from the one thing we started out with—peace. When Ben and I were in college, we had nothing, but we could sit and talk for hours. We could laugh together at the littlest things. We could share nearly everything.

Now, even when our bodies were together, our minds

were spinning ahead—to the next job site, the next round of bills to pay, the next meeting, the next fundraiser, the new house . . . Ben and I had everything, but not the time to enjoy any of it. The problem was, I didn't know how we were going to get off the carousel. It wouldn't do me any good to get off alone. We had to do it together.

I closed my eyes and tried not to think about it anymore. Maybe a few more months at the farm would give us time to reconnect. Maybe Ben felt the same deep need. Maybe that was why he was so quick to consider staying at the farm for a while. Maybe, even if he didn't know it yet, Grandma Rose's magic was working on him too.

But in the morning, he was gone and there was a note saying he had some things to do and would meet us at church for the service.

Grandma had insisted the night before that we would all attend the last service before Christmas, and nobody was getting out of it. I was surprised when Ben said we would go, without even asking me, but I knew he was probably right in agreeing. Grandma would have worked herself into a fit if we'd refused.

I knew Grandma wouldn't be happy to learn that Ben had gone to the office, but there wasn't much I could do about it, so I rose and dressed, then went to the kitchen, where Aunt Jeane and Grandma were already starting breakfast.

Aunt Jeane looked toward the doorway. "Where is Ben this morning?"

"Gone." I tried not to sound as embarrassed by his absence as I felt. "He left a note saying he had some things to do."

Grandma drew back, giving me a horrified look as she set a platter of pancakes on the table. "Well, I hope he won't miss service. We're having the nativity and the handbell choir. *Everyone* will be there. It would be terrible if he missed it. Everyone will ask where he is, and with him using the offices at the church, it won't seem right that he doesn't attend Christmas service."

"He said he would meet us there," I replied quickly.

She went on as if she hadn't heard me. "Now, don't forget Dell Jordan will be coming by to ride to church with us. I told her to be here at ten-fifteen and not a minute later. It isn't right to be late for service. Are you certain Ben knows what time to be there? You know, service begins at ten-fifty, not eleven o'clock. If he comes at eleven, he'll be walking in late, and . . ."

"Grandma, he'll be there. Stop worrying." I sounded more sure than I felt. I hoped Ben didn't get tied up on his computer and forget to come. Grandma would never let us hear the end of it.

As the morning wore on, Grandma latched on like a hound on a bone. Her complaints made me feel even worse about Ben's absence. She fretted all the way through breakfast, getting out of her chair to check the driveway, speculating on what might be keeping him, asking me if he had taken dress clothes with him, or if I should bring some along.

I refused to check his closet and finally resorted to using one of her own lines. "Have a little faith, Grandma. He'll be there." *I hope* . . .

Grandma huffed an irritated breath and went to the car, where she sat for fifteen minutes waiting impatiently for the rest of us to finish getting ready.

Uncle Robert laughed when she started honking the horn. "Sounds like we'd better get out there before she goes into a conniption." He smiled at me as we walked out the door. "This is all Ben's fault, you know. He didn't stick with *the plan.*"

"Make sure you tell him that." I was only partly joking. "All I can say is, he'd better be there."

And he was, waiting at the curb like a valet, helping old ladies out of their cars and saying flattering things about their Christmas dresses. He had the whole over-seventy crowd giggling and blushing like a bunch of schoolgirls when we arrived. Grandma was no exception. He laid on a few compliments, and she instantly forgot that she'd been complaining about him all morning.

Aunt Jeane and I shrugged at each other, wishing we had that kind of magic.

Most of the congregation was gathered on the sidewalk enjoying the beautiful December morning. Standing in groups, they were laughing and talking, discussing what had been said in Sunday school, or how unusually warm the weather was, or sharing their Christmas plans.

We were barely out of the car when there was a knot of people around us, hugging me and Aunt Jeane, and telling Dell how charming she looked in the green daisy-print dress Grandma had found for her. Dell smiled shyly and clung to Grandma's hand as the senior ladies updated Grandma on the progress toward the upcoming workday and delivery of Christmas dinners. The ladies quickly kidnapped Joshua, passing him around and arguing about who would watch him in the nursery. He giggled as three of them gathered the loose children and whisked them off to the church annex.

The high sounds of childish voices drifted away, leaving only the low hum of adult conversation. I had a sensation of being at my mother's funeral. I was overwhelmed with the urge to run to the car and lock myself away.

Ben slipped his hand into mine as if he knew. "Been a while, huh?" he whispered. "Better get inside before lightning strikes us."

Taking a deep breath, I turned toward the door as the chimes rang overhead. I walked slowly forward, clinging to Ben as to a lifeline.

The chapel was as I remembered it—two modest rows of ancient oak pews solemnly facing the pulpit and choir box. Behind the choir box was the wide window to the baptistry, added long after the church was built, so that baptisms would no longer have to take place in the river. I stared long at the old stained-glass window above the baptismal pool, studying the colored beams of sunlight that reflected on the water and floated around the room like angels. There had been no sunlight on the day of my mother's funeral. Only darkness and a cold winter rain. I wasn't certain if that was reality or just the memory of my own pain.

Grandma patted my hand and shifted to put a pillow behind her back as the organ started playing. Standing with our hymnals, we sang "Love Lifted Me" and "Joy to the World." Beside me, I heard Ben's deep baritone and Grandma's high, thin soprano and Dell's light, sweet voice. The words of the song drifted through my soul, lighting the blackness within, taking away old pain. Closing my eyes, I heard the words from my childhood, heard my own voice singing like my mother's, Dell's singing like mine, Grandma's just as I'd always remembered it, crackling high above all the others. A wonderful sense of renewal filled me. Time passes, I thought, but memories do not.

I sat holding Ben's hand, feeling thankful that we were there together as we listened to the handbells play "Away in a Manger," and watched the children file in to complete the manger scene at the front of the church.

Afterward, Brother Baker took the pulpit and began a sermon on the humble birth of Christ and the greatness of God's gift to the world. It was a lesson I remembered from some childhood Christmas visit, spoken in exactly the same way now as then, same words, same inflections, same look of passion in Brother Baker's eyes. There was comfort in the fact that some things never change. It was as if the church had been waiting in suspended animation all the time I was away.

As the sermon concluded, Brother Baker gripped the sides of the pulpit, bowing his head for a moment as he always did, to give his message time to sink in. The silence was more powerful than the volume of the sermon.

The pause was uncustomarily short. Brother Baker took a deep breath but didn't look at us, and spoke almost in a whisper. "This week a young father came to me, confused about his role in the family. He was wondering what his duties were to his child and how he would know if he was fulfilling them. I can't tell you all that he said to me or exactly what I said in reply. I can tell you that he reminded me of myself when I was a young man. There were so many nights when I was busy with my ministry, or away on missions. My children grew up while I was doing other things, all of which seemed very important at the time." He paused, letting out a long sigh, then slowly raised his head and looked at us, his blue eyes glittering.

"I won't be with you this afternoon or next Sunday. My son, John, and my grandson, Caleb, have been put in the hospital after a car accident this morning. John will be going in for surgery this afternoon, and I ask that all of you remember him in prayer. I also ask that this afternoon you spend time with your own families. Young parents, hold your children a little longer today. Kiss them when you put them into bed tonight, say their prayers with them, sit by them while they fall asleep. Your children are the greatest gift God will give to you, and their souls the heaviest responsibility He will place in your hands. Take time with them, teach them to have faith in God. Be a person in whom they can have faith. When you are old, nothing else you've done will have mattered as much."

Tears clouded my eyes as he came forward to kneel with the church elders and pray. No one moved. We sat together and prayed.

When the service concluded, we walked forward to congratulate the children who had performed in the manger scene and to give Brother Baker our best wishes.

The line finally dwindled, and Ben walked Brother Baker to the side door. My mind drifted to the end of the sermon. *Your children are the greatest gift God will give to you, and their souls the heaviest responsibility He will place in your hands. When you are old, nothing else you've done will have mattered . . .*

I wondered if Ben had been listening, if the words would mean anything to him or make any difference. It seemed that he had come to like and respect Brother Baker. . . .

A breeze blew suddenly from the open door, lifting the papers on the pulpit. I glanced over just in time to see Brother Baker take Ben's face in his hands and lean his forehead into Ben's. In that instant, I knew Ben was the young father who had sought counsel.

The fears and doubts in my heart were lifted like the papers from the pulpit and gently cast away.

After the service, Uncle Robert treated everyone to lunch at the cafe. The mood there was subdued because of the tragedy in Brother Baker's family. People dining around us spoke quietly about how terrible it was for such a thing to happen at Christmas, and how it made you realize how fortunate you were to have all of your family together and healthy. Grandma said that sometimes the Lord showed us the suffering of others so that we might be thankful for our own blessings.

She looked at me when she said it, and I nodded with a lump in my throat. I looked at my husband and my son, at my family around me, and I was thankful.

During the drive home, Grandma discovered that

Dell's home had no Christmas tree, and that became her immediate source of concern. When we got to the farm, she insisted that we change clothes immediately and drive the old flatbed truck to the pasture, so that Dell could select a small cedar tree to take home with her.

The old flatbed truck hadn't been used since the last time Grandma's yardman hauled away limbs and trash, so Ben and Uncle Robert spent the better part of an hour getting it going. In the meantime, the rest of us sorted through the leftover Christmas decorations and lights so that Dell would have some to hang on her tree.

When we finally heard the truck rumble to life outside, Grandma had just brought out an ancient can of paint to show all of us how to make angels from fabric scraps and pecan shells, as she had done when she was a child.

"Well, it sounds like the truck is started and you'd better go," Grandma told Dell. Sitting at the kitchen table, she looked pale and tired, but well pleased. "The rest of you go on too. Aunt Jeane and I can stay here and finish these." She smiled at Dell, who smiled shyly in return. "We'll have them all ready to go home with you when you get back with your tree." Raising a finger sternly, she tapped Dell on the end of the nose. "Now don't select one too large. Children always make the mistake of picking a tree that is too large. It must fit in the house."

Dell giggled and nodded; then we hurried away as the truck horn honked outside.

Ben and Uncle Robert were waiting in the cab, looking happy with themselves. Dell and I climbed in the back, and we drove out to find a tree as the coming twilight put a chill in the air.

Darkness had descended by the time we returned with the perfect small cedar tree. Dell hurried to the house for her box of decorations, then climbed into the cab of the truck with Ben and Uncle Robert to take her tree home.

When I entered the kitchen, Grandma was looking out the window with an expression of satisfaction as she tried to wash the gold paint off her hands. "That will be a fine tree," she said. "Christmas trees are best when cut from the pasture and filled with handmade decorations."

"You're probably right, Grandma." I kissed her on the cheek, then stood beside her, washing the cedar sap from my hands. "Dell enjoyed that. It was nice of you to think of getting a tree for her."

Grandma let out a *humph,* as if the compliment offended her. "Every child should have a tree. No matter how poor we were, my father always made sure we had a tree and a kettle of homemade hot cider for Christmas guests." She sighed as the truck disappeared from view. "I wonder when your father will get here."

I stepped back and pretended to be busy drying my hands. "He hasn't returned my message yet. He must be gone on a trip somewhere." Setting down the towel, I turned to leave the kitchen. I was afraid that if she saw my face, she would know the truth. I was convinced that Dad wasn't coming. "I'm sure he'll call soon."

I left her there, staring out the window, because I didn't know what else to do. In the living room, I reminded Aunt Jeane in a low voice that my father still hadn't called, and perhaps she should call him. She looked up from the old photo album in her lap and told me she had already tried. Like my messages, hers had gone unreturned. She was certain he was away on a consulting job and would call soon.

I realized suddenly that Joshua was not in the room with her. "Where's Josh?" I asked, experiencing an instant of panic. Aunt Jeane nodded toward the stairs, the slightest smile curving her lips. "Upstairs," she said quietly. "He was one tired little fellow."

"Thanks for watching him," I whispered, as I sat beside her on the couch to look at the old photo album. Aunt Jeane flipped to the start of the book, and slowly we began turning the pages, laughing at old cars and old clothes as she told me stories about relatives who had died before I was born, ancient farm machinery, and the last team of horses on the farm.

"My daddy hung on to those horses for a long time after we had tractors." She sounded just like Grandma. In the amber light from the fire, she looked like Grandma Rose in the pictures.

"It nearly killed Grandpa to see those horses go," Grandma added as she came into the room. She sat on the other side of Aunt Jeane and touched the picture with trembling fingertips. "He kept horses for years after all the other farmers around here had given them up. Oh . . . and, Kate, your father wanted so badly to get rid of those animals. He was all for the newest machinery. Said it wasn't efficient to have those horses standing here eating when they weren't any use anymore. But Grandpa hung on. When the tractors would get stuck in the mud, he would smile at your father and tell him to go hook up the team, and here those horses would come, prancing across the field, so happy to have something to do. Grandpa would hook them on the tractor, and there they would throw themselves into the harness and pull the tractor right out. Grandpa would smile at your dad and throw his hands into the air and say how there were still some ways that horses were better than that new machinery." Throwing her head back, she laughed, her eyes cloudy with the mist of memories.

Aunt Jeane laughed with her. "My goodness, Mother. I had forgotten all about that." She shook her head, touching the edge of the picture. "Why did Daddy finally get rid of the horses?"

Grandma sighed and looked into the dying flames of the fire, her smile fading. "Your brother and I talked him into it. There was a man down the road with a small farm and not enough money for a tractor. He offered a good price for the horses and the horse-drawn implements. I could see where we needed that money, and I suppose your brother could see that he wouldn't have to take care of those horses anymore, and we just badgered your father until he gave in and let the man buy the horses.

"He was so sad about it, he wouldn't even stay here and take the man's money. He just went off into the field, and your brother and I harnessed the horses and hooked them to a cultivator. The man gave us his money and drove the horses away." Looking at the picture again, she shook her head, then turned the page. "I don't even remember what we did with that money, but I remember the look in your daddy's eye when those horses were gone. It just broke his heart, and he was never the same after." She looked slowly at me, and then at Aunt Jeane, her eyes filled with meaning. "Those horses may not have mattered to us, but they were his heart and soul, and he wasn't himself without them. Sometimes we forget what things are important to other people. I was never as sorry about anything I did in my life."

I swallowed hard and looked at Aunt Jeane, because I knew Grandma was talking about herself and the farm. I wondered if Aunt Jeane understood.

The baby monitor caught my attention, and I listened as Joshua let out a sudden cry, then quieted to a whimper. Finally I heard the hushed rustling of sheets.

"I'd better go check," I said quietly, and left the room hoping Grandma would find a way to explain her feelings to Aunt Jeane. I could hear them talking in low tones as I climbed the stairs.

As I stepped into the doorway of Joshua's room, the sight of the empty crib brought me up short, and I stopped in the doorway, scanning the room. The squeak of the rocking chair caught my attention, and I saw Ben rocking, head tipped back and eyes closed. Joshua was bundled on his chest, eyelashes dark against his cheeks and cupid's lips parted in sound sleep.

Leaning against the doorway, I hugged my arms around myself and watched in the dim window light, capturing details in my mind like an artist painting a portrait—the curve of Josh's hand gripping Ben's, the dark tan of Ben's skin, the pale pink of Josh's, the way Josh's feet were crossed under Ben's arm, the slow rise and fall of Ben's chest. I imagined I could hear their hearts beating close together—one slow, one quick, like a sparrow's.

It was a moment I knew would live with me forever.

I stood watching for a long time, then finally turned and left them to make up for lost time. I wondered, as I walked down the hall, if my mother had sat sleeping with me in that very chair, and if she'd known the sound of my heartbeat.

That night I went to sleep knowing that Ben and I and Joshua would not repeat old patterns. Curled with Ben in the bed, I imagined that I could feel the warm spot on his chest where Joshua had been, where their hearts had touched, and they had finally fallen in love.

Just after dawn, I heard the sound of Grandma moving in the kitchen. I could tell that no one else was up, so I got out of bed and went to check on her. The coffee had been made, but the kitchen was empty. Glancing out the window, I saw Grandma shuffling back to the little house carrying a platter of coffee cups. I wondered if, for some reason, she and Aunt Jeane were up early and having coffee out there.

Watching deer graze at the edge of the lawn, I poured myself a cup of coffee and reached for the sugar bowl, but it was gone. Looking around the kitchen, I spotted it on Grandma's Hoosier cabinet next to two loaves of homemade bread rising in milk-glass pans. Propped between them and the blue batter bowl was the wildflower book.

I glanced toward Grandma Rose's house before picking it up. I wondered how she knew I would find it there.

As before, the old story was removed and a new one written.

Broken Bread, it said.

I glanced out the window before reading the story.

I came to my marriage ill prepared to be the keeper of a fine house and a fine man. My husband did not know my shortcomings, and I was too proud to tell him of them. It was for this reason that he dismissed the woman who had for many years kept his home and cooked his meals. He assumed I would take on her duties. I was loath to tell him that I had no skill in caring for expensive linens, or cooking elegant meals, or baking bread. I did not want him to know the sort of existence from which I had come. I was afraid he would think me not worthy of being his wife.

Left in the house alone, I fretted and cried hour upon hour over cooking and housekeeping. At times, I set out platters of food even the farm dogs refused, and in tears, I washed the pans and began again to prepare a meal before my husband came in from the field. He was angry and critical when his meals were late, thinking that I wasted my day rather than tending to my work. He was angrier still that there was only fried bread on the table, not the fine yeast bread he was ac-

customed to. I was bitter and resentful to be treated so harshly when my body was weary from trying to please. Having no womenfolk around and no recipe to go by, I did not know how I was to learn to bake bread.

When he left in the mornings, I thought many times of taking my belongings and running away. Instead, I brought in the flour sack and struggled each day to create bread. Time after time, I threw my creations in the garbage and served fried bread with our meal. The flour sack, which should have lasted several months, dwindled in less than one. When I asked for more, he chastised me for being wasteful. How, he asked, could a woman who did not bake bread use fifty pounds of flour in a month's time?

I resented his censure so terribly that I could hardly look at him across the table and I dreaded going to his bed. I prayed that God would set me free from his domination.

When the next sack of flour came, God's answer came with it. Sewn into the binding was a paper with the ingredients and measures for bread.

Looking back these many years, I have often laughed at my youthful stubbornness. I suppose, had God not answered my prayer, I would have gone on being angry with my husband and he being angry with me, and our lives would have been wasted, as was that first sack of flour. What foolishness that was, I say to myself now! How wrong I was to resent my husband when I would not admit my feelings to him. How many hours and tears I could have saved if I had not been ruled by pride. Pride and resentment do not create bread that will rise. Bread, like a good life, can only be created by honest measure, patience, warmth, and time.

Closing the book, I propped it against the earthen batter bowl, smiling at the sweetness of the story. I wondered at its meaning and why Grandma had chosen to leave it for me now.

The sound of a familiar voice outside the door caught my ear, and suddenly I knew why Grandma was writing to me of patience and forgiveness.

My father had finally come.

Chapter 11

MY stomach turned over as I heard my father's and Grandma's voices outside the door. Stepping to the center of the room, I stood near the table, my thoughts racing. What should I say? How should I act? What would he look like after six years? Would he be alone or would there be a woman with him? Would he be glad to see me? What would he say? Would we be father and daughter, acquaintances, strangers?

The door opened, and we stood staring at each other for a moment. He looked older than I remembered, his hair almost completely silver now, his face etched with deep lines around his mouth that made him seem sad. In spite of that, his air of dignity remained—the neatly combed head of hair, the carefully pressed sport shirt and cotton slacks, the polished brown leather shoes, the expensive gold-rimmed eyeglasses.

It was hard to believe he had ever lived in Hindsville and easy to see why he seldom found a reason to come back.

"Hello, Kate." His greeting was the same as I remembered—stiff, almost a reprimand, as if he were making a mental catalog of everything about me that was not up to his standards.

I swallowed hard, gripping the back of a chair to keep myself steady. "Hi, Dad." Beyond that, I didn't know what to say. "I didn't know you were coming today." It sounded bad, so I added, "I didn't have a chance to get things ready for you."

"That's all right." His lips gave a hint of a smile that did not touch his eyes. "I didn't know I was coming myself. I had a consultation in Houston yesterday. I finished up late last night and decided to come here instead of flying home."

I nodded, wondering if he had gotten my messages and if they had anything to do with his coming. If they did, I knew he wouldn't admit it. "I didn't know you were still working much." It was the sort of thing you would say to an acquaintance.

He gave that emotionless smile again. "Retirement was too dull for me, I guess. I decided to take in consulting work from time to time. It gives me a chance to travel and keeps me from being idle."

"That's good." It stung me that he was bored at home, yet couldn't find time to come to Chicago to visit Ben and me, or to go to California to see Karen, or to visit Hindsville to keep Grandma company. Why could he find time to work, yet no time for us? Why should things be different now than they used to be?

Grandma closed the door, shuddering from the morning chill. "Mercy. It is too cold to have that hanging open. I'll tell you, it's starting to feel like snow. I hope it doesn't come a blizzard before Karen and James can get here. That airport was closed for three days last year. Maybe Karen and James should change their tickets and come earlier." She glanced at the phone as if contemplating calling my sister and ordering her to come before the blizzard hit.

"They'll be fine, Grandma." I pulled out a chair for her, attempting to distract her from the phone. "They'll be here on the twenty-third. They can't change their plans now." The last thing I needed was a week of Karen and Dad at each other's throats. Four days would be bad enough.

Grandma huffed at me, but sat down, motioning Dad to a seat beside her. "I just don't want anyone trying to come in the snow."

I rolled my eyes, moving to the coffeepot. "There isn't any snow, Grandma. The sun is shining and it's fifty degrees." I stood staring at the coffeepot, wondering what I was doing there. "Would anyone like a cup of coffee?"

"Oh, not me," Grandma answered quickly. "Jackie and I already had coffee out in my little house."

A giggle tickled my throat, and I faked a sneeze to keep from laughing out loud. Dad hated it when she called him Jackie. In years past, he had insisted that she call him Jack, and she had complied.

This time he let the slip pass. "Coffee would be good. Cream, no sugar."

I fixed a cup of black coffee and brought the creamer to the table. Nothing was ever done right unless he did it himself.

We sat silent, listening to the clink of his spoon against the china cup. Even Grandma seemed unable to think of something to say. The clock in the living room struck the hour, and I counted the chimes hopefully. Only seven o'clock. I wondered how I was going to last through a day, much less a week, of tiptoeing around trying to think of something nonconfrontational to say.

Dad looked up from his coffee. "Well, how has Hindsville been treating you?"

"Very well," I blurted out, not wanting him to have the satisfaction of thinking he was right in saying we shouldn't have come. "We're glad we decided to come. It's been good to get away and have some time with Joshua. We're enjoying the peace and quiet." *In fact, we were thinking of staying longer.* "It makes me hate to think about going back to Chicago."

Dad squinted hard, as if he doubted what I was saying. "Well, that's hard to believe. After all the advantages you girls were accustomed to, growing up, that you would find Hindsville so appealing . . ." He paused, perhaps because blood was flooding into my face. Finally he said, "It's unfortunate that you've had to miss all of this time from work."

I stared at him, feeling defensive, my temper hot in my throat. "I have a very capable assistant." Who was practically taking over my job, and probably would if I didn't get back soon. "Besides, Ben and I needed some time with Joshua. Family *is* the most important thing, after all. At least it *should* be."

My father shrugged as if he didn't get my point. "Yes. Unfortunately, family leave isn't looked on favorably by employers. That is the reality of the world we live in." He tapped his spoon crisply against the side of his cup, looking completely nonchalant about the conversation, as if he hadn't an inkling that he was dancing all over my toes.

Grandma sensed World War III coming on and stepped in like Switzerland. "Katie, did you see my bread rising this morning?" she said.

I shook my head, taking a moment to register what she said. "Yes, I did." Her meaning registered also.

"Why don't you put it in the oven?" she suggested.

"All right." I put the loaves in the oven, then stood there trying to figure out what to do next. I felt as if I was onstage and my father was waiting for me to mess up my lines. I could feel him watching me, criticizing my choices, thinking what a waste it was that his college-educated daughter found a reason to enjoy time at the farm. I wondered if he suspected we were thinking about staying in Hindsville, or if Grandma had been filling him with her ideas about us moving into the farm-house. I had a feeling there was more to their earlier coffee conversation than met the eye. Grandma was wearing her wooden-Indian look and Dad was on the attack.

"I guess I'd better get Joshua," I said, desperate to escape the kitchen. "He was in bed early last night, so he should be waking up about now." I hurried from the room, making as much noise as I could along the way, so everyone else would get out of bed, and I wouldn't be trapped alone with Grandma and Dad.

As I lingered upstairs with Joshua, I heard Aunt Jeane and Uncle Robert getting up, and I silently thanked God for the reprieve. I knew Aunt Jeane would step into the empty spots in our conversations, and Uncle Robert would provide his usual calming influence. Ben would find something to talk to my father about, as he did with everyone, and things would probably be reasonably tame for the next few days until Karen arrived. Then disaster was sure to follow.

My father's demeanor had softened by the time I came down with Joshua. The rest of the family had assembled at the table, and Ben was amusing everyone with a description of the Knicks game.

My father smiled when I sat Josh in my lap to burp him. "Well, hello there, Joshua. Aren't you a big boy?"

Joshua watched him intently for a moment, then smiled back, milk drooling down his chin. By the time he had finished his bottle, he had a face only a mother could love. He and Dad were playing peekaboo over and under my arm. It made me laugh in spite of the fact that my father was sitting just over my shoulder.

I heard Dad chuckle also, and I felt a twinge of petty jealousy. Some part of me felt as if he did not deserve Joshua's attention.

I finished feeding Josh and set him in his carrier as I

stood up. "Well, I was planning to drive over to Spring-field today to do some Christmas shopping, so I guess I'd better get going." It was a lie, but I didn't care. I wanted to take Joshua away, to disappoint my father if I could.

I heard Grandma sigh as I rinsed my plate in the sink. "Oh, Katie, not today. Can't you stay home with us?"

I would sooner have driven pins under my fingernails, but I tried to effect a look of regret as I turned around. "I really need to go ahead and get it done. I have to go to the bank and deposit Ben's check, too. Our bank has a branch in Springfield."

Grandma's face fell like a basset hound's. "Well, at least leave Joshua here. We've hardly seen him, and it's no good dragging him around shopping. He won't get a decent nap."

"He sleeps great in the car." I ignored the annoying pang of guilt in my chest and lifted Joshua out of the carrier just as my father was picking up a napkin to continue the game of peekaboo. "He'll be fine."

Ben dropped his hands into his lap and wrinkled a brow critically at me.

"I suppose he will." Grandma stood and shuffled to the oven. "I'd better see about my bread. It should be done. Oh . . . shoot. It's gone flat on top. I guess I've forgotten how to make bread, just like everything else." She closed the oven, her look of sorrow monumental, her eyes glittering with moisture. I knew it wasn't the bread she was disappointed in. It was me.

I looked slowly from her to my father, surprised to see that his expression mirrored hers. Then I gazed into the eyes of my son—laughing, expectant eyes, innocent of the power play going on around him.

Something inside me turned a corner, and I said, "I'll get him dressed for you before I leave. Make sure he takes his naps today."

"We will," Grandma replied gleefully, peeking into the oven again. "This bread doesn't look so bad, after all."

Ben jumped up from the table and followed me to the door. "I'll go get dressed so I can . . . uh . . . ride to Springfield with you." He rolled his eyes as we walked out the door, letting me know he wasn't enjoying my father any more than I was. "Amazing how much of an expert he is on the architecture business," he muttered close to my ear. "He pointed out that I should be sticking with a firm instead of doing structural designs on my own, and I shouldn't take in detailing work because that's a draftsman's job, and it doesn't pay what an engineer deserves. He's pretty much of an expert on the architecture business in general."

"I'm sure he is," I replied under my breath as we parted ways at our bedroom door. "He's an expert on everything."

Ben chuckled, giving me a quick kiss, then kissing Josh on the forehead. "That must be why you're so smart." Ben had the most amazing way of seeing the humor in things.

"Very funny," I said. "Now is not the time to tell me I take after my father."

Wisely, he just grinned, shaking his head, and went into the bedroom to get dressed. I prepared Josh like a sacrificial goat, to be turned over to Grandma and my father. Lying on the bed in the corner of the room, he laughed and cooed and smiled at me as if to tell me he wasn't the least bit worried. I thought of him playing peekaboo with my father at the table, laughing and smiling at my know-it-all dad as if he were the most wonderful thing in the world. I wished I could be that open-minded.

I wondered when I had closed the door on my relationship with my father. I had vague memories of trying to win his affection as a child—drawing pictures for him and bringing home school projects or report cards. His reactions were never what I hoped for—just a quick acknowledgment of the good things and a honing-in on the things that needed improvement. Then a dissertation on how to make everything more perfect, including myself. Then he would end with something like, "But that's the best lopsided flowerpot I've seen. Next time try starting with a round ball of clay and perhaps it will be more symmetrical. It's very nice for a girl your age."

It doesn't take very many lopsided flowerpots before you give up trying and go your own way. It happened first with Karen and then with me. Dad never seemed to notice. He became more and more involved in his research work and maintained a long-term hope of turning Karen and me into medical students. When it became clear that wouldn't happen, we didn't have much left to talk about.

Mom ended up caught in between like a rubber band trying to hold a pack of cards together. No doubt she'd clung to her own sense of self-worth through work since our family life was such a shambles.

When the rubber band breaks, the cards fall and that's the end of the deck—unless someone comes along and needs to play cards. Then you have to start picking them up and putting them back in order. Right now, we needed to find some family unity. For Grandma's sake, and maybe for ours, too.

"It's a mess, Josh," I said quietly, pulling his sweater over his head. "What a mess."

Joshua knitted his brows, as if he understood the problem, then laid his hand over mine, met my gaze and gurgled a long sentence of baby talk. I smiled and kissed him and finished getting him dressed. Somehow, it's hard to feel like much is wrong in the world when you're looking into the eyes of a happy baby.

When Josh was dressed, I took him downstairs and handed him over to Aunt Jeane with a few instructions about feedings and naps.

She listened to the list, then handed him to my father and said, "Did you get that? This is your grandson. You and Mother are baby-sitting. I have some visiting to do around town today."

Dad sat there looking shocked, holding Joshua at arm's length.

I rushed forward to grab my son before he was scarred for life. "It's no problem. I can take him with . . ."

Aunt Jeane stood up and barred my path, then put her arm around my shoulders and guided me toward the door. "Things will be fine, Mommy. Stop worrying. Have a nice day shopping. Grandma and your dad can handle it."

"But I . . ." I glanced desperately at Ben, who was standing by the door.

"Go ahead." Aunt Jeane shooed me away as if I were a bothersome dog hanging around the porch. "You two have a nice time. Grandma can call me at Wanda Cox's if she needs me."

"Yes, that will be good," Grandma chimed in, giving me the bum's rush. "You go ahead. We'll be fine here with little Jackie."

If Dad noticed the slip in the name, he didn't show it. He sat Joshua on the table in front of himself and began clumsily making goo-goo eyes. I stood there for a minute watching, wondering who was this man who had kidnapped my son.

Finally, I followed Ben out the door, shaking my head. "Was that my father?" I muttered as we walked to the car.

Ben raised his hands, palms up. "It looked like him. I guess the ol' Bowman male charm works on anyone."

A tremendous sense of anxiety gripped me as we got

in the car and started down the driveway. "I think we'd better stay." My mind started whizzing through all sorts of terrible scenarios of what might happen while we were away. "What if Josh gets sick or something?"

Ben shook his head and pulled onto the road. "Kate, your father is a doctor."

"But he doesn't know about babies. He won't know what to look for."

"Kate, Josh is fine." He glanced at my hand on the door handle. "You're not going to bail out going fifty miles an hour, are you?"

Pulling my hand away from the door, I clenched it into a fist and pounded it into my lap, frustrated. "I should have stayed home. I shouldn't have said I needed to go to Springfield today."

Ben grinned as if he hadn't a care in the world. "Those little white lies just get bigger and bigger, don't they?"

"I didn't know they were going to steal our child!" I closed my eyes and leaned my head against the seat. "I'm acting like a baby, aren't I?"

"Yes."

"Thanks a lot."

"You're cute when you act like a baby."

"That doesn't make me feel any better."

"Sorry. How about if I play the radio?"

"Good idea." I opened my eyes and stared out the window, watching the miles roll by.

By the time we reached Springfield, my emotions were no longer at hurricane strength. Ben and I managed to have a pleasant day, even though we learned at the bank that one of Ben's clients hadn't wired payment as promised, so our account was in dire straits. Even with the deposit of the new paycheck, there wasn't much left for Christmas shopping, so we just enjoyed walking around the stores, looking at the decorations and planning what we were going to buy for Christmas when the money wire did come in.

We called home only twice, and Grandma assured us both times that everyone there was having a wonderful day. I told her not to worry about cooking, that we would bring home something for supper. Among all the other horrible images in my mind was one of her blowing up the house while we were gone.

On the way home, Ben stopped by the church to send an e-mail about the late payment that had curtailed our Christmas shopping. Then I suggested we write a Christmas message and send it out to our friends, or straighten the office, or finish Ben's reports. Anything but go home.

"Can't put it off forever," Ben teased. "They have a hostage. We have to go back."

"Curses."

"If you hadn't given them our son, we could be in Bora-Bora by now."

"Now, there's an idea." I slipped into his arms, resting my head on his chest.

"Oh, it's not that bad." He said it as though he believed it. "The rest of the family isn't even here yet."

"Thank you for that helpful observation." I pushed away from him and reached for my purse, resigned to the idea of going home.

"Always glad to help." Grinning, he snatched the car keys off the desk. "Let's go by the Chuckwagon and pick up some supper. It's catfish night."

"Good idea," I said, walking down the steps. "My father hates fish."

That thought brought back a memory that made me laugh. "I'll never forget our one and only deep-sea fishing trip. My great uncle, Ruben, invited us on his boat. Dad thought he was a big expert on ocean fishing because he used to fish on the farm when he was a kid, and he'd read a few books about bay fishing and bought all new tackle. He wouldn't let Uncle Ruben give him any advice or loan him any tackle, and he kept giving Uncle Ruben advice from the books he'd read. Anyway, my father didn't catch anything all day, and Uncle Ruben caught a boatload of red snapper."

The memory came back with startling clarity. I could see Uncle Ruben grinning over his basket of fish while my father sat empty-handed with a pasted-on smile as Mom took a picture. Laughter tickled my stomach and coughed from my throat until I could hardly finish the story. "That was the . . . last . . . vacation we ever took . . . with Mom's family."

Ben laughed with me. "Well, I'll make sure to ask your father if he wants to go fishing tomorrow."

We laughed together as we drove up to the drive-through at the Chuckwagon and ordered a gigantic basket of fish.

Dad was sitting in front of the fireplace with Joshua when Ben and I walked into the house. Neither of them noticed us, and I watched for a moment, amazed to see my father splay-legged on the floor with Joshua propped in his lap. Dad was stacking blocks, then making gorilla laughs when Josh knocked them down. I had had no idea he was capable of such folly. I had pictured him teaching my son how to decode DNA.

"Hi, guys," I said, announcing our presence. "Where's Grandma?"

To my surprise, my father merely glanced at us, then went back to building block towers. "In the kitchen. Oh, oh, noooooooo! It's King Kong." Blocks flew everywhere, Dad made monkey sounds, and Josh flailed his arms, laughing hysterically.

I watched a look of joy pass between them. Apparently Josh could work his magic on anybody. My sophisticated, intelligent, educated father was hypnotized.

The strength of the spell became clearer as the evening wore on. My father turned into someone I had never seen before. I wondered where all of that love and worship and interest had been hiding when Karen and I were children. If he had ever felt anything but disappointment and disinterest for us, he never showed it.

My bitterness ebbed as I watched my father kiss Josh and lay him, almost asleep, in his crib. I knew what Aunt Jeane had said was true. They had a right to spend time together. Josh did not care if I harbored ill feelings toward my father. He cared only that a funny man was building block towers and making him laugh. As he grew older, he would call that man Grandpa, or Grampy, or Papa, and they would be special to each other.

"That's quite a boy," my father whispered as we walked down the stairs.

"Yes, he is," I said, strangely grateful that we now had something to talk about.

We entered the living room, and I realized that Grandma, Ben, Aunt Jeane, and Uncle Robert had disappeared while we were upstairs. Their absence was undoubtedly contrived, and I was unhappy with Ben for going along with it.

Dad took the fireplace tool to spread the logs on the fire so they would burn out overnight. "I want to thank you for leaving Joshua here today," he said.

"You're welcome. It looks like he enjoyed it." I wanted to finish the conversation and get out of the room. My emotions were unstable, and I wasn't ready to have a meaningful exchange with my father.

Firelight illuminated the side of his face, making him look old, not like the steadfast image I remembered. He seemed harmless now. "We both enjoyed it. I'm sorry I waited so long to come."

I knew he was reaching out, but I couldn't respond. I

stood there choking on a lump made of bitterness, disappointment, and all the unhappy years that had passed between us.

He stared into the fire, but he knew I was still there. "Kate, nothing I've done in my life was meant to hurt you or your sister. I did what I thought was right at the time."

Sometimes we must try to view the actions of those around us with forgiveness. We must realize that they are going on the only road they can see.

"That's what we're all doing, Dad." Pride coiled around my throat like a snake, and I couldn't say the things I really wanted to. "It's just a shame we've done so much damage to each other in the process."

He dropped his head into his hand, rubbing his eyes. "I don't understand your anger. Your mother and I did our best to give the two of you everything."

Bread, like a good life, can only be created by honest measure. . . .

My emotions broke through the gag and spilled into the room. "You didn't give us *yourselves,* Dad. We were four strangers living in a house together—baby-sitters, day camps, summer camps, separate vacations, separate schedules, separate lives. You don't understand the way I feel because *you don't know me.*"

These were the words I had wanted to say to him all my life, and he only looked into the flames and shook his head.

"Maybe you're right."

It was the first time he had admitted I was right about anything. It was a victory from which I felt no pleasure.

I didn't know what else to say, so I left him there and went to bed, feeling as if the chasm between us would never be breached.

In the morning we acted as if the conversation had never taken place. At least we were somewhat more civil to each other. Dad refrained from commenting about Ben and me wasting our lives. That, in itself, was a success. Perhaps it was the best I could hope for.

Ben, for his part, was gracious with my father, as he was with everyone. It was not in his nature to hold grudges.

I suppose he would have been better than me at following Grandma's bread recipe.

Aunt Jeane and Uncle Robert joined us late for breakfast, and we greeted them as if we were starving refugees and they were the Red Cross. Uncle Robert was quickly overwhelmed and slipped away, looking for a place to hide, but Aunt Jeane stepped into the fray like General Patton. She entertained us with stories about the folly and funny comments of fifth graders. Her anecdotes were a lesson in human nature. As usual, she did well at putting us in our places.

As the days went by, all of us seemed to find our places, and we needed less of Aunt Jeane's mediation. We were strangers who were finally getting to know one another, defining our ground, learning not to step on one another's toes. By the fourth day of my father's visit, we were pretty good at avoiding all of the subjects that stirred up tension. Which didn't leave much to talk about. Dad spent a lot of time with his laptop computer at the kitchen table, and I began working on my files from the office at Grandma's old Hoosier cabinet because it was by the phone. The arrangement kept Dad and me in the same room, which seemed to give hope to Grandma and Aunt Jeane.

Dad was working on his computer with rapt interest when I finally got in touch with Mr. Ducamp about his endowment and the reports in the newspaper that the foundation was being audited and the accounting practices questioned. I turned my shoulder to my father, wishing he wasn't there to hear about the sloppy management of foundation funds. Just one more thing for him to criticize.

The conversation with Mr. Ducamp turned into an exercise in verbal footwork. From the corner of my eye, I could see Dad glance at me, interested but trying not to show it.

His interest bolstered my determination to succeed in keeping the Ducamp endowment. I also felt a strange touch of ego gratification that he was paying attention to what I was doing.

"Well, the fact is, Mr. Ducamp, that the endowment was in no way attached to the coal emissions study. Your funding, as we agreed last year, has been used to support the study on MTBE oxygenate levels in the drinking water supply. The study is still ongoing and is within six months of releasing findings. If you pull your support now, I don't know if we will be able to conclude the study. I guess I'm asking you personally to stay with me on this one. It's looking like our findings are going to be vastly different from the EPA's. We're finding much higher oxygenate levels in many lakes and underground wells. It's critical that we finish the study and publish the results."

Mr. Ducamp sighed on the other end of the line, and I knew I had won the battle. He agreed to continue funding the study, and even increase funding slightly if it would speed up the study results. I thanked him in every way possible, then wished him Merry Christmas before hanging up. A rush of success tingled through my body like a dose of adrenaline.

"Yes!" I cheered, forgetting for a moment that I wasn't alone.

"I take it you were successful." I couldn't see my father's face, but there was a note of admiration in his voice that made me feel good.

"Yes, I was," I replied, feeling larger than life, on top of the world, master of my own destiny. "That funding is for an important study on gasoline additive contamination in the drinking water supply. We're finding high levels of MTBE in—"

"There it is," he muttered, as if he hadn't realized I was talking, or didn't care.

"Anyway, this study is coming up with fascinating findings and—"

"Um-hum. That's good. Well, I know nothing about all this environmentalism." Translation: *I don't care and I'm not interested in hearing any more.*

"Well, the study is very important anyway." Why I felt compelled to drive home my point, I couldn't say. Suddenly I felt like a little girl again, trying to make him notice my report card.

"No doubt." He reached for his pad and scribbled something on it. "I have a good friend at the American Cancer Society. Here is his number. You could put your fund-raising skills to good use there." Which translated as: *You're wasting your time on a meaningless cause where you are.* Which was how he had always felt about my studying environmental science.

"I already have a cure for cancer," I snapped, feeling like a wounded little girl again and angry with him for spoiling my triumph.

He glanced up, cocking a brow incredulously.

"Stop gas additives from getting into the drinking water supply," I shot at him, then turned and left the kitchen without waiting to see whether or not the arrow hit home.

Aunt Jeane met me in the hall. One look at my face, and she deflated like a balloon with the air let out. "What now?"

"He got on my nerves, that's all," I said, taking a deep breath and counting to ten. "I just salvaged a major endowment, and he made sure to tell me that environmental work is a waste of time, and he can help me get a real job."

Aunt Jeane winced. "Oh, Kate, you know he doesn't mean it that way."

I spat a puff of air, and realized I sounded just like Grandma.

Aunt Jeane looked worried. I knew what she was thinking. Christmas Eve was just two days away and my sister was arriving tomorrow. When she did, our fragile detente might come tumbling down like a house of cards.

Aunt Jeane braced her hands on her hips and took on a look of determination. "Well, the two of you can talk about it on the way to Springfield. Remember, you promised you would go with your father today and help him buy Christmas gifts."

I stared at her with my mouth open, choking on a lump of pride that wouldn't let me go back into the kitchen and politely ask him to go shopping. "I . . . but . . . you . . . you go."

Aunt Jeane laid a hand on my arm and turned me toward the kitchen. "I would, but I promised Mother I would spend some time with her today. There's a special ladies' meeting at the church later this afternoon and it's important that I take her."

I grimaced, knowing Aunt Jeane wouldn't take no for an answer.

"Please, Kate," she urged. "You know he didn't mean to hurt your feelings. He's just . . . hopelessly insensitive. Just try to be a little thicker-skinned."

Sighing, I lowered my face into my hand and rubbed my eyes. "All right, but only for you, Aunt Jeane."

"Good girl." She patted my shoulder. "Think of it as a chance to finish your Christmas shopping." She slipped four one hundred dollar bills into my hand as if I were a teenager going on a date.

"Buy some things and let them be from Santa Claus," she whispered.

"Aunt Jeane," I admonished, handing the money back to her. "I don't need you to give me money." Which wasn't exactly true. The money wire still hadn't come in, and Ben and I had only managed to come up with two hundred dollars of mad money. It wasn't much to buy Christmas presents for everyone.

Aunt Jeane pressed the money into my jacket pocket and stared me down with Grandma's blue eyes. "I didn't say you needed money. I just asked if you would do some shopping for me . . . er, Santa Claus."

"All right," I said, knowing that no one but she and I would ever know the identity of Santa's banker. "Thanks, Aunt Jeane."

"Santa Claus." She winked, then shooed me out the door. "Hurry up. The day's wasting. Take all the time you want. Don't worry about Joshua. Ben just saw an ad in the paper for a live manger scene at Pearly's Pecan Farm, and he wants to take Joshua there to see the animals. I think Uncle Robert, Grandma, and I will go along. I haven't been out to Pearly's in years."

I paused in the doorway, wanting to delay the inevitable. "I thought Ben had work to do today," I protested. I couldn't imagine my father and me together for so many hours without Joshua to provide an area of neutrality. "I could take Josh with me."

As usual, she knew what I was up to, and she shook her head resolutely. "Oh, no. Ben wants some daddy time with Josh, and your father needs help with his Christmas shopping. Works out perfectly for everyone." She shooed me toward the door. "Go on now. Have a nice day shopping."

So I did. I grudgingly asked my father if he was ready to go Christmas shopping. He agreed pleasantly, as if he had no idea he'd put me in a rotten mood a few minutes before.

He got his coat and we walked to the car in a strange sort of silence.

Watching him from the corner of my eye as he turned the car down the driveway, I was struck by how strange it felt to be alone in the car with him. Searching my memory, I could not recall a time when just the two of us had gone somewhere together.

We drove without speaking until we were well out of Hindsville and almost halfway to Springfield.

"It's a nice day," he said finally.

"Very," I agreed. "Grandma is still sure there's a snowstorm coming for Christmas."

He chuckled. "She'll probably get her way about it. You know your Grandma doesn't take no for an answer. She used to drive me out of my mind when I was young. I couldn't wait to grow up and get out from under her thumb. I wanted to get away from that farm so bad I could taste it."

I looked at him, not knowing what to say. It was hard to imagine him ever young, or under anyone's thumb, or living on the farm for that matter. "You're not the farming type, Dad," I said finally.

Chewing his lip thoughtfully, he gazed at the winter-browned Ozarks. "Actually, I enjoyed the farming to some degree. I was good at tinkering with the tractors and machinery. It was all the rest of it I could not stand—having my mother and father over my shoulder all the time, working and never having anything, never doing anything different. Everything on the farm seemed so small and unimportant. It seemed as though, if I stayed there, my life would be a waste, and then I'd wake up old. I thought if I got away, got an education and an important job, my life would mean something."

"Well, I guess you were right," I said bitterly, wondering why his children didn't figure into the equation of life's meaning. I wondered if we were one of those small, unimportant things.

He went on as if he hadn't heard me. "But you see, Kate, that was why I didn't want you and Ben to come to the farm. I knew Grandma would work her emotional blackmail on you. She is an expert at loading on the family guilt." He glanced at me, then quickly focused on the road, sensing another fight brewing. "It wasn't my intention to hurt your feelings. I just wanted to prevent the two of you from getting tied up in all of this. It isn't your responsibility. Staying here will be a step backward financially for you and ultimately an unhappy experience for you. Both of you have too much going for you to become tied up in Grandma's web."

His praise only poured salt in my wounds, and I turned to him with my eyes stinging. "In the first place, Grandma Rose isn't a responsibility—she's a person. Her feelings should be considered, not just what is convenient for everyone else. I'm sure Aunt Jeane has told you by now that Ben and I are thinking of staying here for a while longer. If we replace some of the appliances and put in some timers and safety devices, I think she'll be able to stay on her own again when we have to leave."

He shook his head, cutting a hard look in my direction.

I rushed on before he could give me all the reasons why that was a bad idea. "Staying here may not be right for you, or Karen, or Aunt Jeane, or anybody else, but maybe it's right for us, and maybe it's right for Grandma, and maybe it's right for Joshua. He's still so little. I want us to have some time with him, and I want Grandma to have time to fully recover from her stroke."

"Well, that's commendable." His voice was flat and emotionless. "But what happens when you have to go back to the real world?"

"I don't know. We can deal with that when the time comes."

"Grandma will still be in the same situation she is in now, and the same decisions will have to be made." He said it as if it didn't bother him at all, as if we were talking about getting rid of a used car.

"Maybe not. Maybe she will be better by then."

"It isn't likely, Kate." I could feel him looking at me, but I stared out the window. "Grandma is going downhill, and we all know it. She could have another stroke at any time. You have to face that fact."

"No, I don't." I crossed my arms over my chest, glaring at him. "Right now, she is fine and she's happy at the farm. You can't predict the future and neither can Aunt Jeane. Maybe things will work out conveniently for you, and three or four months from now, Grandma won't be around for you to worry about. Then we'll all go back to doing what we did before." It was the worst, the cruelest thing I could say. I wondered what it was about my father that turned me into someone I didn't recognize and didn't like.

He jerked his head back, looking shocked, then stared at the road ahead and clamped his lips into a tight, pale line, ending the conversation.

After that, we stuck to safer subjects, such as tree species and rock formations, Christmas decorations and Joshua's wish list. Dad made me laugh with a story about the origin of the Red Rider BB gun Christmas ornament, and how the gun and hatchet that came with it had been confiscated the next spring when he snapped Grandma's clothesline, sending the laundry into the mud where the pack of farm dogs used it for tug-of-war. I could picture Grandma standing over the wringer washer afterward, issuing instructions as my father scrubbed and bleached each item.

And so the day went by, not unpleasant, but not a point of epiphany in our relationship either. Both of us chose to leave the conversation about Grandma unfinished, but I knew the final discussion would come when Karen arrived and the whole family sat down together. So far, no one seemed to be on my side . . . except Grandma. And she didn't get a vote.

Aunt Jeane probed me for information about the day when we were in the kitchen together fixing supper that night.

"We got the shopping done," I told her. "Not much else." I didn't tell her we had talked about Grandma. I didn't want to give her any more ammunition.

"That's good," she said, loath to admit that she had hoped for more of a reconciliation between me and my father. Maybe she had been hoping he would sway me to their position about Grandma. "You didn't get time to talk?"

I pretended to concentrate on chopping an onion—convenient because it gave me an excuse to cry. "Not much. He told me how much he hated life on the farm, and he couldn't believe I liked it. I got aggravated. That was pretty much it. After that, we talked about trees."

Aunt Jeane bent over the stew pot, gazing in as if she were reading tea leaves. "Well, you have to understand. Your dad had a lot to prove when he left the farm. He was the only son, and Grandpa planned on his taking over the farm someday. When he went away to study medicine and then moved to Boston to live, Grandpa was pretty bitter. They never had gotten along too well, and that just made things worse."

I thought about it for a minute, wiping my eyes with the back of my hand. It was hard to picture my father ever needing to prove himself. "I think Dad and I understand each other about as well as we're ever going to."

Aunt Jeane waited for the pot to settle, then skimmed the shimmering beads of oil from the top. "Well, that would be a shame." She looked sideways at me. "For both of you."

The door burst open, and we glanced up in time to see Grandma shuffle into the kitchen, towing an ancient Radio Flyer wagon stacked high with wrapped Christmas gifts.

She paused suspiciously, as if she knew she had walked in on an interesting conversation and was hoping it would start up again. "Don't let me bother you," she said. "As you two were doing the cooking, I thought I would get my presents wrapped and brought in before Karen gets here tomorrow." She looked from me to Aunt Jeane, then shrugged, giving up on the prospect of finding out any secrets. "We should get busy with making the room ready for Karen and James. There will be no time for that with preparing the Christmas meals for the poor tomorrow afternoon at the church. And then on Christmas Eve we must bake the pies, go cut a tree in the pasture, and get it decorated." She shuffled out of the kitchen with the red wagon squealing behind her like a Christmas goose. "Now, nobody needs to bother with getting any gifts for me," she called back. "I'm too old. It's gift enough that everyone will be together for Christmas."

Handing the vegetables to Aunt Jeane, I met her gaze and smiled, reminded of the real reason for this Christmas gathering, and of how important it was. Grandma needed all of us, and if we had nothing else in common, our coming to the farm proved that all of us needed her.

Chapter 12

DECEMBER twenty-third began in a flurry of activity. Ben and Uncle Robert left for town early to help the Baptist Men's Group cook turkeys at the church for the Christmas meal deliveries. Grandma, Aunt Jeane, and I prepared pies to take to the church in the afternoon. Dell came to our door early in the morning, carrying one of Grandma Rose's handmade tree angels that she said needed repair. Mostly she just looked bored and lonesome and sad. Far too sad for a nine-year-old girl two days before Christmas. She stood shyly in the corner of our kitchen and told us that her granny had said Santa wasn't likely to come to their house because Dell was too grown-up for such things.

Grandma Rose scoffed, shaking her head. "Now that is just nonsense." She wagged a finger at Dell, then reached over and gripped Dell's hand in hers, giving the girl's dark fingers a squeeze. "You're hardly too old for Santa Claus, but with your granny having an attitude like that, Saint Nick probably won't dare come to your house." Grandma looked at us and tightened her lips into a determined line. "I'll wager that he'll leave your gifts under our tree, and you can come here to get them Christmas morning."

Dell glanced at Grandma, a glint of hope in her dark eyes, then looked at Aunt Jeane and me for confirmation. We nodded, hoping Grandma and Santa Claus had something in mind.

Grandma smiled and shooed Dell from the room. "I hear the baby waking in his swing there in the living room," she told the girl. "Why don't you go and play with him while we finish baking? Remember, we'll be going to the church later to help fix Christmas dinners for . . ." She paused, for once thinking ahead of her tongue, and finally finished tactfully, "For people who haven't time to cook."

"Um-hum. I remember." Dell stopped halfway out the door and glanced at me, looking much happier than she had when she'd arrived. "I can watch Joshee in the nursery at church."

"That would be great," I said. "I don't think there's anyone he would rather play with."

She ducked her dark head and hurried from the room, just a hint of a smile showing beneath the curtain of hair.

The three of us paused to listen until we heard Dell talking to Joshua in the living room.

Grandma huffed an irritated puff of air and turned back to chopping apples, her lips a tight, unsmiling line. "Where is Jackie, anyway? I thought he was watching the baby."

"No, Mother." Aunt Jeane rolled her eyes. "Don't you remember? He came through here earlier and said he was going for a walk outdoors. The baby has been sleeping all morning anyway. He's exhausted from all that fun he had with his daddy at Pearly's Pecan Farm. I'll tell you, Kate, you should have seen Ben and Josh feeding the goats. I'm not sure which one of them had more fun."

"I'm glad they got to go," I said, wishing I had been

with them rather than shopping with my father. "Ben said Josh laughed and laughed at the goats."

"Ben is a brave man." Aunt Jeane chuckled. "He was almost goat-nibbled to death taking Joshua through the petting zoo."

Grandma slapped her knife against the cutting board, still murderously dicing the apples, then proceeded to change the subject. "Jackie should have considered that there's no time for lolling around today, what with all the Christmas meals to prepare. At least he could have looked after the baby."

"It's all right, Grandma," I said, trying to settle her down before she and Aunt Jeane got entangled again. The truth was that everyone was on edge about Karen's arrival, including me. I supposed my father's sudden desire to commune with the farm was his way of escaping the tension.

Aunt Jeane was jittery despite the fact that Karen wasn't due for hours. She had less than her normal level of patience with Grandma's complaining, bossing, and worrying. Grandma was doing her part by complaining, bossing, and worrying more than usual, because she wanted things to be perfect for Karen's arrival. It was like cooking in the center of a mine field. My mind was racing so fast that I kept reading recipe cards and forgetting what I had read before I could put the ingredients together. I gave up and took over washing the stack of bowls and pots that had accumulated in the sink.

Grandma finished torturing the apples and moved to her Hoosier cabinet to work out her frustration on a ball of bread dough. Turning her head to one side, she listened to the radio for weather reports, her hands slowly falling into a sedate rhythm, the pinched, worried expression fading from her face. She stared out the window as if her thoughts were drifting away. Watching her, I wondered how many years of her life she had spent in exactly the same way. It must have felt very right to her, to be standing at that ancient breadboard, waiting for the family to come home.

She drew a breath finally. "Karen and James should make it in before the snow. They can come to church with us and help prepare the meals."

Aunt Jeane slapped a spatula against the side of the mixing bowl, and it rang through the kitchen like a Chinese gong. "Mother, will you stop going on about snow? It's clear as a bell outside, and they've been saying all day that all the storms are north of here. Karen and James will be ready for some rest when they get here. They will have had a long day of travel. Kate and I can go to the church and help you."

Grandma raised her chin and turned slowly back to her work. "That weatherman doesn't know his business. My ankles have been predicting snow for sixty years longer than he's been on this earth. And I've already promised that the lot of us would be helping with the meals at church."

Aunt Jeane rang the bowl again. "Oh, Mother, for goodness' sake, I . . ." She fell silent, staring at the hallway door. "Karen! My goodness, where did you come from? We weren't expecting you for another two hours!" Dropping the spoon, she ran to the door, arms outstretched.

I stood paralyzed for a moment, watching Aunt Jeane hug Karen and James, then watching Grandma hurry over to do the same with tears spilling over her cheeks.

Standing silently by the sink, I watched Grandma take my sister's face in her hands and step back to look at her. The past six years had changed Karen more than I had expected. Her hair, which had always been highlighted, was dark now, and pulled neatly into a silver clip in the back. Her face had aged, but she was still beautiful, tall and slim, perfectly dressed in black-check slacks and a red jacket. She looked like my mother.

I was not prepared for the resemblance. Watching her stand in the doorway of the old kitchen with my grandmother was like stepping back in time. My stomach constricted and rose into my throat, and my head swirled with a sudden sense of vertigo. Gripping the counter, I closed my eyes and waited for it to pass.

When it did, Grandma was releasing Karen. I came forward quickly, not wanting her to think I was being standoffish. My mind went blank, and I could not remember what I had planned to say to her.

"Welcome home," I heard myself say. Then I hugged her quickly, not knowing how she felt about me or whether she wanted my affection. "We didn't think you would be here until this afternoon."

She cocked her head, as if she were wondering what I meant. "The airline was able to get us on an earlier flight. They're having a lot of snow north of here, and we didn't want to get caught in it." She winked at James. "Sometimes it pays to be married to a pilot."

James smiled at me, and I shook his hand as I would have any stranger's. We had met only twice—at their wedding and at Mother's funeral. He was an athletic-looking man, about forty now, with salt-and-pepper hair that reminded me of my father's. His manner, too, was dignified and formal like Dad's. They probably would have liked each other if Karen had ever allowed them to socialize.

"It's good to see you again, Kate," he said. "All the Christmas decorations look nice."

I nodded, glad to have something neutral to talk about. "I have to give Ben most of the credit. He scavenged the lights and the gingerbread man display from the church leftovers. He wanted to make sure Josh had a memorable first Christmas."

The subject didn't stay neutral for long. Karen glanced

around the kitchen, frowning. "Where's Dad? Did he decide not to come, after all?" She looked as if she were hoping I would say yes.

"He's here." I watched for her reaction. "He went out for a walk an hour or so ago."

She raised a brow incredulously. "*Dad* went out for a walk?"

The need to defend him came over me, I did not know why. "He would have been back if he'd known you would be here so early. He really was anxious to see you."

She stiffened. "I'm sure he was," she said sarcastically, then glanced at Aunt Jeane and snapped her lips closed.

I wondered if Aunt Jeane had warned her not to start a war in front of Grandma. Even so, I was surprised by Karen's restraint. Normally, she said what was on her mind no matter who it would hurt.

"Would you two like some coffee?" Aunt Jeane asked. "How about a sugar cookie? I'll bet you're exhausted after the trip."

Karen gave Aunt Jeane a smile of genuine affection. "Oh, this is nothing for us. James and I both travel so much, we don't know what to do when we're home. I just got back from Norfolk. It looks like Lansing Technology is going to sew up a megadeal on the East Coast. My team will be designing the networks, so I'll be back and forth to Norfolk for six months or more, but there's a big bonus in it and . . ."

I tuned out Karen's boasting and hurried to beat Aunt Jeane to the coffeemaker. I wasn't interested in being stranded at the table during one of Karen's I'm-an-important-person-and-I-just-got-a-big-raise speeches.

Elbowing Aunt Jeane out of the way, I said, "I'll get it. Go sit down."

She gave me a look of disappointment. I wasn't sure if she was disappointed in me, or in the fact that she would have to sit and listen to Karen. Grandma, meanwhile, was smiling and nodding blankly, as if Karen were speaking in Martian.

Karen was describing the megadeal and I was serving the coffee when my father came in the back door.

He gave Karen a quick look of surprise, then stepped forward and patted her on the shoulder. She did not stand up to greet or hug him. Strangely, I felt sorry for Dad.

"Hello, Karen," he said. "Did you have a good trip?"

"We did," she said. "I was just telling Grandma about the network bid my team just finished in Norfolk." And so she began the story again for Dad's benefit.

Dad took a seat and seemed genuinely impressed. Watching him from the corner of my eye, I felt a twinge of envy. My life was a waste, but Karen's was fascinating conversation. His face was alight with interest and something that looked like fatherly pride. He wasn't advising her to get a better job or calling up his acquaintances to help her get in with a "real employer."

A faint thud came from the living room, reminding me that Joshua and Dell were there. No one else seemed to notice the noise, so I slipped out the door without saying anything. Safe in the hallway, I paused to take a deep breath, shaking my old insecurities from my mind. Karen and I were not in competition. We were two different people. She had her life. I had mine. She had her kind of success. I had mine.

And God bless us, every one. It *was* the season of goodwill, after all.

Dell was rescuing Joshua from the floor as I walked in. "He bumped his head on the floor," she said, grimacing as if she were afraid I would be angry with her. "But he rolled over all by himself two times."

Squatting beside her, I inspected the red spot on Joshua's head. "Oh, that's not too bad," I said, then jiggled Josh and won a smile. "And what do you mean, rolling over when Mommy's not here to see it?"

Dell giggled, arranging Joshua's quilt on the floor. "He might do it again." She rolled Josh onto his back, then teased him with a toy. "Com'ere, Josh, get the toy."

Joshua wormed to one side, then the other, once, twice, three times, then flopped onto his stomach and braced his arms in front of himself, laughing.

Thunderous applause came from the doorway, and I turned to see Ben and the rest of the family gathered there.

"You're just in time," I told Ben. "He has a new trick." Dell set Josh up again, and like a little performer, he repeated his trick, then squealed with glee, bouncing up and down and waiting for more cheers. Laughing, I sat him up and turned him toward the crowd. Ben, Dad, and Aunt Jeane were beaming. Grandma had tears in her eyes.

It was an accomplishment with which no corporate megadeal could compare.

Karen squeezed past Aunt Jeane and hurried to us with surprising enthusiasm, kneeling on the floor in front of Joshua. "Oh, Kate, he's beautiful," she whispered, stretching out a single finger as if she were afraid to touch him. "Hi, pretty boy. I'm Aunt Karen."

Joshua extended a tiny hand and clung to her outstretched finger. Karen smiled nervously, uncertain of what to do next.

"He's really adorable," she said, but the expression on her face wasn't one of admiration. It was a strange look I couldn't quite read.

Joshua squealed and gurgled, then grasped Karen's hand with his other fist, trying to scoot toward her.

"You're cute," she said, smiling at him. "You look like your dad."

"Want to hold him?" I asked, because Joshua was trying his best to get to her. "I think he likes you."

Karen shook her head, gently pulling her hand away and standing up. "I'd better not." She straightened her jacket. "Silk suit."

"Oh," I muttered, picking Joshua up, trying not to look insulted and telling myself I was stupid for feeling that way. It was a mother thing, I supposed.

In the doorway, Grandma clapped her hands together. "Well, we'd best get a-going here and get Karen and James's things brought in. As soon as these pies are done, we must be off for church to help package up the meals. Karen, you might want to change out of that fancy suit." She turned and started down the hall, still talking. "It's bound to be a mess at the church once everyone arrives with their food."

Karen looked at me and then at Aunt Jeane. "What is she talking about?" she whispered.

Aunt Jeane sighed and rolled her eyes. "Oh, Karen, don't worry about it. You and James bring in your bags and relax. I told her Kate and I would take her and the pies to the church and help package the meals. She wasn't supposed to bother you about it."

Karen and James exchanged quick glances of relief. Karen winced apologetically at Aunt Jeane. "I just don't think we're up for an activity right now, and . . . I really need to check my . . . voice-mail messages."

Aunt Jeane wrapped an arm around Karen's shoulders and guided her toward the door. "That's fine. You two enjoy the afternoon and rest."

Ben cleared his throat, rubbing his hands in front of himself. "Well, Uncle Robert, Josh, and I have a date with a football game. We've done our duty. We've been baking turkeys at the church since six o'clock this morning." He stopped beside me and took Josh, who was reaching toward him and babbling happily. Making monkey faces and goo-goo sounds at Josh, he proceeded past me into the living room and sank onto the couch with Uncle Robert following happily in his wake. My father joined them, and everyone else turned to disperse.

Dell got up and stood between me and Aunt Jeane, looking confused as to what to do; then she scurried past me toward the kitchen. Ben turned on the TV and Karen started toward the door with James in tow.

"Now, hold it!" I heard myself say, sounding venomous. Joshua jerked in Ben's arms, looking at me wide-eyed with his mouth open.

Everyone else turned and did the same, as if they couldn't imagine what I would say.

"I can't believe you people, especially you, Ben." My mouth rushed ahead of my brain, and I heard my words echo down the hall. Taking a deep breath, I added more calmly, "You know how much Grandma is counting on all of us being there this afternoon."

My father stiffened and cleared his throat. "Calm down, Kate. You're getting worked up about something pretty unimportant here."

Ben nodded in agreement, looking vindicated. "It's not that big of a deal, Kate. The turkeys are already cooked and sliced. I've done my civic duty. Josh and I were going to do some guy stuff here." Josh looked at his father and squealed, bouncing up and down as if in agreement.

"I'm sure Grandma has church members lined up to help," Karen chimed in.

Aunt Jeane nodded and started to say something, but I beat her to it.

"It *is* a big deal!" I heard my voice echo down the hall again, even as I wondered why I was getting into a red-faced fit. The fact was that the Christmas meals would get made with or without my family. "It's a great big do-or-die deal, and if everyone doesn't go, she'll be upset all day, and we'll hear about it for—"

"Kaaaaaa-teeee?" Grandma's voice drifted from the kitchen like the shriek of a crow. I realized she'd probably heard me yelling. "Stop that kibitzing and come help me with these pies. It isn't good to complain about doing the Lord's work. I don't hear anyone else in there complaining."

Mouth hanging open, I coughed indignantly, looking toward the door.

Ben cleared his throat to hide a chuckle, and Karen rubbed her lips to conceal a smile. Even my father raised his newspaper to hide his face. Finally Aunt Jeane burst out laughing, and everyone in the room joined in. Before I knew it, I was laughing with them, and Joshua was bouncing and squealing in Ben's arms. It felt good, all of it. At least until the general hollered from the kitchen again and spurred the troops into action.

Twenty minutes later, all of us stood in the kitchen like soldiers in the Salvation Army. Grandma inspected the pies and the soldiers and smiled, looking well pleased.

"It's wonderful what a family can do all together," she said, a blush coming into her cheeks and her eyes moistening. "And it's wonderful to have family in the house again." She moved down the line we made, squeezing our hands and touching our cheeks, saying, "It's just wonderful, just wonderful," again and again as she walked out the door.

We smiled at each other, forgetting the football game and the voice-mail messages, the leftover work from the office and the long day of travel, as we followed Grandma out the door to do good in the world.

Sometimes when you're doing good for other people, good things happen to you, too. A measure of amazing grace came over my family as we entered the old church building and began filling Styrofoam containers with

Christmas meals to feed the hungry. As we worked at a
long table together, we talked and laughed. Dad and
Aunt Jeane, together with old neighbors and childhood
friends, recounted events from their years in Hindsville.
The rest of us laughed and listened, and started to understand some things we hadn't before.

Grandma Rose finished straw-bossing in the kitchen
and came to check on us when the level of conversation
at the meal-packaging table became audible across the
room.

"Well, I never thought I'd end up back in Hindsville,
either," Wanda Cox was saying, chuckling, as if at some
private joke. "Now, once upon a time Jeane and I were
going to join the Baptist Mission and go to Africa. Remember that, Jeane?"

Aunt Jeane shook her head, looking confused.

Wanda slapped her on the shoulder, slinging corn ker-
nels across the table. "Oh, yes, ya' do. Remember, those
handsome young fellas came and spoke about the Baptist Mission at church camp, and we just thought that was
the ticket—we'd go off to Africa and live in a tent like
modern-day pioneers. Or maybe we just thought we'd
get a date with those young fellas. Remember? Your
daddy took us over to Dr. Schmidt's and had him show
us the needles he'd have to use to give us our overseas
shots, and next thing I knew I fell dead-out on the
floor."

Aunt Jeane threw her head back. "Oh, my goodness,
I do remember that now. I ran out of that office so fast,
and—"

"And that was the end of our Baptist Mission careers,"
Wanda finished, and everyone burst into laughter.

When the laughter finally quieted, Grandma slipped
into the conversation, "Well, I remember having big
ideas myself." She elbowed her way to the table and
started slicing bread. "When I was fourteen, I went off to

live with a well-to-do lady in St. Louis, on the recommendation of our minister at church who knew my family was sorely in need of money and one less mouth to feed. I was to watch this lady's children and keep house for her. Over time, that lady could see I wanted better, and she helped me move on to a good job at Woolworth's." She paused and glanced up at us, smiling. "Oh, I loved that job. All those fancy things, and money coming into my pocket. I started to buy some things that I'd always dreamed about. Lands! I thought I had it made. After a little more than a year, I was set to move into managing a department."

Shaking her head, she sighed and went back to slicing bread. "But then my father took sick, and I came home. I had to use most of the money I had saved to put a new roof on my parents' house and buy some things my brothers and sisters needed, but I was glad to do it. My family was welcome to all that I had." She frowned, looking far away and a little sad. "I took a job here in town at the dry goods store. My brother asked his friend Henry if he would drive me back home from work at night because my family had no car, and of course, Henry and I went to sparkin' pretty quickly and wound up getting married.

"But, you know, I always thought about what big things I might have done if I'd have stayed in St. Louis." She laughed, just barely, a soft sound of faintly exhaled breath, like the fading of a dream in the first moments of morning. "But now I think, while I was fretting over missing those wonderful big things, I let a lot of good little things pass by me unappreciated." She held the knife above the bread and looked at each of us very directly—Aunt Jeane and Uncle Robert, Karen and James, Dad, Ben and me. "That's the problem with people. We'll starve to death looking over the fence when we're knee-deep in grass where we are."

A pang of regret went through me, and I looked away from Grandma and went back to putting squash into plastic containers. I didn't know quite what to say. Apparently no one else did either. Everyone worked silently for a while until Wanda Cox finally filled the silence with a story about the time my father led the freshman boys' basketball team to district victory.

I stared at my father, amazed that he had ever played basketball, or any other sport. I noticed Karen listening with similar amazement, and I wondered if she was having the same sense of otherworldliness that I was—as if the man blushing at the other end of the table could not possibly be the father we had always known.

My father, for his part, looked as if he were being tortured, and when the first batch of meals was ready, he was quick to volunteer to go with Uncle Robert to make deliveries. Ben and James left shortly afterward, taking Dell with them so they could drop her at home with her Christmas meals. Those of us remaining at the table descended into harmless girltalk, which continued until the last of the meals were packaged. As we worked, I listened to Karen's laughter and thought again of my mother. In the waning light from the ancient stained-glass windows, she could have been my mother . . .

I suddenly felt a strange sense of joy that my sister had come, that all of them had come. Inside me, I kindled a hope that all of these years apart, all the water under the bridge, had worn away our rough edges, smoothed us like pebbles in a streambed.

The last of the evening light faded as we finished carrying the final meals out to cars for delivery. In all, we had prepared Christmas meals for more than fifty people who would otherwise have had none. Grandma looked exhausted but satisfied as she climbed into the Buick with Aunt Jeane and Karen to deliver a few meals and then take Joshua home for his bath and a bottle.

I leaned into the car and kissed him before closing the door.

"We'll take good care of him, Mom," Aunt Jeane reassured me. "Ben and James are probably home by now, so I may drop Joshua and Grandma at the house before taking meals out to Mr. and Mrs. Owens."

Grandma raised her chin. "No, I'm fine. I want to tell Mrs. Owens thank you for the flowers, anyway." She reached out the door and patted my hand. "Thank you for staying behind and helping Wanda clean up. I hated to see her do it all by herself."

"That's all right," I said. "We'll probably be done in an hour or so. I'll see you at home." Something funny struck me as I backed away and the odor of turkey and dressing wafted up from the trunk of the car. "You know, after being elbow-deep in turkey all day, Christmas dinner isn't going to look very appetizing."

Karen, half asleep in the backseat, muttered, "I think we should have ham for Christmas."

Aunt Jeane chuckled and put the car into gear, backing away as I walked back into the church to help Wanda finish cleaning the last of the dirty dishes.

Wanda Cox and I worked for over an hour, and when the job was done, she gave me a ride back to the farm. We sat for a few minutes in the driveway as she finished telling me a story about her granddaughter; then she hugged me as if she'd known me forever.

"Now, ya'll have a merry Christmas," she said, looking me in the eye and patting my arm. "We certainly are glad to have you and Ben here, Kate . . . and the rest of the family, of course. It sure has been a good thing for your grandmother. I haven't seen her with so much color in her cheeks in months. I'll tell you, she had just about dried up to nothin'. It's a good thing ya'll came home this Christmas. I think it was just what she needed."

"I think so, too," I agreed, wondering at the fact that Wanda seemed to have no inkling that the family had come to move Grandma Rose to a rest home. I wondered what she would say if she knew, but I didn't have the courage to ask. "Tell your family Merry Christmas for me," I said finally and opened my door, letting in the winter chill. "Thanks for the ride home and all the stories. I enjoyed it."

"Me too." She smiled, and I had the sense of having made a friend. "Ya'll have a good night. And, Kate . . ." She paused, as if she had something she wanted to say, but she wasn't quite sure whether to let it out.

"Yes?"

"If there's . . . well, nothing. Just if there's ever anything I can do to help you or your grandmother, let me know."

"I will," I said, wishing there *were* something she could do to help. "Thanks."

" 'Bye, Kate."

" 'Bye." I closed the car door and stood watching her drive away, wondering if she knew why the family had come, after all. I wondered if everyone in town knew, and how they felt about us. I thought about how lucky Grandma was to live in a place where so many people loved her and cared about what happened to her—where people were willing to go out of the way to take care of her.

I thought about how wrong it was that her family wasn't willing to do the same. Sometimes it's easier to have sympathy for strangers than it is to have sympathy for your own family. Which isn't right. But that's the damage a long trail of bitterness can do. It dulls the way you look at people—like a wash of watercolor black that makes everything look darker than it is.

The car disappeared onto the road, and I turned and walked into the house. In the kitchen, Ben, Aunt Jeane,

Uncle Robert, and Grandma were engrossed in a game of Scrabble that looked as if it had been going on for some time. James was looking over Grandma's shoulder and whispering ideas in her ear.

I enjoyed watching my family do something so normal, so harmless and peaceful. It was good to hear them laughing together.

Ben glanced up from studying his letters and motioned to me. "You'd better sit down and help me. I'm getting massacred already."

The competitive look in his eye made me chuckle. He *really* didn't want to lose. "Where's Josh?" It was still about a half hour too early for him to be in bed.

"Upstairs with your dad," Ben answered hastily, rubbing his hands together and setting his letters on the board. "There, *zephyr*! How do you like that?"

Shaking my head, I left him to gloat and went upstairs to check on Joshua. I found my baby curled with my father in the rocking chair, his face resting on Dad's shoulder and his soft blue eyes looking drowsily around the room. Karen was sitting cross-legged on the single bed in the corner. Both of them looked up as I came into the room, the expressions on their faces unreadable.

Seeing them together made me stop, my heart frozen in my chest. Swallowing hard, I broke the silence. "If you two are going to fight, I want to take Josh out of here."

Josh raised his head at the sound of my voice, and Dad brought a hand up as if to hold me away. "Joshua is fine. Your sister and I are not fighting. I have some things I want to say to you girls."

Crossing my arms uncomfortably, I came forward and sat on the edge of the bed. All the warm hopes I had kindled throughout the day went cold. The look on Karen's face told me she was ready for a confrontation. My father's expression was stiff and emotionless, like a mask.

I sighed, wishing I were somewhere else. "You know, it's been a pleasant day. Do we have to spoil it now?"

Karen shrugged and said nothing, just sat cross-legged with her elbows resting on her knees and her eyes fixed on my father. She seemed to be waiting for an answer to a question. I wondered how much they had talked before I arrived. I wondered whether it was she or Dad who had started this conversation and why they couldn't just leave things alone.

Suddenly, I wished we could just pretend our way through Christmas, find a way to keep Grandma on the farm, then go back to our separate lives again, the wounds not healed, but not any deeper either.

Dad paused for a moment, settling Joshua on his shoulder and carefully selecting his words. He looked first at me. "I gave a great deal of thought to what you said the night I arrived, Kate. Karen seems to feel much the same way you do about your upbringing. Somehow, I have been painted the monster in all of this, and I feel it's time I set things straight." Another long pause followed before he added, "I feel that your mother and I received very little gratitude for all of the things we gave to you and your sister. However, I do now realize that you are right in saying we were selfish with our time." His face became less earnest, more stoic.

Beside me, Karen shifted impatiently and started to speak, but Dad raised a hand to silence her.

I hugged my arms around myself and kept silent, waiting for his latest line of defense and wishing we weren't having the conversation at all.

He paused again, then went on. "I want you to understand, both of you, that it was not because we lacked love for our children." He looked away from us and out the window, as if the expressions on our faces were too painful to bear. "It is an easy pattern to fall into when you are young. You want so many things, and you want to prove yourself to the world and be successful. Success doesn't come unless you work hard for it, give your time to it, but children grow up whether you spend time with them or not. It's easy to look at your children and convince yourself that everything is fine, that you're giving them enough. Everything *looked* fine with you two. You were healthy and smart. You earned good grades. You didn't give your mother and me any trouble. We were proud of the two of you. We thought we'd been good influences, showing you how to achieve, how to be successful. We didn't really see that there was anything else we needed to do. As time went on and you grew up, we drifted more and more into our own lives."

He trailed off, staring out the window, perhaps into the past at two brown-eyed girls he never knew. "I don't know any better way to explain things. A great deal of your life just happens to you. It isn't a conscious decision at the time, and you end up somewhere you never planned to be."

We must realize that they are going on the only road they can see. . . .

Grandma's words played in my mind, and I glanced sideways at Karen.

She shrugged, looking unconvinced. "I want to know why Mother died," she said flatly, as if we were conducting an investigation. "Aunt Jeane told me Mom called her that morning crying because the two of you had been fighting and she told you she wanted a divorce. I want to know why you left her there in that state of mind to drive herself to the airport."

Dad closed his eyes and rested his head against the back of the chair. "Your mom had wanted the two of us to fly out and see you. You had just told her you were pregnant and asked if she would come. She was concerned about some of the symptoms you described on the phone, and she wanted to leave that day." He opened his eyes and looked at Karen, and I felt as if I were disappearing from the room. "I had critical FDA meetings that day about a research project, and I told her it would have to wait until I could clear some time, or else she could go by herself. The discussion got heated and escalated into talk of a separation. We were both frustrated and emotional. In the end, I walked out on the discussion." He closed his eyes again, lines of pain cracking the mask on his face. "I didn't want to be late for work."

I looked from Dad to Karen, my mind racing. My mother had asked my father for a divorce? Karen was pregnant before my mother died? In all these years, I'd never known. What had happened to the baby? I sat silent, invisible, like the air in the room.

Karen's gaze swept the ceiling like a searchlight, as if the answers might be written there, but her jaw remained in a tight, determined line that said there were no acceptable answers. "I was so angry when she called to tell me she might not be coming that morning," she said. "I said the worst things I could think of." The words were a statement, emotionless. "I was in the hospital when James told me Mom died. I had just lost the baby, and the doctor had told me I could never have children. I was so filled with bitterness. I hated her for driving too fast, and I hated you for getting her upset, and I hated both of you for not getting on the plane that morning when I needed you."

Looking at Joshua, I imagined myself lying in a hospital with emptiness inside me where he had been, facing the idea that I could never have children. Grief and empathy washed over me, and I reached for Karen's hand without wondering how she would feel about it. "Karen, you should have told me. At Mom's funeral . . . I had no idea . . ."

We looked each other in the eye for the first time

since we were girls. The first hints of real emotion glittered in hers, but her lips still held that stubborn, angry line.

"I was just numb," she said flatly. "I didn't want to talk about it with anybody, especially not with someone who could still have children."

I nodded, trying to understand, clinging to her hand as to a lifeline. Guilt and regret went through me, hot and bitter, but cleansing. All these years, all my assumptions about her, all my feelings toward her had been wrong. Everything I thought she was and everything I thought I knew about her was void. Just as my father did not know me, I did not know her.

Silence enveloped us, and Joshua slipped slowly into sleep, unaware and untroubled by the hurricane of emotions swirling around him. My father stood up and laid him carefully in his crib, then looked at Karen and at me.

"You may feel as if your mother and I did not love you enough. Please don't let that guide your lives. That is not reality." His focus turned to me, intense, insistent. "We loved you as much as you love your son, Kate. In hindsight, I can see that perhaps we let other things *seem* more important, but that was not the truth. I promise that your mother's last thoughts were of the two of you, and that she would not have wanted her family to disintegrate as we have. I would be ashamed to have her see what we have become."

Tears rushed into my eyes. I nodded, tormented by the time that had passed, but afraid to move forward and unsure of where to go.

Get on a different road, end up in a different place . . .

I didn't know how to act toward them if not angry and indifferent.

For a long time, no one spoke. I wondered if all of us were sitting there, trying to decide how to feel about one another.

Finally, I said what I was thinking. "We can't change the past." I looked at Karen and hoped the ice inside her was softening. "We probably can't even change the way we feel, but it would be better for Grandma if we could at least try to act like a family. She is really counting on this Christmas being a family time."

Standing up, Karen nodded, looking at Joshua in his crib, her grim frown softening. "Well, as far as I'm concerned, what Grandma wants, Grandma gets. Beyond that, I'm not sure how I feel about anything," she said quietly. "But it won't kill any of us to sing Christmas carols and smile for a few pictures. Grandma Rose is too old to be worrying about us."

It probably wasn't appropriate, but I laughed under my breath. "She'll find something else to worry about. She wouldn't know what to do if she didn't worry."

"Grandma?" Karen questioned, and I wondered if she really knew Grandma Rose at all.

I rolled my eyes, glad to be breaking through the oppressive cloud of emotion. "You can't imagine. She'll worry about anything. One night she woke me at midnight to ask how much toilet paper we'd been using."

Dad shook his head, stepping away from the crib with us. "She's been going on about that since 1959, when they put that septic line through the basement." Even he chuckled. "You know, that thing never has backed up."

The three of us looked at each other as we filed out Joshua's door, and in spite of everything, we smiled at each other. Grandma Rose had managed to bring us to a point of common understanding after all.

Chapter 13

CHRISTMAS Eve dawned sunny but cold, with a billowing mass of gray clouds swirling on the horizon that seemed unable to decide whether or not to blot out the fledgling winter sun. Inside the house, the mood was much the same—quiet uncertainty, with the faint rumbling of distant thunder. Everyone seemed to be aware that something serious had gone on between my father, Karen, and me the night before, but no one asked for details, not even Ben. That was probably for the best, because I couldn't have explained to him all that was said, and all that was in my mind and heart now. I wondered how Karen felt after a night's rest, and whether she felt any differently this morning, and whether she would keep her promise to act like a family for Grandma's sake.

It was hard to say whether we were in the wake of the storm or in the eye.

I was relieved when Grandma ate breakfast quickly, then left for town with Uncle Robert and James to pick up some last-minute groceries and to buy some Christmas gifts for Dell before the stores closed at noon.

The door was barely shut behind them when Karen brought up the subject of Grandma. "So, has anyone talked to her yet about moving to a home?"

A sick feeling slid to my stomach, and suddenly I couldn't look at my half-eaten breakfast. As usual, Karen's timing was terrible.

Everyone at the table looked grim, and we all sat silently, not knowing what to say.

Aunt Jeane finally spoke, her voice hushed as if the walls had ears and would report to Grandma. "I've tried to talk to her about it a couple of times and she keeps getting off the subject. I think we're all going to have to sit her down and force her to hear what we have to say."

I looked narrowly at Aunt Jeane, angry that we had to be talking about this on Christmas Eve, and even angrier that no one seemed to be considering my opinion, or Grandma's. "She hears you, Aunt Jeane. She just doesn't like what you're saying. I told you she wouldn't."

Aunt Jeane laid a palm gently on the table, trying to quiet me. "I understand her feelings, but—"

"No, you don't," I interrupted. "If you did, you would be trying to find another way. Didn't you hear her talking about Grandpa and the horses the other night? She's trying to tell you how she feels about the farm, how much it means to her. She's asking for help, but no one's listening."

Dad leaned forward, and I could tell he was going to come to Aunt Jeane's defense. "Kate, we're doing the best we can. There's no reason for you to be hostile with your aunt. Arrangements have to be made." His voice was almost a whisper, as if he, too, thought Grandma could hear, even though she was somewhere on the road to town.

"Kate and I thought we could stay while she is on leave," Ben said, jumping into the conversation so suddenly that we all sat staring at him. "I was talking to some people in town the other day, and they suggested that for fifteen hundred a month or so we could proba-

bly hire someone to live here and take care of
Grandma. With the two houses, it's a perfect setup. We'd
just have to put in some ads and do some interviews
over the next few weeks, or a month or two, whatever it
takes to find someone who's right for the job."

He finished, and everyone remained silent. I reached
under the table and squeezed his hand, and he closed
his fingers around mine, letting me know he understood
what I was feeling.

Dad came to his senses first. He addressed me, rather
than Ben, as if he thought Ben might be acting as my
mouthpiece. "Your staying here isn't a workable solution. It just isn't practical. You aren't a nurse, Kate. She
needs medical supervision."

"She needs her home and her family," I said, determined not to let him reduce me to feeling ten years
old again. "She needs us to care about her and take
time for her at least as much as her friends and neighbors do. Everyone in this town does more for her than
we do."

Aunt Jeane sat back in her chair as if I'd slapped her.
"Kate, that isn't fair. Friends and neighbors aren't responsible for her. We have to do what is best for her."

I rubbed my eyes, sorry that I'd hurt Aunt Jeane's
feelings, and determined not to cry. "We also have to
make sure she's happy. She won't be happy in some
nursing home in St. Louis."

Aunt Jeane shook her head. "Well, you can't—"

"I agree with Kate," Karen interrupted. Everybody
looked at her in surprise, including me. "Grandma has
the farm rental income, plus her Social Security and the
railroad stock. It might as well go to pay a live-in as a
nursing home. And if Kate and Ben don't mind staying
here for a little while, then fine. Hopefully we can get
someone hired pretty quickly."

I glanced sideways at Karen, surprised to hear her lining up on my side of the argument, though I wondered if she was doing it just to goad my father. Whatever her reasons, I was grateful that the odds were a little closer to even.

Aunt Jeane tipped her head to one side and laid a hand on my arm, giving me a pleading look. "Kate, I think you and Ben are feeling this way because Grandma has been working on you the last few weeks. I understand how she works. I really do. She can lay on the guilt. But we all have to be sane about this."

My father nodded in agreement, sitting back in his chair and tipping his chin up as if the discussion were over.

Which only made me more determined. "I'm not on a guilt trip, Aunt Jeane. I'm just trying to go for the least drastic option first. If getting a live-in doesn't work out, or if Grandma's condition deteriorates, we can always go the nursing-home route later, if we have to. Meanwhile, she may be perfectly fine and perfectly happy here at the farm for years. You can't say, and I can't either. Only God knows how all this will work out."

Everyone looked surprised to hear me talking about God. I was a little surprised myself, but I had a feeling that His hand was involved in what was happening.

Aunt Jeane tapped her fork against her plate, then looked deeply at me, as if she were starting to seriously consider my idea. "Well, I think it would only be fair to help you and Ben with the expenses of staying here, for however long it takes to hire a live-in."

Karen nodded. "I agree with that. Grandma's money might as well go to make Grandma happy."

I breathed a huge sigh of relief as I felt the tide turning. "We can work that out later, Aunt Jeane. The main thing is, I just want to know you're willing to give it a try."

Aunt Jeane skewed her lips to one side and tapped a finger to her chin. "Grandma's so tightfisted, she'll hate to see the money being paid to a live-in," she pointed out. "We'd have to take over her checkbook, or she'll refuse to pay the monthly salary."

Aunt Jeane, Karen, and Ben went on talking about how the financial arrangements could be made, where ads should be placed, and what sort of person would suit Grandma.

No one seemed to notice that my father hadn't said anything. I looked across the table at him, and he just shook his head, then turned his attention to his breakfast, stabbing irritably at his eggs. He knew the battle was lost and he was outvoted.

He finished eating quickly and left the room.

Aunt Jeane sighed, watching him go as she carried dishes to the sink. "I hope he doesn't say anything to Grandma until I've had a chance to talk to her. I don't think he's very happy with this idea."

"He'll get over it," Karen snapped, plunking a pan into the dishwater. "He's just mad because it didn't go his way." Her face took on a look of satisfaction that made me again wonder whether she was taking my side just to spite my father.

"Now, Karen," Aunt Jeane soothed. "Don't be so hard on your father. He's concerned about her well-being." She let out a long breath of air, looking up at the ceiling and stretching her neck. "Let's swear off of all this angst now and just have a nice Christmas Eve."

"I'm sorry." Karen shrugged. "Habit," she added and almost looked as though she regretted stirring up discontent. "You're right. It's Christmas. I won't say another unkind word to anybody."

I chuckled under my breath—I couldn't help it—and Aunt Jeane did, too. Karen looked sideways at us, then smiled wryly and started washing dishes.

By the time the dishes were finished, we were actually singing along with the Christmas carols on the radio. My father came through the kitchen, seeming a little less irate, but nobody said anything.

The day pretty much passed that way—everybody busying themselves with wrapping presents, baking pies, and making cheese balls and baked goods for Christmas Eve and Christmas dinner. Grandma returned home at midday with a few groceries and some Christmas gifts for Dell. Shortly after, neighbors started stopping by, bringing homemade goodies and small gifts for Grandma. We sat at the table having coffee with one, then the next, laughing and talking, listening to Christmas music crackle on Grandma's old hi-fi. Grandma hummed along under her breath, laughed, chatted and told stories, looking completely content. I thought of her story about how Christmas had been when she was young and wondered if she was thinking of those old times now.

The angst that Aunt Jeane had been worried about evaporated as the day continued. Even Karen and my father seemed to enjoy socializing and sampling the home-baked goods. Grandma had brought Ozark cider from the store, so we brewed a pot and served it to everyone as they came and went.

By late afternoon, the sky was beginning to darken and the wind was rising. Grandma shooed the men off to get the old flatbed farm truck for Christmas tree hunting as the last round of neighbors finished their cider.

"We'd best go out and get a tree before the snow," she said.

Aunt Jeane shook her head. "Mother, the snow is north of here. They just said so on the weather report."

"My knees have been predicting snow for sixty years longer than that weatherman on Channel Five has been alive," Grandma repeated her litany from days before. "I know when snow is coming."

"All right, Mother. Let me round up some old quilts for the back of the truck."

Ben stepped in the door and clapped his hands together in the doorway, drawing everyone's attention. "Well, is everyone ready to go find a tree? The Vongortler farm chariot awaits. Wear warm clothes. It's getting blustery out there." He winked at Grandma. "Smells like snow's comin'."

Grandma lifted her chin and shot Aunt Jeane a self-righteous snub. "See."

"Yes, I see, Mother."

"I know when snow is coming."

"Yes, Mother. I'm sure you do."

In short order, we were all dressed and hoisting Grandma into the front of the truck to cut a Christmas tree before the blizzard. I placed Joshua, dressed in a red snowsuit, in Grandma's lap, as everyone else climbed onto the flatbed.

Grandma held the door open and looked around the yard, seeming confused. "That ol' mutt of Dell's is wandering around by the yard fence. That's odd that he would come here without her. She never did come by today. You don't suppose something is wrong, do you?"

"I'm sure they just got busy or had company." I helped her move her foot onto the floorboard and closed the door. "I'm sure nothing is wrong." But in the back of my mind I had been wondering about Dell all day. Hardly a day went by now that she didn't show up at our door.

Grandma frowned, rolling down the window. "Well, they haven't a phone to call . . ."

"Grandma, it's Christmas Eve. You shouldn't be calling, anyway."

"When we get back, I'll call Larry Leddy and see if he's been by their place today. He rents them that old shack, and . . ."

Ben turned the key, and the rest was drowned out by the rumble of the engine. Grandma was still talking and shaking a finger as I climbed into the back of the truck.

"Let's go tree hunting," Ben cheered over the engine roar as the truck sputtered forward. Aunt Jeane began a round of Christmas carols, and after a tentative start, we soon all joined in. By the time we had selected and cut an eight-foot-tall cedar from the pasture, we had exhausted our repertoire and were too cold to sing anymore.

The icy weather must have broken the last of the ice around us, because we were laughing and jostling one another as we hauled the enormous tree into the dogtrot and set it up next to the front door. After adding lights, we took the old decorations from the garlands on the banister and hung them carefully on the tree.

Grandma pulled me aside as the others were finishing. "I've spoken with Larry Leddy, and he said he was by their house this morning and there didn't seem to be anyone around the place."

"What?" I said, only partly listening to her. My mind was occupied with watching Karen hang ornaments and my father try to reengineer the tree lights.

"There's no sign of anyone around the place. That old granny of Dell's doesn't have a car. I just can't fathom where they are."

"Maybe a relative came and got them for Christmas." A pang of concern went through me, too, because I knew Dell had been planning on decorating our tree with us.

"Pppfff!" Grandma spat. "They haven't anyone, and besides, that old woman doesn't leave the house. I think we'd better drive over there and see that nothing is wrong."

"Now?" I asked. "We can't just drop by someone's house on Christmas Eve. It's practically dark outside."

"Well . . ." She chewed the thought for a moment.

"We'll take one of those cakes. That way if that old woman is home, she'll just think we're neighboring."

"But I—"

"I have to go, else I'll worry about it all night and I won't sleep a wink. That old mutt of Dell's has been scratching around my little house all day like something's wrong." She looked out the window. "I don't see him just now, but he's been there all day, whining and scratching around."

I sighed because I knew she was determined, and in the back of my mind, I too wanted to make sure nothing was wrong at Dell's house. "All right. I'll get my keys."

Karen looked up as we started toward the kitchen. "Where are you two going?" She sounded suspicious.

"Just to deliver a cake to Dell's house," I said, trying to sound casual so as not to disturb everyone's Christmas Eve. "We'll be back in a minute."

Karen nodded and went back to hanging ornaments. "All right, see you in a bit. Hey, remember these, Aunt Jeane? We made these in Girl Scouts. We couldn't have been more than ten or twelve years . . ."

I followed Grandma into the kitchen and out the door as Aunt Jeane's laughter echoed through the house like the warm draft from the glowing hearth.

On the way through the kitchen, Grandma grabbed a gingerbread cake that a neighbor had brought. "We'll take this. Mrs. Allen will never know." She slipped on her coat and tucked the gingerbread underneath as if it were contraband.

The wind threw open the door as soon as Grandma turned the handle, and the thrust nearly toppled her onto the floor. Outside, the sky had begun to look ominous.

I caught her as she stumbled backward. "Why don't you stay here? I can run over there by myself."

She righted herself, giving me the wooden-Indian look. "You won't know your way to their house without me."

"All right," I said. "Hold on to my arm so you won't get blown over." We headed out the door, the wind whipping our coats around us. "This is some wind!" I hollered.

"Storm coming!" she yelled back. "I was certain there was a storm coming!"

Shuddering and shivering, we climbed into the old Buick. Neither we nor the Buick was ready for the sudden burst of arctic winter. Grandma pumped the floorboard with her foot as if to help the engine crank.

The last afternoon sunlight streamed through the windows as we emerged from the shadow of the house. "I hope this wind hasn't knocked the power out at Dell's house," Grandma said, her lips moving in a worried line. "They wouldn't have a phone to call it in. They could freeze to death on a night like this."

"Grandma, I'm sure they're fine."

"That old house probably has propane radiators anyway, so they won't be out of heat, even if the electric is out. It's too cold this evening to be out of heat. Why would that dog be running around scratching on my door all day?"

"Grandma!" I said it louder than I meant to, and she jumped in her seat. Her conjuring was more than I could stand. "We don't know that anything is wrong. Dell has probably just been home helping her grandmother. Things are probably fine."

Chin jutting out stubbornly, she gazed out the window as we pulled onto the highway.

"You can wager they don't even have a detector in that hovel of theirs." Grandma was determined to break the tranquillity of the evening. "John Morris almost died from that monoxide gas two years ago, and I went to

Wal-Mart and got a detector the next day. Dell's granny is too busy buying cigarettes."

"Grandma, please." I was caught between laughing at her and getting ill at the horror of what she was suggesting.

"Well, it's true," she muttered, and went back to looking out the window, moving her lips. "Turn here. Mulberry Road."

The warning came too late and I had to make the turn quickly, causing the car to skid.

"For heaven's sake, Katie, you'll run us in the ditch." She took a death grip on the dashboard. "It's just two miles up here, past the old school." She paused, gazing at the side of the road as we descended into the valley of Mulberry Creek. "Oh, this place is horrible. It's worse than I remembered."

For once, Grandma was right. Even the golden evening light could not hide the ugliness of Mulberry Road. On either side, the ditches were littered with remnants of trash and rotting furniture, interrupted by narrow gravel driveways leading to trash-filled yards and cracker-box houses on the verge of caving in.

Dell's house was no better. Despite the howling wind, the odor of trash made my stomach turn as we pulled into the drive. Leaving Grandma in the car, I took the cake and walked slowly to the door.

I knocked, prepared, I hoped, to finally come face-to-face with Granny.

No one answered, and I tried again, so loudly that the entire place seemed to rattle. No answer. Glancing over my shoulder, I saw Grandma Rose craning sideways to get her head out the car window.

"Look in and see if there's anyone inside." Her shrill voice slashed the stillness like a knife. The dog appeared at the corner of the house, raising his fur at first, then recognizing me and trotting forward. He escorted me as

I walked to the front window and peered in. A couple of dim lightbulbs with no shades lit the interior.

The place was surprisingly neat inside—just one ancient couch and chair, an end table, a lamp with a torn shade, and a broken coffee table held up at one end by a stack of magazines. More magazines were stored in one corner of the room in three neat piles, each probably three or four feet high, as if someone had been keeping them there for years. One faded print of a wagon train hung crooked on the wall above the sofa. Other than that, the room was empty except for Dell's Christmas tree, propped in the corner.

Twisting my face to the left, I peered into the kitchen, not much more than a freestanding sink with two cabinets overhead, a stove on one side, and a squatty round-topped refrigerator on the other. Dirty dishes were piled in the sink, which was full of water, as if someone had started to wash the dishes and then been interrupted.

"Well, do you see anyone?" Grandma's voice from the car startled both me and the dog, and we bumped into each other. Legs tangled, we fell against the door. It gave way under our weight and flew open with a crash, depositing us on the ancient shag carpet.

Any other time, the situation would have been comical. As it was, I stood up with my heart pounding and stared at the bedroom doors, waiting for someone to come out with a shotgun. Rolling to his feet, Rowdy shook off the aftereffects of our encounter, then walked into the living room like a king entering his court.

I was torn between going after him or backing politely out the door. Rowdy disappeared into one of the doors off the living room, and I stood waiting, hoping that was Dell's bedroom and not Granny's.

An eternity seemed to pass, and nothing happened. Choking on the scent of mildew and cigarettes, I stepped forward.

"Hello," I called out, standing in the center of the tiny living room.

No answer. Rowdy came out of one door and trotted into the other, which I could now tell was a bathroom. I stepped sideways and peeked inside. Empty.

"Hello," I said again, feeling like a cat burglar about to be caught in the act. "Is anybody home? It's Kate Bowman." I moved slowly toward the other door, my heart fluttering against my chest. "I just wanted to make sure everything was all right here. . . ."

The bedroom was empty. Bringing a hand to my chest, I paused, took a deep breath, and let my head clear. Moving a step closer, I stood in the doorway and looked around the room, gaping in curiosity at the place where Dell curled up to sleep at night and dreamed dreams of her baby brother living in a perfect house. Just a mattress on the floor with one soiled sheet and a faded comforter thrown over the top. Atop the comforter lay the pink-and-white pajamas she and Grandma Vongortler had gotten from the church. Beside the mattress was a sagging bed, which I assumed belonged to Granny. It and the dresser next to it were strewn with flowered housedresses and slippers. It looked as if someone had been searching for clothing in a hurry.

More confused than ever, I called the dog and started for the front door. At least I was assured that they were not lying in their beds, dead from carbon monoxide poisoning, or freezing from lack of heat. What I didn't know was where they were, or why Dell hadn't said anything about going away. Their things were still in the house, so they must be coming back. That, at least, would be comforting to Grandma.

I took a final look around as I shooed the dog out and reached for the door. One last glimpse of Dell's reality—a world where the ceiling was caving in and the floor dipped in the middle, where the windows were opaque with filth, and the covering was rotting off the sofa. A world where Santa wouldn't visit and Christmas dinner came in Styrofoam containers. A world where the smells were stifling and the sights turned your stomach. Yet somebody had found time and money to build an altar of periodicals in the corner.

My stomach turned over as I closed the door and hurried back to the car. Grandma was waiting with one leg out the door.

"I was just coming after you." Her words were breathless, and I could tell she was more upset than was healthy.

"Nobody's home," I said, trying to hide the sick feeling inside me. "Maybe they were invited somewhere for Christmas."

Grandma shot me a cynical look. "I doubt that. I'll call Larry Leddy again when we get back. I'd like to give him a piece of my mind, anyway. This place is shameful."

I nodded, saying nothing. A lump of tears was forming in my throat, and I knew the slightest utterance would crack it. I didn't want Grandma to see me cry, especially not on Christmas Eve. Watching the road, I tried not to listen as she rattled on about Larry Leddy, white trash, welfare, garbage collection, and Mulberry Road.

When we got home, Grandma exited the Buick quickly, determined to call Larry Leddy and tell him her opinion of his rental property, Christmas Eve or not. I sat in the car, staring at our house, the windows glowing warm against the darkness, and I was more ashamed of myself than I had ever been in my life. Only a few miles away, people had nothing. No food, no family, no secure shelter, no Christmas. We had everything, and yet we'd failed to fully appreciate it.

Stepping from the car, I stood in the cleansing rush of winter wind, watching through the window as the family gathered by the Christmas tree, Ben holding Joshua, Karen rearranging a few decorations, Aunt Jeane watching from a nearby chair with her feet propped on a footstool. Above the windows, red lights glittered from the eaves, and around the porch posts, white twinkle lights were wrapped with pine garlands. The tree, impressive in its stature, shone through the beveled glass window in the front door, and hickory smoke billowed from the chimney. It was a perfect scene of home, hearth, and Christmas—what many people wished for, but only some received.

I realized how truly fortunate we were, and how wrong to be petty and cruel with one another. Standing alone in the winter cold, I closed my eyes and asked God to show us the way to forgiveness and peace, and to protect little Dell, wherever she was. I opened my eyes again and just stood there for a long time, watching as the family wandered away and only the tree remained.

Finally, the winter chill and the icy wind forced me inside, and I hurried through the starless night into the house.

I went to bed that night beginning to understand who we were, who we could become, and what wonderful gifts we had been given in life. Cradling the old photo album in my lap, I looked into the eyes of my mother, holding me when she was close to my age. I realized that she had been the same as I—feeling her way through life without all the answers. If she had lived, we might have become close. As it was, I felt her near the family that Christmas Eve, drawing up the quilts and kissing our cheeks as we lay down, listening to the prayers of our hearts and trying to answer.

The clock on the mantel chimed midnight, and the wind ceased howling through the maples. A light snow drifted to the ground like flour falling from Grandma's sifter, covering the old leaves and dressing the barren trees in white lace. The world became clean and new, born as the Christ child on Christmas night.

In the dark hours of the morning, I heard Grandma get a glass of water in the kitchen, then slowly shuffle past our bedroom. Drowsily, I looked at the alarm clock, then rolled over and drifted back to sleep. The sound of Joshua fussing pulled me to consciousness some time later, but he quickly settled, and I snuggled into Ben's arms, floating away again.

The first rays of dawn were lighting the new snow like a field of diamond dust when I awoke again. I sat up quickly, and Ben muttered a sleepy complaint, clumsily stretching out an arm to pull me back.

"Go back to sleep," I whispered. "It's early."

Filled with the excitement of Christmas morning, I walked to the window and looked at the sugarcoated world outside. Grandma's ankles were truly more accurate than the young weatherman on Channel Five. The snow probably measured only an inch or two, but it was a white Christmas.

Shivering from the cold draft near the window, I slipped into my robe and house shoes and walked silently through the house, enjoying the solitude. Filled with a sense of joy and anticipation, I plugged in the Christmas lights so the house stood ready for the family to awaken.

I found Grandma sound asleep in the recliner by the fireplace, undisturbed as the mantel clock chimed six-thirty. On the table beside her lay the wildflower book. Slipping it away, I moved to the window to read by the glow of early-morning light.

For Joshua at Christmas, it said. I had a sense that this story was not for me, but I could not stop myself from reading on.

Ssshhhh, little one. No more cries. Everyone is sleeping but you and I. Nothing new for me to walk the halls at this late hour. In my old age, sleep and I are so seldom paired. But how many years since I have tramped the floor with a colicky babe!

How many years ... Since your father was born ...

Oh, listen to me! Not your father. My son is your grandfather. How could so much time have been whisked from me so quickly? Like the silent stroke of a broom, the years have swept me clean of youth, and worth, and loved ones. In my mind, I held your babe grandfather in my arms just yesterday. In my mind, you are he ... sometimes ... Yet he is grown, and his daughter is grown, and now you are born.

Come, come, don't cry. Look at this fine Christmas tree your mother has set up—the colored lights twinkling like so many stars, reflecting in your bright eyes. In mine also, but not so bright.

Oh, the best times of my life were at Christmas, when my family gathered together. In those days, they came in box sleighs hooked behind their good farm horses, hooves crunching dully on the packed snow. We were poor folk and had no autos, but those old-time cars were of little use in the snow.

We children would sit by the hour on those Christmas Eves, listening for harness bells to bring our loved ones to us. Oh, the air was so still, the bells sounded like butterflies dancing! We pressed our hands and noses to the frosty glass and watched and listened.

There was barely enough space for the line of us at the eight-paned window on the front porch. I had five brothers and sisters, you see, and many, many aunts, uncles, and cousins. You never knew any of them. They were gone long before you came, and I am the last.

These days, families are spread like cottonwood fluff, but back then! Back then we were all together— so many we filled the floor when we laid our pallets beneath the claws of the big black stove. And dutifully, we children fought for sleep against the ticking and striking

*of the mantel clock that came from the old country. You
see, there it is on your mother's mantel. She does not always wind the chimes. The new clocks are not so noisy
and need no winding. Ssshhh . . . If you listen, you can
hear it ticking now.*

*Oh, like a drum, it once struck in my ear . . . One—
"Santa won't come." Two—"Until you sleep." Three—
"Gifts won't come." Four—"Gifts won't come." Yes, it
once rang in my ear, and in the ears of my children, and
their children, and now for you.*

*On Christmas morn, that clock called us to our bright
Christmas tree, a humble product of our forest, hung
with such things as we could find or make. In my day, a
Christmas tree did not come from a shop. It came from
our land, and our hearts, and our hands. We sought it
out in the snowy wood in our box sleighs—not three
weeks early, mind you, but on Christmas Eve. Always
on Christmas Eve.*

*My, what fun we children had going on the sleigh for
tree choosing! And carefully, with much discussion, we
would stop to consider every tree along the path. The
horses would toss their shaggy manes, and rattle their
bells, and snort smoke from their nostrils, impatient for
their warm stable. But we would not be hurried. Youth
is never hurried. . . .*

*But listen to me. I go on like an old lady, remember-
ing.*

*What fine Christmastimes I had in my own little
home, when I held the hand of my lover and watched
my children hang their tree with ribbons, and bows,
and strings of chokecherries. And I clipped the can-
dles to the branches, lit the wicks with a twig from the
fire, and watched them burn . . . before electric tree
lights . . . before anyone I ever knew had died. . . .*

*Years have mellowed my joy in Christmas, as in all
things. The packages, the tree, the fire, all carry memories to me—reminders that I am the last. Looking at*

*them, I relive, remember, regret. And an ache blossoms
in my breast that I am no longer young.*

*But you . . . you in my arms are my blanket when my
grief lies naked like a babe in the cold night. You are
my youth, my sleigh bells, my nose pressed to the frosty
window. You are me, repeated, sleeping unaware of the
ticking and striking of the clock. . . .*

Closing my eyes, I hugged the book to my chest, sad
for all the things Grandma Rose had lost and happy
that we were able to give her one more Christmas with
family, and a tree chosen from the field on Christmas
Eve, and a baby to rock in her arms in the dark hours of
the morning.

I set the book beside her and stood looking at her in
the dim light. She seemed so pale, so fragile. Yet she was
strong in her determination to make us a family again.
Perhaps determination was one thing age could not
take away. Pulling the quilt over her shoulders, I left her
there to rest and went to the kitchen to make coffee and
start breakfast. Everyone would be up soon. A wonderful
sense of anticipation came over me, and I knew that,
just like the white-cotton landscape outside, this Christmas would be perfect.

Chapter 14

THE smell of the coffee and the sound of the pans clanking slowly awakened the family, and they wandered into the kitchen until all were present except for Grandma, who was still catching up on sleep in her easy chair, unaware that Christmas morning had come.

I glanced around the table as I set out a stack of dishes. The expressions on our faces were pleasant, and the conversation a harmless and chatty one about the snow outside, and how Dad and Aunt Jeane remembered Grandpa playing with them on their sleds one year on the hill above the river, sliding right onto the ice and falling into the water. After that, he hadn't cared much for sledding.

Even Karen laughed at the story. "Do you remember when Mom got Grandpa and Grandma on a sled to take a picture that one year we came for Christmas?" she asked. "Remember that, Kate? We were laughing so hard, you wet your pants and Mom told you to go inside and change. You were so mad, you threw a fit and flopped down in the snow, and Mom said that was the first time she'd ever seen someone make a snow angel facedown." Everyone at the table chuckled, and Karen lost her usual control, laughing with them, and finally gasping with tears in her eyes, "You got so mad at everybody for laughing at your fit that you stomped off to the closet and wouldn't come out the rest of the day."

"I did?" I had no memory of it, but laughed anyway. It was good to hear Karen mention my mother without bitterness. "I don't remember that."

Karen wiped her eyes on a napkin. "You were probably only four or five." She sniffed hard, regaining her composure. "Wow, that was funny."

Joshua let out a cry over the baby monitor, and Dad, Ben, and Aunt Jeane jumped up as if they'd been shot from rocket launchers.

Aunt Jeane prevailed with her usual determination. "It's *my* turn. I didn't get one kiss from that baby all day yesterday. Everyone was hogging him."

"One baby, so many fans," I joked with the pride of a mother whose child is being adored.

Karen shot me a hard look that went right to the pit of my stomach. She quickly turned back to her coffee as if she hadn't meant for me to see what she was thinking. Or perhaps she was ashamed of it. I felt like a little girl competing with her over report cards again, then felt guilty for being so petty when I knew she was still hurting over the loss of her baby.

No one else seemed to notice our exchange, and I was glad. I didn't want anything to spoil the day.

Ben sat down again, waving Aunt Jeane toward the door. "Be my guest. That morning diaper always comes with a nice little present in it."

Everyone laughed, and I turned back to the stove, letting out a breath. Whatever Karen thought, whatever she felt, it wasn't up to me to change it. She was doing the best she could to be pleasant and make this a good day. All I could do was try to do the same and stop letting my little-girl self do my thinking. Funny how you never quite outgrow sibling rivalry.

I scooped the scrambled eggs into the bowl, and she was at my shoulder. "Here, let me take those." Our gazes met for just a second, and she smiled—an apology, I thought. "What else can I help with? Here I am just sitting at the table like a guest while you're doing all the work."

"It's all done." I pulled the platter of bacon from the oven. "I was up early this morning."

Ben glanced over his shoulder as Aunt Jeane came in with Joshua. "You think we ought to wake Grandma up?" he asked.

"She's still sound asleep," Aunt Jeane said, looking a little worried. "I hope she's feeling all right."

I had a nagging worry in the back of my mind too. It just wasn't like Grandma to sleep through breakfast, especially with everyone here. Usually, she was up with the first signs of life in the morning, marshaling breakfast and directing us around like actors on a stage. "She was up wandering around in the middle of the night." I sat down and reached for the eggs, hoping Aunt Jeane would sit down also. "I think she's probably just tired. We'd better let her sleep."

To my amazement, no one argued. Aunt Jeane put Joshua in his carrier, then sat down. Somehow over the past weeks, I had become the supreme authority on Grandma Vongortler.

We had finished eating and washing the dishes before Grandma finally made it to the kitchen.

"We left you a plate on the table, Mother," Aunt Jeane said as she entered the room. "You feeling all right this morning?"

Grandma ignored the food and the question and went to the window to look out. "Oh, it's a white Christmas!" she breathed. "I've half a mind to call that weatherman at

Channel Five. It must be two inches of snow. I told you young people it was coming."

"From your lips to God's ears," Ben joked as he set a stack of plates in the cabinet, then gave Grandma a kiss on the cheek. "When you talk, Grandma Rose, everyone listens."

Grandma flushed like a schoolgirl. "Oh, Benjamin. For heaven's sake. You stop that."

I smiled, watching them. It was good to see some color back in Grandma's face. She had looked so pale sleeping in her chair.

Putting the last pan in the drying rack, Aunt Jeane wiped her hands and pronounced the kitchen work done. "Time to open gifts," she said, rubbing her hands together. "Let's get on with this Christmas! I can't wait any longer." With a schoolteacher's air of command, she ushered Dad, Ben, and Uncle Robert out the door. She glanced over her shoulder at me and Grandma as she followed them. "Come on, you two. You're going to get left behind."

"We're coming," I called after her, then stacked the last of the plates.

Grandma stood looking out the window as if she hadn't heard Aunt Jeane. "My goodness, what a morning!" she said, in awe of the world outside. "A body could not ask for a more perfect Christmas."

Standing beside her, I looked out, and a brief memory flew through my mind. "I remember sledding down that hill with Mom. I wonder when that was. I had a new pink snowsuit."

Grandma laid her hand on my arm. "Oh, you were little then. I bought you that snowsuit at the dry goods store when they cleared them out in the summer, and I saved it until you came for Christmas. It was only five dollars, and there was just one, and oh, my, was your sister jealous over it! I never did that again. From then on, two of everything, or none at all."

I chuckled, remembering some of what she was talking about. Mom and I were sledding alone that day because Karen was sitting by the tree pouting. "I had forgotten all about that."

"You could probably find a lot of lost memories here, if you took the time to look," Grandma said quietly. "Of course, if the family has its way, none of you will ever have the chance."

I stood with her for a moment, listening as she let out a long, somber sigh. "No sign of my little neighbor girl this morning."

"No," I said. "Did you find out anything from Larry Leddy last night?"

"No." Grandma turned away from the window, looking sad. "I've called everyone I can think of, but no one seems to know where they've gone." Her lips started to tremble. "I hope she comes today. I have her gifts all wrapped and under the tree. It's an awful thing for a child to spend Christmas morning with nothing." A tear slipped from her eye and traced the lines of her cheek, and I knew she was talking about herself. "Christmas is the hardest day of the year when you have nothing."

Her hand fell from my arm, and she turned and left the room.

I stood a moment longer, thinking of Dell and wondering where she was this Christmas morning. Wherever she was, I hoped she was warm and happy, and waking to a Christmas tree with surprises underneath. . . .

Then suddenly, there she was, slipping through the back gate like the answer to a prayer with Rowdy yipping and jumping behind her. Smiling, I watched her dash across the flawless blanket of snow, a little Christmas angel. I opened the door as she clattered onto the porch.

"Come on in. We were wondering about you. We missed you yesterday." I fought the urge to grab her and give her a big hug, because I knew it would make her uncomfortable.

She held up a crumpled grocery bag, smiling from beneath her curtain of bangs. "The lady come to take us to Springfield Hospital for my granny's medicine. They got her medicine messed up, and she didn't feel good. But she's O.K. now. She's home sleepin'." She spoke as if it were nothing unusual to spend Christmas Eve in a hospital. "I brung some Christmas presents." She jittered with excitement. "Did ya'll open presents yet?"

"Not yet," I said. "We were starting to think you weren't going to make it in time." I held the gift bag so that she could take off her coat.

Underneath was a red sundress, hopelessly wrinkled and two sizes too small, a pair of soiled white tights with a big hole in the knee, and two soaked Mary Janes with the patent leather scuffed off the toes. Dell smoothed the front of the dress and smiled at me, clearly proud of herself for dressing up for Christmas.

"I have a feeling there might be some things waiting for you under the Christmas tree." I ushered her toward the door, handing her bag of gifts back to her. "We'd better get in there before Joshua opens everything."

Ben was just warming up his Santa act when we entered the living room. Glancing at us, he registered a moment of surprise at Dell's dress, then quickly turned to the pile of gifts that had been moved from under the tree in the dogtrot. Grandma paused in the middle of picking at the bow on her first package and surveyed Dell with a critical eye.

Please, God, don't let her say anything, I prayed. Trying to guess what would come out of Grandma's mouth was like trying to predict the path of a tornado.

She seemed to stare at Dell forever, moving her lips as if she were chewing the words before spitting them out. "Well, hang!" she said finally. "Dell already has a new Christmas dress. I guess that means she won't be wearing the one that's hanging in the laundry room." She let out a huge sigh, looking terribly hurt and pitiful; then she waved a backward finger at Dell's soggy dress shoes. "Of course, the little shoes that go with *my* dress are dry."

For just an instant, I thought Dell was going to say something, which would have been surprising considering how many people were watching her. Then she just shoved the grocery bag into my hands, broke into a sheepish grin, spun around, and dashed into the hall.

Grandma huffed a mouthful of air and crossed her arms over her chest, looking completely put out. "That old woman! Letting the child go out like that on Christmas morning!"

"Oh, Grandma, be nice," Karen scolded, chuckling as Joshua turned around in her lap and began fiercely trying to strangle her with the string of gold beads she was wearing. Laughing, she wrestled the beads from his fingers and tossed them over her shoulder where he couldn't reach them. "I think we've got a little wrestler here. He's got quite a grip."

I think we've got . . . I replayed it in my mind. *We've got.* It made me feel warm and connected. It was the first time I'd heard her refer to our family as a unit.

Grandma caught my eye and gave just a hint of a smile, as if she were thinking the same thing. Her grin widened as Dell appeared in the doorway wearing a green velvet dress with a wide white-lace collar and a sash bow at the back. It made her look as precious as she was.

"Now, doesn't that look nice?" Grandma said. "Do you know that Iris Craig was going to sell that dress in her yard sale because it was too little for her granddaughter?" She motioned Dell closer and leaned forward to fix the bow in the back of the sash. "I told her, no, ma'am. I know a little girl who would look just right in that dress." Scooting over in the big chair, she patted the seat beside herself. "Now sit down here beside Grandma and help me open these gifts. My fingers don't work well enough to untie these ribbons. I don't know why everyone bothered to buy me so many things anyway. I don't need anything, and I'm too old to get any use out of them. No one should have wasted their money on . . . Oh! Look, a new wristwatch! Oh, now won't this look fine at church. I think this might be the one Doris Crumpler was looking at in Wal-Mart the other day. Won't she be . . ."

And so the morning went on. Grandma kept up a running commentary on the gifts—hers and everyone else's, and what they might have cost, and what store they might have come from. Her favorite, she said, was a flat, round piece of river slate on which Dell had painted a picture of our farmhouse. Both she and Dell were beaming as Dell opened some jeans, shirts, and tennis shoes from Santa Claus, and a new bicycle basket from Aunt Jeane and Uncle Robert. Aunt Jeane had bought that and sneaked it under the tree herself, which just showed how sweet and kind and truly good she was. Nobody's needs escaped her attention. When I finally grew up, I hoped I would be just like her.

Joshua's pile remained in the middle of the floor unopened after everyone else was finished. He was preoccupied with shredding the loose wrapping paper and had no interest in finding out what was in the boxes.

"Open your presents, Joshee," Dell said, scooting out of Grandma's chair and into the middle of the floor. "Here, look, open this one. It's got a . . . Look, a big yella truck!"

Leaning against the hearth with the fire crackling softly behind me, I watched as she and Joshua opened the packages one by one, becoming lost in a sea of wrapping paper and ribbons. I watched Aunt Jeane snapping pictures and James shooting videotape, Karen directing him to make sure to get some footage of the kids and Dad saying that Joshua was unusually bright for a baby his age and Ben throwing a sheet of wrapping paper over Josh's head. I looked at Uncle Robert almost asleep in his chair with a stack of new shirts in his lap, and Grandma with her head propped against her favorite crocheted pillow, slowly nodding off, smiling at the sounds around her.

My heart swelled until I felt as vast and as light as the air in the room. This Christmas morning was everything I had hoped for and yearned for and thought we would never have. The expressions on the faces of those around me told me they had been yearning too. I understood now that all of us have that place inside that wants to be part of something, that needs the comfort and companionship of loved ones. Within each of us, there is an empty room, and when we open the door, light flows in. The wider we open it, and the longer we leave it open, the brighter our souls become.

I tried to put my feelings into words later that day, after we had eaten Christmas dinner and Ben had left to take Dell home with her Christmas gifts and a plate of food for her granny. Karen and I stood washing the dinner dishes, alone in the kitchen. Aunt Jeane had taken Joshua up to bed and the men had retired to the living room to watch football on TV.

"This has been a great day." I didn't know exactly what to say or how to thank her for trying to make Grandma's Christmas wonderful, and for supporting me in my plan to let Grandma stay at the farm. "Thanks for being so good about it."

Karen gave me a rueful sideways glance, and for a moment I regretted saying anything. "Did you think I was going to come in here like the Grinch and steal Christmas?"

"No . . . Well, I didn't know how you felt about coming."

"Me neither." It was an honest admission, for Karen. "I just felt like it was important that I come . . . and maybe I felt a little jealous that you were here at the farm spending so much time with Grandma and Aunt Jeane when I never get to see them."

Holding a wet pan dripping above the dishwater, I stared at her openmouthed. "Are you serious?"

Chuckling, she took the pan from my hands and rinsed it. "Yes, but one butt-chewing yesterday from Grandma got me over it, believe me. Honestly, Kate, you must be some kind of a saint, wanting to stay here with her for weeks. I could never stand it day in and day out. She's always lecturing or griping or worrying."

"Pretty much," I agreed, to my surprise not offended by her less-than-flattering assessment of my daily life. It didn't feel like an insult, just Karen telling what she thought, as usual. It struck me that she and Grandma were alike, and the idea made me laugh. "Anyway, as long as she's lecturing, griping, or worrying, I know there's nothing wrong with her. When she quits all that, I'll know I need to call an ambulance."

We grinned at each other, and I had another flashback to when we were girls, standing at the sink washing dishes and making plans to sneak out our window at night.

"You remember the time we sneaked out and went skinny-dipping in the middle of the night?" I asked, the memory as clear as if it had happened yesterday.

Karen nodded, her eyes bright, so much like my mother's. "That was so much fun. And then, remember, a bobcat screamed in the trees, and we were just sure somebody had been murdered over on Mulberry Road?"

I nodded, having almost forgotten that part of the

story. "You called Sheriff Carlton the next day to see if anything had happened, but you wouldn't tell him who you were."

She set a pan in the rack with a loud clank and pointed a finger at me. "And you caved in when the grown-ups asked us about it—remember that? You never could keep your mouth shut. We got grounded for the rest of the visit."

I rolled my eyes at her berating, not wounded as I would have been in younger years when I lived for her approval and never got it. "We ought to come to the farm and do it again next summer. Go down to the river, I mean. Just us girls." The words came out of my mouth before I had time to think about whether I should invite her, or what she would say, or how I would feel if she said she wasn't coming back.

She gave me an odd look, as if she were also wondering if I meant it, then gave a noncommittal shrug. "We'll see what next summer brings." After a long pause, she seemed to reconsider. "Maybe I can fly here between jobs sometime instead of going home. A lot of weekends, James isn't there anyway."

"That would be great," I said, and I meant it. "Let me know when you can make it. If we're not still here, I'll plan to fly in too. Maybe we can meet at the airport and rent a car to drive out together."

There didn't seem to be much left to say, so we went back to the dishes and fell into an uneasy silence until Karen took a deep breath and gave me a serious look.

"Speaking of Grandma," she said, "Dad seems convinced that she has given you the guilties and that's why you feel you need to stay here. You know, Kate, it's not your duty to be the family lifesaver. You and Ben have your own lives to live. I'm all for your staying, if that's what you and Ben want, but not if you feel you have to."

"It is what we want." I wondered what Dad had said to her. "Dad needs to stop trying to shove his opinions about the farm onto everyone else. I like it here. I've always liked it here. The quiet time has been really good for Ben and me. It's helped me realize that I'm not ready to hand Joshua over to a baby-sitter and go back to work."

She looked at the dishes, not at me. "Um-hum. Well, you know, a lot of friends of mine went through that, but once they got back to work things just kind of settled in. Being off all this time won't do your career any good. Management frowns on women who want to stay home."

"To tell you the truth, that doesn't seem important right now."

"Are you sure it won't seem important later?"

I wondered why she was pressing so hard—if the sentiments were hers, or if Dad had put her up to talking me out of staying. It was odd to think of her and my father on the same side, but Karen wasn't usually the type to show deep interest in other people.

Glancing up, I caught her gaze, dark, earnest, and my mind flashed again to my mother. I found myself confessing all the things I had been afraid to say, or even think. "The truth is that we're still waiting to see whether Joshua's heart is developing normally, and whether he'll need another heart surgery. We'll know more when he has his six-month checkup."

Karen dried her hands and gave me the towel. "Kate, you should have told us. We could have done . . . something. Been there at least."

"There's nothing to do." My darkest thought, the one that had hidden in the corner of my mind since the day Joshua was born, came spilling out in a veil of tears. "The truth is, I'm afraid all the time for Joshua. I worry about him getting sick. I worry about him exerting himself too much when he cries. The doctors told us to treat him like a normal baby, but it's hard, knowing what he's been through." I closed my eyes impatiently, not wanting to go back to that horrible time in the hospital. "It makes everything else seem pretty unimportant."

Rubbing her forehead, Karen let out a long sigh, then stretched out her arms with surprising tenderness and embraced me. "You know what, Kate? You're right," she whispered. "It does."

I hugged her back, realizing there was something special between us, after all. Whatever else we felt, however we had failed each other in the past, or would in the future, we were still sisters.

When we let each other go, Grandma was standing in the door looking very benevolent and happy. "I guess we aren't doing so badly, after all. This has surely been a fine Christmas day," she said, then shuffled across the kitchen to the back door. "I'm going out to my little house for a while. I've eaten too much turkey dinner, and it has given me the heartburn." Wrapping her coat around herself, she opened the door. "Now, don't worry about me. I'll just take some seltzer pills and go watch my shopping program. I'll be back after a while. I want to get some visiting in before everyone packs up and leaves again. I certainly don't care for that football on the TV . . ." She was still talking as the door blew shut behind her.

Karen and I looked at each other and laughed, taking comfort in the fact that some things never changed.

We gathered in the living room later that evening to enjoy the fire, roast marshmallows, and look at old photo albums. Grandma told a story about Grandpa spouting off and getting his horses into a pulling match with a neighbor one summer. The neighbor had a newly broken field that was filled with rocks, and he volunteered his place for the contest, in which a sled was loaded with rocks, and the teams took turns proving they could drag it thirty feet. Rocks were added to the sled until finally one team couldn't pull it. In the end, Grandpa's team won, but the victory was bittersweet. He looked at the neighbor's field, now cleared of rocks for free, and realized the neighbor had bamboozled him on purpose. After that, Grandpa was a wiser man.

When the story was over, all of us laughed.

We went on looking at old photos while Josh rolled around on the floor with a sheet of leftover Christmas wrap. Finally, I untangled him from the mess and pulled him into my lap.

"You're a rascal," I said, and he snuggled close to my chest, patting me gently with his hands. Letting out a long sigh, I cuddled him and rested my chin atop his head, losing myself in his baby-powder smell and the fuzzy-soft feel of his pajamas, and the sweet circle of his tiny arms, and the low, scratchy refrains of "Silent Night" playing on Grandma's old hi-fi.

When I looked up, Grandma was watching me, her lips trembling into a smile filled with love and her blue eyes as bright as the Christmas lights outside.

That benevolent smile was still with her as she gathered her things to go out to the little house. "I do hate for this day to end," she said. "But I have to be off to bed if I'm to be up in the morning to cook a breakfast before Karen and James leave." She sighed, looking slightly crestfallen. "Lands. It seems like everyone just arrived."

"Maybe we can do it again at Easter," Karen said, and Grandma seemed instantly cheered. Across the room, Dad looked a little surprised. Karen glanced sideways at me and gave a quick wink.

Aunt Jeane brought up the subject of Grandma as soon as the back door closed. "All right, I talked to her this afternoon about the idea of getting a live-in and, of course, she doesn't think she needs a live-in and doesn't want to pay the money, but she's acquiesced to the fact that she doesn't have any choice. So I think we're all set."

"Good," I said. "You and I can sit down and write some ads in the next day or two before you leave."

On the other side of the room, my father cleared his throat, and the rest of us stiffened visibly.

"Everyone can relax," he said. "Since I am hopelessly outvoted, I was going to suggest that you put an ad in the Springfield paper, rather than just the local one. There isn't much to pick from in Hindsville. In Springfield, you might have a chance of getting someone with nurse's training or EMT experience who wants to move into the country."

Everyone breathed a collective sigh of relief.

"Good point," Aunt Jeane said. "If you like, you can help me write the ads, Jack. You are going to stay a couple more days, aren't you?"

My father nodded, noting my look of surprise. "A few, at least. Maybe a week. I have a consulting job shortly after the first of February. So for a while, at least, I think I'll stay and take care of some things that need to be done around the farm."

All of us stared at him in openmouthed amazement, and he just shook his head with a rueful smile. "Lest all of you forget, once upon a time, I was a farmer."

We chuckled at that, and the conversation turned harmless again as Dad recounted farm adventures, I told everyone the story of Joshua's birth, Aunt Jeane talked of finishing her last years before retirement from teaching, and Karen described the nightmare she and James had gone through building their new house.

In the end, the evening was a success. We spread the logs on the fire and wandered off to bed feeling as if we knew each other a little better, feeling closer, feeling like a family.

I wondered if Grandma Rose, asleep in the little house, felt it, too.

Chapter 15

THE end of the Christmas holiday came too soon. After dreading our coming together, we now found that we were reluctant to part. Perhaps we were afraid that the miles between us would destroy what we had built.

After Karen left, Aunt Jeane and I wrote ads to place in the papers and questions to ask potential live-in care-takers. We convinced Grandma to add Aunt Jeane's signature to her checking account and went to the bank to fill out the forms the day before Aunt Jeane left. Grandma followed us as if she were being dragged to the gallows and made sure to tell the bank teller that she was doing it to appease the needless worries of her children, and that we were welcome to all that she had.

The house seemed vacant after Aunt Jeane left. I was actually glad that my father had decided to stay longer, even though I suspected he was staying because he thought we would need advice on how to properly look after Grandma.

Dad spent long hours walking the farm, examining the rusting implements behind the barn, finding his initials on trees and fence posts, reconciling himself to his past. He worked on repairing the barn and the fences, and met with the farmer who was contracting out the land. He often took Joshua with him on his walks. When he thought I wasn't looking, he would talk to Josh and tell him stories about things on the farm. As the weeks passed, Dad and I admired Joshua and laughed at Grandma, and slowly learned to get along, even to enjoy each other a little. He knew more about environmental issues than he had let on, and, being a doctor, he was able to give me valuable advice on Joshua's future treatment. Never in my life could I remember the two of us being so relaxed with each other.

Dad seemed to have reconciled himself to Ben and me staying longer at the farm, and to the idea of hiring live-in help for Grandma, though he admonished me regularly not to feel guilty about returning to our lives in Chicago once we found someone to care for her.

But the truth was, the more time that passed, the farther away that life seemed. When I called my boss to tell him I might need to take my full six months of leave, I felt as if I were talking to a stranger. I hardly got upset when he complained about it, barely felt a twinge of jealousy over the fact that my assistant was rapidly taking over my job and my contacts were quickly becoming her contacts. I wondered sometimes if I was losing my edge. The job, the office, the commuter train, the fund-raising parties all seemed like part of a former life—like an old movie playing in a projector with the light slowly burning out.

I hoped I could remember how to play my part when we returned to our lives in Chicago. I considered going along when Ben drove up to Chicago to sell the boat, discontinue the club membership, and help Liz rearrange some of our belongings at the town house, which she had agreed to rent until we came home. If Ben was upset about having to give up his boat and cancel his memberships, he didn't say. He just got it done, returned to the farm, and started on another consulting project so we could keep our heads above water.

On the February morning that Dad was scheduled to leave, Grandma didn't come in for breakfast, nor did she poke her head out the door to tell Ben to drive carefully as he left for the church office. I figured she was sulking in the little house, trying to shame Dad into staying longer.

Dad must have been thinking that too. He shook his head, looking out the window as he put his coffee cup in the sink. "I really can't stay any longer. I've been here for over a month. That ought to be enough to make her happy. I have to be in Dallas in three days for a consulting job. I'll have only two days at home to get ready, as it is. I don't know why she has to try this emotional blackmail." He pointed a finger at me. "Be prepared, Kate. She'll try this on you, too, when it's time for you to leave. You do realize she means to sabotage every live-in candidate Aunt Jeane finds?"

"I know," I said. "But the next good one that comes along, Aunt Jeane is going to go ahead and hire her without having her call here to interview with Grandma. We think that once the check is paid, Grandma won't have much choice except to accept the situation. She can't stand to waste money."

"Probably a good idea," Dad agreed. "Time is passing. You need to get things settled. I don't know why she feels the need to make things so . . . impossible for everyone."

"Don't let her get to you," I said as I wiped Josh's face. "You know she's a master manip—" I stopped as I heard the sound of my bedroom door banging against the wall, then the clatter of dresser drawers being opened and closed. "Looks like she finally made it to the house. I wonder what she's doing in my bedroom."

The clatter grew louder, followed by the sound of Grandma muttering words I couldn't quite understand. Feeding Josh the last of his bottle, I picked him up as the commotion grew alarming. "What in the world is she doing in there? It sounds like she's tearing the bedroom apart."

Dad followed me from the kitchen and into my bedroom, where Grandma, dressed in one of her church dresses with the zipper still undone and her hair sticking up in all directions, was rifling through my bedside table. Most of the dresser drawers were hanging open and clothes had been strewn everywhere.

"Grandma, what are you doing!" I said, setting Josh down and starting to pick up the clothes. "What in the world is going on?"

Without looking at me, she paced around the bed to the other nightstand, bumping unsteadily into the corner posts on the way. "I can't find my pearls!" she said, sounding angry and desperate, as if she were about to cry. "Henry's waiting in the car and we'll be late for church. I can't find my pearls or my lesson book."

Alarm bells rang in my head as my father pushed past me just in time to stop Grandma from falling over the stool at the foot of the bed. Holding her by her arms, he forced her to look at him, and my heart went to my feet. The expression on her face was like nothing I had ever seen—complete panic and nonrecognition, like a person gone crazy.

Dad leaned down, trying to capture her attention, but her gaze darted haphazardly around the room.

"Mother, you're not making any sense. Today is Thursday."

"No," she said, trying to pull out of his grasp and knocking both of them off balance so that they fell against the bed. "It's Sunday. Henry's waiting in the car for church." She looked at me, beseeching me to help. "I can't find my pearls."

I stood frozen to the spot, unable to say anything.

Dad helped Grandma up, his hands clasped firmly

on her shoulders, guiding her toward the door. "Mother, you need to calm down. Let's go in the kitchen and get something to drink. It will make you feel better."

"I have to have my pearls!" She flailed her hands in the air, screeching so loudly that Josh started to cry.

Picking him up, I followed them to the kitchen, my heart hammering and my stomach rising into my throat as Dad forced her into a chair and grabbed a wet towel, wiping the perspiration from her forehead. "Mother, listen to me. You're confused. There is no church today. It's Thursday. Dad's been gone for thirty years. He's not waiting in the driveway."

She stopped struggling and looked at him blankly, her eyes searching his face, then slowly filling with tears. When he released her arms, she covered her face with quivering hands and wept, her body trembling as if it would shatter.

Fifteen minutes later, she stopped crying, wiped her eyes on the towel, then tried unsteadily to rise again to look for her pearls for church. Like a record with a scratch, we repeated the same litany, and she wept a second time.

Not having seen her like that before, I watched with a growing sense of panic. It must have shown in my face, because Dad laid a hand on my shoulder and looked me sternly in the eye.

"Calm down, Kate. You look like you're about to faint." His voice was steady and controlled. "Get her things together. We need to take her to the hospital."

"Can you stay?" I choked, knowing that his plan was to fly out that morning.

"Of course." He seemed surprised that I would even ask. "Are you sure you're all right?"

Embarrassed, I waved him off, not wanting him to think I was out of control too. "I'm fine. That pecan pie

I ate for breakfast didn't agree with me. I'll get her things. We can drop Joshua with Ben on the way."

Dad nodded. "Be calm about it, Kate. We don't want Grandma to panic. She's probably had a slight stroke."

Swallowing my churning stomach, I walked past Grandma. Tears pressed at my eyes, and I bit my lip, frustrated with my emotions. *She's probably had a slight stroke.* I didn't want to believe it, but I knew that my father, who had worked in the medical profession all his life, could spot the signs.

The doctors confirmed it at the hospital later that day. They also discovered that her electrolytes were badly out of balance, causing some of the dementia. After an IV treatment, she stopped muttering about the past. By nightfall, she was beginning to come to reality.

She quickly made sure that my father would spend the night with her, and then she started in on me. "Katie," she whispered, capturing my hand beneath hers and urging me closer to her hospital bed. "What is wrong with you? You look terrible."

Laughter tickled my throat and burst from my lips. The comment was vintage Grandma. "Too much pecan pie," I told her. "But you gave us a scare. Do you feel all right now?"

She nodded weakly, her eyes falling closed. "You should have somebody check you over. They have good doctors here."

Dad and I looked at each other and smiled, both relieved that within that pale, fragile-looking shell, Grandma Vongortler was still scheming.

At home that night, I stood in the kitchen looking at the darkened windows of the little house. A part of my mind told me Grandma was out there sleeping, even though I knew she was in the hospital. Somehow I could not frame the idea—as if the farm could not possibly exist without her. I wondered how I was going to prepare myself for the day when her absence became permanent.

Ben came into the kitchen and caught me watching her house. Wrapping his arms around me, he held me close. Neither of us spoke, but I knew our thoughts were the same.

"It'll be all right," he whispered. "Let's take it one day at a time."

Then we closed the shade and went to bed, with the house seeming quiet and the farm too empty. Even the winter wind was silent, as if it, too, did not know how to exist without Grandma.

Dell appeared at our back door the next morning as Ben was eating breakfast and I was nibbling on saltine crackers, nursing my case of the flu. Still only 6 A.M., it was bitterly cold and almost pitch-dark outside.

Dell slipped through the door on a gust of frigid air and stood on the rug shivering, with her coat still bundled around her face.

"Dell, what's wrong?" I stood up and unwrapped her, then pushed her toward the warm oven. "Stand here by the stove. You're about frozen to death. Why in the world did you walk here in the dark?"

I realized instantly that I had been too harsh with her. She looked at me with tears sparkling in her eyes. "I'm sorry," she whispered. "I was afraid about Grandma Rose. I wanna go to the hospital with you."

My heart twisted at the sight of those dark, pleading eyes. "Dell," I said soothingly, knowing there was no way I could take her out of school and to the hospital an hour and a half away, "you don't need to be afraid. Grandma's fine. But you know you have to go to school." Tears rolled down her cheeks, and I felt like an ogre. "I'll tell you what. Maybe you can stop by Ben's office at the church on your lunch break and call her on the phone."

The tears ebbed, and she sniffed, wiping her eyes. "Can I make a picture for her before I go catch the bus?"

"Sure," I said. "Have some of those eggs, too, if you're hungry."

She did both, then was off to catch the bus at the end of our driveway. Sticking her carefully folded note in my pocket, I got my things together and headed for the hospital, leaving Ben to take care of Josh.

When I reached her hospital room, Grandma was sitting up in bed nibbling at food on a breakfast tray.

"It is a sin to call this food," she complained. No *Good morning, Kate*. No *I'm so glad to see you*. Just: "Lying is a sin."

Taking off my coat, I stepped a little closer. "Oh, Grandma, it can't be that bad," I said, although the sight of it made me ill. "The sooner you start eating, the sooner they'll let you out of here."

She jutted her chin out and gave me and the hospital food her wooden-Indian stare. "You shouldn't have brought me here anyway. I was just fine."

"No, Grandma, you weren't." I sat in a chair by the door and grabbed the TV remote, realizing that this was going to be a long day. "But I can see you're back to normal now."

My attempt at humor went unappreciated. "And it's a good thing I am," she retorted. "Your father's just gone off and left me before I even awoke this morning. I have no idea where he is."

"He's probably getting some breakfast," I said.

"I hope nothing's happened to him."

"I'm sure he's fine."

"Will you look at that foolishness on television? That is why there are so many crazy people in the world. They watch too much television."

"I can turn it off."

"There's nothing else to do. It's too quiet in here."

"I can make it louder."

"Then we'll disturb the old lady next door. She was up all night screaming that she was dying. Come to find out, she's only having gall bladder surgery."

"Well, she's probably in pain."

"She ought not to be screaming and keeping everyone awake."

And so the conversation went for an hour or so, Grandma making it clear that she would not be content until we sprung her from prison. Even Dell's note only cheered her up momentarily. By the time a nurse came in to draw her blood, I had a splitting headache and was feeling woozy from lack of breakfast. Standing up, I took some money from my purse to go to the snack machine.

"Katie, will you look at this?" Grandma motioned to me from behind the nurse. "I haven't a vein left that isn't bled dry. They've . . ."

I didn't hear the rest. Images of needles and blood came into my head, blackness swirled before my eyes, and stars danced just for me. I dimly felt the coins falling from my hand, and I heard them ring against the floor. The last thing I remember was falling also.

When I awoke, Dr. Schmidt, a nurse, and my father were crouched over me. Grandma, in the bed, was straining to see over their shoulders.

"Ooooohhhh," I groaned, feeling leaden and weak. "What happened?"

Dr. Schmidt smiled, dabbing a wet towel on my forehead. "You fainted. How do you feel now?"

Like I'm in the middle of a bad dream, I thought, supremely embarrassed to be laid out on the floor. "All right. Can I sit up now?"

They helped me into a slightly more dignified position. Dr. Schmidt pressed a digital thermometer against my ear. "You're not running a fever. Let's go down to the lab and take a blood sample. Do you think you can walk?"

"Yes," I said, trying to think of any way to avoid having a needle stuck into my arm. "Do we have to take a blood sample? I just missed breakfast this morning, that's all."

Dr. Schmidt gave me that wise, fatherly look with which there was no arguing. "I just want to make sure this isn't something your grandmother could catch."

"All right, I'll go," I conceded, then climbed to my feet and teetered into the hall between Dr. Schmidt and the nurse. As we left, I could hear Grandma theorizing on what might be wrong with me.

Dr. Schmidt was not nearly so arbitrary. In the lab, he gave me a Twinkie to eat, then drew a blood sample.

Fifteen minutes later, he was back with a diagnosis. "It definitely isn't something your grandmother can catch." He smiled, sitting in the chair across from me and fiddling with his pen while I held my breath, wondering what he would say. "Kate, you're pregnant."

I stared at him in complete disbelief, unable to comprehend what he was saying. "What?"

He looked at me squarely and said it again. "You're pregnant."

Blackness descended on me, and I closed my eyes, leaning my head against the wall.

"I take it this wasn't news you expected," Dr. Schmidt said. I felt the warmth of his hand over mine.

"No," I choked, not laughing, not crying, just numb.

"There's nothing to worry about physically." His voice seemed to be coming through a long tunnel. "You're slightly anemic, and I'm going to give you a prescription for prenatal vitamins and iron. I'd like to see you in my office later this week so we can run all the normal tests."

"O.K.," I muttered, clutching the paper as he slipped

it into my hand. "Thanks, Dr. Schmidt." But at the moment, I was anything but grateful.

He patted my shoulder as he stood up. "Sit here until you feel better. I'll tell your dad and your grandmother that you're fine, but you need some fresh air and lunch. You can decide what you want to tell them after that."

"Thanks," I muttered, and then I was alone with the faint humming of machines and the soft buzz of hospital lights. And the terrifying reality that I had a five-month-old baby at home and another one on the way. It felt like the most horrible revelation of my life.

Two days before, things had seemed perfect. Grandma was well, the family had mended, Ben and I were ahead of the bills . . .

Now all of it was coming down like a house of cards. Grandma was in the hospital, the family was gone, there would be thousands of dollars of insurance deductibles and baby expenses to pay. . . .

I sat there with my head in my hands, unable to comprehend it all. How was I going to tell Ben? What was my boss going to say when I told him I was pregnant again? How would I be able to work with a toddler and a newborn? How would we survive financially if I didn't work?

What was Ben going to say? What would he think? Fighting over the responsibility for one child was almost our undoing. How would we raise another so soon? Was it fair to Joshua, when he still needed so much of our time?

I don't know how long I sat with those questions spinning through my mind. When I stood up, I felt as if I were watching myself in a movie—as if the person walking back to my grandmother's room was not me.

Entering the room, I had the sudden fear that Grandma would see through me and know what was going on. I wasn't ready to talk about it with anybody. Not yet.

Dad gave me a casual glance as I came in, and Grandma studied me with only a modicum of suspicion. Obviously, Dr. Schmidt had done a superior snow job on them.

"Are you feeling better?" Grandma asked.

I nodded, pretending to search for something in my purse because I couldn't look her in the eye. I felt as if the truth would be obvious, even though I hadn't known it myself until an hour ago. "Yes, but I have a splitting headache from landing on the floor. Would you mind too much if I went on home?" I felt guilty for asking, but I desperately needed to be alone.

My father didn't give Grandma a chance to answer. Standing up, he handed me my coat. "It doesn't make much sense for both of us to stay here, and there's no point in my driving back to Hindsville when I have to catch a flight tomorrow. I'll stay here again tonight and see you in the morning before I leave. You can bring my suitcase with the rest of my things."

Grandma, who so seldom got my father's undivided attention, was quick to chime in, "Yes, Katie, you go on home. There is no sense all of us sitting around this horrid place. If you see Dr. Schmidt on the way out, tell him I am fine and it is time he let me out of here."

"You listen to what Dr. Schmidt says," I scolded, then kissed her on the cheek and departed as quickly as I could. I wanted to leave the antiseptic smell, and Grandma's problems, and Dr. Schmidt's revelation behind.

Unfortunately, they were passengers in my car as I drove home. Rolling down the window, I let the cold afternoon air flow over me.

The antiseptic smell finally subsided, and my stomach started to rumble. Halfway to Hindsville, I stopped at a mountaintop cafe—the kind of place where tourists come in the summer to take pictures of themselves high atop the mountains, to buy handmade Ozark baskets, wooden popguns, grapevine furniture, and other souvenirs. At two in the afternoon on a cold February day, it was deserted except for the waitress and someone rattling pots in the kitchen.

I ordered the beef stew special from the chalkboard as I walked past the counter, then proceeded into the empty dining room. The solitude felt good. Taking a seat at the far end by a long row of windows, I gazed at the miles of rolling, tree-clad mountains below. The view was serene, and I stared at it intensely, hoping to soothe my jumbled thoughts.

Only a half-hour drive waited between me and Hindsville. When I got there, I would have to tell Ben the truth. In my mind, I pictured him going about his daily routine, having no idea a bomb was coming and he was at ground zero. I imagined what he would say when I told him. I imagined him angry, sad, happy, depressed, somewhere in between, but the truth was I didn't know what his reaction would be.

An hour and a half later, I had eaten my meal, looked over all the souvenirs, and walked the short path to the lookout point nearby. I could find no more reasons to avoid going home, so I climbed into the car and slowly proceeded.

Ben was in a good mood when I arrived at the church. He had just gotten a new consulting job and was on top of the world. I considered not telling him about the baby.

But I also knew that wasn't fair. "There's something I have to tell you." I swallowed hard. "I found out at the hospital today that . . . I'm pregnant."

Openmouthed, he stepped backward, catching himself against the desk, his face washing white. For a long moment, he stared at me, as if waiting for me to take back the words.

"I'm sorry," I whispered, the heat of tears in my eyes.

He shook his head in disbelief. "B-but we've been . . . careful. We used . . ." He rubbed his forehead impatiently, then slapped his hand against the counter. "How could you be pregnant?"

I had asked myself the same question. Unfortunately I didn't have the answer. "Birth control isn't a hundred percent," I said. The look of panic on his face made me feel sick inside.

He snapped suddenly to life and came forward, taking my hand in his. "Don't get me wrong, Kate. I'm not unhappy about another baby. It's just"—he grimaced, closing his eyes—"the timing."

"I know." And I did, perhaps more than Ben realized. I was contemplating being pregnant, trying to take care of Josh and Grandma, trying to go back to work, trying to keep all the bills paid. I took my hands from his and covered my face, feeling the hopelessness of the situation. "How are we going to pay for all of this?"

I felt him take me into his arms, the warmth of his closeness driving away my misery. "We'll make it," he promised, as if he knew it would be so. "We can do it. Things looked bad six months ago, and everything worked out."

Stepping back, he drew my hands from my face and leaned down until our eyes met. "I think we just need to have a little faith." He smiled that take-on-the-world smile. "If Grandma Vongortler were here, she'd say, 'The Lord doesn't give us more than we can bear,' or the ever popular, 'Be patient. Everything doesn't have to work itself out today.'"

His imitation of a high-pitched old-lady voice made me smile in spite of myself. I couldn't count how many times she had said that to me. Strangely, it always turned out to be true. "She uses that line on you, too?"

He shook his head. "Not directly, but I read the Baptist Buzz."

"I guess I'd better start," I joked, feeling my mood brighten as if someone had opened the window and let light into my world. Faith. It was time I gave mine a try. "How do you feel about being a father of two?"

Taking a deep breath, he pursed his lips and then exhaled slowly. "Strange," he admitted. "But I can get used to it . . . I think."

"You're sure?" I pressed.

"Are you?"

"I guess I am."

"Then I guess I am, too."

Chapter 16

BY the end of March, Grandma had spent nearly eight weeks in the hospital battling a prolonged bout of pneumonia that she contracted while bedridden from the stroke. Dad, Karen, and Aunt Jeane had been back periodically to visit her. Aunt Jeane came to stay for a week while Ben and I took Joshua back to Chicago for his six-month heart checkup, where the doctors pronounced him healthy and normal in every way. No further surgery would be needed, just yearly checkups with a heart specialist. In a time when everything else in our lives seemed to be caving in, Joshua's clean bill of health was an indescribable blessing.

We stayed in Chicago for a few days, enjoying the company of friends and checking on the town house. But Chicago didn't feel like home, and the town house seemed strange, with its barren white walls and flawless plush carpet. Liz had moved in some of her furniture, and the place seemed to belong more to her than to us.

"Whenever you're ready to move back in, let me know," she said as we were getting in the car to return to Missouri.

"We will. Aunt Jeane says Grandma is still recovering from the pneumonia. We hope she'll be out of the hospital soon, but we don't want to leave her with a live-in until she's somewhat better." The truth was, I couldn't imagine going back to Chicago and leaving Grandma alone with a stranger. I wasn't sure how Ben felt about it. I was afraid to ask, and we didn't have much choice, anyway. My leave would run out in May.

Liz laid a hand on my shoulder. "It's a great thing you're doing, taking care of your grandma like that."

"Thanks," I said, feeling the press of tears. I didn't feel heroic. I felt I was failing Grandma by being unable to make her well. "I guess we'd better get on the road."

Liz nodded, stepping away from the car. "Have a good trip."

I waved, and we drove away from our house. Yet I felt as if we were heading home.

On the way, Aunt Jeane called us and told us she was headed to the airport to catch her flight out, but that we could go to the hospital the next day and pick up Grandma. Dr. Schmidt had told us that her condition had not improved much, but Grandma was strong in her determination to return to the farm. She insisted that if she was going to die, she was going to do it there. Dr. Schmidt had finally given up and admitted that the hospital stay was doing more harm than good.

I wasn't at all prepared for what greeted me when I entered Grandma's hospital room the next day. In the week since I had seen her, she seemed to have lost thirty pounds, and her skin hung sallow and loose on her face and arms. Her legs seemed too weak to carry her as the nurses helped her out of the bed and into a wheelchair for the trip to the car.

Grandma batted the nurse away impatiently, motioning to me. "Oh, there is my girl!" she said as if she hadn't seen me in a hundred years. She clasped her hand around mine and hung on. "Everything will be all right now that my Katie is here."

The nurse tried to lift Grandma's foot onto the footrest, and Grandma kicked at her impatiently.

"Grandma!" I gasped.

She looked at me with a pursed-lipped scowl. "Well, Katie, you don't know. Ever since your Aunt Jeane left yesterday, they have been horrible to me. I told her they would be, but she insisted she had to go home to her job." She raised the lecture finger and wagged it at all of us. "*This* is the thanks I get. I never once left that child's side when she was deathly sick with the mumps, pox, strep throat, and rubella."

Laying a hand on her shoulder, I tried to soothe her as the nurse wheeled her down the hall. "Grandma, Aunt Jeane stayed as long as she could. She had to be back this morning, and she knew I was coming to get you."

"Yes, well, everybody just shuffles me around. . . ."

Her one-sided conversation went on like that for an hour and a half until we reached Hindsville and picked up Joshua at Ben's office. The sight of Joshua brightened Grandma's spirits, and on the way home, she talked about how much he had grown and changed, and how glad she was to hear about his clean bill of health.

By the time we reached the farm, she was exhausted. I helped her into the downstairs bedroom, which Ben and I had vacated so that she could stay in the main house. She fell asleep looking pale, and tired, and sad. I stood in the doorway watching her and wondering what would happen now that she needed more care than a live-in helper could be trusted to provide. I kindled a faint hope that before my leave ran out, she would be well enough to stay at the farm. Aunt Jeane had temporarily put on hold our plans to hire help for her and had made arrangements with a nursing home, in case her health deteriorated.

As the days went by, Grandma was in better spirits, happy to be home at the farm and determined to get

back to normal. But her body, which seemed to have op-
erated on will alone over the past months, was slowly
becoming her enemy. Nearly everything seemed to take
more effort than she could muster. Most of the time she
was reduced to lying in the recliner, asking us to bring
things to her.

She frequently forgot events that occurred, or people
who came to visit, or what we told her. Each time she
caught me having morning sickness, she asked me what
was wrong, and I was forced to confess again and again
that I was pregnant. Each time she would remark on
how young Joshua was, and how close together the babies would be, and how I would have my hands full.
When she had managed to reduce me almost to tears,
she would realize what she'd said, pat my hand or my
stomach, and say, "What a blessing."

On days when she felt well enough, I took her to
town and left her at the church office or the Senior
Citizens' Center across the street. When she didn't,
Oliver Mason came to our house to sit with her—an
arrangement that irritated her to no end. She had always been certain that she would survive him by many
years. Now he was bringing her cups of tea and pillows
for her feet. It was not what she had planned, and she
hated it when the world did not turn according to her
say-so.

Dell Jordan visited often in the afternoons, bringing
little drawings or pretty rocks and pine cones and, finally, the first wild daffodils of an early spring. Grandma
looked forward to her visits, and they sat for hours
going over Dell's schoolwork or looking at the old
photo albums. Grandma told Dell about all the things
she had done without while growing up, and I think Dell
understood.

As the weeks passed, I felt lousy and looked worse. I
lost weight because I was too sick to eat, and changing

Joshua's diapers and taking care of Grandma didn't help. I was worried about my leave of absence running out in May, and about the fact that I still hadn't told my boss I was pregnant again. He was already irritated enough about all the leave I was taking. He didn't have much sympathy, and in a way, I didn't blame him. It was hard to understand about Grandma Rose's situation unless you were living it. It would have been hard for me to understand, sitting at my desk in Chicago six months ago.

Sometimes, I fell into feeling sorry for myself, burdened with the work of taking care of Grandma and Joshua while I was frequently sick from the pregnancy. Then I would look at Grandma, exhausted in her chair, and feel guilty. I reminded myself of her story about the roses, and of how I had felt when I read it—glad to be young, surrounded by activity and noise, not caged in the silent solitude of old age. I wished I could read the story again, but the wildflower book was nowhere to be found. I tried asking her about it, but she looked at me with confusion and told me where to find a pad of paper. I wondered if the stroke had taken away some of her memory and if the book was finished, or even lost, forever.

Whether it was the pregnancy hormones or the stress, I don't know, but I sat and cried daily. It was only a matter of time before Grandma Rose caught me at it.

"What's wrong, Katie?" she asked, coming into the kitchen with her walker just as I was closing the back door.

"Ben forgot his lunch," I said, keeping my back to Grandma. Ben forgetting his lunch was nothing to cry over, but I was disintegrating into tears once again.

The floor groaned softly as she moved toward the table. I heard her labored breathing as she pulled out a chair and sat down. "Well, he can eat over to the cafe.

It's not worth worrying about." Her voice was steady and understanding, as it used to be before she went to the hospital.

Wiping my eyes impatiently, I turned around, not wanting to miss the chance for a lucid conversation with her. So much of the time she was either muddled in her thoughts or angry about being stuck in her recliner. We were as much her jailers as her caretakers.

"Oh, I know," I said. "It's just that we don't need to be spending any extra money."

She spat a puff of air. "One lunch won't make any difference." This from a woman who had forced me to gather and store enough discarded potatoes to feed an army.

"You're probably right," I agreed, raising the shade so that the morning sunbeams danced into the kitchen like a troop of pixies. Pouring a cup of coffee, I sat in the chair across from her.

She stared at the sunbeams and took a deep breath, her eyelids drifting downward, then rising again. "I feel very well today."

"I'm glad," I said, harboring a hope that this might be a sign of recovery, though the doctors had told me not to expect it.

She looked at me very directly, as if she knew what I was thinking. "There are some things I want to say while I can. I don't want you finding out when I'm gone."

"Grandma," I admonished, "you're not . . ."

She impatiently raised a hand to silence me. "I haven't time to waste. I do not know how long my mind will stay with me. First of all, I spoke yesterday with Reverend Baker about Dell's situation, and I've told him I would like to leave a small stipend in his charge so that he might help to look after Dell and get her the things she needs for school, so that the other children will not be cruel to her. Also, I have encouraged him to begin making regular visits to her home, and to consider organizing a church workday to clean up and repair that awful place. She is a good girl, and she deserves better."

"You're right," I agreed. "Ben would probably like to help plan the workday."

Grandma nodded, seeming pleased. Then her expression became serious again, and she looked at me very directly. "Second, I know what a struggle you and Ben are having with your money, and I want to do what I can to help you raise my babies. I am leaving the main farm to you and Ben. There is no debt attached to it, so you'll always have a place to live, and you will receive a rental check every month for the farmland."

"But, Grandma, that isn't fair to everyone else." *And we're supposed to be going back to Chicago in six weeks.* But in my heart, I knew I had turned that corner a long time ago. I didn't want to go back, but I had no idea how Ben would feel about it.

She raised her hand, again impatient with my interruption. "Let me finish, Katie. I have thought this through." Her tone brooked no argument. "Your father, Aunt Jeane, and your sister will each receive one hundred acres of the land your grandfather and I purchased on Grayson Road after the war, and also a division of your grandfather's railroad stock. It won't be as much as your part, but I spoke about this to them on the phone already, and we've settled things." Reaching across the table, she took my hands in hers, her pale blue eyes bright and determined. "This land has been in the family for a hundred-and-twenty years. It is to remain in the family. Your grandfather is buried on it. I will be buried on it. If it is gone, the family will be scattered to the wind. You and Ben must keep it alive so the family will have a place to come home to."

"I'll talk to Ben," I promised, feeling the importance

of what she was asking. "Are you sure this is all right with Karen? I don't want her to think I'm getting more because I'm the only one who . . . has children."

Grandma shook her head, silently admonishing me. "Kate, you must let go of the idea that the two of you are running against each other in a race. Your children are not your accomplishment to hold up to her, nor is her work and her money hers to lord over you. Both are gifts God has given, by His grace, not by your works. God has put you where you are, and He will show you where you should go from here. Be humble. Be gracious and grateful. Bring the family closer together. I wish I had not waited until the end of my life to begin this task. Now I have no choice but to leave it for you to finish." She smiled, giving my fingers a squeeze. "When you feel burdened, listen to the laughter of your children. Take delight in them. They will make your load seem light."

"I will. But you stop talking like this. You're going to be around for a good long time."

Patting my hands, she sat back in her chair. "Oh . . . long enough to watch my roses bloom. I'm certain about that," she said quietly. "Could you help me back to my chair? I want to rest before that McCamey boy comes out with my legal papers."

Carefully, I helped her from the kitchen, and we moved along the dogtrot with painful slowness. One tiny step, then another, no larger than a baby's and no more steady.

As we passed the stairway, she turned her head to look at the images of old picture frames yellowed into the wall. "You need to paint that wall, Katie," she said. "You can hang pictures of my babies there."

"It can wait," I whispered, a lump rising in my throat. Those yellowed squares of paint were our history. In my mind, I could see which portrait went in each space— like puzzle pieces that fit together to create my grandmother's life. I wondered if my children would someday take my life off the stairway wall and replace it with their own.

A great gasp of air rushed from her as I lowered her into the recliner in the living room. She groaned deep in her throat, closing her eyes but keeping her grip on my hand.

"Do you need a drink of water?" I asked, wondering if she still had something to say to me, or if she just didn't realize she was holding me there.

"No." Her voice was faint, little more than a breath exhaled. "You'll remember your promise about the farm?"

"I'll talk to Ben this afternoon." Sitting on the arm of her chair, I rested my cheek atop her head and listened as her breathing became long and deep. Slowly, her fingers loosened, and her hand fell away from mine.

Standing up, I took an afghan from the couch and covered her, then watched her for a moment, the way I sometimes did with Joshua, just to make sure everything was all right. She looked peaceful, more so than usual, her lashes fluttering slightly and the pleated line of her lips curving into a smile. I pictured her dreaming the dream about yellow bonnets, her mind making her once again into that barefoot, tawny-haired girl with the sky-colored eyes.

Joshua called me from his crib, and I went to get him, closing the living room door so he wouldn't bother Grandma. It was impossible for him to comprehend the fact that she couldn't play with him anymore. When they were in the same room, he tried with great determination to convince her to build block towers, play puppets, or roll his ball to him. She seldom felt well enough, and I knew that only made her situation harder to bear. It was difficult to know whether to let them be together or to try to keep them apart. His baby antics made her happy. The fact that she couldn't participate made her sad. It was hard to say which outweighed the other.

I woke her when the lawyer came. Oliver Mason arrived just after the lawyer. Bundling Joshua, I told Grandma good-bye and left her to her legal papers. I didn't want to be there to hear about the dividing of her estate. It made me feel like a vulture waiting to gain from her life. I wondered if that was what the lawyer would think of me.

Grandma seemed to be feeling well as she held Joshua in her lap and kissed him good-bye. "You keep those ears covered," she said, opening the Velcro fastener on his hood and examining it with fascination. "I declare," she said to the lawyer. "They have simplified everything these days. I suppose soon no one will know how to tie a bow or fasten a button."

The lawyer laughed at her. "You know, Mrs. Vongortler, you're probably right. I'm not sure that's such a good thing."

"I'm not either," she agreed, handing Joshua to me. "You take your time and have supper in town with Ben this evening," she suggested. "Oliver can stay with me. We'll slice some of that ham and have sandwiches for supper."

Half asleep in the corner, Oliver nodded like a trained hound. "I don't have any place to be. I'd be happy to stay until this evening."

"Don't wear yourself out," I told Grandma. "You can call me at Ben's office if you decide you need me."

She waved me off as if I were a fly buzzing in her face. "Go on, now. I'll be fine. Enjoy some time with your family." So I gathered Joshua and left her there with Oliver and the lawyer. I knew why she wanted to give Ben and me time together. She wanted me to tell him about our inheriting the farm, and she wanted to know that he would accept the responsibility of keeping it for the family.

On the way to town, I thought about how to tell him and wondered what he would say. Over the months, he had settled in to life in Hindsville and had made friends in town. He had even joked about someday retiring there and playing dominoes Tuesday nights with the old men at church. But we hadn't talked seriously about staying.

When I got to the church office, I closed the door and told him everything Grandma had said.

It took him a moment to digest the news. He stopped making funny faces at Josh and started looking serious. "Well . . . but . . . wow," he muttered, shifting Josh on his lap. "Is she sure she wants to do that? I mean, isn't this going to cause some hard feelings with the rest of the family?"

I wondered if that was his polite way of saying he didn't want the responsibility of the farm. "She says she's already talked to them about it. She's leaving them some of the land she and Grandpa bought in later years and some railroad stock. She's afraid if she wills the main farm to them, they might decide to sell it. She asked me to promise we would keep it for the family." I took a deep breath and plunged headfirst into the private dream I had been building. "Ben, it could be a perfect solution for us. I don't see how I'm going to work with two babies, and I don't want to right now. I want to take the time to be with the children. They'll only be babies for a little while, and I don't want to miss it. I don't want to wake up someday with regrets."

He fell silent for a moment, looking at the computer screen, as if the answer might be somewhere in his electronic blueprint. "What did you tell Grandma?"

I swallowed hard, hoping he wouldn't be angry. "I told her I would talk to you, but you know Grandma. She had her lawyer out there this afternoon so she could change her legal papers. She doesn't want to take no for an answer, but we have to do what is right for us. If we take the farm, it means staying in Hindsville for good."

He gave me that devil-may-care grin and turned to put a disk into his computer as Joshua stretched out his hand to touch the flickering screen. "Well, Kate, you know I'm not the practical kind. I've been thinking about staying for a while now. It just seems to make sense." A logo came up on the computer screen, and he pointed to it. "You know these plans I did for Williams and Bernhardt? Well, those are on ComCAD software, and ComCAD is a little company based out of Springfield, of all places. I was talking to a guy there the other day, and it just happens they need a tech support person for their structural design module. Steady work, salary negotiable, stock options, insurance—the whole works. I can do a lot of the work remote. No need to commute every day."

"You're kidding!" I gasped, staring at the ComCAD logo on the screen, and feeling as if God had just answered all our prayers. "Ben Bowman, why didn't you say something! You've been wanting to get into the software end of things. Why didn't you tell me when I came in?"

A wicked twinkle danced in the corner of his eye. "Well, you had all this *important* stuff you wanted to talk to me about . . ." He did a perfect imitation of Grandma's wistful, martyred tone. "I just didn't figure you'd have time to listen to my little bit of news."

Wadding up an extra sheet of paper, I threw it and hit him in the head.

"Ow," he complained, glancing over his shoulder at me.

"You deserve it." I laughed. "You should know better than to tease a pregnant woman."

Standing up, he grabbed me in his arms and kissed

me, squeezing Josh between us. "You're pregnant?" He pretended to be amazed. "We couldn't tell."

"Benjamin," I scolded, sounding like Grandma, "you'd better watch what you say. You're skating on thin ice here." It was the first time the two of us had talked about the baby since I told him the news, but suddenly everything seemed all right.

Ben seemed to feel it too. The stress lines were gone from around his eyes. "How about if I take you to dinner to celebrate? Grandma called and said she'll be dining with Dell and old Oliver. She suggested we go over to that German place on the way to Springfield. I can show you my new office while we're over there. And she told me to tell you not to worry about her, and to leave Joshua at Wanda Cox's, because she'd already called Wanda and made sure it was all right."

Shaking my head, I chuckled under my breath. "I think she's decided we need a little time off."

Ben reached to turn off his computer, but I could tell from his profile that he was smiling. "She's probably right. These past few months have been something else."

"Yes, they definitely have," I agreed, hearing the bell ring on the church tower. Opening the door, I stood in the March sunlight, feeling the promise of spring in the warm afternoon air.

Ben stood beside me, looking out at Town Square Park, bustling with kids headed home from school. "I wouldn't trade it, though. Would you?"

I didn't have to think about the answer. This had been the hardest year of my life, when all the colors ran outside the lines I had drawn, but also the year when I finally discovered myself. "No," I said. "This year has been worth it."

We had started the year adrift, lost on a river of conflicting desires and uncertain plans. Now we were anchored to this place, our family, the farm, our children, each other. The prayers of our hearts had been answered, even if we had not known what to pray for.

We talked about the future that night with a wonderful sense of joy and anticipation. We talked about the children growing up, about Joshua starting school, about the new baby and what he or she would be like. We talked about names—Jared for a boy, and Rose for a girl, after Grandma. We imagined ourselves retired on the farm, waiting for the grandchildren to visit. We talked about ourselves, and how lucky we were to have each other, and how long it had taken us to find out what was really important in life.

When we returned to the farm, the house was quiet. Grandma was asleep in the downstairs bedroom she had once shared with my grandfather. Stepping into her room, I watched her in the dim light of the reading lamp on the night table. Her face was as pale as milk, her breathing raspy and labored. Coming closer, I touched her forehead and listened. She felt warm, but not feverish, so I didn't wake her, but decided to sit up for a while instead. Ben came by the door, and I whispered for him to go on to bed, then turned back to Grandma.

Something familiar caught my eye beneath the lamplight. I stretched out my hand and touched the pressed wildflowers on the cover, just to make sure I wasn't imagining the book's presence. Grandma hadn't forgotten it, after all. A sense of joy filled me, and I picked it up, sitting on the chair beside the bed and opening to the first page.

The Snow Dancers, it said, and I thought of the silent Christmas snow that Grandma Rose had willed into existence. Warmed by the memory, I read the handwriting, now faint and drifting downward across the page.

> *Winters were long and deep when I was young, a slumber during which I held close to my family, huddled*

against cold, and darkness, and hunger. With my young brothers and sisters, I slept on a mound of quilts by the old black stove in that ancient white house where the wind howled through like a marauding ghost. At night we sat by the dim hearth and thanked the Lord for the meager blessings of our table.

Ofttimes we had only fried cakes for our supper. Buck flour sold at twenty-five cents each bag, and in those lean days it was the only means by which my father could feed so many mouths. Many nights he stood over the heavy black stove, his shoulders stooped from a long day of selling firewood. He mixed the flour with milk, or water when there was no milk. We watched, hungry for better things, but grateful for what we had. We knew the pain of empty stomachs and were thankful for each night we went to bed with food in our bellies.

My mother seldom took care of the household work. The hardships of birthing so many had left her bitter and frail in her thoughts. She was not born to a life so filled with want. Winter, with its dark, silent storms, made her sullen and quiet. She sat alone in the oak rocking chair saved from a rich man's rubbish, and sang quietly, nursing the youngest of us in her arms, weeping from the burdens life had brought her.

I often heard her rise with the babe late at night when we were all in our beds. The sounds of the baby nursing, and of the rocker creaking, and of my father sleeping nearby, were sounds of comfort for me.

I remember a night when she called to us so suddenly that we jumped from our beds. We went to her hesitantly, nervous and afraid, for we were often uncertain of her. We found her not in the rocking chair, but standing in the blue spill of moonlight from the eight-paned windows. She did not scold us, but gathered us round her knees and stroked our tangled heads with gentle fingers.

"Look, children," she whispered so that my father

would not hear. "The snow dancers have come out tonight."

Looking out, we saw them with our own eyes, tiny fairies of ice, no larger than grains of sand, dancing and twirling like diamonds in the moonlight. My mother told us how she often watched the snow dancers from the big house she had lived in as a child—before she came from the old country. Before she became a wife and a mother of so many. She told us how the snow dancers only came at special times, when the moonlight was like spun silver and the snow touched with magic.

Tugging at her hands, we begged to go among the snow fairies. She smiled like an angel, then bade us dress in our warmest clothes, but quietly so our father would not hear, for he did not believe in such foolishness.

When we were dressed, she wrapped our heads in white flour-sack towels to keep the dampness from our hair, and we dashed from the prison of the old white house—away from the scent of coal oil and buck-flour cakes. Stretching our fingers, we ran through the glittering air, catching the snow fairies, passing through them and sending them swirling on the smoke of our breaths. Laughing, we unwrapped our linens and let them billow from our hands as we ran, twirling and dipping, floating on the moonlit breeze, as light and free as the snow fairies themselves.

I looked back at my mother as the dampness fell on my hair, but there was no hint of scolding in her face. She stood by the frosted window glass, the baby asleep in her arms. As I watched, she closed her eyes, and she danced in and out of the window light, swirling and dipping, unaware of the burden in her arms, free and light as the snow dancers.

Setting the book on the table, I sighed and laid my hand over Grandma's, wondering what I was going to do without her and thinking how sad it was that we had waited until these last months of her life to get to know each other. She had so much to teach me, but time was running out. I could hear it in the raspy sound of her breathing, feel it in the icy coolness of her hand.

Closing my eyes, I thanked God for the time we had been given together, and I prayed for one more thing— the last thing, I felt, she wanted to do in her life.

Please, God, let her live long enough to see her roses bloom once more.

Chapter 17

THE family came home at the end of April to be with Grandma on her ninetieth birthday. She had suffered another small stroke two weeks before, and her pneumonia was ongoing. For the most part, she drifted in and out of sleep, waking sometimes in the present, sometimes in the past. Occasionally, she confused Ben with my grandfather and me with her sister, Maggie, but mostly she was aware of who we were. All of us knew she would not be with us much longer. Dr. Schmidt said she was holding on by will alone.

I knew she was waiting for the roses.

The day of her birthday, the first of May, dawned bright and perfect, with a warm spring breeze and a cloudless blue sky. The irises were bright around the edges of the yard, and the roses were opening their first blooms. Grandma woke feeling well, so we wheeled her out to lie in a big chaise longue, and we held a birthday party in her rose garden. For those few hours, with friends, family, and neighbors around her, she was more alert than she had been in weeks. Her cheeks were flushed and her eyes sparkling as we raised glasses of lemonade to toast her.

After the toast, someone in the crowd called out,

"Hey, Mrs. Vongortler, tell us the secret to a long life."

Looking into the crowd, Grandma set her lemonade aside. "I need more time to figure it out." She laughed at her own joke, and everyone chuckled with her. "I don't know about a long life, but I can tell you the secret to a happy one, and it isn't what you young people think." She raised her lecture finger, and we all fell silent. "The secret to a happy life is not in getting what you want. It is in learning to want what you get. Don't waste your time crying over what you're not given. When you have tears in your eyes, you can't see all the beautiful things around you." She swept her hands, fingers curled and trembling, to the rose garden, then let them fall into her lap, the pleated line of her lips curving into a quivering smile. "That's all I know, after ninety years."

The guests rose into a cheer, and we toasted her wisdom, then cut the birthday cake, a beautiful, three-tiered affair covered with icing roses, courtesy of the Baptist ladies. Before it was gone, Grandma fell asleep in her chair. She protested when my father tried to take her inside, so we left her where she was. The party went on around her, children laughing and chasing among the flower gardens, parents conversing, and old people recounting stories from the past. It was, we decided, exactly the kind of birthday party Grandma Rose wanted.

The family stayed for the rest of the weekend after the party. Their visit and the birthday party seemed to recharge Grandma's spirits. While we were all together, we had talked about Ben and me staying at the farm, and she was satisfied that the place would remain the heart of our family. I started to hold out hope that she might be experiencing a recovery.

The day after the family left, she sat in the kitchen

feeding cracker bits to Josh as I washed and put away the good dishes. The last of the evening light faded from the windows as she told me an old story about Grandpa buying their first electric washing machine. It was almost too dim in the kitchen to work, but neither of us turned on the light. To do so would mean it was time to close up the house and admit the day was over. That transitional time of evening always made me lonely if Ben wasn't home.

I think it made Grandma miss Grandpa.

"Is the power out?" Ben's voice surprised both of us.

Grandma started, knocked her cup of water off the table, and uttered a word that wasn't usually kosher around the house.

"Grandma!" I laughed. I'd never heard her curse before.

She grinned sheepishly, then grabbed one trembling hand with the other and placed them both in her lap, looking frustrated. "I'll repent in church on Sunday."

We laughed as Ben walked in the back door, setting his papers and a jar on the table. The jar twinkled suddenly to life.

Grandma leaned forward to get a better look. "What is that?"

"Lightning bugs," Ben said. "Dell handed them to me on the porch. She said they were for Joshua. Then she took off for the river path like a bat out of—"

"Benjamin!" Grandma admonished with a sobering glare. "Don't curse in front of the baby."

Chin dropping, he looked at me and pointed at her back.

I couldn't do anything but shrug my shoulders. Grandma's rules usually applied to everyone but her.

Picking up the jar, Grandma stared at the twinkling lights inside. "Aren't they beautiful?" Her voice was as quiet as the air in the kitchen. "I didn't know there were any left."

Ben and I exchanged questioning glances. The yard was alive with lightning bugs every evening, and tonight was no exception.

"What time of the year is it?" Grandma was mesmerized by the lights in the bottle. Setting them on Josh's high chair, she sat beside him, watching.

"It's only May, Grandma."

"Oh," she muttered. "Then I guess there would be. Look at how pretty they are, Jackie."

Wide-eyed, Joshua reached out and touched the glass, a tiny hand exploring the wonder of tiny things.

Spellbound, I sat down at the table and watched Joshua discover the magic that was beyond the circle of glass. Ben sat beside me, as rapt as I. The air around us was silent, as if the farm were holding its breath as the kitchen grew dark and the sun seeped below the blue-black hills. We didn't consider turning on the electric light. Each of us was seeing fireflies for the very first time.

I don't know how long we sat watching. Outside, the night was as black as pitch when Joshua finally grew tired. Cupping his face in trembling hands, Grandma kissed him on the forehead, then told us good night and walked slowly to her bedroom, leaning heavily on her walker, looking sad. I went after her, but she had closed the door, so I left her alone.

Ben sat down to watch the evening news, and I went upstairs to bathe Joshua and put him to bed. I sat rocking him in the chair for a long time, listening to the night insects, feeling his heartbeat against my chest, his tiny hands drowsily patting my shoulder. I thought about Grandma's hands touching his face and about how much her fingers had trembled. I knew that she wasn't recovering, just determined to be with us a little longer.

Finally, I left Joshua and went downstairs to finish the dishes. The room was quiet and dark. The uneven rhythm of green light drew my attention to the table. Watching the lightning bugs, I stepped closer. The wildflower book was lying open beside the jar.

In the glow from the yard light outside, I sat down to read the spidery writing.

When Did the Fireflies Stop Dancing? I read the title, then looked at the lightning bugs, twinkling as if to a melody I could not hear. I thought of Grandma's face as she watched them with Joshua, her eyes bright like his, mesmerized, thoughtful, as if she, like Joshua, were trying to figure out the secrets of the world.

When Did the Fireflies Stop Dancing? I read again, then plunged into the story as the glow flickered against the paper.

I often found moments of silence and solitude as I walked from the barn to the house on that crooked, worn path I had trod a thousand times. In light or in darkness, in the damp hours of morning when my feet went silent through the low mist, I knew each step, each rise and fall of ground, each scent that drifted on the air—apple blossoms in the spring, honeysuckle in the hot months, curing hay in the fall . . .

When my bones were not too weary from work done, and my thoughts not too frazzled from chores left to do, I stopped there and looked over the valley. The breeze combed my hair from my face like my mother's fingers, whispering of peace, of contentment, of time passing. I looked upon those waving trees, or knobby-legged yearlings in the pasture, or the flowers by the road, and wondered how they grew so tall while my back was to them. Then I turned my back again and hurried on to my tasks. The workings of God are often too painful to face.

I stopped on the path once in the autumn, on a night when the moon was full, like a fresh cake of butter. Below, I saw the farmhouse, saw bits of my life through the windows, heard the faint sounds of my children laughing the way children do—about nothing at all.

I smiled as I gazed at the moon. There, in soft shades of blue and rose, was the celestial face I once knew from my storybooks. One I once shared with my lover. I thought of how many times as a girl I stared into that faraway moon and dreamed impossible dreams—wishing for the same treasures I heard my children ask for when I passed their doors at night. I thought of that part of me that once created bigger worlds and I mourned. . . .

Through the trees, the light from a nearby farm twinkled as the leaves shivered apart like a curtain. The flicker brought me in mind of neighbors, and then of fireflies. I looked for them in the field, but the darkness was complete. It seemed only a day ago when I ran with my children catching the tiny bits of light to make a lantern jar. Now the grass contained only the whisper of the breeze. How long had they been gone? Days or weeks, I could not say. I suppose they flew away one night as I lingered over mending, or soiled tableware, or a child's lessons. They flew away while my head was bent to task and took no time to bid good-bye.

But I knew they bade farewell to my children. I knew my children saw them fly away like sparks from summer's waning flame. My children mourned their passing, as I once had, and knew, I was sure, the very hour when the last of them stopped dancing.

I laid the book on the table and carried the jar outside. In the darkness of the yard, I lifted the lid and promised myself I would remember to look for the fireflies tomorrow night.

Dell came a few days later to retrieve her jar. Grandma was worse again and was staying in bed. Dell sat with her a while, telling Grandma about the lightning bugs, how many there were and how they had hatched out early this year because it was so warm. When Grandma grew tired, Dell left with her jar and some books and other keepsakes Grandma had wanted to give her. As they said good-bye, I heard Grandma tell Dell that people get old and go to be with God, and she shouldn't be sad.

That night, Grandma slipped into a peaceful sleep and she didn't awaken. Dr. Schmidt came and confirmed that she had suffered another setback and was hanging on through will alone. He suggested that we call the family together and tell her good-bye so she would feel free to finally let go.

The family arrived the next day, but the house remained hushed. None of us knew what to say. For three days Dad, Karen, Aunt Jeane, and I took turns keeping vigil by Grandma Rose's bedside, first waiting for her to awaken, then believing she would simply slip away in her sleep. Each of us talked to her in private moments, telling her what she meant to us and how much we loved her. We told her that Grandpa was waiting for her in heaven and that we would be all right after she was gone. We told her that she need not hold on for us any longer.

I knew that all of us would somehow find our places in the world without her, or perhaps because of her. But I was worried about Dell, who came by several times and didn't understand why Grandma couldn't talk to her.

Grandma must have known, because it was for Dell that she finally brought herself into the world again. Waking, she looked into Dell's dark, solemn eyes as Dell slowly leaned over and laid her head on the other pillow, their faces only inches apart, Dell's hand over Grandma Rose's. For a long time, I sat and watched them lie motionless, looking into each other's eyes with expressions of understanding, as if something silent and profound were being said between them. Slowly, Dell's hand moved to intertwine with Grandma's—small, tanned fingers interlacing with long, thin ones as cool and as white as milk. Raising their hands together, they wiped the moisture from Dell's cheek; then their fingers parted, and Dell rose silently from the bed, leaving the room without a word.

Grandma reached for me as I stood beside the bed. "I'll go get Dad and Karen," I whispered.

Shaking her head slowly, she motioned for me to come close, and I sat on the edge of the bed, staring into those stubborn, determined, wise blue eyes for what I knew would be the last time. I saw the little girl with the tawny curls and the summer-sky eyes, the one who led me through the yellow bonnets in my dream.

"In . . . a moment." Her voice was little louder than the rustle of a bedsheet, and she shook her hand at the glass of water on the nightstand. Raising her head, I put the cup to her lips and she swallowed painfully, closing her eyes again.

"Grandma Rose?" I said, afraid she had slipped away.

"Ssshhhhh," she whispered, opening her eyes. "It's all right. I won't go with them just yet. I still have . . . something to say."

I smiled, touching her cheek as tears rimmed my vision. "Grandma Rose, you always have something to say."

Moisture glittered in her eyes as she looked out the window and then at me, taking my hand. "I am in this farm, Katie," she said quietly, her voice suddenly stronger. "A mother cannot say good-bye to her children completely. I am in this farm. You tend it. Tend my roses. Tend the family." She looked out the window again, and her expression grew distant. Letting go of my hand, she touched my swollen stomach with fingers trembling like fall leaves caught in the wind. The baby kicked, and she smiled, then sighed and let her hand fall to the bed again. "The roses will need to be dusted soon. The rose dust is in the . . . storage room."

"I'll take care of it," I said. It was like Grandma to be giving instructions to the last.

"Good girl." She let her eyes fall shut. "Go bring Karen and Jackie and Jeane now . . . and my baby."

I stood up to do as she had asked. "I love you, Grandma."

"I love you too, Katie. You're a good girl."

Leaving her there, I hurried to find Dad, Karen, and Aunt Jeane, and sent them and Joshua to Grandma while I went looking for Dell. I wanted her to be able to say good-bye to Grandma while she was awake and could talk. I felt it would make things easier for Dell.

I found her coming in the door, carrying a large willow basket filled with dozens of flowers in every color. I helped her as she struggled to fit through the doorway.

"Grandma asked me to bring in her flowers." She looked at me with wide dark eyes filled with joy. "She wants to take them to heaven with her."

The joy in her face lifted my heart, and I threw the door open wide, welcoming in the scent of green grass and roses, maple trees and early-summer sunshine. Carried by the breeze, Dell and I took the basket to Grandma's room.

Through tear-filled eyes, Karen looked at us from the bedside, and Dad shook his head slowly. Even Joshua was silent in Aunt Jeane's lap, as if he also knew that something somber was happening. Grandma's eyes were closed and her breath was coming in rapid, shallow gasps.

Dell came into the room and laid the flowers on the tables, windowsills, and at the corners of the bed. Watching her, Karen covered her face with her hands. When her basket was empty, Dell stood close to the bed, the last few roses still held carefully in her hands. "I brought the flowers like you told me," she whispered, holding them close to Grandma's face.

Grandma's eyes fluttered open, and Dad sat back in surprise. "Good girl." Grandma Rose looked lovingly at Dell. "You heard me." And I knew that in those silent moments when they lay together on the bed, thoughts had passed between them as clearly as any words ever spoken.

Grandma's lips trembled into a peaceful smile as her gaze reached lazily around the room, taking in the colors and the perfect soft shapes of the flowers she had cared for with such devotion. "Oh." It was little more than a breath exhaled. "They look . . . like . . . heaven." Closing her eyes, she seemed to drink in the scent of summer and roses, drifting slowly away, skyward, above the house, above the rose garden, above the fields filled with yellow bonnets, until she floated like a dove from the bluffs of the river.

Grandma Rose was buried on the eighteenth of May beneath a blue sky in the plot beside my grandfather. Never before had I noticed the loaf of bread engraved on the headstone between their names. Now I knew what it meant.

Family and neighbors crowded around Grandma's resting place, as numerous as the roses blooming on the old iron fence. Because the weather was perfect, we set tables outside and held the wake on the hillside by the family graveyard. Below us, Dell and the other children ran in the shallows of the river, forgetting the somber occasion. In my mind, I saw a girl with tawny golden curls and sky-blue eyes, barefoot, running with them, laughing.

*   *   *

A week later, Dad, Aunt Jeane, and Karen had left. Ben was back at work, and for the first time I was alone in the house. It was a strange day, too quiet, too lonesome, but I was comforted by the news that Dad would return to visit in a few months, and Aunt Jeane and Uncle Robert were making plans to build a retirement home on the hundred acres they had inherited down the road. Grandma would have liked that. I wondered if, eventually, she would convince all of the family to come back.

During the cleaning and sorting of Grandma's belongings, I never found the wildflower book, and I think I was more saddened by that than anything. I wished I had kept it that last night when I read it in the kitchen. I could not imagine how she had managed to put it where I could not find it. I didn't want to believe that part of her was gone forever, and I held on to the hope that the book would turn up somewhere.

Overwhelmed by the emptiness in the house, I decided to fulfill my last promise to her and dust the roses. While Josh crawled after butterflies in the yard, I opened the storage room off the side of the house and stepped into the dim interior to get the rose dust. Leaning against the can was a brown envelope with my name on it. Chuckling to myself, I picked it up. Instructions, no doubt, on how to care for the flowers.

Bending back the clip, I turned the envelope upside down, and something heavy slid into my hand. I knew the feel of it immediately.

The wildflower book.

My heart soared as I lifted the cover, turning from one story to the next—yellow bonnets, roses, fragile things, breaking horses, broken bread, Joshua at Christmas, snow dancers, fireflies—all of the stories were there, carefully bound between the pressed-flower covers, tied with the blue ribbon. At the end was one last entry: *Hymns and Lullabies.*

By the time I was a young married woman awaiting my first child, my own mother was gravely ill. It fell to me to return home in those last days to care for her and to help my father set his house in order. How strange it was to come back to that old white house after years away! I felt half woman, half child—half my new self and half who I had been growing up. My feelings for my mother came from those two sides of me—half pity, for she was wasting from tumors, and half anger, for she had given me wounds that still bled inside me.

But I came to know her in those last days and, perhaps, to understand her a little. More than that, I came to understand the cycle in which life moves.

As I sat at her deathbed, she laid her hand on my stomach, round with life soon to be born. This babe, she told me, was the end sum of her existence, the part of her that would go on. The reason she had existed at all.

She smiled as the babe stirred inside me. Then she fell into a sleep, but clung to life. She was waiting for the babe, I knew, and when we whispered news of the birth to her, she left behind the hardness of this world.

I cannot put words to the feelings within me on the day we brought her out for burial. It is an odd thing to stand so close to life's beginning and life's end. Birth and death are such strange cousins.

We carried my mother to the graveyard, shed tears and sang hymns, then returned home, stood over the cradle, smiled, and sang lullabies. . . .

Katie, do not be sad.
You must smile at my babies for me.
I love all of you,
Grandma

A sense of peace came over me as I laid the book on the porch and went to care for Grandma's flowers. The farm wasn't empty, I thought, watching Joshua on the lawn. It was being filled with new lives, which was as it should be.

Toward evening, Joshua and I drove to the graveyard to tend the flowers there. When the work was finished, I stood by the gate, closed my eyes, and breathed in the scent of coming summer. On my face, I felt the last rays of the descending sun, and in my hand the warm softness of Joshua's fingers. Inside me, the baby fluttered like a butterfly—my daughter, Rose, waiting to be born. Below I heard the music of the river passing by, and above the hush of new maple leaves rustling against the sky.

The light around me dimmed slowly as another day surrendered its grasp on the land. On the hillside, the roses nodded on the breeze, as if inviting the fireflies to come out and dance.

Tending Roses

LISA WINGATE

This Conversation Guide is intended to enrich
the individual reading experience, as well as
encourage us to explore these topics together—
because books, and life, are meant for sharing.

A CONVERSATION
WITH LISA WINGATE

❖

Q. Tending Roses has such a wise and universal message. What inspired you to write this book?

A. The seedling for *Tending Roses* was planted along with a flower bed my grandmother and I tilled in front of my house ten years ago. As we worked, she gave instructions about simple things she had learned through long years of experience—how to wind the roots around an iris bulb, how to prune the branches on a rosebush, how to cut the blooms without harming the plant.

When my newborn son was fussy, we had to go inside instead of finishing the garden. My grandmother settled into a rocking chair, bundled him on her shoulder, and patted his back lightly—quieting him with a special sort of grandma magic.

Closing her eyes, she rocked slowly back and forth and told me about the time in her life when the roses grew wild. When she finished the last words, a tear fell from beneath her lashes, and she let out a long, slow sigh filled with sadness and longing.

Something profound happened to me then. I understood so much about her and about myself that I had never considered before. I had an almost painful sense of life passing by. I had a sense of life being not just a trip from here to there, but a journey with lots of good stuff, maybe the best stuff, in the middle. I realized that I was so focused on goals down the road, I was missing the value of where I was.

Q. *How did this epiphany evolve into a novel?*

A. That night, when the baby was asleep and Grandma had gone to bed, I sat down and wrote the story longhand in a notebook. Over the next several days, I added more of her stories. They remained in the notebook for several years, but I never forgot them. I shared them occasionally with other writers and got a powerful response, but beyond that, I had little idea of what to do with them. They weren't appropriate as stand-alone works, and there were not enough of them to make a book.

So I just left them in a drawer and waited. The idea to use my grandmother's stories in a novel came at a time when I was beginning to feel a strong sense of meaning in my life, about four years after I wrote them. I was now the mother of a newborn, as well as a four-year-old. Because of my husband's career, we had moved to a place deep in the countryside. Life was quiet, and there was much less of familiar noises and busy schedules, shopping trips, dates with friends, phones ringing. I had a great deal of time to reflect on what I valued and what gave me joy and peace. Peace, I determined, was centered around my faith in God, my children, my family, and a desire to do something good with my life.

I think *Tending Roses* grew out of a need to communicate that process of soul-searching. I stumbled upon my notebook of Grandma's stories while cleaning out a desk drawer, and the idea just came to me. I started writing, and the words flowed so fast, I could hardly keep my hand on the keyboard. When I was finished the first day, I had written two chapters of something that was unlike anything I had ever done. I had never before poured so much of my heart into something or written something that was a combination of my own life and fiction. I had a strong desire to create something that had a sense of goodness to it, where good people do the right thing and wonderful things happen to them.

Q. *How long did you spend writing the book?*

A. The original manuscript took about four months to write. It was more like catharsis than work. The words just seemed to flow, almost as if I was typing a book that had already been written somewhere in my mind. Of course, then I had to revise it about four times!

Q. *How much of the book is from your own experience?*

A. Kate's feelings about motherhood and the struggle between career, a sense of self, and the demands of motherhood were from my own experience. The difficulty of maintaining self-esteem while being "just" a stay-at-home mom was from my own experience. The power of finding faith in God and forgiveness for those around us were from my own experience, and certainly so were the sense of the importance of parenthood and the need for closeness and the support of extended family.

Happily, a lot of the family problems in the book were fictional. The members of my family are an understanding lot, and we have never suffered the pain of being estranged from one another, though we have often lived at opposite corners of the country, which can create some of the same loneliness and longings.

Q. *Your book deals with so many important themes. Which ones do you hope will generate the most discussion?*

A. I think some of the more nebulous themes are the importance of family, the need for forgiveness, and the value of faith. Some of the more concrete themes include the question of motherhood versus career, the notion of quality time versus quantity time with loved ones, the duty to care for one another, especially the elderly, and the difficulty of deciding how best to care for elderly parents and grandparents. Secondary themes include the importance of active fathers, the materialistic focus of society, the needs of disadvantaged children, and the loss of the family homestead.

Q. *What do you see as the most important secondary themes in the book?*

A. Dell's situation is certainly a secondary theme in the book. Thinking about my grandmother's hardships growing up made me realize that, even in this wealthy, advanced, speed-of-light society, many children still grow up with seemingly insurmountable difficulties and desperately need the kindness of strangers. The materialistic focus of today's society is also an important secondary theme. These days, we're convinced we are failures if we don't have everything. My grandmother had a lot to say about that.

The importance of community is an inescapable theme in the book. Human beings are basically tribal animals, and I think that these days a lot of us are missing a tribe.

Q. *Where are you personally at this stage of your life?*

A. Well, I am the mother of two young sons who keep me running and keep me laughing. I wanted girls. I got boys. I never dreamed that boys could be so wonderful. But that is another story.

My husband and I live on a small ranch in the Texas hill country—a beautiful area filled with rugged vistas, ancient trees, and a strong sense of the past. We are avid horse people and spend a great deal of our spare time in various equine pursuits. We think we may have watched too many cowboy movies when we were young.

I have always, always, always been a writer, and cannot remember a time when I didn't write. My older brother, Brandon, taught me how to read and write before I started kindergarten. I wrote and illustrated my first book at five years old and have never stopped writing. I had a very special first-grade teacher, who recognized a little ability and a lot of desire in a small, shy transfer student and started reading my stories to the class. I quickly discovered the joy of having an audience and set out on many, many writing projects, with childhood dreams of one day being published.

Somewhere in between writing projects, I attended Oklahoma State University, received a B.A. in Technical English, and married my husband, Sam, also an OSU grad. After college, I took a job as a technical writer and continued writing and selling freelance projects on the side. Over the years, I have published various fiction and nonfiction titles, and have written more computer manuals than I can count. Fiction has always been my first love, particularly anything with a sense of history and triumph of the human spirit.

Q. *What things inspire you?*

A. People inspire me. God inspires me. Love inspires me. Life's everyday miracles inspire me. I think most of us are stronger than we know, capable of more than we have ever imagined. I like to write about people pushing aside life's confines and roadblocks and setting the spirit free. I like to write about people forgetting the destination and enjoying the journey.

Q. *Are you working on another book now?*

A. I am working on another novel that combines fiction with true stories and a sense of the past. The main character is very different from Kate, but is also in a rut and searching for her life's meaning. The themes are in some ways similar to *Tending Roses* and in some ways different. Just as no two people are the same, no two characters are the same, and no two stories the same.

Which is what makes life interesting, and fiction fun, and keeps writers writing. It's all just . . . sort of . . . potluck. You never know what's going to be in the next dish until you open it.

QUESTIONS FOR DISCUSSION

1. Lynne Hinton, bestselling author of *Friendship Cake*, a novel that celebrates female friendship, has praised *Tending Roses* as a "rich story of family and faith that reminds us of the bittersweet seasons of life and our call to care for each other." What do you think she means by "the bittersweet seasons of life"?

2. How do the various characters in *Tending Roses* care for each other? Do you agree that we are all called to do so? Are we as obliged to care for people outside our families as we are for immediate family members? In your own life, how are you heeding or not heeding that call?

3. The wildflower journal continues to make mysterious appearances throughout the novel. Do you think Grandma deliberately leaves the book for Kate to read? Why does she choose to convey her advice in this way rather than verbally?

4. After reading *Tending Roses* and calling upon your own experience, do you think a mother or father can have a demanding career and still be a good parent? Is it naive to think you can "have it all"—both a satisfying career and an active role in raising children?

5. The author suggests that focusing on obtaining a lot of "stuff" makes it more difficult to nurture a healthy family. To what extent do you agree or disagree? If you wanted to simplify your own life, where would you start?

6. Some of the tension between Kate and her sister, Karen, arises from their very different situations—Kate's as a stay-at-home mom and Karen's as a childless career woman. Have you experienced a similar tension in your own family or community? What's at the root of this kind of problem, and how might you begin to diffuse it?

We invite you to read the following excerpt
from Lisa Wingate's NAL Accent novel

Good Hope Road

Available now

Jenilee Lane

THERE is a moth in a cocoon outside the window. It has been there for months, twisted by the wind, dampened by the rain, a reminder that the windowframes should have been cleaned and painted last fall. It is spring, and there is a tiny hole in the end of the cocoon, a tiny probe pushing through, sawing back and forth, struggling to free the creature inside.

The moth has labored for hours, and only now has it pushed two legs through the hole. Inside in the darkness, does it know why it must struggle? Somewhere in the mass of cells and neurons that make up its tiny body, is it aware that the struggle is God's way of pumping fluid into its wings? If not for the struggle, it would come into the world with a swollen body and flightless wings. It would be a creature without strength, unable to fulfill its purpose.

I wonder if it can sense the warmth of my hand on the other side of the glass as night falls and another spring storm blows in.

On nights like this, I do not sleep. I sit awake and listen as the storms howl through the valley. Like the moth, I have emerged in a place that was once beyond my imagining.

Outside, I hear a gust of wind, and I remember. I remember where I have come from, and it is as if every blessing in my life has been showered anew around me.

I fall to my knees, and I thank God for everything. Even for the wind. For the fragments of my life that survived it, and the fragments that didn't, and the things that were changed forever....

On the afternoon of July 29, the entire town of Poetry, Missouri, was cast to the wind. The town rained down around me for what seemed like an eternity as the tornado receded into the sky and disappeared, spitting out what was left of Poetry.

I stood watching, thinking it was the most horrible, awesome sight I had ever seen, unlike anything I had experienced in my twenty-one years of living. If Daddy had been home he would have yelled at me for not having sense enough to go to the cellar. But once you start watching something so enormous and so vile, it pulls you in just as surely as if you were caught in the vortex itself. I don't know what it is that makes people want to look into the face of evil....

"Dear God. Dear God," I remember saying. My mind couldn't comprehend what was happening. Only a few minutes before, I had been fixing dinner for Daddy and my younger brother, Nate, listening to an old Bob Wills record, and wondering if the coming storm would bring rain. I was thinking about leaving again—having that fantasy where I packed Mama's old suitcase and went ... somewhere. The dream always came wrapped in a tissue-paper layer of guilt so that I couldn't see the contents clearly. Perhaps that was a merciful thing, because I knew Daddy and Nate couldn't get by without me.

I heard branches slapping against the house as if the

oak tree knew about the dream and was angry. Outside the window, a car sped by, a black Mercedes going too fast on the gravel, like it was running from something. It fishtailed back and forth on the curve, throwing rocks against the yard fence before it straightened and rushed onward.

Probably one of those doctors or lawyers leaving the resort on the lake, I thought. *Probably doesn't want his high-dollar car to get wet. They should stick to the paved roads where they belong.*

The car disappeared down Good Hope Road, and the wind came up, roaring like a freight train. Hail pounded the roof, and debris whipped through the air, crashing into the house and barn.

When I ran to the screen door, the sky was swirling like a giant black cauldron. I watched as the cone of the tornado slowly separated from the ground and disappeared into the sky. Not a half mile away, a wall of rain was falling, but at our house, the hail stopped suddenly. The roar faded, and destruction lay everywhere—pieces of wood and metal, tree branches, shredded furniture, torn clothing, shards of glass glittering like diamonds in the afternoon sunlight.

Bits of paper floated from the churning clouds, drifting, swirling, dancing, as if they had all the time in the world. They filled the sky like snow.

The air was so quiet I could hear the papers falling, rustling slightly against an eerie silence, like a battlefield after the battle, when only the corpses remain. I wondered where so much paper could have come from, and if it had been blown all the way from Poetry, three miles across the low hills.

The big oak tree in the yard moaned, its limbs heavy with a crusty coating of fresh hail. I stared at the ice, then turned around in disbelief, looking at our single-story brick house and seeing everything as it had always been—the peeling paint, the overgrown bushes, the torn window screen where Nate sneaked out of his bedroom at night.

A piece of paper fell lightly on the screen and hung there, fluttering against the window like a bird trying to break free.

I remember thinking, *Why not us? Why not our house? Why is everything the same as it was yesterday, last week, last month, last year, ten minutes ago? Why wasn't anything destroyed, or changed, or carried away. . . .*

I had the strangest sense of wishing that it had been. Then I realized how crazy that was. I should have been thanking God I was alive.

Turning around, I gazed at the wall of rain, now moving away toward the east, revealing the footprint of the beast—an enormous path of stripped earth and strewn debris, ending in a narrow swath of twisted trees just past Daddy's wheat field. From there, it carved a jagged scar toward the horizon, toward Poetry. Where farms had been, there was nothing.

I wondered how God could let something so terrible happen at all.

A mile down the valley, the pecan orchard that had hidden old lady Gibson's farmhouse stood splintered, the limbs hanging like broken bones. Near the road, a geyser of water sprayed into the air, mixing with the falling ran.

I realized the tornado had passed across the Gibson farm. Gasping the gritty air, I ran down the porch steps and across the yard. At the sound of the yard gate opening, Daddy's bird dog rushed from under the house and slammed against my legs, sending me sprawling into the litter on the grass.

"Get away, Bo!" I hollered, grabbing his collar as he tried to bulldoze his way through the gate. "Get back in the yard, you big, stupid dog!" Daddy's dogs were always big and stupid, and always trying to escape.

I held on as Bo plowed a furrow into the long, scrappy grass outside the gate and pounced on a bit of paper blowing by. Scrambling to my feet, I dragged him into the yard and struggled to hook him to his chain while he cavorted with the paper, grabbing it, then dropping it and pouncing on it again. I caught a quick glimpse of a face. A photograph. A baby. A birth announcement.

Securing the chain, I snatched the photograph away, dried it on my jeans, then looked at it with the same horrible fascination that had forced me to stare at the tornado.

Somebody's baby. Just newborn. A girl. Seven pounds six ounces. The space where the name would have been was torn away.